8/2 £1.60

written by
Sean Dylan

First published in paperback by
Michael Terence Publishing in 2021
www.mtp.agency

ISBN 9781800942318

This book is dedicated to my wife Jacky.
Without her love, patience and help it would never have been possible.

1

The thirty-year-old Russian Antonov An-124 Ruslan cargo plane shuddered violently, as it picked up speed down the runway at Moscow's Domodedovo Airport. Gradually as Captain Vladimir Cauchemer pushed the throttle slowly forward, the plane's four engines sprang to life in a defining roar, as the plane gradually lifted off the ground in a huge spray of freezing water. As the cargo plane gradually climbed up to a cruising height of 30,000 feet, rain and hail crashed onto the cockpit window, whilst the plane continued to creak and groan. Once above the grey storm clouds, which appeared to float endlessly in a vast wilderness of space, the plane appeared to settle down and relax. All you could hear then was the repetitive drone of the engines. Both the men turned and looked at each other.

Captain Cauchemer glanced again at his young co-pilot with a broad smile. "Alexei, I bet you thought we were not going to make it."

The co-pilot, who was also the navigator, did not answer at first. His face was ash white and looked frozen. "I almost shit in my pants," he eventually stuttered.

Vladimir started to laugh. "My friend you should trust me, this old box will get us anywhere. If you recall, she was completely re-overhauled a couple of years ago which included new engines, she will last for another ten years."

"We should be in Khatanga in just over six hours if the weather holds up."

"I am afraid not, we have to touch down at Norilsk."

"I have never been there."

"It is the capital of Yamalo-Nenets, which is the world's largest gas producing region. Alykel airport is about 7km from the city."

"Is Norilsk a large city?"

"Relatively small for a city but this is Arctic Siberia, it only has a population of about 175,000, but it does have a very important airport. It is designated as an emergency airport for commercial airliners flying cross-polar routes."

"You are a mind of information Vladimir." The captain smiled but didn't speak. "Why are we flying to Norilsk?"

Vladimir still did not answer. "When you called me on Saturday about this flight, I was taken aback, as I thought our last flight on Monday the 11th October was the final one, before the diamond mine at the Popigal Creator on the Taymyr Peninsula, closed down for the winter months. We evacuated most of the miners on our last flight home, apart from a maintenance crew and four security guards, who will stay the winter there. What is going on Vladimir, this is not a normal flight?"

The captain then broke his silence. "You are quite right Alexei this is not a normal flight. We are landing at the Alykel Airport, Norilsk to pick up two armed security guards. We should be able to take off again within forty minutes, the plane's engines will have to be kept running as the outside temperature is down to -10c. The airport maintenance staff will also have to spray the aircraft with de-icer, we don't want the wings iced up on take-off."

There was then a change in the conversation.

"Vladimir, will you be taking a holiday when we return to Moscow for our winter break?"

"I sure will. Next week my wife and I are heading to Tenerife for a month, with a bit of luck the weather will be warm and sunny. We will sunbath, drink vodka and martinis in the hotel bar, and eat fine food. And you my friend what do you intend to do?"

"I shall just sit at home relaxing and waiting for my wife to give birth to our first child, it is due at the beginning of December. Mind you I am certain that I won't be able to relax, as I have still not finished painting the baby's bedroom."

Vladimir laughed. "I remember those days very well, our three children are now grown up and married with families of their own. They were happy days."

The flight to Norilsk was proving uneventful. There was hardly any wind and no blinding snow storm. Down below in between breaks in the white soft clouds, the trees had disappeared as they flew north towards the Arctic Circle, all they could see from the cockpit window was a barren landscape covered with endless miles of frozen snow.

This was Siberia in winter, a frozen wilderness.

"Why did the security guards not join us in Moscow?"

"Alexei, I keep asking myself the same question. I was not informed about the flight change or about picking up the two security guards until five minutes before we left Moscow Domodedovo Airport. All I was told was that this particular flight was ordered by the Kremlin, to pick up an extra large quantity of diamonds and precious gems from our usual destination Khatanga Airport on the Taymyr Peninsula."

"Surely we could have brought the diamonds back on our last flight to the peninsula?"

"Room and weight was the problem, if you recall we had almost seventy miners on board plus baggage and a damaged snow plough for the return flight. At least we both get an extra pay day, the money will be useful."

"I agree with you. To have security guards travelling with us the diamonds must be worth a few bob."

"They are worth over seventy five billion roubles or one billion Euros on the European market."

"You are joking."

Vladimir shook his head. "No, this is what the guy told me before we left this morning. Diamonds from the Taymyr Peninsula are now in big demand due to their purity, but during the winter months there is always a world shortage of them, due to the mine being shut down. However this winter our Government are making certain that they have their house in order. We are about to make history Alexei, this consignment of diamonds will be the largest ever transported. I presume this is why everything is so secret."

The cargo plane was now descending through the icy clouds, snow was starting to fall but luckily there was no wind.

"Ten minutes to touch down captain. What a desolate city Norilsk is, it is treeless."

"That is due to a nickel smelting plant which pumps out toxic smoke twenty four hours a day. There are no living trees within a thirty mile radius of the smelter."

"Christ, what a miserable life the population must have here. Their lungs must be in a bad way, and on top of that they have to put up with incredibly harsh winters. I am glad I live in Moscow."

"You can say that again."

A loud grinding noise came from the undercarriage. "The wheels are down captain."

Passing huge mounds of snow which lined the sides of the single runway, the cargo plane gently touched down. After slowly taxing to the front of the terminal building, the cargo plane came to a halt with the engines still running. As far as they could see the Antonov An-124 was the only aircraft at the airport.

Vladimir glanced at his Russian Vostok wrist watch; it was a few minutes before mid-day. The 1,800 mile flight had taken them four hours thirty minutes.

"Captain, a mobile Stairway is being fixed against the outer door of the aircraft by airport staff and a military jeep has just drawn up alongside us. There are eight personnel in the vehicle, one of them has just jumped out of the jeep, and he looks like he is in charge. He is now climbing the staircase."

"Alexei, open the outer door and let our guest in."

Once the door was opened freezing air rushed in, the interior of the cargo plane now felt like a giant meat freezer. Alexei pulled the collar on his flying jacket closer to his neck.

"Captain Vladimir Cauchemer." A military looking guy aged about forty wearing a fur hat pulled down over his ears, dressed in a long grey trench coat which had a thick fur collar and heavy black military boots, held out his gloved right hand.

"The captain is in the cockpit. I am his co-pilot and navigator Alexei Petrov."

"Would you please tell your captain that I would like to speak to him? I am Major Boris Mikhailov from the Military Police."

"If you would please step inside I will take you to the captain."

Once the Major was inside the aircraft, Alexei closed the outer door. "Would you care to follow me Sir?"

The two men walked down the fuselage of the cargo plane and stopped at the cockpit door. Alexei then pressed a buzzer on the right hand side of the door and entered.

"Captain this is Major Mikhailov from the Military Police he wishes to speak to you." The Major then removed his gloves and the two men shook hands.

"What can I do for you Major?"

"I have two security guards in the Jeep waiting to board your plane."

"No problem, bring them on board."

"Unfortunately we do have a slight problem."

Vladimir and Alexei stared at the Major.

"I have a third security officer who will be joining you; he is also a pilot and navigator. As you only have room for four people in the cockpit we have a slight problem. Anybody travelling in the fuselage will freeze to death. As it is essential for my man to be on board, there is only one option open. Your co-pilot will have to leave the plane."

Captain Cauchemer objected strongly but to no avail.

The Major then turned to the co-pilot. "Don't worry my friend, you will be flown back to Moscow on the next available plane."

"I am sorry captain but these arrangements are out of my hands, I have to follow the Kremlin's instructions."

"I'm sorry Alexei, you heard the Major."

Vladimir and Alexei then embraced. "I will call you on your mobile when I arrive back in Moscow, let us hope there is a flight back for you later today."

"Captain, when you fly north to Khatanga Airport you will refuel as usual and take on eight sealed metal containers, which hold the diamonds. From that moment you and your aircraft will be under the protection of the Military Police, until you arrive back in Moscow."

Without another word Alexei and the Major left the aircraft and got into the Jeep. Three heavily armed men carrying submachine guns then jumped out of the Jeep, climbed the Stairway and entered the aircraft. Captain Cauchemer then closed the aircraft's outer door.

"Which one of you three guys is a pilot?"

"I am." The guy who spoke was in his late twenties, clean shaven with short dark curly hair, slim and standing about six one.

"I shall need your help, would you please sit in the co-pilot's seat next to me. By the way what is your name?"

"Sergei Aslanov."

"Are you familiar with this type of cargo plane?"

"No problem captain. I have just spent the last six months flying supplies three times a week into Syria for President Bashar al- Assad on behalf of our Government. I know the Antonov An-124 cargo plane like the back of my hand."

"Excellent. Welcome aboard Sergei."

After clearance from the Air Traffic Control Tower, the cargo plane then slowly moved onto the runway. There was a slight pause then a huge roar from the aircraft's four engines as it started to move down the runway at speed. After about quarter of a mile the plane lifted off from the ground shuddering and creaking violently.

"Sergei, retract the wheels and close the under carriage."

As usual there was a loud grinding noise as the under carriage closed.

"Captain it sounds as though your aircraft is on her last legs."

Vladimir laughed. "That is nothing my friend, just wait until we have to land."

The flight to Khatanga Airport which was only 371 miles took an hour and ten minutes. As the cargo plane descended from its cruising height of 30,000 feet the weather started to deteriorate. Freezing snow, driven by a strong Arctic wind was hitting the cockpit window making visibility poor. The aircraft was rocking violently making it difficult to control.

"Captain, the airport runway is straight ahead and the landing lights are on. Everything is clear for you to land." Captain Cauchemer touched down perfectly with only a slight bump as they hit the runway; by some miracle the wind had lost some of its ferocity but it was still snowing. To his left Vladimir could see a giant snowplough and blower struggling to keep the runway open. This was Khatanga, one of the northern most inhabited localities in Russia, situated on the banks of the Khatanga River with a population of about 3,500. Both men and women had to be tough to live here, in the winter temperatures frequently dropped as low as -35c and in the very short summer, which only lasted for about two months, never crept above 45 Fahrenheit.

Vladimir was pleased they had departed from Moscow at 6.30am just as it was starting to get light. It was now 1.35pm in the afternoon; they had made good time considering the inconvenience of stopping at Norilsk to pick up three passengers. In another hour the little daylight they had would fade and it would be dark, this was the Arctic Circle where winter really was winter, dark, freezing cold and unforgiving.

After taxing to the small concrete terminal building the cargo plane came to a halt, all the engines were still running. Next to the terminal there was a large hanger, this too was constructed of concrete, the rusting metal door rolled open and a small fuel tanker came out and drove up to the side of the aircraft. Within minutes, the two men in charge of the tanker were pumping aviation fuel into the thirsty tanks of the cargo plane. Fifteen minutes later a large dark blue and white snow tractor came from behind the terminal building and drew up by the side of the fuel tanker, just as it was uncoupling the fuel pipe from the aircraft. Four heavily armed security guards then jumped out of the snow tractor, one of them shouted to Captain Cauchemer to open the outer door which he did. This allowed a sudden rush of freezing air and a flurry of snow to enter the fuselage. After carrying the eight sealed metal containers up the Airstairs with the help of the co-pilot and the two other security guards who were already onboard the aircraft, one of the security guards from the snow tractor asked to speak to Captain Cauchemer.

"I need your signature captain, and then you can be on your way back to Moscow, before the weather closes in and the airport is shut down."

Ten minutes later Air Traffic Control at Khatanga Airport gave them clearance to take off. Vladimir was relieved to get away, no way did he want to spend winter in this God forsaken frozen wilderness. Once the Antonov An-124 cargo plane had climbed to its cruising height of 30,000 feet Vladimir felt relaxed, he was now on his way home to Moscow, it was two thirty and they had made good time.

"Any chance of a warm drink and some food captain" enquired one of the security guards.

"Help yourself from the kitchen galley at the rear of the plane. Whilst you are there bring some food and drinks through for us all. There is plenty roast ham, cheese, bread rolls and tea and coffee."

The security guard nudged one of his colleagues who was nodding off "Petro, give me a hand."

"I will put the heater blowers on for you in the fuselage otherwise you will freeze to death."

"Thank you captain," Vladimir acknowledged him with smile and a nod of his head.

The cargo plane had only been in the air five minutes, when new co-pilot Sergei Aslanov suddenly dropped a bombshell. "Captain, I have just been informed that we have to make a detour to Dikson, which is a small port of 650 people on the Kara Sea. It appears that a couple of Government geologists have to be picked up otherwise they will have to spend the winter there. The airport is 5km west of the settlement on a small deserted island."

"I don't know the area, how far is it from Khatanga?" Sergei immediately checked the co-ordinates on the navigation chart. "Four hundred and sixty one miles, we should make it in about two hours."

"I hope so, the weather is shit at the moment, if the snow increases landing will be a major problem especially in the dark."

"They have runway lights and flares."

"Ok you win. I hope you have no more surprises for me."

There was a buzz and the cockpit door opened. The two friendly security officers had returned with warm drinks and food, which was appreciated. Strong cross winds were now starting to buffet the aircraft, so the captain took the plane higher to 32,000 feet, which certainly helped. All the guys in the cockpit appeared quite friendly apart from one. He sat in one of the cockpit's brown leather chairs behind the captain and never spoke. Most of the time, he appeared to doze off. Never once did he remove his fur hat, even though it was warm in the cockpit. The submachine gun he carried never left his lap.

Time was passing by quickly.

"Have you always been a pilot?"

"No, I qualified as a gemmologist from Moscow State University and then went to work in South Africa to gain experience." The cockpit then went quiet.

"Captain we are approaching Dikson, we shall be landing in twenty minutes."

"Thank you Sergei."

The aircraft then started to descend through the clouds into a clear dark sky; there was no wind or blinding snow.

"There ahead of us is the settlement. Dikson Airport is 5km to the right; I can now see landing lights and flares. I am now in contact with the airport. The flares point out the start, halfway point, and the end of the runway. Landing wheels are down captain."

Vladimir's eyes were transfixed on the small landing strip ahead. Thoughts were going through his head. Had the snow been removed from the runway? Was the runway frozen? Was the runway long enough or would they crash into the huge mounds of snow at the end? When the wheels hit the runway and the air breaks applied, he immediately knew the answer. There was an intermission of grip on the runway, he could feel the aircraft sliding and he was struggling to control her. As they reached the halfway point down the runway, he could see a small concrete structure, which he presumed was the terminal building, but it was in complete darkness. All of a sudden four powerful search lights lit up the whole area. Parked to the right of the terminal was an Mil Mi-26, the military's largest and most powerful helicopter, with her giant rotor blades spinning round. The outer door slid open, and ten men dressed in white military camouflage uniforms jumped out. As the cargo plane shot past the helicopter at speed, Captain Cauchemer knew instantly that the large mounds of soft snow piled further down the runway would either be their saviour or destruction. As they hit deep dry snow the aircraft's wheels started to clog up. Eventually they started to slow down before coming to a complete halt.

"Brilliant flying captain, you are one hell of a pilot. I hold my hands up to you."

Vladimir smiled put didn't say anything. He was more concerned how he was going to get the aircraft back into the air again. What the hell was the Military helicopter doing here; surly they could have transported the two geologists to safety. Something sinister was going on and he did not like it.

"Sergei, what the hell is going on why the Military helicopter?"

The co-pilot turned and faced Vladimir, for a few moments he didn't speak. "I am sorry you have been dragged into this, you are a great pilot and a nice guy."

The security guard, who had hardly spoken throughout the flight, got out of his chair and walked behind Captain Vladimir Cauchemer. He then pulled out from under his long grey coat a Russian Lebedev Pl-15pistol and shot him in the back of the head twice. Blood immediately sprayed over the cockpit."

"You bastard there was no need to do that," said Sergei as he whipped away specs of warm blood from his face. "He has done you no harm, he was a good guy and his incredible skill as a pilot saved our lives today."

"He could have identified us." He then waved the pistol menacingly in front of Sergei's face. "Are you with us or not?"

2

London - England

Whenever Jack Sinclair visited his parents at their luxury apartment overlooking the River Thames in Central London, he always opened the balcony door and went outside, whether it was summer or winter made no difference. The view was always stunning, especially when daylight was fading and thousands of lights flickered on all over the city. The Thames, with illuminated river traffic darting back and forth, looked from a distance as though it was full of florescent river snakes. For no apparent reason he glanced at his gold Gucci watch as he stood on the balcony it was 5-15pm. There was a distinct chill in the air but then again it was the 8th November, another three weeks and his parents Edward and Rachelle would be back from their six week holiday in Australia and Singapore.

Jack was a 28-year-old bachelor and gemmologist with Hatton Garden diamond dealers Franks. Occasionally in the evenings he worked as DJ Ramos performing anything from house music to the latest chart hits. Friends told him that he was very good but friends often do. He knew he was good and enjoyed their praise, but he had to admit, he was no Calvin Harris. Calvin was the young DJ from Dumfries, Scotland, who was finding international fame partying his way through the Balearic holiday islands of Ibiza, Mallorca, and Menorca on the sun soaked Mediterranean.

Placing his hands on the balcony's stainless steel safety rail, he looked across the Thames to the *MI6* and Foreign Intelligence Service Headquarters on the Albert Embankment by the Vauxhall Bridge. The huge building looked quite spectacular, like many other people he often wondered what went on inside this bomb proof building. Today had been a great day, after a late lunch at Joe's Café Bar by the river, where he had his usual ham omelette and latte coffee, he returned to the apartment with a couple of cans of lager to watch his beloved football team Chelsea play Liverpool live at Anfield on Sky Television. An incredible result for Chelsea who won 2-1; they had now won fourteen consecutive matches. Going back inside the apartment, he laid full length on the soft cream leather sofa, intending to have an hour's shut eye, before having a shower and a change of clothes. Then, he would hit the road; find an upmarket wine bar which had glamorous barmaids and then get down to some serious drinking. What else could he do? He was single and free but he was not interested in shagging every pretty girl he chatted up, that was probably why he was still alone.

He would be the first to admit that he had been brought up to a very privileged life style. Jack could not sleep but instead he just lay there relaxing. His mind drifted back to late May when his father called him in Johannesburg, South Africa a week before he returned home to the UK. He had spent the last eighteen months, working for the world famous diamond mining company De Beers, where he gained valuable experience.

"Your mother and I are going to Singapore and Australia for a six week holiday. I have taken early retirement. As you know, your mother was born in Australia and I always said that I would take her back there again. I now think it is about time I kept my promise."

"I fully agree with you dad."

"If you like, we will pick you up at Heathrow International Airport when you arrive in the UK, just email us with the final details of your arrival."

"Thank you dad, I appreciate your offer."

"You can stay at our London apartment whilst we are away, infact you can stay there permanently until we decide to sell it, which we will do eventually. Your mother and I will be spending most of our time in our house in Ludlow, Shropshire as well as having a few holidays abroad. By the way Jack, you will need a job when you return home." My father always came straight to the point. "My close friend Jim Richardson, who is the Chairman of Franks the Hatton Garden diamond merchants, which are the largest importers of precious gems in the UK, may have a vacancy. Give him a call when you arrive home. They employ three full time gemmologists and one of them is retiring, I will give you Jim's telephone number when I see you."

"Thank you dad, I appreciate what you are doing for me."

Jack did call Jim Richardson and he offered him a job, which he accepted.

His mother Rachelle at fifty eight was a lovely looking woman, and could give any woman ten years younger a run for their money. Her parents had originally come from Brighton on the south coast of England. At the age of twenty four, they moved to Perth in Western Australia, which was known as the windy city and one of the most inaccessible cities in the world. His grandfather had answered an advertisement in the Times for skilled industrial electricians, which were desperately needed in the mines in the hinterland of Western Australia. The money was fantastic. After five years they intended to return home to England with enough money to buy a house and start up their own electrical business, as they never intended to live permanently in Australia. After two years his mother was born and became an Australian citizen. His grandparents were having a fantastic time. They owned an attractive three bedroom bungalow by the sea, a car and were not short of money. Every Monday morning at seven, his grandfather along with hundreds of other employees, used to fly out to the mining communities near Kalgoorlie and return at six on the Friday evening. Every weekend was party time for them, with either a barbecue or beach party. Life was fantastic. Then everything changed in the fourth year. His grandfather was killed in an explosion at one of the gold mines he was working in. His grandmother was devastated and once she had sorted out her affairs, which included a large insurance pay out for her husband's death, she moved back to England settling in Slough, which was is in commuting distance of London. Four years later she remarried but within fifteen months she was a widow again after her second husband died of cancer. She never married again and used all her energy to bring up her daughter. She did a marvellous job; his mother was extremely bright and ended up at the London School of Economics and Political Science. This is where she met Jack's father who was in his final year. They kept in touch and dated, love blossomed and eventually they got married. His father worked for Global Investments, he was a brilliant businessman with an incredible brain and soon worked himself up into a top management position. When the guy who owned the business retired, he did a financial deal with him, which allowed his father to take control of the business and eventually buy him out. Within months the company name was changed to Global International Investments. When his mother left University two years later, she went to work in his father's business until their family came along. Our family home was a detached four bedroom property by the river in Maidenhead. Jack has an older sister Lilly who is thirty two and a maths teacher at some posh Academy in London. She is happily married to her husband Bret Washington, who works for an International Bank in the city. They have two delightful children, seven-year-old twins a boy and girl. Jack also has a famous older brother Lex, who is a professional footballer. Not only has he played for Australia fifty six times because of our mother being Australian, he has also played for West Ham and Chelsea in the English Premier League as a mid-fielder. For the last three years of his career he has had one injury after another. Eventually Chelsea gave him a free transfer and he ended up in the Spanish Premier League La Liga with Malaga. After two seasons, his injuries flared up again forcing him into retirement. After gaining his coaching badge, he is now a respected coach with Malaga. Last year he married a stunning Spanish girl seven years his junior, she is now pregnant with their first child. They live in a fantastic villa with a swimming pool, on the coast between Malaga and Torremolinos, which has incredible views of the Mediterranean. He reckoned his brother must be worth at least fifteen million. Good luck to him, he loves him dearly."

Well what about Jack? He studied at Manchester University for three years to become a gemmologist, then to gain experience, he worked for several high class jewellers before deciding to specialize in the diamond market. For the last three years he has been working for De Beers in Amsterdam, Barcelona and Johannesburg, South Africa before joining Franks in London. Without sounding conceited, Jack rates himself as one of the top gemmologists in the business, but that does not guarantee you a top job, it is your reputation which counts.

What about his father? He built up Global International Investments into a massive company. Small investors were discouraged; he was not interested in the little guy with just a few thousand to invest. He wanted the high rollers with their millions. The UK Government's past and present had welcomed all wealthy foreigners, many of them dodgy to our shores with open arms, providing they had millions to invest. They even gave them residency permits. His father used these people, many who were on the run from their native country, to make his company millions. These clients never once complained, as they normally doubled or tripled their investment. Interest rates in the 80's and early 90's were high worldwide especially in offshore countries like Luxembourg, Channel Islands, Isle of Man or Cayman Islands in the Caribbean, where you could get as much as 15% interest tax free. At the age of forty nine according to Google, his father sold the company to a large American Bank for over two hundred million pounds. For twelve months he retired and then he became a Civil Servant. It wasn't until later years, that Jack found out that he actually set up and ran a department for *MI6* looking into the financial affairs of very wealthy people. You could be famous, a drug dealer, a Russian Oligarch or a deposed Dictator. His father even discovered that deceased dictators, Presidents Saddam Hussein of Iraq and Colonel Muammar Gaddafi of Libya, had invested millions of dollars in property in Central London under pseudo names, they all came under his father's scrutiny. Edward Sinclair knew so many powerful and wealthy individuals, that he was a natural for the job.

Jack had just finished having a shower when the intercom buzzed in the apartment. Switching on the CCTV camera he could see his sister Lilly and her husband Bret downstairs in the foyer.

"Hi folks please come up."

"Jack, we need to speak to you urgently."

There was something wrong; Bret had his arm around Lilly supporting her, she looked as though she had been crying.

Minutes later after taking the elevator to the fourth floor the buzzer rang again. On opening the door, his sister immediately put her arms around Jack and hugged him tightly. Tears were flowing uncontrollably from her eyes. At first he thought something terrible had happened to their children. Lilly tried to speak but she seemed paralyzed with shock. Bret touched Jack's shoulder, there were tears running from his eyes. He knew instantly that something terrible had happened to their parents. It could not be their brother Lex, he had received a text twenty minutes earlier from him in Malaga about Chelsea's famous victory over Liverpool. It had to be their parents.

Bret then composed himself. "Jack, I have some terrible news," he came straight to the point, "Your parents have been involved in a terrible helicopter accident in Australia. Neither of them has survived."

Whatever his brother in-law said next he never heard, the shock and pain almost caused him to pass out. Both brother and sister sat down on the sofa and held each other in their arms. It was years since they had both cried like this. They both loved and admired their parents; all they had ever wanted was to be with them as they grew old, not to have them snatched from their grasp without even a whisper.

After about twenty minutes Jack turned to his brother in-law. "Do you know what happened?"

"Yes, Edward and Rachelle had gone on a two day trip from Alice Springs to Ayers Rock some 450km away. If you recall Ayres Rock or Ulura as it is known by the Aborigines or the Indigenous Australians, is a massive red sandstone monolith in the heart of the Northern Territory. With another couple from New Zealand, they took a twenty minute helicopter ride around the rock. The weather appeared to be perfect, warm and sunny with no wind. Ten minutes into the flight and close to the summit of the rock, they struck severe wind turbulence. Whether or not the helicopter was flying to close to the rock I don't know at the moment, but the strong air currents circulating around Ayres Rock appeared to have dragged the helicopter into the cliff side, causing the rota blade to catch protruding rocks. The pilot, who was very experienced, tried everything to keep control of the helicopter but it went into a violent spin and plunged to earth. Though there was no fire or explosion, everybody on board was killed instantly, due to the intensity of the crash. The police identified your parents, with the help of a mobile phone and passports which were in your mother's handbag. Jack, they noticed that your mother had spoken to Lilly the day before so they called her number. Thank God I took the call."

"Lilly, we need to call Lex, he will be devastated. We don't want him finding out about the accident via the media. If you like I will call him."

"Thank you Jack, I was dreading having to call Lex." Lilly then leaned over and kissed him.

Lex was devastated; in fact their parent's death had ripped the heart out of the family. His elder brother was so emotionally distressed that he was unable to continue with the conversation, he said he would call back in twenty four hours which he did. He was now in more control but he knew Lex was finding it hard, even so he insisted on knowing all the details about their parents' dreadful accident.

"Jack, as the eldest sibling I will take charge of bringing our parents back to the UK for burial."

"Lex, you don't have to do it alone I am here to help you if you need me."

"Jack, this is something I have to do alone. Over the last few years, I have not seen our parents as much as I should have because of working and living in Spain. It is the least I can do for them." He then paused for what seemed eternity before continuing again but his voice was full of emotion and he started to cry, tears were now running from Jack's eyes.

The following day, Lex contacted the Foreign Office in London and he was put in contact with the British Diplomatic Commission in Canberra, Australia. They made all the arrangements to have their parents' bodies flown from Ayres Rock to Sydney. In the meantime, Jack's brother took a connecting flight from Malaga International Airport to Sydney to repatriate their parents to the UK.

Ten days later their parents' joint funeral service took place at St Peters Church, Vauxhall and London were later cremated together. Jack knew his father was held in the highest esteem in the financial world; both the media and television networks showed great interest and portrayed him as one of the leading financial experts of his generation. No mention was made of his involvement with *MI6*, only that he became a Government Civil Servant at the age of fifty until his retirement. As expected many important people attended the service but what took the family completely by surprise, was the sudden arrival of the Prime Minister, Foreign Secretary and Minister of Defence. They all then realized what an important man their father had been. After the service as guests were leaving the church, the Prime Minister shook Jack's hand warmly. "Your father would have been knighted in the coming New Year's honour list. He was a remarkable man, who served his country, you must be very proud of him."

His brother Lex and his wife stayed at their parents' apartment with Jack for a few days and then returned to Spain. Lilly was finding life extremely hard, she was very close to her mother and they spoke most days, losing her so tragically was a huge loss. Most people you speak to who have lost loved ones, say eventually your life slowly gets back to some sort of normality. Everyone is different; some people take months and even years, before they can see a light at the end of the tunnel.

Six weeks later solicitor Richard Webber contacted Jack about their parents' will, which was very straight forward. Everything was to be divided equally between the three siblings. The value of their parents' estate shocked them, almost two hundred and fifty million pounds. To avoid inheritance tax, their father had placed the majority of the estate in a trust. Jack decided to keep their London apartment as he needed somewhere to live. Lilly and her family, after selling their London property, moved into their parents' beautiful detached stone residence in the market town of Ludlow in South Shropshire. In medieval times Ludlow Castle was a summer haven for many Kings and Queens. Her husband Bret resigned from the International Bank, who employed him, and joined a small investment company in Kidderminster, Worcestershire as a partner. Jeremy Banks, who owned the company, had studied at University with Bret. They had kept in touch and knew each other well. Jeremy had worked hard building up the business, but urgently needed an influx of capital to take the company forward. Bret had the experience and now the money. He also had no intention of retiring at his age.

Regarding their parents' two properties, Lilly and Jack compensated their brother Lex, there never was going to be any problem over the property's valuation. Lex is continuing his idyllic life in Spain as a football coach, whist waiting for the birth of their first child. To an extent everyone was now happy and life carried on but Jack had a problem, loneliness. He needed to settle down with a loving wife. Having large wealth had its drawbacks. If he found the right girl, would she be with him because she loved him or would she be after his money. Fortunately at the moment that scenario was miles away. After spending Christmas with his sister Lilly, her husband Bret and children at their home in Ludlow, he flew to Spain to celebrate New Year's Eve with his brother Lex and his wife Maria at their villa near Malaga. He loved Spain, probably because of the many happy family holidays he had spent there.

He happened to mention his feelings to his brother Lex.

"I completely understand what you are saying. Why not come over for a few weeks and see if you like the Spanish way of life? You can always stay with us, we have plenty of room. You don't have to work, you could become an international playboy." Jack laughed out loud. "If on the other hand you decide that you want to work, you may be able to get employment at the diamond and gem importer Cobra Jewellery. They also have a number of upmarket stores along the Costa del Sol, and have recently opened an office and workshop in Marbella."

Jack smiled at his brother. "I will certainly give it some thought. I may even find myself a lovely looking Spanish wife like you."

"If you do come over, I will get Maria to introduce you to her two younger sisters, they are both very good looking girls."

Jack enjoyed the four days relaxing with his brother Lex and his wife at their villa in Spain, it went too quickly and then it was time to fly back to the UK and return to work at diamond dealers Franks. To be honest he was enjoying his job with Franks and the responsibility that it held. Even so, he certainly intended to give his brother Lex's suggestion a great deal of thought.

3

Moscow - Russia

Colonel Alexander Stepanov was more than a little surprised to receive a telephone call from the FSB, the Federal Security Service of the Russian Federation, formerly known as the KGB. He was now a private citizen, it had been many years since he had served in the military. The woman who spoke to him was very sure of herself and precise. "Colonel, Major Ivan Pavlov would like a few words with you. A serious problem has arisen and he feels you may be able to help him."

"Please tell the Major that I am certainly willing to help him if I can."

"Of course I will Colonel. A limousine will pick you up at your apartment at 10.15am tomorrow morning for an 11am appointment, and then return you to your home when the meeting has been concluded."

The Colonel could not help wondering why the FSB wanted to talk to him; he had been retired from active service for almost six years. He had not even spoken to anyone directly from the military for at least three years; it was as though his career had never existed. Ever since his early teenage years he had kept a diary even to the present day. The Colonel was extremely methodical, probably due to his military upbringing. His late father and grandfather had both fought for their country in Afghanistan against the Taliban and died bravely in action, both had posthumously received bravery awards. Opening his desk diary for Tuesday 4th May 2010 he wrote a few notes, "11am meeting with Major Ivan Pavlov of the FSB at the Kremlin. They will pick me up by limo at 10.15am." On the morning of the meeting Colonel Stepanov was very tempted to wear his old military uniform. Perhaps that was pushing it too far as he was now officially retired from active service. In the end he wore his dark grey suit, white shirt with a dark tie and black shoes. Glancing in the long gilt edged mirror in the hallway of his modern upmarket apartment overlooking the Moscow River, the Colonel felt more than pleased with his appearance. At sixty two and six two in height with broad shoulders he was still an imposing looking man. His hair which was swept back was still thick and dark, but now with streaks of grey. His neatly trimmed beard was also streaked with grey. The Colonel had always been a fitness fanatic, every day he would either go road running or train in his local gym; no way did he want to end up like some of his military colleagues who were fat and old looking.

The door buzzer to the apartment rang. When he opened the door a woman in her early thirties greeted him.

"Colonel Stepanov, I am Natasha, Major Pavlov's personal assistant and chauffeur. I have been instructed to drive you to the Kremlin to meet the Major."

Once outside the Colonel secured the apartment door, and then followed Natasha to the car park, where the Government black Mercedes limousine was parked. The early May weather was unusually good, the winter snow had receded and now it was mild and sunny. The view looking down the Moscow River, a tributary of the Oka River, which in turn was a tributary of the Volga Europe's longest river at 2,300 miles which emptied into the Caspian Sea, was stunning. Once they had hit the 'Special Highway' a wide flat lane down the middle dividing both the left and right roads, that ran directly from the President's residence and was reserved for very important people, Colonel Stepanov could see Red Square and the Kremlin creeping up on them. After driving through a heavily fortified side entrance, the limo was parked in a cobbled court yard with several other vehicles.

"If you would please follow me Colonel, I will take you to Major Pavlov's office."

As they walked down several faceless corridors, they were stopped twice by armed security and body searched. Eventually they reached the Major's office. Natasha knocked twice on the dark mahogany door.

"Enter."

"Major, this is Colonel Alexander Stepanov."

The Major, a slim bald headed man in his mid-forties of average height, immediately stood up from behind a dark mahogany office desk which was littered with paperwork, a computer which was switched off and two telephones, one white the other red. The walls and ceiling were covered in light mahogany and the room illuminated by two florescent lights. There were also several prints of uniformed officers on three walls; he recognised only one of them, a younger President Vladimir Putin when he was head of the KGB.

"An honour to meet you Colonel, I have heard so much about you. Please take a seat."

There were three very modern stainless steel, red and black leather chairs facing the Major's desk. The room felt stuffy, so the Colonel sat down on the one nearest to the only window in the room, but he then realized that it was closed.

"Would you care for tea or coffee Colonel?"

"Yes please, tea with milk but no sugar,"

"Would you mind Natasha?"

"Not at all Major she replied,"

"Would you ask my two assistants to join us and also bring in two extra mugs," the young woman smiled as she left the room.

Minutes later two men entered the room both in their early thirties, of average height and build. Both were clean shaven like their boss Major Pavlov. The Colonel looked at them closely. He had the distinct feeling that they were both FSB operatives.

"Gentlemen, I would like you to meet Colonel Alexander Stepanov. He is the Russian Federation's most decorated soldier with two Gold Stars for outstanding bravery in the war with the Chechen Republic. At the time the Colonel was a helicopter gunship pilot and commander, who under extreme enemy fire, rescued over seventy of our soldiers after their military transport plane had been shot down by a Sam missile. Twelve months later the Colonel also rescued twelve soldiers from certain death when their helicopter was shot down. I might add that Colonel Stepanov insisted on flying his helicopter gunship alone, in case he too was shot down."

Both the men then walked over and shook the Colonel's hand warmly.

"Major, what can I do for you?"

Major Pavlov then picked up the white telephone on his desk. "Natasha, would you please make certain that we are not disturbed for the next couple of hours." Seconds later Natasha arrived with four mugs of warm tea. After she had left the room, Colonel Stepanov repeated his question to the Major.

"Major, what can I do for you?"

"Colonel, we are trying to contact your son Sergei."

"I have not seen my son since he was six months old. My former wife walked out on me with our child and fled to Grozny in the Chechen Republic. The only contact I have had with her has been an official looking document to say she had divorced me. Our son is now twenty eight and I have never stopped thinking about him."

"You have a daughter Colonel."

"I most certainly have Sasha, she is thirty two and married to the only son of the President of Georgia. Sasha and her husband Christian have two young sons. When my wife walked out on me, I was left to look after my four-year-old daughter by myself. I could never understand how my wife, who had always been a loving mother, could abandon her."

"Where did your daughter meet your son in-law?"

"At Saint Petersburg State University where they both studied to be doctors, once they had both qualified they married and then set up home in Tbilisi, Georgia. They both now work as doctors in the city's main hospital." "Your daughter has done well for herself Colonel,"

"She certainly has, I am very proud of her."

"I am unable to help you with the whereabouts of my son Major, but why do you wish to speak to him?"

There was a brief silence, before the Major continued with the conversation. "On the 20th October last year, an Antonov An-124 Ruslan cargo plane was hijacked in Siberia with an estimated one billion Euros worth of diamonds and other precious gems on board. We believe your son Sergei was involved in this hijack."

"Why has it taken you almost seven months to ask for my help?"

"The weather Colonel. Most of Siberia is snowbound for more than half the year before nature gives up her secrets. At first we thought the Captain and Co Pilot of the cargo plane had hijacked the aircraft. We now believe they touched down at Norilsk to take on several passengers, a military vehicle was seen parked by the cargo plane.

Three weeks ago as the snow started to melt the frozen body of the Co-Pilot Alexei Petrov was discovered dumped on the outskirts of Norilsk. His body had been preserved in perfect condition apart from two bullet holes to the back of his head. We believe that your son Sergei boarded the cargo plane as the new Co-Pilot at Alykel Airport Norilsk. The cargo plane then continued on its flight to Khatanga Airport on the Taymyr Peninsula, where the cargo of diamonds and other precious gems were transferred onboard. We know from checking back on the flight radar, that the cargo plane for some reason then headed to the remote Siberian settlement of Dikson, eventually touching down in heavy snow and darkness on the small island airport, which is about 5km from the settlement. No one in Dikson saw the plane land, and as the airport was closed for the winter due to heavy snow, no one had any reason to visit the airport until a few weeks ago. A maintenance crew discovered the missing Antonov An-124 Ruslan cargo plane buried in deep snow whist clearing the runway. Using a mechanical digger they managed to gain entrance to the aircraft. Inside the cockpit, they found the frozen body of Captain Vladimir Cauchemer, like his Co-Pilot he too had been shot in the back of the head twice. No trace was found of the cargo. We are certain the eight metal containers carrying the diamonds and gems were loaded onto a helicopter and flown to an unknown destination. A MIL *Mi-26* fully fuelled Military helicopter, was taken by twelve heavily armed men dressed in white Military Police camouflage uniforms, from an airport hangar at Alykel Airport Norilsk. The airport staff thought nothing of it, as the officer in charge had paper work which was signed by our President, stating that they were on a secret Government mission, and must be given all the help they needed. The guy who flew the helicopter was obviously very experienced and knew what he was doing. It took real guts to fly that big bird in bad weather conditions."

"Where is the helicopter now?"

"We have not got a clue. The helicopter and hijackers along with the cargo have disappeared without trace."

"What makes you suspect my son was involved in the hijack?"

"Colonel, there is obviously a great deal you do not know about your son." The Major then turned to his two assistants. "My boys here will fill you in; they have done some excellent detective work over the last few weeks." The assistant who had short ginger hair opened the conversation. "Where did you first meet your former wife Colonel?"

"Here in the Kremlin." The three men looked at each other. "My wife was studying to be a lawyer at the Moscow State University. She had been invited to an award ceremony at the Kremlin, along with nine other female students, to serve drinks to the guests who were all from the military. Alina, that was her name, stood out from the other girls, she was an extremely attractive young woman and looked more Mediterranean than Russian. Over the next few hours we spoke to each other often. I discovered that she was twenty and came from Southern Georgia. At the time I was a handsome thirty-one-year-old helicopter pilot and squadron commander. I had never been married and had no children. We were immediately drawn to each other and started dating, fourteen months later we got married. There were no guests from Alina's side of the family, she said her parents had both died when she was a young child, and she had been brought up by an aunt who had since died. At the time I thought it was very strange. Once Alina had got her degree, she worked in the Kremlin for one of our MPs for about fifteen months before she became pregnant with our first child Sasha. I was rising quickly through the ranks; I was now a helicopter gunship squadron commander. Just as the Soviet Union disintegrated in 1991 the Chechen separatists declared independence. Three years later in 1994 the war broke out between Russia and Chechnya. It was terrible war with atrocities on both sides, with very heavy fighting and many losses both civilian and military. This was the time when I was awarded my first Gold Star and twelve months later my second Gold Star. I noticed at the time Alina showed little interest in my bravery awards. She said at the time "I hate all the killing, I just want peace and you to come home to me safely and then we can be a real family." After two years our forces withdrew from Chechnya, it had become Russia's Vietnam. Five years later in 1999 war was declared again and I was back again fighting. Again thousands of innocent people died, as Chechen separatist insurgents made direct attacks on the Russian people in their own cities. Even Moscow was not immune, with attacks by a group of women who called themselves the 'black widows'. They had all lost their husbands or partners in the war.

It was a terrible war in 2004, 333 Russians including 186 school children, who were being held hostage in their school on the Russian – Chechen border in North Ossetia, were murdered. Separatist gunmen who had invaded a Beslan School were attacked by Russian soldiers using hand grenades and submachine guns in a three day siege. This terrible atrocity pricked the conscious of both countries and sent shock waves round the world, even so it took until 2009 before a peace treaty was finally declared, in the meantime thousands of innocent civilians on both sides continued to die.

Three years after our first child was born, my wife gave birth to our second child Sergei. Life was becoming very difficult with Alina, she was constantly asking me to leave the military, but I loved my life serving the motherland. By the year 2000 I was a Lieutenant Colonel, after a great deal of deliberation I relented and left active service in the military, to become the Principle at the new purpose built Aviation and Aircraft Engineering Academy in Moscow. I was now promoted to a full blown Colonel. The year was 2002. My wife Alina was still not happy, and continually blamed the Russian military for all the deaths in Chechnya. "Look at all the orphans in the country, who is going to care for them? you are no different than the rest of the military. All you wanted to do was to wipe the Chechen people off the face of the earth." If she said this once to me, she must have repeated it half a dozen times. I was convinced Alina was on the verge of a mental breakdown, I desperately tried on many occasions to get her to visit a doctor but I got nowhere. One minute she would be a loving wife and a wonderful mother. If there were reports in the press or on the television news about the hardships the Chechen population were experiencing, she would then flair up."

The Major then interrupted. "Would you care for another drink Colonel?"

"I would love one, coffee if you don't mind"

The Major looked at his two colleagues who both smiled and nodded their heads. Picking up the white telephone on his desk, he spoke to his assistant Natasha in the adjoining room. A few minutes later Natasha entered the room with a white plastic try holding five mugs of coffee.

As soon as she left, Colonel Stepanov continued with his conversation. "As I was saying before Alina was causing me great concern, then suddenly my whole life changed and I might add not for the better. I had just finished a lecture in the academy to forty new students. I remember the day very clearly, it was a warm summer's day in late June. The mobile phone in my jacket pocket rang. It was Mai a close neighbour of our family. She and Alina took it in turn to pick the children up from a local nursery school. Alina had dropped the children off in the morning but had failed to collect either of the four-year-old girls at 2pm. Mai was extremely worried so I immediately rushed home, but there was no trace of Alina or our six month old son Sergei. At first I thought my wife had gone into the city shopping and had simply forgotten to collect the children. When she had not returned home by seven I called the police. They did a thorough check, even the possibility of them being kidnapped by Chechen extremists was mentioned, but to no avail. There were even suggestions because of Alina's health, that she had committed suicide in the Moscow River taking our son with her. Neither Alina or Sergei turned up, then out of the blue eighteen months later, I received an official looking letter from Alina saying that she had divorced me and was now living in Grozny, Chechnya. I passed the letter onto the police, but they had an impossible task as there was still a great deal of fighting and unrest in many parts of Chechnya and diplomatic relations had not yet been fully restored. From that day onwards my life has been in limbo, and I have never heard or had any further contact from my former wife or our son."

The Major then turned to the Colonel. "You will be pleased to know that due to the incredible efforts of my two assistants we can now answer most of your questions. Officer Sokolov, would you please continue?" The officer cleared his throat and then started to speak. "Your wife Alina was born in Tbilisi, Georgia. Her mother was Georgian but her father was from Chechnya. When the first Chechen war broke out with Russia, Alina's father went back to his homeland to fight for his country, her mother insisted in going with her husband. Rather than put Alina in any danger, they left her in Georgia in the care of a relative who had no children. Alina's parents then went to Grozny, but a couple of months later died together during one of the heavy Russian bombing raids. Alina's relative a close aunty had no option but to bring up the child as her own daughter. She did a marvellous job and Alina ended up going to the Moscow State University to study law and of course she then met you."

The Colonel took a long drink of his coffee. In fact they all did. "Please continue officer."

"We have also discovered by perseverance and good luck what has happened to your former wife. When she walked out on you with your son Sergei she flew to Tbilisi, Georgia. She left your son with the same aunt who had brought her up. Alina then made her way alone to Grozny in Chechnya. It was her intentions to try and help the hundreds of children orphaned by the war, which she most certainly did. Shortly after sending you the divorce papers she was killed in one of the last bombing raids on Grozny. Though the city was now a wasteland of bombed buildings, the memorial garden in the city centre was completely untouched, it was as though the good Lord had preserved it for posterity. A memorial plaque in her honour has since been erected." The officer then opened the file he was holding and passed a photograph to the Colonel, which had been emailed to them by one of their operatives in the city. Tears formed in the Colonel's eyes as he read what was on the memorial plaque. "Alina Aslanov. In honour of a very remarkable woman from Georgia who came to Grozny to care for a generation of orphaned children and died fulfilling her dream."

The officer then continued. "Again like her own mother, her elderly aunt had no choice but to bring up your son Sergei as her own child. Once again she did a wonderful job and young Sergei eventually attended the Military Academy in Moscow, where you are the principle. Your paths probably passed, but you would not be aware who this young man really was, as he had been brought up to use his mother's maiden name. When Sergei was originally accepted at the Academy at the age of eighteen, he was one of twenty elite orphaned students who immediately bonded with each other. They had arrived from Georgia and Chechnya to be trained as pilots or aircraft engineers. At the age of twenty three Sergei qualified as both a helicopter and aircraft pilot. We understand he was an exceptional student. Colonel with you being his natural father, it is easy to see where he got his talent from." The Colonel smiled. "Once your son was qualified he did not return home to Georgia as expected but instead enrolled at the Moscow State University to study to become a gemmologist. He eventually qualified at the age of twenty five. For the next twelve months he worked at the Popigal Creator diamond mine on the Taymyr Peninsula, Siberia as a gemmologist and helicopter pilot. After leaving there he went to Grozny in Chechnya for a few weeks and then travelled to Georgia to see his ageing aunt. Three months later, he flew to Johannesburg South Africa to take up a twelve month contract with the famous diamond mining company De Beers. When Sergei returned to Georgia and this is where our investigation starts to come up against a brick wall, the only discovery we have made is that for six months, he was contracted by our Government to fly cargo planes into war torn Syria for

President Bashar al Assad, who desperately needed medical supplies and vital military hardware. Once his contract was up he just disappeared off the radar, it was as though he had never existed until now."

Major Pavlov then got involved in the conversation. "Do you see your daughter often?"

"Yes, every month without fail. She means the world to me, we have always been extremely close and I love being with her and my grandchildren and of course her husband. I normally take an early morning flight from Moscow to Tbilisi, Georgia and stay for a long weekend or a couple of weeks in the summer. Why do you ask?"

"Has your daughter ever mentioned her brother to you in conversation?"

"Yes, occasionally when we are alone, we will both talk about Sergei and wonder where he is now and what he is doing. My daughter is fully aware about my wife leaving with our son but you must remember, it was many years ago and Sasha was only four."

"I understand Colonel but I had to ask you. When will you be seeing her again?"

"Later this week, I am taking an early morning flight out to Georgia on Thursday, and will return on Sunday evening. I am due back at the Academy on Monday."

"Perhaps you will ask her again? May I suggest you ask her husband as well? He may know him socially as Sergei Aslanov, but may not be aware who he is."

"When I arrive in Georgia, I will speak to both my daughter and her husband and if there is anything urgent to report I will call you."

The Major then passed the Colonel a black and white business card, which had his office and mobile telephone numbers on. The Colonel took the card and slipped it into his left inside jacket pocket.

"We urgently need to contact your son Colonel, he may have been hired just as a pilot and knew nothing about the hijack, and he could be completely innocent."

"You think my son is alive?"

"There is no reason for us to think otherwise; apart from the pilot and co-pilot of the cargo plane we have found no other bodies."

"Major, where do think the *Mi-26* helicopter is now it is a huge bird to hide?"

"Possibly in an old military aircraft hangar somewhere in Chechnya,"

"Maybe, but they would have had to refuel, Dikson to Grozny is over 2,300 miles. Could be that the hijackers want you to think that. They could have abandoned the helicopter at some old air strip and camouflaged it, so it is not visible from the air. There are dozens of these air strips all over Russia, especially in the region bordering the Ural Mountains. These guys are obviously well organised, they could have even had a small cargo plane waiting for them at one of these remote air strips. Perhaps this is where my son comes into the scenario, though it is only hypothetical; his job could have been to fly the hijackers to some pre-arranged destination. What about the Chechen Mafia otherwise known as the Obschina? I believe they are now the most dominant crime group in Moscow. It would have taken big money to set up this operation, they certainly have the rubbles and the contacts to move the diamonds out of the country and on to the international market, but there is something wrong." The three men in the room looked at the Colonel waiting for an explanation. "If the Chechen mafia are behind the hijack, why involve these young men from my academy? None of the students are violent or gangsters. The mafia have enough foot soldiers in Moscow to build a small army. Why involve my boys?" The Colonel stroked his beard with his right hand. "There is something else going on. When I speak to my son in-law in Georgia over the weekend I may gain more information. His father the President may have said something to him." The Colonel then turned to the Major. "On the other hand if my students and the mafia are not involved who the hell are the hijackers? There can only be one other possibility, the military it has to be, there can be nobody else."

Major Pavlov did not answer but glanced at his watch, he then got up from behind his desk. "Colonel, thank you for coming to see us we won't detain you any longer. When we have any further information we will contact you." The Major then picked up the white telephone on his desk. "Natasha, would you please drive Colonel Stepanov back to his apartment?"

"Major, I am not happy. You continue to point accusations in the direction of my son and his fellow orphaned students from Chechnya.

What proof do you have?" There was then a knock on the door and Natasha walked in.

The Major hesitated. "Natasha, something has just cropped up so would you give us another hour."

The girl smiled. "May I remind you Major, that you have a meeting with the Defence Minister at 2pm?"

"Please remind me again in forty-five minutes."

Natasha replied. "Certainly Sir," and smiled as she left the room.

"You want proof Colonel; perhaps this may open your eyes?"

Walking back behind his desk Major Pavlov took a large red file from the bottom left hand side drawer and passed it to the Colonel, who had sat down again.

"Normally this information would never be available to you, but because of whom you are and your high rank I am making an exception. Please go ahead and look through the file."

The Colonel opened the file which contained twenty plastic sleeves; inside each was a photograph of a young man. Some had red stars attached them.

"Colonel, the first photograph is of your son Sergei. He is a fine looking boy and he certainly has a clear resemblance to you. All the other photographs are of his orphan friends from Chechnya, the photos with red stars attached to them are considered to be suspects.

Colonel Stepanov had great difficulty taking his eyes off his son's photo. "Major, I now recall my son and several of his colleagues. They were a very talented group of young men, quick learners and spoke the Russian language perfectly. If you are able to, please tell me more."

"This group of young men, including your son spent most of their free time frequenting the bars and night clubs in the city which are owned by the Chechen Mafia. They have become very close friends of the Suleimanov brothers, whose gangster father Nikolay took control of the city in the 1980's. The violence the Chechens used to become the dominant crime group in Moscow is unparalleled. They often strung up and tortured their enemies to death with a blow torch. The Major then took a purple file out of the same drawer and passed it to the Colonel. "Take a look at these photographs; they prove without any doubt that these young men from Chechnya including your own son know the Suleimanov brothers well."

"May I ask how you have come across all this information?"

"I will just say Colonel that we have a most reliable insider. We at the FSB believe there are two major operations going on. Firstly the mafia are out to make big bucks out of the diamond and gem hijack. If they dispose of them even at a fraction of their true value they will still make a huge profit. We believe that they will need the services of your son, who is an expert gemmologist to negotiate the sale of the gems to overseas buyers. Secondly, the Chechen orphans have never forgiven the Russian Government for the death of their parents. Our contact tells us, that there is talk about the mafia supplying the Chechens with arms and explosives to launch a new insurgent movement against Russia. Since this revelation, we have been in touch with the Chechnya Government. They are convinced that it is just talk from the deep hatred they still feel towards the Russian Government. We also believe that several of the so called Military Police, who boarded the cargo plane at the Alykel Airport Norilsk, were former students at your Aviation Academy along with several Chechen Mafia gangsters. The bullets removed from the back of Captain Vladimir Cauchemer's head, match a gun used in several killings in Moscow three months ago. The executioner was more than likely the same guy. Can you now see why we urgently need to speak to your son?"

Colonel Stepanov looked at the three men and shook his head in disbelief. "Are you absolutely certain about all these facts and that my son is involved."

"I am sorry Colonel but the facts speak for themselves. Your son Sergei has to be one of our chief suspects, as in the past he worked at the Popigal Creator diamond mine on the Taymyr Peninsula as a gemmologist and helicopter pilot. We must also not forget that your son attended the same Aviation Academy as the Chechen orphans." The Major then stopped speaking for a few seconds whilst he took a final drink of his coffee. "Because of who you are, we are prepared to hold an olive branch out to your son. If he comes forward, that is if he can be contacted, and gives us all the information he knows, we will overlook everything that has happened providing he co-operates. It is far better than being blown away by the mafia, as he most certainly will be when he is of no further use to them."

"I wish I could help you, but I do not know where Sergei is at the moment. Do you know?"

"Our contact in the mafia, informs us that he currently lives in Moscow but where we have no idea. There is a possibility that he could be living in a dacha on the outskirts of the city. Many wealthy and influential Russians, often have second homes away from the hustle and bustle of the city. We suspect a number of these guys have mafia links. The problem is the FSB are unable to mount a raid, unless we have absolute proof that Sergei is hiding in one of them. If we target the wrong dacha and the owner happens to be a friend of the President, we are in the shit big time. We have to be patient and very careful but sooner or later we will find him."

"Major, before I leave, could you let me have a photo copy of the photograph of my son? My daughter Sasha would love to see him as would my son in-law, it may prompt his memory."

"Of course I will."

One of the Major's assistants then removed Sergei's photo from the red file and went into the adjoining room. A few minutes later he returned with two copies both in a plastic sleeves.

"For you and your daughter Colonel,"

"Thank you."

The Major then picked up the white phone on his desk and called Natasha back into the office.

Colonel Stepanov was deep in thought as he relaxed in the rear seat of the Mercedes limousine as Natasha drove him back to his riverside apartment. He was glad to have left the Kremlin; it had felt more like an interrogation. He was extremely worried about Sergei and knew that when his son was eventually apprehended, the full force of the law would come down on him. No way did he believe Major Pavlov, when he said his son would face no charges provided he co-operated with the authorities. From experience he knew it just did not work like that in Russia. When he arrived back at his apartment he would have a large glass of Jack Daniel's Whisky, he had never been one for vodka and had no intentions of starting now. Next week when he returned to the Military Academy after the mid-term break, he intended to search through data computer records of all the students from Chechnya and

Georgia, who had attended the Academy over the last five years. With a bit of luck, he would then have an insight into who were the fellow conspirators with his son Sergei.

4

London - England

Life was slowly returning to some form of normality for Jack Sinclair, since the tragic helicopter death of his parents in Australia. Though if he was perfectly honest it will never be normal again, it was now more of a routine. He missed his mother and father immensely and had spoken to them most days, even when he was living thousands of miles away from home. His father Edward had done him a great favour, by recommending him to Franks in London, who urgently needed an experienced gemmologist. He enjoyed working for the diamond and precious gem merchants. After a few months the chairman Jim Richardson, who was a close friend of his late father, put him in charge of the purchase of rough diamonds. A new life opened up to him. Gone was his 8.30am to 5pm job, instead he was frequently jetting off abroad to Antwerp, Belgium, the diamond centre of the world, where he would often purchase on behalf of Franks, several million pounds worth of rough diamonds. Trips to New York, Beijing and Dubai and other Middle Eastern countries followed; these countries had an insatiable demand for a girl's best friend and Jack was a most persuasive salesman. Jack Sinclair was now a celebrity in the diamond market where he had formed contacts worldwide, even so he was still not a happy guy. There was no one in his life. Sophisticated night clubs had never been his scene; he would much sooner spend the night sat by the bar in one of the trendy wine bars along the Thames embankment where he lived. The only problem was that single pretty girls very rarely visited these bars alone. Most nights unless he was watching television he would end up in his favourite haunt Sam's Café Bar, having a meal and a couple of pints of Peroni. This evening was no exception, he had just arrived back from a tiring trip to New York and Beijing and he didn't feel like cooking his own meal. It was a gloriously warm late July summer's evening when Jack walked into his favourite café bar. The pavement outside the bar opposite the River Thames was overflowing with locals and tourists of all nationalities. Most of them were enjoying a meal and a drink under the large multi-coloured umbrellas. Inside the bar was just as busy, fortunately the air conditioning was switched on. Looking to the right of the long modern curved bar, he saw that his usual black and red leather bar stool was vacant in the corner. Eventually he sat down and managed to order a bottle of Peroni.

"Good to see you Jack, it must be a couple of weeks since we last saw you."

The young woman, who was about the same age as himself, kissed him on both sides of his stubble face. He could feel the warm of her soft breasts through the thin white short sleeveless dress she wore as she pressed herself against him, as well as the lingering allure of Channel perfume.

"Can I get you a drink darling?"

"I have just ordered a Peroni. I know you are very busy but is there any chance of some food?"

"Could you give us half an hour? Mattia is run off his feet in the kitchen." Jack smiled and nodded his head. "What would you like to eat?"

"Chicken pasta,"

"No problem. If you will excuse me, I will speak to you later."

Jack liked Sophie and Mattia who owned the bar; they had worked extremely hard building up the business. Their overheads were high, but with Mattia being the main chef it saved them thousands a year in wages. With three kitchen assistants Mattia could cope with any number of customers. His wife Sophie ran the bar and restaurant with four assistants. She was a lovely looking girl at about five four with long blond hair and a stunning figure. Her warm smile and infectious personality could put anyone at ease. When Jack ran his eyes over her, the same thoughts always went through his mind, perhaps one day, hopefully sooner than later he would meet a girl like Sophie. Half an hour later Sophie brought him his chicken pasta. Punters, mainly tourists were now slowly starting to drift away to their hotels. After pouring herself a glass of red wine, Sophie came over and sat on the vacant bar stool next to him. Her tanned legs looked beautiful as she crossed them seductively on the stool. She was obviously a girl who took a great pride in her appearance and loved to be admired by the opposite sex.

"Have you just been away on holiday?"

"No, I have been abroad on business for my employers Franks. I spent three days in New York before flying to Beijing China."

"Aren't Franks a diamond and precious gems company?" "You have been doing your homework." Sophie laughed. "China is our largest market."

"Have you had a good trip?"

"Could always be better but I should not complain."

"You look tired Jack."

"I am absolutely shattered. I didn't get into Heathrow International Airport until this 3pm this afternoon after an 11 hour 5,000 mile flight. I am going to head for home in a few minutes, fortunately I don't have to be in the office until mid-day."

"Have you anything lined up for this weekend?"

"Yes, as soon as I finish work tomorrow, I am going to drive to Ludlow to visit my sister Lilly and her family. I shall have a long weekend with them and then return to London on Monday. I start work again on Tuesday."

Ten minutes later Jack left Sam's Café Bar and by ten he had hit the sack.

After sleeping for almost twelve hours the jet lag had virtually disappeared. Once he had showered, shaved and eaten a light breakfast Jack took the elevator to the ground floor. The security doors instantly opened as he walked towards the exit. Once out of the building, Jack walked a few yards to the road before waving down a cab. It was a beautiful day, warm with a clear sky and no wind. The Thames was already busy with water taxis and working barges going back and forth and it was only eleven fifteen in the morning. The black cab, due to heavy traffic, took about thirty minutes to arrive at Franks in Hatton Garden. He could easily have got there in less time had he walked. Security at Franks was extremely high as expected at the UK's largest diamond merchants. Along with CCTV, there was an armed security guard on the outer door, who checked out all clients. If the guard was happy, you were then admitted to a small room which had a bomb proof door, through which you could gain entrance to the main building; this could only be opened via photo and finger print recognition. Once inside you were in another world, a modern twenty first century building with all the latest computer technology.

"Have you had a good trip Mr Sinclair?"

"I have June, but I am glad to be back in the UK, it has been very tiring. Would you give me ten minutes in my office and let Mr Richardson know that I have arrived back in the building?"

"Of course I will Mr Sinclair."

June on reception was a lovely woman. In her early thirties, she was extremely attractive with long blond hair, about five six and quite slim, with a beautiful smile, she was married with an eight-year-old daughter. Franks which was situated in a two storey building had a staff of thirty. All the offices including the director's boardroom were on the ground floor. On the second floor, eight gem cutters or lapidarists as they are called in the industry worked under stringent security measures to cut and polish millions of pounds worth of precious gems, which were then exported to clients worldwide.

Ten minutes later the internal phone rang in Jack's office. "Mr Richardson said would you mind going through to his office now."

"Thank you June,"

Jack knocked on the chairman's office door and walked in. "Jack, good to see that you have arrived back safely." The two men shook hands.

"Have you have had a good trip?"

"Business has been excellent especially in New York, but it has been very tiring due to the time differences."

"Coffee, Jack?"

"I would love one, milk but no sugar if you would please." Jim then picked up the black and grey internal phone on his desk. "Sakura, would you please bring us two coffees with milk but no sugar."

A few minutes later, a young Asian girl who he presumed was Sakura walked in with two white mugs of coffee. After she left the room, Jim beckoned to the two black leather chairs, by the light mahogany office desk. They both sat down.

"Tell me Jack how is our friend Chang Yang."

"He and his family are in excellent health; Mr Yang sends his kindest regards to you and Mrs Richardson."

"Next year my wife and I intend to visit him in Beijing." "Chang told me something in complete confidence, as he has known and done business with you for over twenty five years, he thought you should know. We may have a new serious competitor."

Jim immediately placed his half empty mug of coffee he was drinking on the office desk. "Tell me more."

"A smart looking Russian guy in his late twenties, who was extremely knowledgeable, has approached Chang and several other leading gem dealers offering them rough diamonds and other precious gems at ridiculously cheap prices. He said that he represents a new Russian precious gem company called Gem Stone International. They have offices in Moscow, Spain and Tunisia. He says that Gem Stone International, have bought vast quantities of diamonds and other precious stones direct from a mine on the Taymyr Peninsula Siberia. As we both know, diamonds from that area are almost perfect."

"Did Chang buy any of the stones?"

"No, but several of his competitors did. They formed a consortium and purchased fifty million dollars worth of rough gems mainly diamonds. Chang Yang says there is no way he can compete with them on price but he is not concerned at the moment. He has a bad feeling about this Russian gem dealer and wonders if he really is Russian. If Gem Stone International did flood the world market with cheap pure gems, then the market will collapse. He can't believe that the Russian Government would have sanctioned this operation, but he has not heard anything to the contra." "Have the Chinese gem dealers received their consignment of precious stones?"

"Yes, within ten days, once they had deposited their fifty million dollars with the Arab Banking Corporation in Sousse, Tunisia. Their precious stones were then actually delivered from Spain by a direct flight from Malaga International Airport to Beijing."

"Was the paper work in order?"

"I am unable to say, we never discussed that but I am sure it was otherwise there would have been problems with customs."

Jim Richardson then shook his head. "Obviously something is going on. I will make a few discrete calls, including one to Antwerp to see if anyone has heard anything." Jim then rose from his chair. "Jack, thanks for bringing this to my attention, I will speak to my fellow directors after I have made the phone calls."

The two men then walked towards the office door.

"Let me have your written report on your business trip as soon as possible, and then I can show my fellow directors when I speak to them."

"Of course I will, it will be in your office before I leave for home this evening."

"By the way, before I forget. Mr Yang has a present for you." Jack then reached into his left hand jacket pocket and took out a small purple velvet box and passed it to his boss, who looked most surprised.

"Go ahead and open it, it is your gift."

A broad smile crossed Jim Richardson's face as he opened the box, he then looked up at Jack as his glasses slipped to the end of his nose.

"This is one of two rough samples which the Russian businessman gave Mr Yang. It is flawless; you may need it to further your enquiries."

"Thank you Jack, I will email Chang Yang and thank him, I appreciate his loyalty."

When Jack left Franks shortly after five, he decided to walk back to his apartment, rush hour traffic was just far too heavy to call a cab, in any case it was a beautiful evening and the walk would do him the world of good. After eating a frozen beef lasagne which he had recently purchased from M&S, he made his usual Friday night call via Skype to his brother Lex in Malaga, Spain. Once the apartment was secured Jack took the elevator down to the underground car park. He was looking forward to the 155 mile drive to Ludlow, which would take him about three and a half hours. This would be his first long drive in the new Firenze red and black metallic Range Rover Sport, which he had recently bought. Once he had placed his dark blue sports bag into the boot, he got into the driving seat and fired the vehicles powerful engine and headed out of the car park. As he waited for a break in the traffic, he slipped on his dark designer shades and glanced at his gold Gucci watch, it was just leaving six- forty. Traffic was still very heavy as he made his way to the M25 before finally slipping on to the M40. Though traffic at times was quite heavy the journey was quite uneventful.

About forty minutes from Ludlow, Jack called his sister Lilly on the mobile. "I will be with you around ten-fifteen."

"No problem, be careful Jack it will be almost dark when you arrive. The children will be both in bed but Bret and I will be waiting for you."

"See you shortly sis."

Thirty five minutes later the Range Rover Sport pulled up outside the black wrought iron gates leading to the property. Jack jumped out of the 4x4 and pressed the intercom on the right hand side of the stone gate pillar. Seconds later the gates slowly opened and then closed as he drove up the tree lined drive to Lilly and Bret's impressive five bedroom detached stone house. Every time he returned to Castle View, his late parents' house, he half expected one of them to open the front door and welcome him. He was happy his sister had decided to keep the family home and allowed the urn containing their parents' ashes to be buried in the rose garden below a memorial plaque.

As he pulled up outside the property everywhere came to life as the security lights flickered on illuminating the surrounding gardens. Everything was the same as always, the lawns were perfectly manicured; flowers and bushes were in full bloom. Even the water fountain with Eros standing guard was in full flow. The solid dark oak front door opened just as Jack switched off the ignition. He immediately got out of the Range Rover as Lilly and her husband Bret came out of the house. Coming over to her brother, Lilly put her arms around him and held him tightly whispering in his ear. "Jack, good to see you again, I love you," before kissing him on both sides of his face.

Lilly was so much like their mother Rachelle. She always used to say the same words when he used to come and stay with them.

Bret shook Jack's hand warmly. He was a lovely guy, a good husband and a wonderful father. Lilly was very lucky she had found such a very special person.

"When did you get the Range Rover?"

"Three weeks ago, I decided to splash out rather than keep hiring cars."

"It looks a million dollars Jack and I love the colour."

Jack then removed his sports bag from the vehicle and followed Lilly into the house. Bret was slightly behind them. Lilly then went through into the spacious modern grey and white kitchen, whilst Jack was in the lounge with Bret.

"You are in your usual room upstairs, looking out over the side garden." She called.

"Thank you Lilly."

"Would you like tea or coffee?"

"Coffee if you would but no sugar."

"Can I get you anything to eat?"

"I am fine. I had a light meal before I left London."

A few minutes later Lilly came into the lounge with three light blue mugs of coffee.

"You look tired Jack?"

"To be quite honest with you, I am extremely tired. I only returned from a business trip to America and China on Thursday afternoon and with the long drive from London to Ludlow, I am shattered."

Lilly then walked across the room and linked his left arm. "Darling, you get to bed and we can talk tomorrow."

Jack then kissed his sister's forehead. "Thank you for being so understanding, I will see you both in the morning." He then left the room, picked up his sports bag from the hallway and headed upstairs to his bedroom. The room which was south facing was stuffy and warm, so he opened the window to let some air in. After hitting the sack he was asleep in a matter of minutes.

Saturday was another beautiful day warm and sunny and it was only eight in the morning. Swallows were darting back and forth. Several birds were perched on the edge of the water fountain pruning their feathers. Jack quickly took out the mobile phone from his left trouser pocket and took a few photos of the birds.

After parking the Range Rover, which he had left in front of the house last night, he made his way to their parents' small memorial garden in the rose bed. The flowers were in full bloom and looked exquisite, so he took several more photos with his mobile phone. Tears started to form in his eyes as he said a prayer to his loving parents. He missed them terribly but he knew his sister Lilly would always look after them. When he finally returned to the house, all the family had risen and were in the kitchen. Lilly was in the middle of preparing breakfast. When the twins saw Jack they immediately rushed up to him shouting out "Uncle Jack, Uncle Jack." Putting his arms around them he gave both Bethany and Paul a hug and a kiss. They were lovely children, Lilly and Bret must be very proud of them.

Lilly was a fine chef and the full English breakfast she prepared was excellent, it was a long time since he had sat down and enjoyed a meal so much that early in the morning. About an hour later leaving Lilly in the kitchen, Bret and Jack went outside and sat on the dark green wrought iron chairs on the stone patio, which overlooked the rear garden.

"Bret, how is your Investment Company in Shrewsbury progressing?"

"We are doing extremely well. I have recently managed to do a deal with the International Bank I used to work for, this will allow us to arrange loans through them for our clients. Joining up with Jeremy Banks has been a great move, I have no regrets."

Jack smiled. "You Lilly and the children appear to be so happy here."

"We are but we all miss your parents terribly." Bret then changed the subject. "How did your overseas business trip go?"

"Very good, Franks are an excellent company to work for but I can see huge problems ahead." Jack then told his brother in-law about Gem Stone International approaching their clients in China.

"If it is not the Russian Government, then who is it?" "There can only be one other explanation, the Russian Mafia. If it is them, somehow they have managed to get hold of an enormous supply of rough diamonds and other precious gems probably by fraudulent means."

Bret raised his eyebrows. "This could have very serious repercussions on the world market."

"The chairman of Franks, Jim Richardson, who was a close friend of my father, is currently looking into the situation. Jim has many friends in high places in and out of government, I am certain he will find out what is going on. At the moment there is nothing I can do, so I intend to enjoy my weekend with the family."

As the sun was getting stronger Bret and Jack slipped on their dark shades, and then went for a walk in the garden with the children, who were becoming a little restless. The weekend turned out to be most relaxing. On Saturday evening they dined at home and opened a couple of bottles of German white wine, as Lilly was most reluctant to use a babysitting service. Jack could not have agreed with her more. On Sunday they went to the Unicorn Inn in Ludlow for a late Sunday lunch. The food was excellent, the children were happy and so was Lilly.

Shortly after ten on Monday morning Bret left for his office in Shrewsbury and Jack headed back to London. He had thoroughly enjoyed his weekend break with the family; it was his intention in future to visit them every month. Apart from his brother Lex who lived in Spain, they were all he had and he loved them dearly.

5

Colonel Alexander Stepanov felt slightly uneasy as he got out of the black Mercedes taxi at Moscow's Vnukovo International Airport. It was not the eight-thirty morning flight to Shota Rustaveli International Airport Tbilisi, Georgia which concerned him, as he had made this journey on numerous occasions. He was most concerned what the reaction would be from his daughter Sasha, when she saw the photograph of her long lost brother Sergei.

The warm sun was just starting to break through the overcast sky, as the Georgian Airways Boeing 737 lifted off runway two. The flight to Shota Rustaveli International Airport Tbilisi, Georgia which was a little over one thousand miles, normally took about two and a half hours. The Colonel was travelling light for his long weekend break. All he had was a small black wheelie suitcase, which he had placed in the overhead locker. As well as his personal belongings, he had also placed inside the suitcase for safety, two photographs of his son Sergei.

Time literally flew by. The flight was uneventful, no food was served which was normal, but complementary hot and cold drinks were always available. The three attractive Georgian air hostesses, who were always smiling, said very little until the plane was due to land. Then the aircraft became a hive of activity with the girls rushing around making certain all one hundred and thirty two passengers had their seat belts fastened, as they were due to land in twenty minutes. There was not even an announcement over the intercom from the senior air hostess or captain before they landed; it was though the aircraft was being flown by computer on autopilot. With a huge roar from the plane's four engines, the air brakes were thrown into reverse as they made a perfect landing. Once the captain had gained complete control of the aircraft, he taxied to gate number two by the Terminal Building, and shut down the Boeings engines. One of the air hostesses then opened the outer door of the aircraft. It felt like an oven as the warm Georgian air rushed in. After the Airstairs was attached to the fuselage the passengers slowly left the aircraft and walked across the tarmac to the Terminal Building. The Colonel immediately removed his dark shades as he passed through passport control and customs before entering the arrival lounge. He had no difficulty recognising his beautiful looking daughter

Sasha; she was the mirror image of his late wife. She looked stunning in her pink and blue summer dress as she walked towards him.

"Hi dad, it is lovely to see you again." Sasha put her arms around her father and then kissed him on both sides of his face. "My Toyota 4x4 is parked nearby but I am only allowed twenty minutes. I think we should go before I get a parking ticket. Can I help you with your suitcase?"

The Colonel laughed. "I am not that old." His daughter laughed. "You look lovely darling." Sasha smiled fondly at her father, as she took hold of his left hand.

"How are you dad?"

"I am absolutely fine. What about you and your family, are you all well?"

"Yes, we are all in good health. Christian has now qualified as a heart surgeon."

"You must be very proud of him."

"I am. He has worked so hard to get where he has."

"Are you still working as a doctor at the Central Republican Hospital?"

"Yes, but only three days a week, Monday to Wednesday."

Once the Colonel had put his suitcase into the boot of the Toyota and sat in the passenger seat next to his daughter, they left the airport complex. After slipping onto the main duel carriageway, they headed in the direction of Tbilisi the charming capital of Georgia, some eleven miles away. The scenery was stunning, with little traffic on the road. After a mile or so, both the Colonel and his daughter slipped on their dark shades to protect their eyes from the strong clear sun. The temperature outside was rising towards 28c according to the on-board temperature gauge, and it wasn't even mid-day. As they approached the city they could see the centuries old ruins of the Norikola Fort on the hillside overlooking Tbilisi. Once through the old area of the city, with its cobblestone roads and quaint buildings, which still retained an influence from when Georgia was part of the Persian Empire, the Toyota 4x4 headed towards the modern suburbs of the city. With a population of over one million there was a great deal of development in progress and many twenty first century buildings were springing up.

Sasha and Christian's home was a modest detached three bedroom single storey villam with whitewashed walls and a rustic tiled roof, down a quiet tree lined road with several other similar properties. The large garden was lovingly maintained and full of flowers which were normally only found in Mediterranean countries. Georgia's location in Europe on the Black Sea was the reason for the perfect climate. The Colonel was sorry to get out of the air conditioned Toyota into the searing heat, but soon acclimatised once he was in the house drinking a cool glass of orange.

"What time will Christian be home?"

Sasha glanced at her gold watch. "About five-thirty, his first patient was at eight this morning."

"Dad, you are in your usual bedroom at the back of the bungalow."

"Where are the children?"

"With one of our neighbours, I am going for them now. I will be back in about ten minutes."

"Grandad, grandad,"

He could hear the voices of the boys as they rushed into the property. Colonel Stepanov loved his monthly visits to Georgia to visit Sasha and her family, even though it always brought back so many memories of the family life he could have had, if his wife Alina had not left him. Luka and Anri who were eight and six were lovely boys. Sasha and her husband were bringing them up well. Both the boys, who were bilingual in both Georgian and Russian, always gave him a hug and a kiss.

Christian arrived home shortly after five-thirty. He looked tired from a long day in surgery and now having to face the high evening temperature. After a cool shower he came outside with the children onto the veranda overlooking the garden. Sasha was inside preparing the evening meal.

"Christian, have you never been interested in politics?"

"Not really but my younger brother Thomas is. At the last election, he became the youngest MP in parliament at twenty five.

I have the feeling that one day, he will follow in our father's footsteps and become President of Georgia. What about you?"

"I have always kept out of politics in Russia, though I have been asked on many occasions to get involved. It can be very dangerous if you happen to be on the wrong side. As you know you still have to be very careful what you say or do in my country. You are very fortunate here in Georgia, everything has changed dramatically since you became a Republic. You now even get on with the Russian Government providing you do not criticise them." Christian laughed. "They have us by the balls as they supply all our oil and natural gas at vastly reduced prices, so as they say in the west we have to watch our p's and q's."

Sasha then popped her head round the kitchen door. "Food is now being served. I have also opened a bottle of Georgian Carta Roja red wine."

The kitchen which was the hub of the house was quite large and modern. By the open patio window was an equally large round light mahogany table with five chairs round it.

"I hope you don't mind darling but I have prepared my dad his favourite meal tonight Chicken Khinkali (better known as chicken dumplings)"

The food was delicious, even the children loved the meal and the Carta Roja was far superior to any wine the Colonel had drank in Russia.

Shortly after nine the children went to bed. It was still light and very warm, so the Colonel his daughter and her husband went back outside onto the veranda to finish off the bottle of wine, in fact Christian ended up opening a second bottle.

"I need to speak to you both but what I am going to tell you must not go any further." For the next half hour the Colonel told them about his meeting with Major Ivan Pavlov of the FSB and the probability that his son Sergei, Sasha's brother, was somehow involved with a number of fellow Chechen students, who attended the Aviation and Aircraft Engineering Academy in Moscow where he was the principle, in the hijacking of a cargo plane carrying one billion Euros of rough diamonds and other precious gems. It appears that Sergei had attended the academy for five years but neither of them was aware of the family connection to each other.

The Colonel then looked straight at his son in-law. "I need some help Christian to track down my son, before the FSB get to him. Major Pavlov said that if Sergei handed himself in there would be no charges, as my son may have just been hired as a pilot and could be completely innocent. To be honest with you, I trust the FSB no more than I did the KGB."

Christian smiled. "Alexander, I sympathise with both you and Sasha but what can I do.?"

"Perhaps you would speak to both your father and brother. It is possible they have heard rumours about the hijacking. The young Chechens who are suspected of being involved are all orphans from the war. Losing their parents and what the Russian's military did to their country has created deep hatred towards the Russian Government, though not the people."

"I promise you I will speak to my brother and father over the weekend."

"Thank you Christian."

"Would you care for another glass of wine?"

The Colonel nodded his head and smiled. "Before I forget I have something to show you both. Would you excuse me for a moment whilst I pop into my bedroom, it is in my suitcase?"

Without another word he went back into the house, a few minutes later returning with a thin yellow plastic file. Opening the file he took out the two photographs, passing one to his daughter the other to Christian.

"Sasha, this is a recent photograph of your brother Sergei."

"Dad, he is so handsome, I can see where he gets his good looks from." There were tears in her eyes as she spoke. "Do you really think he is involved in the hijacking?"

"I truly hope not, that is why I have to find Sergei as soon as possible and prove his innocence."

Christian who had never spoken but continued to stare at the photograph suddenly blurted out. "I have known the guy in this photo for several years; we have often trained together in the local gym. He told me that he was a gemmologist and a qualified pilot. Every so often he used to disappear, sometimes for months. He once told me, he had taken a contract with the Russian Government to fly urgent supplies into Syria for President Bashar al-Assad. I have not seen him around for about six months. I just presumed that he was working away from home."

"Do you know where he lives?"

"I most certainly do. I used to drop him off at his Aunty Sarina's house in the old town. I saw her sat outside the house on an old wooden chair on several occasions, she looks to be in her late eighties and was quite frail with a walking stick, but she always found time to speak to me. She is a lovely old lady. Sergei thought the world of his aunty saying she had been both a mother and father to him." Christian then thought for a moment. "As I am not on duty at the hospital tomorrow, I will take you to see her."

"Thank you, I would appreciate that." Sasha smiled her approval.

It was shortly after mid- day when Christian and the Colonel arrived in the old town, it was a beautiful part of the city with many tourists especially from Russia and the weather was perfect. Christian parked the burgundy Toyota 4x4 on a recently opened car park, as the street where Sergei's aunty lived was now pedestrians only. The street in question was like a picture post card, quaint with several huge rustic urns full of Jasmine, Blanket Flowers, Tickseed and Corn Flowers. About halfway down the street on the right, Christian stopped and knocked on the white door of a terraced property. There was no reply so he knocked again, this time the door slowly opened. An elderly grey haired lady dressed in black with a shoal over her head and resting on a walking stick appeared. It took a while before she spoke. "Christian, what on earth are you doing here?"

Her voice appeared very strained as she spoke, as though it was an effort. The doctor then kissed her on both cheeks.

"I had not seen you or Sergei around for some time, so as we were passing by I thought I would call round with my father in-law Alexander to see you both."

The Colonel held out his hand which she shook. She then looked up at him. "Have I not seen you somewhere before?"

"I don't think so."

"Perhaps you will help me to my chair by the door and then I can sit down. This is what happens to you in old age. Thank you Alexander." She then looked the Colonel in the face. "I have certainly seen you before."

Christian then spoke. "Is Sergei around?"

"No, he flew to Moscow several months ago. He has landed a contract to fly helicopters and cargo planes. It will make him a great deal of money. He told me that when he returns, he intends to find himself a beautiful looking Georgian girl, get married and start a family. I am certain he will, he is a lovely young man and has always looked after me financially."

"Do you ever hear from him?"

"Yes, he never fails to telephone me every week."

"You have a mobile."

"No, only a land line, Sergei had it installed shortly before he left. I am unable to call him but he can call me at any time."

"When you next speak to him, would you please tell him that you have been speaking to me? Perhaps he could give me a call." Christian then gave her a white business card which had his name and telephone number on.

"I will certainly tell him doctor next time we speak, I won't forget." The old lady then coughed a few times. "The heat always gets to me at this time of year." Her voice faltered a little before she regained her composure. "I may be ninety two but I can still remember many things. Alexander I have been thinking, you remind me of my nephew Sergei and he looks so much like you, even the beard. You are not related to him are you?"

Both the Colonel and Christian looked at each other. For a moment they did not know what to say.

Christian then took the initiative by taking hold of Sarina's hand. "Please prepare yourself for a shock."

"Stop fussing me young man just tell me who Alexander is."

"He is Sergei's father and my wife Sasha is Sergei's sister." The old lady looked up at them both, tears started to run down her weathered face. "I knew this would happen one day." She then turned to the Colonel. "I believe you are very famous in Russia?" The Colonel smiled but didn't speak.

"Alexander only found out a few days ago that his son was still alive and where he lived, it is almost twenty eight years since he last saw him.

It was only yesterday that my wife Sasha discovered that Sergei was her brother."

Sarina looked at them both. "Though I have expected something like this to happen for years I am still shocked. Sergei hasn't done anything wrong has he?"

The Colonel spoke. "No, nothing is wrong, I just want to make contact with him for my sake and for his sister Sasha's sake as well, we have a great deal to talk about and many years to catch up."

"Now if you boys will excuse me, I need to go inside and rest. Christian will you please help me?"

The Colonel smiled at Christian as he helped Sarina into the house. "You have done a wonderful job bringing up Sergei, you should be very proud of yourself." The old lady smiled but did not say anything.

"Will you be all right?" enquired Christian.

"Of course I will. It has been a bit of a shock but I am not ready to go to heaven yet." Both the men laughed.

"Sarina, I will call and see you tomorrow on the way to the hospital."

"Thank you doctor,"

Once they had returned to the Toyota 4x4 they headed back to Christian and Sasha's home.

"I think we made the right decision telling Aunty Sarina."

"I fully agree with you Christian. We did not tell her anything which would cause her any undue stress and on reflection, I am glad we did not. If Sergei should make contact with you, please don't give him my landline, it may be tapped, just pass on my mobile number to him. Would you tell him that I am prepared to fly anywhere to see him?"

"Of course I will."

The Colonel's daughter Sasha was most concerned when they told her all about their meeting with Aunty Sarina.

"I hope the shock does not cause a heart attack."

"I don't think so, she has been expecting your father to make contact with her one day. In any case I will call in and see her tomorrow on my way back from the hospital. I have to prepare for major heart surgery, which I and my team will be performing on Monday."

The weekend continued to go well for the Colonel, he got great pleasure from being with his daughter Sasha and her family. Christian spoke to both his father and brother over the weekend but neither of them had heard even the whisper of any rumours about an aircraft hijack in Russia. His father the President said that he would speak to his security chief, once he was back in his office on Monday, to see whether he had heard anything.

"If my father comes up with anything I will call you immediately, infact I will call you anyway."

"Thank you."

"As your return flight to Moscow leaves Shota Rustaveli International Airport at 2pm, I will drop you off at the terminal at mid-day on my way to the hospital. It will save Natasha having to take the children along to the airport to see you off."

Shortly after breakfast on Sunday morning before leaving for the airport with Christian, the Colonel had a long chat with his daughter Sasha.

"I am seriously thinking of retiring and moving to Georgia to be with you and your family."

"Are you serious dad what would the Russian people say? You are a national hero. They would call you a traitor. The Georgian and Russian Governments are always falling out over this country's closeness to the west since the breakup of the Soviet Union, and we became a democratic republic. Given half the chance I am certain the Russian Government would love to invade us and bring us back into line."

"The Georgian Government appears to be having a better relationship with the Russians at the moment."

"It would appear so, but to put it bluntly as Christian says the Russians have us by the balls. If we get too close to the West they threaten to cut off all our supplies of oil and natural gas. Without either of these we have no electricity or heating, the economy would collapse. The Russians like to dangle a carrot in front of us; if we stay neutral they will supply Georgia with cheap oil and gas."

The Colonel smiled. "I understand what you are saying." "Dad, if you do retire why not spend the winter months in Georgia from November to late March? The weather in Tbilisi in winter is normally milder and drier than Moscow which can have heavy snow and temperatures of -10c. You could stay with us or even rent your own apartment."

"Thank you darling, I won't make a decision at the moment but when I return to Moscow I will give it more thought."

Shortly after an emotional farewell with Natasha and the two children, the Colonel left for the airport with Christian. Fifty minutes later they arrived at the airport terminal. Christian embraced the Colonel warmly as they departed. Once he had checked in, the Colonel headed for passport control and customs with his small wheelie suitcase case, before entering the departure lounge which was fairly quiet. Whilst relaxing in the airport's only café with a glass of sweet tea, the Colonel had time to think about many things. He quite fancied moving to Georgia especially if his son Sergei ended up there as well. Once they were reconciled his family would be united again. Frequently he wondered why he had never remarried but he knew in his own mind that he would never find another woman to replace Alina. Until the past caught up with her, she had been the perfect wife. Moscow was the city where he was born and loved. The winters were harsh but in the summer it was perfect. He had a few retired military friends who he socialised with. In the warm summer months, they would meet and reminisce over a few beers, a glass or two of vodka or whisky in the café bars by the river close to where he lived. At sixty two he could take retirement whenever he wanted to. It had been his choice to continue as head of the academy, he loved his job and it gave him the opportunity to pass on his vast knowledge and experience to the next generation. He had a deputy who was twenty years younger and one day he would make a fine head. Perhaps now was the time for him to take over. He would have to give it some serious thought.

The woman's voice over the loud speaker suddenly brought him back to reality. "Would all passengers for the 2pm flight to Moscow, please make their way to gate two."

The Georgian Airways Boeing 737 flight was only half full. Sitting at the rear of the plane on the right hand side by the window, the Colonel had a perfect view of the white stone terminal building on take-off, the weather was glorious and he had enjoyed the last few days.

Two hours thirty-five minutes later the Boeing made a perfect landing at Moscow's Vnukovo International Airport. Quickly making his way through passport control and customs, he headed to the main entrance of the arrival lounge and hailed a taxi to his apartment overlooking the Moscow River.

6

London - England

Receptionist June, at Franks the diamond merchants, was her usual bubbly self as Jack Sinclair walked in. Monday morning blues were not in her repertoire.

"Jack, Mr Robinson has been in his office since seven- thirty, he wants to see you as soon as possible. By the way did you enjoy your business trip to Amsterdam?"

"Business wise it was good but the city was far too busy for me, the bars in the narrow side streets and on the canal sides were packed and the weather was extremely warm, just like here in London. Amsterdam was full of young people on cock and hen nights."

"I would have thought with you being a young guy, you would have enjoyed yourself." Jack laughed.

"Most of the young people were between eighteen and twenty five. In the evening I felt like an old man as I was by myself. I am not into smoking marijuana or watching girlie shows alone. Late August is always a very busy time in Amsterdam, I was glad to get back to London. Unfortunately there was a two hour delay on the KLM flight to Gatwick on the Sunday evening, so it was well after midnight when I finely arrived home. Next time I will go mid-week."

"I will tell Mr Richardson that you are now in the building." Jack smiled and whispered thank you.

He then walked along the grey tiled corridor and knocked on the second door on the right.

"Please enter."

Pushing open the light oak door of the chairman's office, Jack walked in.

His boss Jim Richardson, known to his friends and senior staff as JR, immediately got up from behind his desk and held out his hand. "Good to see you Jack, how did the trip go?"

"Excellent, the managing director of Van Amstel Diamonds was so impressed with the quality and workmanship of the jewellery I showed him, that he intends to fly over to London a week on Monday to meet you. He is convinced we can do a great deal of business together, but his company will need some designs which will be exclusive to them in the Netherlands."

Jim smiled, "I expected him to say that, that should not be a problem." He then paused whilst he took a drink of coffee from the blue mug on his desk. "Would you care for a coffee Jack?"

"No, I am ok thanks."

JR then continued. "If you recall, about five weeks ago when you returned from your trip to Beijing, we discussed what our Chinese friend Chang Yang had told you about the Russian guy selling cut price high quality gems." Jack nodded his head.

"I spoke to a friend who is a Government Minister; he in turn has spoken to someone in MI6. Our intelligence service at first denied all knowledge, but a few days later the whole situation had changed. Our Foreign Secretary had been visiting Moscow to discuss a new trade deal when the Russian Foreign Secretary confided in him, that there had been a cargo plane hijacked in Siberia. The aircraft had over one billion Euros worth of diamonds and precious gems on board. Though the hijack had taken place almost twelve months ago, the Russians had kept quiet. No way did they want the world market to collapse, by being flooded with cheap diamonds and other precious gems. The Russian Foreign Minister said that his government needed the help of the British Government to track down the hijackers, as it was in everybody's interest to keep the market stable. A week later Major Ivan Pavlov from the FSB flew to London to meet his counterpart in MI6 Miles Coburn. It would appear that the discussions went well at the highest level and the British Government said they would co-operate with the Russians. The Russians said that they had isolated eight of the original twenty Chechen students who attended the Moscow Aviation and Aircraft Engineering Academy as taking part in the hijack, along with several known gangsters from the Russian Chechen Mafia. There were rumours flying around, that the Chechens were only involved so that they could raise money to buy arms for a new separatist movement, who wanted to start a war with Russia again. Major Pavlov said this story was nothing but bull shit. The Russian military would crush them instantly. Even the Chechen military who had great sympathy with the separatists, would never allow a new movement to be established, as it was not now in the country's interest. Time had moved on. A senior official from MI6 Miles Coburn wants a meet up with you; he believes you can help him."

"How an earth can I help MI6?"

"It would appear that when you recently worked in Johannesburg, South Africa for the De Beers diamond mining company, you met a Russian guy called Sergei Aslanov, his father Colonel Alexander Stepanov is a national hero in his homeland. Sergei like yourself was also employed as a gemmologist."

"Yes, I remember him well; he was a very pleasant guy and we got on well. We worked closely together for twelve months and frequently socialized.

"Well, this very pleasant guy from all accounts, is now suspected of working for the Russian Mafia selling the hijacked diamonds and gems to traders worldwide at ridiculously cheap prices." JR then finished drinking the remainder of his coffee. "Jack, I know it is highly irregular but I have made an appointment for you to meet with Miles Coburn in your office tomorrow morning at eleven. I believe you should meet him, as your father knew him very well and trusted him. What he has to say could affect the whole future of our industry so I hope you agree?"

Jack paused for a few moments before he spoke. "Jim out of respect for both you and my father I have no objections meeting Miles Coburn, it should be a most interesting conversation."

Mondays for Jack were always exceptionally busy after an overseas business trip. Today was no exception, after leaving his office at Franks at five-thirty he made a leisurely walk in the late evening sun to his riverside apartment. Normally on a Monday evening he would make his own meal rather than dine out. Today he felt exhausted and even after a shower he felt no different. The rushed business trip to Amsterdam and too much alcohol over two days had taken its toll. Joe's Café Bar was only ten minutes away so that is where he would dine, but firstly he needed to call his sister Lilly and discuss the final details of their parents' first anniversary get together, which they had talked about when he visited her in Ludlow three weeks ago.

"I will pick Lex up from Gatwick Airport at five. We will then make our way to Ludlow via the M25 and M40 and stop and have something to eat on our way there. We should arrive at Castle View before ten."

"Darling, I don't mind making you a meal when you arrive."

"Lilly, you are a treasure but you have enough to do with looking after your family. In any case it will give me the opportunity to have a good chat with our brother." Their conversation went on for another twenty minutes before it ended, as always he told her how much he loved her. Lilly's reply was always the same. "Thank you Jack and I love you."

Shortly after seven Jack made his way to Joe's Café Bar. Before he went in, he walked across the pavement to the grey stone wall which ran along the Thames embankment. It was another beautiful evening; it had been a glorious summer's day. Slipping on his dark shades he looked across the river towards the MI6 Headquarters, a magnificent building overlooking the Albert Embankment. He could not help wondering what they wanted to talk to him about, and what Miles Coburn's connection was with his late father. Tomorrow after eleven he should be a little wiser.

Joe's Café Bar as usual was busy, mainly with visiting tourists. As he was about to walk inside, the proprietor Sophie was coming outside to serve customers who were sat outside under the large floral umbrellas. As she was about to pass him, she stopped and gave him a kiss on his left cheek. "Your usual seat is free by the bar I will be with you shortly." Sophie was a lovely looking young woman, always happy with a smile for everyone. The Italian perfume she wore was exquisite. He had asked her what it was called. She replied. "That is a secret which only my husband knows. You must ask him." He never did.

The meal Jack had was excellent, fresh Scottish sea salmon and boiled Jersey potatoes with tomatoes and a light green salad. For once he had no alcohol, instead one cup of white Americano coffee with no sugar. By nine-fifteen he was back in his apartment. After watching Sky News for half an hour, he decided on an early night and hit the sack.

The early night proved to be one of his better decisions. On Tuesday morning he felt back to normal. The temperature was warm and the sun was very bright as he made the short walk to Franks, another couple of days and it would be September. The lovely June was her usual happy self on reception as he walked in. Jack was a young handsome looking guy with over eighty million in the bank, a top job, a fabulous apartment and a top of the range 4x4, but why was it that all the girls he fancied were either happily married or had partners, was he too fussy or perhaps setting his heights too high?

"June I am expecting a Mr Miles Coburn at eleven. When he arrives, please call me and I will escort him to my office."

"Certainly Jack."

The white internal telephone rang on Jack Sinclair's mahogany office table. He immediately picked up the phone.

"Mr Sinclair. Mr Coburn has just arrived in reception." "Thank you June, I will be with you in a moment."

Miles Coburn was obviously a man who always made a point of arriving on time.

A few minutes later Jack left his office and walked into the reception area.

"Miles, Jack Sinclair a pleasure to meet you." Both men smiled and shook hands. "Would you please come this way?" After walking a few yards down the corridor they entered Jack's office on the right. "Please take a seat." Jack then sat down behind his office desk. "Would you care for a coffee?"

"I would love one, milk but with no sugar please."

Jack then picked up the white internal phone on the desk. "June, when you have a moment could we have two white Americano coffees with no sugar? Please cancel all my calls for the next hour,"

"Certainly Mr Sinclair,"

"Now what can I do for you Miles?"

"Would I be right in presuming that Jim Richardson has told you who I am?"

Jack smiled. "Only that you are with MI6 and knew my father extremely well."

"I most certainly knew your father. He was a brilliant financial expert and we are all indebted to him for setting up his department. Though your father was in complete charge of his section, I was head of the division but I always agreed with everything he did. He more or less had a free hand and it paid dividends." There was a sharp knock on the office door and June entered with two mugs of coffee. As soon as June left the room Miles continued. "Jim Richardson told me about your trip to Beijing a few weeks ago and what Chang Yang told you. Last week I had a meeting with Major Ivan Pavlov from the Russian FBS, who put me in the complete picture about the Siberian cargo plane hijack. No way do the Russians want any information to leak out about the hijack and I might add neither do the British Government. Neither country can afford for the world diamond market to be affected. After I informed Major Pavlov about your conversation with Mr Chang Yang in Beijing the Major spoke to his counterpart in China. All Chinese gem traders have been instructed not to deal with Gem Stone International. Any freight deliveries to China from this company will be confiscated."

The two men then took a drink of their coffee. Jack was a little taken aback with Miles Coburn. He was certainly no James Bond. Probably in his mid-fifties, with receding light brown hair and a bald patch on top. Slim and standing at about five ten he wore dark tinted glasses with gold frames. His smile and personality were most friendly. Jack also noted that he was immaculately dressed in a dark grey suit, white shirt with a black and yellow tie; his shoes which were dark brown were highly polished. Had Jack been asked to guess what Miles Coburn's profession was, he would probably have said a solicitor or barrister not a Spymaster.

"Major Pavlov tells me that the Russian Government believe that Gem Stone International has their headquarters in Marbella in Southern Spain, but at the moment they are unable to prove it."

"What makes them think that?" Miles then took another drink of his coffee before continuing. "For the last fifteen years, a former Chechen separatist leader Aslan Maskhadov who fled to Spain after the first Chechen war when the Russians were after him, has lived in Marbella and built up a very successful upmarket jewellery business. He owns the exclusive Cobra Jewellery Emporiums, which are dotted along the Costa del Sol from Nerja to Estepona including Malaga, Marbella and Puerto Banus. Recently he opened a new emporium in Gibraltar.

Maskhadov applied for and received Spanish citizenship much to the Russian annoyance. He has been a perfect citizen, paying his taxies and raising money for various charity organizations. The Spanish knew if they handed him back to the Russians he would be executed. The

Russians are convinced that the Chechen Mafia must have provided Maskhadov with funds to build his business empire, if so he must have a lifetime debt with them. About eighteen months ago Maskhadov opened another company which designs and manufactures exclusive jewellery. The business has become so successful that they are supplying clients all over Europe and North Africa. This new company now employs around twenty full time staff."

"Where is the company based?"

"On the outskirts of Marbella close to the new motorway, where he has his head office and workshop."

"Maybe he is helping to dispose of the hijacked diamonds and gems through his company."

"That is a possibility, but at the moment we have no way of finding out. Neither the Russians nor the British want to involve the Spanish Government. Fortunately your boss Jim Richardson came up with a possible solution." Jack never responded to the statement. "He suggested that you may be interested in getting a job with the Cobra Jewellery chain. With a man on the inside, we could certainly find out whether Aslan Maskhadov is involved. What do say Jack, would you be interested in being that man?"

Jack felt slightly pissed off but didn't show his annoyance. "This is the first time I have heard about this suggestion, Jim Richardson has never discussed anything with me."

Miles Coburn looked slightly embarrassed. "Jim never suggested you, it was my idea. With your late father working for MI6, I thought perhaps you would like to follow in his footsteps. By the way, Jim did say he would have no objection releasing you from your contract if it meant helping the industry and your country. He also made it clear, that your position with Franks would still be available for you on your return." Coburn paused for a moment before continuing with the conversation. "Jim Richardson tells me that until a few months ago you worked for 'De Beers' in Johannesburg South African?"

"Yes I did. Why do you ask?"

"My counterpart Major Pavlov tells me that the FSB suspect that one of the hijackers, who is a gemmologist and a qualified pilot, also worked in Johannesburg South Africa for 'De Beers' around the same time you were there. You may have met or even worked with him. Sergei Aslanov, his father Colonel Alexander Stepanov is a National Hero in Russia."

"I certainly knew a Sergei Aslanov but he said he came from Georgia and he never mentioned anything about his father. We got to know each other very well and usually socialised together. He spoke perfect English and told me he trained to be a pilot at the Moscow Aviation and Engineering Academy. Later he studied to be a gemmologist at Moscow State University. He then came to South Africa like me, to gain experience by working for De Beers. He never once talked about his parents and said very little about his past. I did ask him if he had any brothers or sisters and he said no. Sergei also said he had lived in Tbilisi, Georgia all his life until he moved to Moscow to study. Do you have a current photo of him?"

"I am sorry but I don't."

"A pity, I could have identified him for you."

"I have already emailed the major asking for photos of all the suspects, but so far I have not received a reply. I will try again when I return to the office."

"May I ask a question?"

"Fire away."

"What about my salary, who pays me?"

"We will at MI6, your wages and expenses will be paid the first Friday in the month by us. Should you find employment with Cobra Jewellery your salary from us will be adjusted, I might add we are throwing in a £50.000 bonus if you are successful." Coburn then paused again and drank the remainder of his coffee. "Jack, please think about my offer, and let me know what your decision is within the next two days."

Jack smiled and looked as though he was going to shake his head. "I can give you my answer now." Coburn touched his glasses, which were slipping down his nose and pushed them back into position. "I am in, you can count on me."

Miles Coburn then got up from his chair and shook Jack's hand. "Welcome to MI6 Jack."

"Miles, if you will excuse me for one moment I need to put a call through to Jim Richardson." Jack then picked up the internal phone on his office desk and called his boss.

"Jim, it is Jack Sinclair. I am with Miles Coburn; we need to have a word with you. Would you mind if we come through to your office?"

"No problem Jack I will see you in a few minutes."

Jack then turned to Miles Coburn. "When will you expect me to fly to Spain?"

"As soon as possible,"

"It is impossible for me to go before the 10th September. We have a family memorial service in Ludlow to remember our departed parents."

"That will be ok Jack don't worry, a few more days will not make that much difference."

The two men then left the room, and walked a few yards down the corridor to chairman Jim Richardson's office. Jack knocked a couple of times before a voice called out. "One moment please." Seconds later JR opened the door. "Good morning or perhaps I should say good afternoon. Please come in. Good to see you again Miles," he then shook his hand firmly. "Would you care for coffee?" They both replied yes. Picking up the internal phone he spoke to June on reception, "June, when you have a moment could we have three white coffees with no sugar? Take a seat guys." The three of then sat down on the soft black leather chairs.

"You must have made a decision Jack?"

"I have, it is obvious the hijack diamond situation can't continue, sooner or later the word will get out, the press and media will find out. A hell of a lot of rogue countries, especially in the Middle East and Africa will put two fingers up at us and buy the cheap diamonds; they are not interested in price control. As I said earlier to Miles, I am with you all the way. Once my parents memorial service is over I shall be free to travel." Jack then turned and faced his boss. "Miles tells me, that my job here will still be open when I return?"

"Of course it will be Jack."

"Good, it has been a pleasure working for you Jim."

"The pleasure is mutual Jack, you are highly thought of throughout the company."

Coburn then got into the conversation. "In the next few days we will meet to discuss everything in more detail." The MI6 man then glanced at his watch. "If you two guys will excuse me, I need to get back to my office. Jack I will call you tomorrow and arrange a meeting."

"That will be fine."

Coburn then turned to Jim Richardson. "Jim, thanks for your help. Once Jack is working for Cobra Jewellery we should then be in a position to sort this problem out."

Shortly after Miles Coburn left the office and the building, Jim Richardson then turned to Jack. "If the situation turns nasty in Spain you can always pull out, remember you are volunteering to help MI6 and the Russians. Whatever the outcome, you must never put your own life in danger." Jack smiled; he knew that Jim was right.

Miles Coburn called twenty four hours later. They arranged to meet at Jack's Thames Plaza apartment the following evening at seven.

Normally the weather in September in London is usually warm and mild but today was different with light rain and no sunshine, it looked and felt miserable. Whilst it had been another very busy day at work, Jack's mind had been on another planet, he was worried that he had made a mistake by volunteering to help MI6. If Miles Coburn put any doubts in his mind this evening he would pull out. By the time he had arrived home at his Thames side apartment after a brisk walk through very busy pedestrian walkways, the rain had disappeared, the pavements had dried up, and the sun was now breaking through a cloudy sky. It was just before six. After a quick shower, Jack put a frozen beef lasagne which he had bought from M&S into the microwave. Twenty minutes later he was sat on the balcony eating the lasagne and a couple of white bread rolls with a large glass of red Spanish wine. Not the most exotic meal but it was still very satisfying.

The apartment intercom buzzer rang promptly at seven.

"Jack Sinclair."

"Who is enquiring for him?"

"Miles Coburn,"

"Please come in Miles. If you would take the elevator to the fourth floor, my apartment is number thirty-two. I will see you in a few minutes."

Walking over to the CD player he switched off his favourite singing star George Michael. His CD 'Older' which he had recently purchased from HMV was stunning. The door buzzer rang, virtually at the same moment the CCTV automatically switched on. From the small video screen by the door, he could see Miles Coburn in the passage way.

Jack opened the cream door. "Hi Miles please come in." "Good to see you again Jack." Both men shook hands. "You haven't changed your mind?"

"No way, but I do have several questions to ask you."

"That is why I am here. Whatever you want to know go ahead and ask me."

"Can I offer you a drink? A coffee or may be a glass of wine or a Budweiser."

"A bottle of Budweiser would be fine."

"Should we sit outside on the balcony, it is surprisingly a warm evening after the rain today."

As they spoke, Jack walked into the open plan kitchen and took a couple of bottles of Budweiser out of the fridge. He then passed one to Miles Coburn. The sun was still shining brightly when they went onto the balcony; they both then sat down on the white wicker chairs which had matching dark grey cushions.

"You have a stunning apartment Jack."

"Thank you, it was my parents. As I needed a base in London, I decided to keep it. I love the property and its position overlooking the River Thames." Both men took a drink of Budweiser.

"Now Jack what do you want to ask me?"

"How can you be certain that I will be able to get a job with Cobra Jewellery?"

"I can't be certain but they are an expanding company and are more than likely taking on staff. There are not many gemmologists with your experience and qualifications in Spain. I believe in the past you have also worked as a DJ?"

"You appear to know a hell of a lot about me?"

"We have done our homework. One of our operatives in Spain owns the trendy Med Beach Club in Marbella, it is one of the top beach clubs on the Costa del Sol. Pedro the owner will give you one or possibly two nights a week playing House Music, which will be an excellent additional cover for you even if you land a job with Cobra Jewellery. To be honest Pedro Gonzales is not the owner but the general manager, though everyone believes he owns the club. He is actually English and there is quite a story behind how he ended up in Spain. As Pedro will be your contact I will give you an insight into his past. Many years ago his mother who is English met a guy in Spain whist on holiday with her parents. At first she thought he was Spanish but he turned out to be from Argentina, South America, he too was on holiday. They had a passionate holiday romance and then went their separate ways but kept in touch. Some weeks later Pedro's mother Fran found out she was pregnant and contacted her lover who immediately offered to marry her. They were married in the beautiful city Buenos Aires, Argentina several weeks later. There was a lot of unrest at the time in Argentina, with the President General Leopold Galtieri threatening to go to war over his ambitions to take back the Falkland Islands (known in Argentina as the Islas Malvinas) by force for his country from the British, so the couple decided to move to the UK and that was where Pedro was born. His father, who was also called Pedro, was called a traitor by his family and friends because he had left Argentina and gone to live in the UK. Even local papers carried articles about him, accusing him of running away when his country needed him to fight for them. Everything got too much for Pedro and after a great deal of soul searching he returned to Argentina and joined the army just before the invasion of the Falklands took place. Fran and their son decided to stay in the UK. After the war, it was Fran's intention to join her husband in Spain with their son and start a new life together in a country where they would be made welcome. Fate can play terrible tricks. Pedro senior was part of the young ill equipped and badly trained conscripts, who invaded the Falklands landing at Port Stanley. When the British flotilla of more than a hundred ships finally arrived after a three week 8,500 mile sea journey and attacked the Argentine soldiers at Port Stanley, the invaders were overwhelmed. The commander of the British task force Admiral Sir John Fieldhouse said it was like sending lambs to the slaughter, as the Argentine soldiers defending Port Stanley were so badly equipped. Hundreds died including Pedro from injuries and the freezing temperatures before they finally surrendered. Sir John went on to say that General Galtieri should be held responsible for their deaths. After the war, all the soldiers from both sides were buried with dignitary in the military cemetery in Port Stanley. In recent years peace has returned to the Falkland Islands, and the proud people of Argentina have been allowed to return to Port Stanley to exhume their loved ones and take them back home for reburial as war heroes in the military cemetery in Buenos Aires. Some years ago Pedro and his mother flew to Argentina to meet her husband's family and visit his war grave."

"A most intriguing story,"

"There is more to come,"

"Would you care for another bottle of Budweiser?"

Miles nodded his head. The sun had now dropped below the horizon and it was a little cooler so they moved back inside the apartment.

Miles then continued. "Fran returned to live with her parents. Pedro who was a bright child from an early age was brought up and educated in England. He studied telecommunications and IT at Nottingham University gaining a first class honours degree. In his last year he was head hunted by MI6 due to his outstanding ability. Whilst working for MI6 he got to know your father. Pedro programmed the information your father had compiled for the security services into a data base. To cut a long story short as time is going on." Miles then glanced at his watch before continuing. "Pedro and his mother were very close and used to visit the Costa del Sol frequently. On one of these holidays Pedro was invited to an exclusive beach party and met a beautiful young girl called Nada, whose father was Sheikh Ali Bin Falih, a property and construction billionaire from Abu Dhabi in the United Arab Emirates. They met on several occasions unknown to his mother. When Pedro returned to the UK he and Nada kept up their relationship via emails, text and mobile calls. Every few months, they would meet alone in a Marbella hotel for a romantic holiday. Eventually Nada broke the news of her relationship with Pedro to her father. Instead of him going into a violent rage and banning her from leaving the country, he asked to meet Pedro and his mother. Mother and son flew to the Emirates to meet the Sheikh. The meeting went extremely well and Nada's father gave his permission for them to be married, providing the service took place in Abu Dhabi, which it did. After a sumptuous wedding Nada and Pedro returned to London were he continued to work for MI6. About twelve months later, Pedro was asked to set up as a MI6 operative living in Spain as he spoke the language fluently, but he needed a cover for his activities. Nada, who thought her husband was a civil servant earning a living as an IT expert in a Government Department, suggested they open a night club when they moved to Spain, as they would need to make a living.

Pedro thought it would be great cover for him. "Fantastic idea but we have not got the money to do that."

"My father has and he will do anything for me."

Sheikh Ali Bin Falih jumped at the idea of opening a night club in Marbella. For years he had been considering expanding his property empire to Europe and now was the golden opportunity to do so. But there were three conditions, one he would own the property, secondly Nada and Pedro would run the club and finally thirdly the club was not to become a rich couple's play thing but had to make a profit. Pedro agreed to everything Nada's father said and a few months later, the Sheikh purchased for fifteen million Euros a property in Marbella, which used to be an apartment hotel on the Golden Mile facing the beach. The property was very run down having been empty for a couple of years. Though the building complex was small, there was a considerable amount of land which could be redeveloped. The previous owner, who could not pay his tax bill and had many debts, had gone bankrupt.

After spending a further five million Euros converting the property into one of the most exclusive beach clubs on the Costa del Sol, the Med Beach Club and Restaurant was launched in a blaze of publicity. Six months later Nada was pregnant with the couple's first child a boy, four years later a girl arrived, and eight years later the Med Club is still the place to be seen in and business is booming. The couple and their two children have recently moved out of the penthouse apartment they built over the club, and now live in a stunning villa between Marbella and Puerto Banus. Pedro's mother who has never remarried now lives with them."

"What does Pedro actually do in Spain apart from run the Med Club? Earlier you said he was MI6's man in Spain." "You are quite right I did; he is what we call a snooper.

He listens into mobile conversations in government buildings, bars, clubs, restaurants and also plants bugs in apartments, villas and cars.

Pedro is a whiz kid with electronic devises and computers. Spain is the premier country in Europe for the trafficking of drugs from North Africa, much of which ends up in the UK. For years we have been convinced their police and border control could do more. We know that many of these officers are on the pay roll of the International drug cartels. Maybe it is coincidence, but since Pedro Gonzales has been based in Spain the situation has drastically improved, you would be amazed what he has discovered."

Miles glanced at his watch again. "I am going to have to leave you now; I have a train to catch at ten."

"How far do you have to travel?"

"Richmond. I will be home in forty minutes."

"Are you married?"

"Yes, very happily with two grown up daughters and three grandchildren." Miles then suddenly stopped and turned, as he walked across the whitish grey tiled lounge floor towards the exit door. "You can trust Pedro Gonzales he will always be there for you. I will call you early tomorrow morning then perhaps we can meet for lunch in Hatton Garden, we can discuss a few more details then."

"Yes no problem. Do you want me to call a cab?"

"No, I will pick one up on the main road. Thanks for the Budweiser's."

After shaking Jack's hand, Miles Coburn disappeared down the corridor in the direction of the elevator. Half an hour later Jack hit the sack, he needed an early night.

Miles Coburn was true to his word and called Jack on Friday morning at nine-thirty, they agreed to meet at the Eat Coffee Bar at twelve-thirty. Jack spent most of the morning finalizing paper work for several overseas deals he had made during the week. At twelve twenty-five he left Franks, and headed to the Eat Coffee Bar a few hundred yards away. The weather was mild with no breeze and the sun was still fairly strong so he slipped on his dark shades. Hundreds of tourists and staff from nearby offices made the area very congested. As he approached Eat Coffee Bar he could see Miles Coburn sat at one of the white tables inside the coffee bar. Miles raised his right arm and smiled when he saw Jack. Once inside they shook hands.

"Jack, what would like to eat?"

"A bacon baguette and a latte coffee,"

"I will have the same." Miles then got up and went to the counter and ordered. "One of the girls will bring it to us in a few minutes."

"How much do I owe you?"

"Nothing I will put it down to expenses." Jack smiled.

"I gather your brother Lex is a football coach with Malaga?"

"Yes he is."

"He was a fine player when he was at Chelsea, I saw him several times. It was a great pity his career was cut short with injury. How is he doing in Spain?"

"Very well, at the end of the season he is expected to become the manager-coach of Malaga. Their current manager, I forget his name, is returning to Italy. If Lex is appointed, he will then be the youngest manager in the La Liga at thirty four."

"I gather you two are very close?"

"Yes, we always have been, even more since our parents' death. Why do you ask?"

"I think you should put him in the picture about why you moving to Spain but be very careful what you say and do not mention Pedro Gonzales by name." Jack smiled and nodded his head but didn't say anything. "If anyone should ask you why you have moved to Spain, always keep to the same story. Tell them about your parents, and being single you decided to move to Spain to be near your brother, who is a first team coach with Malaga. You are now a DJ at the Med Beach Club but if anyone needs a gemmologist you are available."

"What about my sister Lilly?"

"Tell her Franks are opening an office in Marbella and they want you over there for a few months until it is established. There is no point of causing her undue stress by telling her the truth."

"Good idea."

"Your parents' memorial service is this Saturday the 10th September in Ludlow?"

"Yes."

A young female waitress with spiky red hair then arrived at their table with the bacon baguettes and coffee. "Sorry for the delay guys but we are so busy today."

"No problem." The girl smiled at Jack, she was very attractive with a lovely smile and had perfect white teeth. "When will I be leaving for Spain?"

"Wednesday the 14th September."

"When is your last day in the office?"

"Monday the 12th September." On Tuesday, I need you to call in at the MI6 Headquarters on the Albert Embankment at eleven-thirty. If you possess a laptop would you please bring it with you? When you arrive at reception just ask for me. You will need to sign the Official Secrets Act before you can depart on your mission. I will then give you your one-way flight ticket, Pedro Gonzales will meet you at Malaga International Airport, he will be holding up a card saying Med Club. I will also give you a couple of emergency numbers, only to be used if the situation is a matter of life or death."

"Did you catch your train last night?"

"Yes, I was in bed by midnight. Miles then glanced at his watch. "I need to be getting back to the office." He then lowered his voice to almost a whisper. "The Russians are convinced that six or possibly eight of the former Chechen students from the Moscow Aviation Academy along with several senior Mafia foot soldiers are now living in Marbella, either working for or liaising with Cobra Jewellery. All these guys are bachelors and frequently visit the Med Club and other upmarket clubs and restaurants looking for pretty girls."

"What about my accommodation, where will I be staying?"

"The company own a two bedroom apartment in a gated complex by the Mediterranean twenty minute's walk from the city centre. I will give you the address before you leave for Spain. All your bills will be paid, apart from food. Be very careful who you take back to the apartment and if anyone asks, a wealthy friend of yours in London owns the pad."

Both men then got up and walked outside, shook hands and then went their separate ways.

7

Jack was lucky he had the hindsight to leave his office at Franks by mid-afternoon. The traffic heading for Gatwick Airport was heavy. His brother Lex was due to land on an EasyJet flight from Malaga, Spain at five. In the end he arrived at the Arrival Lounge with forty minutes to spare, which gave him time for a quick latte coffee in Starbucks. There was no mistaking his brother, when he walked through the security gates at customs, looking deeply tanned and carrying a black and red Malaga FC overnight sports bag. The two men warmly embraced, it was obvious to anyone that there was a special closeness between the two. Once out of the Arrival Lounge they quickly made their way to the short stay car park. As they walked towards Jack's Range Rover Sport, he opened the doors with the automobile key.

"I like your car Jack, a great choice, and I love the colour."

"I thought I would splash out."

"I don't blame you."

"What are you driving these days?"

"His brother laughed. "The same as you and believe it or not the identical colour. They say brothers think alike."

"I thought that was twins." They both laughed.

After opening the boot, Lex dropped his sports bag inside and then got into the passenger seat. Twenty five minutes later they were in a traffic jam on the M25, eventually they slipped onto the M40, gradually the traffic thinned out and they made up time.

Jack turned to his brother as he drove. "How are Maria and the little one?"

"Fantastic, Maria sends her love. She couldn't see the point of flying over with a young baby, as she hardly knew our parents."

"She did right." Lex smiled, he was a handsome man just like his brother Jack. "Malaga has got off to a good start this season."

"I can't believe it myself, second in La Liga behind Real Madrid with a very small budget, but there is a long way to go."

"Do you think you will get the manager's job next season?"

"All most certain, and it is highly likely to happen in the next few days. I was speaking to our manager Roman Russo yesterday, his wife is poorly with breast cancer and they also have two teenage children. She is finding it difficult coping by herself. Roman intends to ask our chairman over the weekend to release him from his contract, so he can immediately return home to Italy. It is a great pity as we work well together. I am a tracksuit coach, whilst Roman has the ideas and I follow out his instructions. If you recall in the English Premier League, Kenny Dalglish and the late Ray Hartford operated in the same way with great success at Blackburn Rovers."

After a couple of hours driving they pulled into a service station for a meal. They both decided on a beef burger with chips, not the healthiest of food but it was tasty. Whilst they were relaxing in Costa Coffee with a couple of white Americano coffees, Jack decided to inform his brother that he would be moving to Spain on the 14th September and would be based in Marbella. He took Miles Coburn's advice and was careful what he said to Lex, but more or less told him everything."

"So our father worked for MI6 after he sold his investment company and you are now doing the same?"

His brother shook his head in disbelief; the look of shock on his face said everything. "Man, you could end up in a box blown away by the Russian Mafia." Lex meant every word he said.

"Whatever you say please do not tell your wife the truth. Tell her I always fancied being a DJ on the Costa del Sol and managed to get a gig at the Med Beach Club."

"Have you told Lilly?"

"No, but I intend to tell her tomorrow."

"She will have a fit."

"As far as Lilly is concerned I will be opening an office in Marbella for Franks."

"Good idea brother. We must keep in close touch whist you are in Spain."

"I most certainly will, perhaps you will invite me to the Malaga home matches?"

"Of course I will, you will be my guest." His brother looked at him. "Jack, please be careful, I don't want to lose you as well as our parents."

"You won't, I shall be extremely careful and please remember this conversation is just between you and I."

Two hours later they arrived at the entrance to 'Castle View' the property now owned by their sister Lilly and her husband Bret. Once through the security gates, the Range Rover purred its way up the short drive to the imposing stone built two storey detached house. The garden looked immaculate even though darkness was creeping in. As usual at this time in the evening the children were in bed, but Lilly and Bret were waiting for them at the entrance to the house, and gave them both a huge welcome. Lilly was very emotional as she kissed and hugged both her brothers affectionately, her eyes were tearful with the occasional tear running down the side of her beautiful face.

"Lovely to see you both, it has been a while since we were all together. Please come inside and take your bags upstairs whilst I make us a coffee, you boys are in your usual rooms."

Ten minutes later the four of them were in the kitchen drinking coffee.

Bret who rarely said anything just smiled. Lilly was always the most talkative.

"Is your insurance investment company still doing well?" "Very well Jack, thank you for asking. It has been a great move for me and I can also spend more time with Lilly and the children."

By eleven-thirty they had all made their way upstairs to bed, it had been a tiring day, especially Lex who looked worn out.

The following morning after an excellent full English breakfast, which was cooked by Lilly, they all went outside onto the patio. The weather was perfect, dry and warm, with only a slight breeze which gently rustled the trees. The two seven-year-old twins Paul and Bethany were having the time of their lives running across the large lawn.

Lilly turned to Lex and Jack. "I have arranged for a short memorial service at three in the rose garden, where our mum and dad's ashes are laid to rest. The Reverend Sheila Preston from St Laurence's Church in Ludlow, where we often attend, has offered to do the service."

I looked at Lilly and my brother. "I found it hard to believe that it was twelve months since our parents passed away, I miss them terribly." Both my brother and sister said the same.

Most of the day was spent relaxing, talking and playing with the children. At around two forty-five the security buzzer on the entrance gate rang. Bret glanced at the CCTV screen in the kitchen. "The Reverend Preston is at the entrance, I told her to come in. She will be with us shortly."

To say the Reverend Preston was different would not be an exaggeration. Firstly, she arrived at Castle View on an old black Raleigh bicycle, with a wicker basket fastened to the handle bars. The Reverend had told Lilly, that it was the easiest and cheapest way to get around her parish and visit her flock. She was certainly right on both accounts. Probably in her late forties, she stood no more than five two and was quite plump. With her short darkish grey hair and spectacles as well as no makeup, she looked several years older than she was. Born in the attractive seaside town of Tenby in South Wales, she originally moved temporarily to St Laurence Church, Ludlow after the previous vicar suddenly died. Fourteen years later she was still there.

After Lilly had introduced the Reverend Preston to Lex and Jack they began to converse, they soon realised what a compassionate and interesting person she was. It was very easy to see why she was so popular in the community. Though she was single with no family she wore a thin gold wedding ring. My sister Lilly said it showed that she was married to the church.

At almost three o clock, the Reverend Preston gently clapped her hands. "Ladies and gentlemen and children would you all make your way to the rose garden."

Following Lilly and Bret, we walked across the manicured lawn to the rose garden, the sun was shining and it was warm, there were even a few swallows darting back and forth, everything looked perfect.

The ceremony took less than twenty minutes. After blessing the rose garden, the Reverend Preston told us this would be a place where we could always remember our loving parents and talk to them in private. She then sent a message of comfort to them from all our family members, including my brother Lex's wife and baby son in Malaga, followed by the Lord's Pray. The whole ceremony was extremely moving. Later we all moved back to the house for light refreshments of tea, cake and biscuits, before the Reverend Preston left.

"Lilly, will you and your family be attending the ten-thirty service on Sunday morning?"

"We most certainly will. We shall all look forward to seeing you at St Laurence Church. Thank you again Sheila."

"No problem, I am always here to help you."

The last Jack saw of the vicar she was with Lex walking down the drive with her Raleigh bicycle, to the gated entrance. Lilly told me later, that if we all agreed it would become a yearly event. We obviously did and my brother Lex said next year his wife Maria and baby son David would be joining him.

Instead of dining out for our evening meal, Lilly decided with the help of her husband Bret to cook a Sunday roast, as Lex and I would be leaving for Gatwick Airport, London shortly after breakfast on Sunday morning. Lex's flight was due to depart for Malaga at 3pm. Later on in the evening I plucked up courage to tell Lilly about my pending move to Marbella for a few months.

"Could Franks not have sent anyone else?"

"I am afraid not, they want a single guy who was young and handsome."

Lilly laughed, but I knew secretly that she was upset; we had always been extremely close. "I will call you every week, that is a promise and if I am able to, I will fly over every so often." Lilly was now happy with the arrangements.

Lex turned to me. "You certainly know how to keep our sister happy. Dad was the same with our mother."

Lex and Jack left 'Castle View' at nine-thirty on Sunday morning. It had been fantastic seeing all the family together. The journey to Gatwick Airport was uneventful and the Range Rover Sport made good time. Once we had arrived at the entrance to the airport check in, Lex got out with his overnight sports bag.

"I will call you when I arrive at my apartment in Marbella." "Be very careful brother I don't want to be going to another memorial service."

We then warmly embraced and went our separate ways. Within the hour Jack was back in his Thames Plaza apartment.

Monday the 12th September at Franks was no different than any other Monday, apart from when he was leaving on an overseas business trip. Today everything appeared normal; nobody was to know that Jack would be out of the office for possibly several months. Once he had left, if anyone asked, they would be told that he was on a sabbatical.

"Jack, you be careful, remember you are only helping MI6 and the Russians out, if the situation gets too hot to handle then get out. I eventually want you back in one piece." Jack liked Jim Richardson and could see why his father spoke so highly of him.

"When do you fly to Malaga?"

"This coming Wednesday on a 3pm EasyJet flight, I will receive my one way ticket when I visit the MI6 Headquarters tomorrow, to sign the Official Secret Act, and receive more information about my trip."

"They will then have you by the balls." They both laughed. Receptionist June was her usual happy self when Jack left Franks shortly after five-thirty. It was a great pity that he could not confide in her; she was a good friend and always brought a breath of fresh air into the building with her ever present happy smile.

On Tuesday morning, the journey from Jack's Thames Plaza apartment to the MI6 Headquarters on the Albert Embankment over the Vauxhall Bridge, took about forty minutes due to heavy traffic. In hindsight he could have walked there in thirty minutes, but the weather was overcast and light rain had been predicted around mid-day, fortunately he had left early and managed to park his Range Rover Sport without much trouble. According to the parking meter he had three hours, before he would get a ticket. Entering the prestigious white marble entrance through the automatic bomb proof glass doors, he walked up to the two smartly dressed young women on reception. He was about to address the younger one of the two, when she turned and spoke to him.

"Can I help you sir?"

"Yes, my name is Jack Sinclair I have an appointment with Miles Coburn at eleven-thirty."

The girl who was seated then glanced at the computer screen in front of her. "One moment please Mr Sinclair." Picking up the grey telephone on the glass and stainless steel desk, she tapped in a number and spoke to someone. "Mr Coburn will be with you very shortly. Can I get you a coffee whilst you wait?"

"No thank you." Jack smiled and the girl did likewise.

Glancing round the foyer which was quite bare apart from three large portraits of the Queen on the wall opposite the main entrance, he observed several CCTV cameras, two of which appeared to follow his every movement. The ceiling was full of white halogen lights which looked most effective, whilst the room was painted in off white to match the whitish grey floor tiles. As he waited a door immediately behind the reception area suddenly opened. A police officer, in full body armour carrying a submachine gun and a Glock automatic hand gun in a right sided holster, walked out and then positioned himself by the entrance just outside the building.

"Jack." His name rang out, turning he could see Miles Coburn standing at the other side of the security scanner by the reception desk. "If you would walk through the scanner I will give you your security pass."

Jack immediately followed Miles's instructions, and went through the high tech scanner and then shook the MI6 man's outstretched hand.

"Good to see you Jack. Slip this ID round your neck I don't want you being arrested."

Jack looked at the security pass. "When did you take my photo?"

"Immediately you started to proceed through the scanner. The new technology we have recently installed is very impressive."

The two men then took the elevator on the right hand side of the room to the third floor. Jack was completely taken by surprise when they got out. The third floor reminded him of the Daily Express news room in Fleet Street. Rows of small desks and faceless personnel sat behind computer screens and telephones. Walking down the central aisle of the long office, they attracted several glances before stopping at a glass door, which had Miles Coburn's name on. Miles then tapped in his security pass number into the key pad on the door and the two of them entered. The room was quite small, with a light oak desk and three dark green leather chairs and a portrait of the Queen on the wall behind the office desk. There were no windows but the wall and the entrance door facing the office was one way glass, which was covered by a grey blind.

"Take a seat Jack. Would you care for a coffee?"

"I don't mind if I do."

Miles then picked up the green telephone on the desk. "When you have a moment Liz, would you please let us have two Americanos with milk?"

Miles then slid open the left hand drawer of his desk and took out a narrow brown envelope, which he opened with a thin brass paper knife, before passing it to Jack.

"The envelope contains your flight ticket, the address of your apartment and two emergency telephone numbers. 0044-757575 is my number and 0034-886688 is your contact in Spain Pedro Gonzales, we can be contacted twenty four hours a day. For security reasons such as losing your phone, do not put a name against these numbers in your mobile phone, just leave them blank. The same applies to my private mobile number."

"Will Pedro be my only contact in Spain?"

"Yes. Listen to any advice he offers, he is a very experienced operative."

There was a knock on the door and a young woman who Jack presumed was Liz walked in with two mugs of coffee and placed them on the office desk.

"Thank you Liz." The girl smiled and then left the office.

Jack continued with the conversation. "If I do make contact with Sergei Aslanov and gain his confidence and discover that he is involved with Gem Stone International and the hijacking, what then?"

"We are expected to inform Major Pavlov of the FSB. He will then take over."

"I presume the Russians will then send a hit squad to eliminate Sergei and his Chechen friends."

"There is a distinct possibility they will do that, unless the diamonds and other precious gems are retrieved. Mind you, I still think their lives are in danger even if they come up with the diamonds. Accidents often happen; people are found dead for no apparent reason or even commit suicide. The outlook does not look rosy for them, the Russians will want redemption."

"What about the Russian Mafia?"

The police and military will give them hell. They will raid dozens of mafia owned businesses, twenty-four hours a day. Violent shootouts and arrests will be made, and wherever possible the police will blow some of the mafia gangsters away, rather than put them on trial."

Jack and Coburn then took another drink of their coffee.

"If Sergei Aslanov knows where the diamonds are, try to find out where they are. The Russians, have offered to pardon him in exchange for the relevant information because who his father is."

"If the Russian Mafia is involved, they will have control of the diamonds and Sergei; his friends are just being used as pawns."

"You could be right." Miles then changed the conversation. "Just to remind you, your wages will be paid into your bank account at the end of each month. You can use your debit card to withdraw cash."

"What about the money I will be paid at the Med Club for gigging as a DJ?"

"Sorry Jack, that will have to be a free as Pedro did not really need a DJ. You never know, when this assignment is over he may offer you a permanent gig. In any case don't forget the £50,000 bonus if you are successful."

Jack glanced at his watch. He had been in Miles Coburn's office for almost two hours.

"Just one final point, once you have identified Sergei Aslanov and the Chechens, try to socialize in the venues where they hang out."

"It would be far easier if I had photographs to identify them." "Christ! I almost forgot, the Russians have now emailed us photographs of Sergei and the eight suspected Chechens who studied at the Moscow Aviation and Aircraft Engineering Academy."

Miles then opened his desk drawer again and took out a large brown envelope which he passed across to Jack. "Please take a look." After removing the photographs he ran his eyes over them, when he saw Sergei he stopped.

"All these photos could be several years old, probably when they were studying at the Moscow Aviation and Aircraft Engineering Academy."

"Why do you think that?"

"If you recall I worked with Sergei in South Africa twelve months ago, he had a dark short beard then. It suited him so there is no way he would shave it off." Jack then put his left hand inside his jacket pocket and took out his Apple iPhone. "I have just remembered that I took a couple of photographs of Sergei Aslanov whilst we were in South Africa, they are more recent." Jack then ran through the phone's photo albums from twelve months ago. "Here we are." Jack then passed the phone to Miles.

"Good looking guy, the photos are excellent. We need to take a copy from your phone."

"Go ahead."

Miles picked up the internal phone on his desk. "Richard if you have a moment."

Minutes later a guy in his late twenties, about six foot and slim, with a thick head of ginger hair and a full beard to match, knocked on the glass door and walked in.

"Jack, this is my assistant Richard Montague, he knows all about your pending trip to Spain." They shook hands. Miles then passed him Jack's phone. "We need to take photocopies of this guy." He also passed him the brown envelope containing the other photographs. "Richard, is it possible to transfer all these photos to a stick?"

"No problem, give me fifteen minutes." He then turned to Jack. What make of laptop do you use?"

"An Apple,"

"Excellent. I will put you a link on your laptop to our office here. All you have to do is tap in our emergency telephone number and you will have direct contact with us on Skype."

Jack then turned to Miles Coburn. "I presume you will let Major Pavlov have Sergei's new photograph?"

"Naturally, we have to help the Russians. It is to our benefit as well."

It was more like twenty minutes when Richard returned with Jack's mobile phone, laptop and the computer stick.

"Does everything work?"

"There is no reason why it should not." Richard then opened up the laptop and slipped in the computer stick. All the photographs including the two from Jack's mobile came up on the screen. He then tapped in the emergency telephone number, seconds later the laptop Miles was using on his desk was activated.

"Thank you Richard."

"My pleasure Jack, have a safe trip." He then left the office.

Miles Coburn then turned to Jack as he opened a red file on his desk. "I need you to sign the Official Secrets Act." Taking out a couple of white A4 sheets of paper from the file, which was marked Jack Sinclair, Miles read out in detail what Jack had to sign. Once signed, Miles placed the two sheets back in the red file. He then went over to a medium sized grey filing cabinet, took a key out of his pocket and opened both doors. Jack noticed that the cabinet contained several other similar files. Miles placed Jack's file on the second shelf down. He then proceeded to relock the cabinet before placing the key back in his left trouser pocket.

"Jack, I will not detain you any longer, you must have a lot to do before you fly out to Spain tomorrow."

"I have."

"I will walk you down to the reception area."

As they took the elevator to the ground floor, Miles turned to Jack. "Once you have arrived at your apartment in Marbella, send me a text to confirm your arrival. Use my office mobile number only, not the emergency number. All my telephone numbers are printed on a card in the brown envelope I gave you. On Thursday you will have a meeting with Pedro Gonzales. As I said earlier trust Pedro, he knows what strategy we will be taking."

"I most certainly will."

Once out of the elevator the two men embraced.

"Be careful Jack and don't take any undue risks, and remember, both Pedro and I are available twenty-four seven."

After leaving the MI6 Headquarters, Jack made his way quickly back to where his Range Rover Sport was parked. He returned just as a parking meter attendant was making his hourly check. He had twenty minutes left on his ticket. Once he had got into his Range Rover, Jack fired the vehicles powerful four litre engine, and sat there for a couple of minutes looking at the MI6 Headquarters. He was now officially on their payroll, but he certainly did not feel like James Bond. On the way back to his Thames Plaza apartment, Jack called in at his local Esso Service Station, where he took on extra fuel and gave the vehicle a car wash and valet, before driving to the security of the Thames Plaza underground car park. As the Range Rover was going to be parked for several months, he just hoped the battery would not be flat when he finally returned home.

The afternoon flew by as Jack packed his large dark blue wheelie suite case and his black and yellow sports bag with both summer and winter clothes. Over the last two weeks he had also managed to download onto his laptop almost two thousand songs, most of which were House Music, electronic dance music, black South African disco music, Caribbean, Latin American and European chart hits. If he was going to be a top DJ at the Med Beach Club, he had to make certain there would be no mistakes from his side.

Around six-thirty he headed for Joe's Café Bar for his evening meal. There was a chill in the air and it felt like rain. This time tomorrow he would be in Spain, where the temperature in the evening would be in the late seventies. The café bar inside was fairly busy as it was far too cold to sit outside. Jack's usual bar stool was still vacant, so he pulled the stool closer to the bar and sat down. Punters were now starting to drift in, it was a good job he was early. Both the owners Mattia and Sophie were on duty.

"Hi Jack, you are in earlier than usual." He liked Sophie she was always happy with a lovely smile.

"I need to get an early night tonight because ten-thirty tomorrow morning I am away on a business trip."

"Where are you going to this time Jack?"

"Europe and then followed by the Middle East and North Africa; however my first port of call is Spain."

"How very exciting"

"Franks are expanding worldwide, so I have volunteered to be their International salesman. I have no ties and I love travelling, especially to warm climates. I shall probably be away several months."

Sophie then passed Jack the menu. "What can I get you?"

"A mixed vegetable omelette and a pint of Peroni followed by a latte coffee, was the reply."

"No problem, give us about twenty minutes, I will get you your lager." Sophie then disappeared into the kitchen with the food order, minutes later she was back behind the bar pulling Jack's Peroni. "Mattia wants to speak to you before you leave; I have told him about your business trip." Jack smiled.

The Peroni was cool and refreshing just what he needed. Twenty minutes later another attractive young woman who had recently started working in the bar brought him his meal.

"Thank you."

Jack glanced up into her eyes, they were large and exciting, and he also noticed how white her teeth were when she smiled. She was good looking, like all the other staff in the café bar. Jack looked at his gold Gucci watch, it was almost eight forty-five, he needed to get back to his apartment and sort out whatever else he would be taking with him, before he hit the sack for an early night.

"Sophie." She was at the far end of the bar.

"Yes Jack."

"I am going to have to make a move, I need to get an early night. By the way the food was excellent."

"Thank you Jack, I will just tell Mattie you are leaving."

A few minutes later she returned with her husband who was still wearing his chef's uniform.

"You take care Jack, don't forget to keep in touch with us." He then passed Jack a business card with their mobile number on. The two men embraced. If you will excuse me I have to get back into the kitchen, we are quite busy for a Tuesday at this time of the year."

Sophie then put her arms around Jack and gave him a huge kiss. "You are a lovely man Jack Sinclair, some lucky girl out there is waiting for you, and sooner or later you will meet her. As Mattie said, please keep in touch."

"I will I promise you."

As soon as Jack left Joe's Café Bar he felt cold, he was glad to get back to his apartment. Passport checked, one thousand Euros in cash. Designer shades, sun cream, and electric razor, the list was endless but eventually they were all crossed off. By ten-fifteen Jack was in bed with no time to listen to the ITN News.

When he slid out of bed at eight on Wednesday morning he felt rejuvenated after a great night's sleep, the adrenalin was now starting to flow. The first thing he did, was to book a cab for ten-fifteen, which would take him from Thames Plaza to Charing Cross Underground Station for the eleven thirty train to Gatwick Airport. He glanced out of the balcony window, it had been raining during the night but at least now it was beginning to dry up. The apartment looked spotless just like his mother had always kept it, she would have been proud of him. After a light breakfast he had a shave and shower. Changed into smart casual gear and then slipped on his favourite pair of black and yellow Reebok trainers. Once he had made certain his wheelie suitcase and sports bag were secure he put on his black soft leather zip jacket. It was now leaving ten, picking up the laptop case and his two travel bags, he left the apartment after a quick look round to make certain everything was secure, and then took the elevator to the ground floor. Nelson the immaculately dressed middle aged black security officer was on duty at reception.

"You look as though you are going on a long journey Mr Sinclair."

"I am but not as far as usual. This time I shall be visiting Europe, the Middle East, and North Africa."

"Will you be away for long?"

"Could possibly be four to six months? There is no one staying in my apartment and my Range Rover Sports is parked in the basement."

"Would you like me to keep an eye on your property for you Sir?"

"Thank you Nelson, I would appreciate that." Jack then passed him the Range Rover's key. "Perhaps you would give the vehicle a run on the road every so often to keep the battery charged up."

"No problem Mr Sinclair, leave everything to me, I can see your cab has just drawn up outside the entrance."

"Thank you, I will see you when I return."

"Do you need any help Mr Sinclair?"

"No thanks, I am fine."

"Have a safe trip."

Without another word, Jack put his gear into the black cab. Minutes later they were heading through the city to Charing Cross Underground Railway Station. Twenty minutes later, even in London's heavy traffic they arrived at Charing Cross. After paying the cabbie, he headed down the escalator to a ticket machine and booked a one way ticket to Gatwick Airport, this was a journey he had made many times before during the last twelve months. The eleven thirty train which was fairly full was on time, the twenty eight mile journey took about fifty five minutes. Once on board the free airport bus, which ran from the railway station to the airport terminal, Jack felt more relaxed. "Why the hell had I not taken a taxi from the Thames Plaza to Gatwick Airport, I could certainly afford to, rather than have all this inconvenience." The thought went through his mind several times. After checking in at the EasyJet desk with his flight ticket and baggage, Jack made his way with his laptop to passport control and customs. Once through he entered the departure lounge and then went to the nearest Starbucks. There was a long queue but eventually he ordered a large latte and a couple of buttered croissants. Taking his mobile out of his jacket pocket he switched it on, the time came up, one-thirty. Bringing up his sister's number he called her, she answered the phone. "Lilly it is me Jack, I promised to call you today."

"Where are you Jack?"

"I am sat in a Starbucks at Gatwick Airport drinking coffee whilst I wait for my 3pm flight."

"I am so glad you called. It was lovely to see you and Lex last weekend; mum and dad would have loved the get together."

"You are absolutely right Lilly they would have." Their conversation went on for another ten minutes. Lilly worried Jack. He had been concerned for some time that his loving sister was still struggling with grief over the loss of their parents. Last weekend whilst in Ludlow, he mentioned his concern to her husband Bret. He too had noticed how she was and said if there was no improvement they would go and see their doctor. Bret promised to keep him in the picture.

Before they parted company Lilly told her brother how much she loved him. "Please be careful Jack and keep in touch regularly with me."

"Of course I will and try not to worry." After their call ended, Jack sat there for several minutes thinking about his sister and the stress she must be going through. Her husband Bret was a compassionate guy and would take good care of her. For the next hour to pass time away, he scrawled down Facebook, which he had not done for many months. Nothing had changed mainly idle gossip and people with big egos making unsavoury comments. Frustrated he brought up Sky News. After ordering a second latte, he moved to another table which was closer to the flight information display screen. A few minutes before two his Malaga flight came up, it was leaving from Gate 10. More or less at the same time a female voice came over the airport public address system, asking all passengers for the 3pm Boeing 737 Easy Jet flight to Malaga, to make their way to Gate 10. Along with 143 other passengers Jack made his way down the glass window corridor. As he approached Gate 10, he could see the Boeing 737 on the tarmac ready for take-off. There was no delay and once boarding cards were checked, all the passengers entered the plane via the Jet Bridge. Jack was sat at the rear of the aircraft on the last row by the aisle, next to two attractive young women, who gave him the impression that they were lesbians, from the way they were flirting with each other and holding hands. Within minutes the Boeing's four engines came to life and the plane slowly taxied to the end of the runway for take-off, but not before the senior stewardess had made the passengers aware of all the safety regulations. For a good thirty seconds all the passengers and crew sat in silence waiting for the inevitable. Some had the look of fear on their faces, others closed their eyes, and many held hands whilst others just sat there with a passive look on their face. All of a sudden there was a defining roar as the Boeing 737 picked up speed and thundered down the runway to make a perfect lift-off. As the aircraft's wheels contracted, they gradually climbed to a cruising height of 35,000 feet and headed out over the English Channel in the direction of Malaga Spain.

8

The three hour, 1,023 mile flight to Malaga was uneventful; no food was served apart from snacks and drinks. Jack could have downed a cool pint of lager but his better judgement wisely made him stick to tea, in any case there were only cans and shorts on sale. Touchdown was perfect with only the slightest bump. As the Boeing737 taxied to a vacant gate, the Captain came over the planes public address system. "Ladies and Gentlemen this is your Captain Hugh Morgan. We shall be embarking in the next few minutes. The time in Malaga is 7pm, as Spain is one hour ahead of the UK. The temperature outside is 26c (78 Fahrenheit) and there has been no rain for over four months, you will be pleased to know that so far there are no water restrictions."

"There would be in the UK," someone shouted out and got a lot of laughs.

The Captain continued "EasyJet would like to thank everyone for travelling with us." The door of the aircraft then opened allowing the heat to rush in; it felt like an open oven. Along with all the other passengers Jack left the aircraft down the Airstairs. As he walked across the tarmac he slipped on his dark shades and took off his black leather zip jacket. Immediately he felt the heat of the sun on his body. It was warm, very warm. Once in the air-conditioned airport terminal, he removed his dark shades as he passed through passport control on his way to collect his luggage from the baggage carousel. Twenty five minutes later, he was heading down the green customs exit for the arrival lounge. Even at seven-forty in the evening Malaga International Airport, the fourth busiest in Spain, and the Costa del Sol's premier airport, was still extremely busy. Holiday reps filled the entrance to the lounge, directing tourists to the numerous waiting coaches, mini-buses and taxies. With all the commotion Jack was having problems finding his contact, the guy with the Med Club sign. Then he saw the sign and the man himself Pedro Gonzales, well he presumed it was him. Pushing the airport trolley in front of him Jack walked over to him.

"Pedro." The guy turned and smiled.

"Good to meet you Jack, I recognised you from the photo Miles Coburn emailed to me." The two men shook hands. "I have parked in the short stay bay, we had better move as they are hot on tickets if you overstay your time." Pedro Gonzales was a very good looking guy in his early forties. Standing about six two with dark eyes, he was slim with broad shoulders and large biceps, his shoulder length dark hair was tied in a short ponytail. Apart from a small goat like beard he was clean shaven. As his complexion was very Mediterranean, you would never have known that he was not Spanish by birth. Dressed in dark shorts and a black t-shirt, which advertised the Med Club on the front, Pedro also had a solid gold rope chain around his neck, as well as a gold wedding ring on the second finger of his left hand. On his feet believe it or not, he wore identical black and yellow Reebok trainers like Jack. He also had a tattoo on his left leg of a Japanese Samaria Warrior.

"Let me help you with your luggage then we can leave the trolley here."

The two men then slipped on their dark shades and left the arrival lounge, Jack with his wheelie suitcase and laptop, whilst Pedro carried the sports bag. As they left the terminal and walked across the road to the parking bay, Pedro took out his car key from his right pocket and pressed the open button. Immediately the lights flashed on the Hyacinth Red Metallic C-Class Mercedes opposite them. Pedro then opened the boot. Once Jack's luggage had been taken on board they got into the car, which was extremely warm.

"Don't worry once I fire the engine and we move out the air conditioning will kick in. Within minutes they had left behind the hustle and bustle of Malaga International Airport and joined the new Mediterranean Motorway the A7, which was due to be completed in the next two years. Eventually the motorway would run in two segments from Malaga to Estepona and then from Estepona to Guadiaro a distance of sixty-five miles. Pedro was right, the air conditioning kicked in. The motorway was no way near as busy as Jack had expected. Many drivers still used the fast main road, the longest road in Europe, which hugs the Mediterranean Sea, allowing tourists easy access to the holiday resorts of Torremolinos, Benalmadena and Fuengirola. After thirty five minutes, Pedro slipped off the motorway and followed the signs for Marbella and Puerto Banus.

"I am going to take you straight to your apartment. I presume you have not eaten?"

"No not since breakfast."

"There are several excellent bars and restaurants only minutes from your complex who serve food until late; you will have no problem finding somewhere to eat."

Twenty minutes later they were driving through the busy city centre towards the Esplanade Paseo. The area was much quieter with several impressive looking hotels and luxury apartment complexes, whose gardens were a mass of colour with exotic flowers and palm trees set amidst meandering manicured lawns. All had open air swimming pools, which were now completely deserted, as most of the clientele were either dining or getting ready to hit the city nightspots. These properties all had one thing in common, apart from the high-tech security fencing, they all faced a white sandy beach and the sea, where visitors to Marbella both rich and famous stayed. Many of who spent most of the day either posing around the pool, or on the beach in skimpy swimwear, showing off their slim toned bodies, or drinking endless cocktails and white-wine spritzers with Caesar Salads at the bar.

"There on the left, that is where you are staying, the Marbella Beach. It is a plush apartment complex, sixty percent are residents and the other forty percent are owned by wealthy individuals and used mainly for family holidays. Only about twenty Brits live here, as prices start at two million Euros upwards. The owners, who are from all over Europe and the Middle East, also include several Russians. By the way, the entrance to the complex in a car is by intercom only. You can use the small gate on the right by the entrance if you are on foot; I will give you a key card to use before we part company."

Pedro then jumped out of the Mercedes and went over to the large double wooden and metal gates and pressed the intercom. He was obviously known to the security guard who must have been observing him on the CCTV, as the gates immediately opened allowing him to drive the Mercedes to a private parking area by the side of the complex. Here they parked next to a black Porsche 4x4 and a red Ferrari and several other high priced cars, which included a black and gold Bentley Continental GT Convertible.

After removing Jack's two bags from the boot of the car, they walked towards the glass door entrance of the complex.

"The end apartment on the second floor on the right belongs to the company."

Jack must have had a blank expression on his face.

"We try not to refer to MI6 but instead us the name of the company." Jack nodded his head and smiled.

As they approached the main entrance, Jack noticed the two large terracotta urns on either side of the entrance, which were full of sweet smelling yellow Jasmine. The doors automatically opened and then closed as they entered the air conditioned white marble foyer. The foyer was spotlessly clean, in fact clinically clean.

A guy with a bald shaven head, in his mid- thirties was sat behind a black marble reception desk with a computer and CCTV screen in front of him. When he saw them he immediately stood up, he was about six feet tall and quite slim and looked impeccable in his black silk shirt and cream suit. He was in fact a very good looking guy, and like most men in this part of Spain had a fairly dark complexion.

"Good to see you Pedro."

"And you too Roberto." The two men embraced, they obviously knew each other very well. "I would like you to meet my friend Jack Sinclair from London." They then shook hands. "Jack is a top DJ in the UK and will be resident at the Med Club for the next few months. He will be staying here in my father-in-law's apartment whilst he is with us, so you will be seeing a great deal of him." Pedro then turned to Jack. "Roberto is a frequent visitor to the Med Club, we see him most weeks when he is not on duty."

Pedro and Roberto exchanged a few more words before he and Jack took the elevator to the second floor. As they walked down the dimly lit corridor to apartment eighteen, Pedro turned to Jack. "I could not very well say I or the company owned the apartment, it just so happened that my father-in-law Sheikh Ali Bin Falih being from the United Arab Emirates, fitted the bill perfectly." Jack smiled.

When they finally entered the company apartment shortly before nine-thirty it was with a sense of relief, he was tired and hungry. Pedro showed him around the spacious modern two bedroom apartment and kitchen dinner, making certain he was familiar with everything.

"You will need two key cards. One is to gain entrance to the Marbella Beach Complex and foyer, the other is for entrance to your own apartment." Pedro placed both the key cards on the grey granite top table in the kitchen. "Tomorrow we need to talk; perhaps you could be at the Med Club by two. Bring your laptop with you and we will work out a programme and decide which nights you will be gigging at the club." Pedro then started to walk towards the door. "I am going to leave you now and let you find somewhere to eat. Just turn left out of the complex onto the Esplanade Paseo and you will have no problem finding a restaurant." A couple of minutes later Pedro left the apartment.

There was little point in unpacking his luggage until he had eaten. He was casually dressed from the flight but he always looked smart and trendy. After throwing some cold water on his face and running a comb through his dark hair, he opened the glass door and went outside onto the balcony. Quickly he sent a text to his sister Lilly and brother Lex, telling them he had just arrived at his apartment, and was now heading out to find somewhere to eat. Tomorrow he would give them a call. Darkness was descending quickly but it was still very warm with no wind. The gardens looked stunning in the security lights which had flickered on. Putting his hands on the balcony rail, he stood there listening to the sound of the crickets down below, every so often a fire fly darted back and forth, it was a world away from the River Thames and London. This was Marbella, the largest and most exciting city on the Costa del Sol, said to be full of beautiful sexy women. Jack laughed to himself, what was wrong with letting your imagination run away. After putting his passport and cash, which included his English sterling and most of his Euros, along with Miles Coburn's contact details in the apartment's security safe deposit box, he headed down the white marble stairs to the foyer.

Roberto was who was still on duty, smiled when he saw Jack.

"You work late."

"I am on duty until midnight if you need me personally Mr Sinclair, you can then contact me on the emergency telephone number on the desk."

"My friend Pedro tells me if I turn left outside the complex, there will be bars and restaurants where I can get a late meal."

"There are several but it is getting late, they don't normally serve food after ten-thirty." Roberto then glanced at his black Sekonda wrist watch. "Ten minutes past ten. Head for Albatross the owner Roscoe is my cousin, I will call him and tell him you have just arrived, he will look after you. You will love the restaurant and bar, it is a fabulous venue to hang out at." Roberto picked up his mobile and put a call through to his cousin. After a brief conversation in Spanish, Roberto put his mobile back on his desk. "My cousin will be expecting you in ten to fifteen minutes. Just ask for him."

"Thank you Roberto." The security officer smiled but didn't speak.

Once out of the Marbella Beach Complex, Jack headed left along the Esplanade Paseo passing several busy bars and restaurants. It was now almost completely dark but the bright florescent street lights illuminated the winding Esplanade, which ran along the side of the Mediterranean Sea. Every time Jack passed by any bushes or trees he could hear the sound of crickets chatting away, even above the crashing waves rolling onto the beach to his right. Marbella was now starting to wake up. The multi- coloured stone tiled pathway was very busy with young guys flying by on skateboards, couples walking arm in arm, whist others were amorously involved in each other whilst sat on the low sea wall, which snaked along the edge of the coastal path. A head of him maybe a hundred metres away, he could see the illuminated pink and blue sign of the Albatross Bar and Restaurant. The place was alive with smiling faces, young, middle-aged and occasionally quite old, but always very glamorous. There must have been close on one hundred and sixty punters sat outside dining and drinking. Many of the older men were with skimpy dressed stunning looking girls, who were at least twenty years younger than most of them. Not to be out done, there were older women adorned with expensive jewellery and wearing off the shoulder dresses, which showed off their tanned bodies, with handsome young guys. Sex- Sex -Sex, it was everywhere but then again this was Marbella.

Jack urgently needed to find the owner Roscoe, so he gradually made his way past tipsy punters and headed indoors to the restaurant and bar. There was only one way he could describe the Albatross, it was sumptuous, and had an incredible position on the waterfront, it oozed opulence with a huge polished oak and brass bar, lavish velvet and soft leather furniture and a stunning golf ball light installation above the bar.

"Mr Sinclair, if you would please follow me, I will take you to Mr Rodriguez. He is in the lounge with friends."

He looked at the girl who was a pretty young thing, no more than seventeen or eighteen. "How did you know I was Jack Sinclair?"

The girl smiled. "You are already famous in Marbella we have been waiting for you to arrive. Aren't you DJ Ramos, the UK's top House Music DJ?" Jack couldn't help but smile. "Your posters are up everywhere in Marbella advertising your forthcoming gig at the Med Club. We shall all be there to see you." She then started to laugh. "My Uncle Roberto described you perfectly to my father but he never said you were such a good looking guy."

Jack was now feeling slightly embarrassed, so he quickly changed the conversation. "You speak perfect English."

"I should do. I have studied your language since the age of ten. Later this year I shall be going to the University of Malaga to study to be an English teacher."

"Good luck to you."

"Thank you, Jack."

She certainly was a good looking girl and she knew it, slim and well developed for her age, with her long black hair and a Mediterranean complexion, but it was still hard to believe she was only a teenager.

"By the way what do I call you?"

"Valentina,"

"What a beautiful name."

"Thank you Jack," she then fluttered her eye lashes at him; the look in her large brown eyes said everything.

The Albatross was just as busy inside but eventually they made their way into the lounge. Valentina immediately went over to a guy with a pony tail who looked to be in his late forties. He was sat talking to another guy, who was a good five years older than him, who in turn was sat next to a handsome young man, who was probably no more than twenty five or twenty six.

"Excuse me Papa, may I introduce you to Jack Sinclair otherwise known as DJ Ramos."

"Jack this is my Papa, Roscoe Rodriguez."

The man stood up. "Good to meet you Jack, I have heard so much about you." He then shook his hand. "May I introduce you to my very close friend Aslan Maskhadove who owns the famous Cobra Jewellery chain on the Costa del Sol, and of course his very good friend George."

The mention of his name immediately rang alarm bells in Jack's head. He certainly did not sound Spanish with his broken accent. It then dawned on Jack who he actually was. This was the Chechen Separatist leader, who was given citizenship by the Spanish Government when the Russians tried to extradite him. He had since built up the Cobra Jewellery Empire into a multimillion Euro company, and now lived in luxury in an exclusive villa between Marbella and Puerto Banus. The Russians were still after him, as they are convinced he is somehow involved in the Siberian cargo plane hijack. They also believe that the Chechen Mafia, who were now part of the Russian Mafia, had funded his empire building.

Aslan was a handsome man, tall with an excellent physique and a full head of short dark hair. Jack presumed he was gay and George was his boyfriend. Aslan then stood up and embraced Jack, and introduced him to George, who had a handshake like a wet lettuce.

"Sit yourself down Jack and join us." Roscoe then called a waiter. "What would you like to eat my friend?"

"Whatever you can recommend?"

"The seafood paella was excellent tonight."

"That would be fine by me and a pint of Peroni lager if you would."

The male waiter then left, returning almost immediately with the food and drink.

Roscoe turned to Jack. "My good friend Pedro Gonzales from the Med Club speaks very highly of you. He tells me you are the top guy in the UK for House Music."

Jack laughed. "Certainly not the top guy, that honour falls to Calvin Harris, but I am certainly not far behind, until it comes to appearance money and then there is a big gap."

Aslan then got into the conversation. "What is House Music Jack?"

Jack turned to Valentina. "I am sure you know, perhaps you would care to explain."

"Of course I will. House Music is a genre of electric music which was created by DJ's and music producers in Chicago in the early 1980s. It is very popular in clubs all over Europe. Once Jack starts his residency at the Med Club you and George will have to go and watch him."

"We will."

"If you guys agree, we could all attend Jack's opening night?"

Roscoe then spoke. I will speak to Pedro about tickets.

"Have you known Pedro Gonzales long?"

"No, only a few months, it is my brother Lex who knows him well and has recommended me."

"You are not by any chance related to the new head coach and manager at Malaga FC?"

"I most certainly am. Lex is my elder brother."

The two men suddenly came to life. George still did not speak; he just looked pissed or was taking something.

Aslan then opened up. "He was one hell of a player, I saw him many times until he retired due to injury. We were all delighted he got the manager's job when Roman Russo returned home to Italy to look after his seriously ill wife. "You must join us in our company's Corporate Box, when we have our next home match?"

"Thank you for the invitation, I shall look forward to that."

Roscoe then got into the conversation. "You don't have a talent for football like your brother?"

"I am afraid not, as a teenager I was never interested in football, all I wanted to do was to become a top DJ. However all that changed when I went to University to study to become a gemmologist. I have travelled all over Europe and even went to work in South Africa for two years to gain experience. Eventually I ended up working for Franks the Hatton Garden, Diamond and Gem dealers in London.

"And now your dream has come true, and you are about to start a new career as a top House Music DJ at the Med Club in Marbella."

"Not really Aslan, fate has a strange way of changing your life forever. Just over twelve months ago, my brother and sister and I lost both our parents in a helicopter accident in Australia. From that day on, my life completely changed and I decided to live one day at a time. On the spare of the moment, I resigned from my job at Franks and moved out here to fulfil an old ambition."

For a moment nobody spoke, the three friends just stared at him, whether it was pity or shock he did not know. Jack then broke the silence. "Guys, you are going to have to excuse me, I am shattered from such a long day and need to get some shut eye." He then turned to Roscoe and spoke in a low voice to him. "How much do I owe you?"

Roscoe shook his head. "On the house Jack, any friend of Pedro is a friend of mine."

"Thank you. You have an incredible restaurant and bar." Roscoe smiled and then shook Jack's hand.

"I will certainly be spending time here."

"You will always be very welcome; we shall look forward to seeing you again."

"Before I make my departure, perhaps you could give me directions to the Med Club, I have a meeting with Pedro tomorrow?"

"No problem, continue walking down the Esplanade for another ten minutes, you can't miss the Med Club."

Jack then headed for the exit. Valentina was outside talking to a male member of staff, when she saw Jack she waved and came over to him smiling. "Are you impressed with the Albatross?"

"You have a beautiful place here, you must be very proud of your Papa?"

"I am, my mother and he think he works far too hard. "When I am eighteen will you take me out clubbing? I like older guys, especially if they are as handsome as you." "You are now making me blush." She was obviously amused and started to laugh.

"Perhaps I will see you tomorrow?"

"More than likely Valentina, you take care."

Without another word Jack made his way back to the Marbella Beach Apartments, it took less than twenty minutes. All the bars he passed were still very busy. It was still warm with hardly a breeze and the sea was crashing onto the nearby beach, it may have been his imagination but it appeared to be calmer. After slipping his key card into the security pad by the side of the small entrance gate, he entered the Marbella Beach Complex. There was an eerie silence, apart from several fire flies fluttering past as he walked up to the main entrance door, which did not automatically open as he approached it. Inside he could see a security guard but it wasn't Roberto. He immediately pressed the intercom buzzer and the guard looked up. He was young, probably only in his early twenties.

"Can I help you Sir." He had a broken accent which certainly was not Spanish.

"Yes, it is Jack Sinclair apartment eighteen, I need to gain entrance."

"One moment please Sir." The security guard who was average height and build, clean shaven with dark short hair, ran his eyes quickly over the computer screen in front of him, before opening the door.

Jack then entered the foyer. "Good evening Mr Sinclair." Jack nodded his head and smiled. "Roberto told me he was going off duty at midnight; I had no idea that we had twenty four hour security."

"Roberto Sanchez is my boss, he owns Costa Security. He always makes certain that five star complexes like the Marbella Beach Apartments and the more exclusive hotels always have twenty four hour security. As there are many wealthy guests and celebrities staying on the Costa De Sol, Mr Sanchez also offers a personal armed protection service to VIP's."

"Roberto Sanchez appears to be a very successful business man."

"He is, but he certainly puts the hours in. That is why he is the premier security operator on the Costa del Sol."

"Is he married?"

"No, but he has a gorgeous looking blonde Latvian girlfriend called Tanya, who he spends time with. Even though they have only known each other for less than three months he wants her to move in with him. Roberto has a beautiful villa in the hills overlooking Marbella and drives a red Ferrari Portofino. He also owns an Ocean going speed boat called the Black Prince, which is moored in the marina at Puerto Banus. As I am used to driving Ocean going speed boats, he allows me to use it when I go sea fishing.

"You are not Spanish?"

"No, I come from Sousse in Tunisia. Six months ago I came to Spain to make my fortune and ended up in Marbella."

"You speak very good English."

"Yes, thanks to my parents. My father met my mother, who is English, when he was studying in London to be a pharmacist. They fell in love and eventually got married and moved back to Sousse, were they now own a large pharmacy in the city centre. I speak both English and Arabic fluently.

"A fascinating story, tell me, what is your name?"

"Youssef Beji."

"Well Youssef, it has been a pleasure to meet you but you must excuse me, I need to get to bed. I only arrived around nine this evening from the UK and the lack of sleep is catching up on me."

"It has been a pleasure to have met you Mr Sinclair. Before you take your leave one final point, if there is no one on duty and the foyer door is closed, just slip your apartment key card into the security pad and the door will open. The software we use automatically checks if you are a resident at the Marbella Beach Apartments, and either gives you clearance or refuses you entry."

"Technology these days is incredible, thank you for the information Youssef; I hope I will see you tomorrow." Without another word, Jack headed up the white marble staircase to apartment eighteen. As he opened the door he was hit by the heat. Walking over to the balcony door, he opened it slightly, within minutes the room had cooled down. Stripping off his clothes he lay down on the king size bed in his light blue boxer shorts. He then realised he needed to set his mobile alarm for ten which he eventually managed to do, but it was an effort, he could hardly keep his eyes open. Minutes later he lay back and fell into a deep sleep.

9

Jack was relieved that he had set the alarm for ten otherwise there was a distinct possibility, that he would still have been asleep at mid-day. The apartment was still very warm, even with the balcony window open all night. When he finally came too, he realized he had not closed the window blinds, leaving the rooms open to the warm rays of the sun. Walking into the open plan kitchen, he opened the fridge door more out of curiosity than expecting to find anything inside. There were a couple of bottles of Mountain Spring Water and a dozen cans of mixed fruit and baked beans, as well as a dozen eggs and a tub of olive spread butter. On the kitchen table was a white envelope with his name on, which he had not noticed when he first arrived. Opening the envelope, he ran his eyes over the note inside. It was from Pedro. "I have left you some water, a carton of milk, food and eggs in the fridge; you will find bread and croissants along with tea and coffee in the kitchen cupboard. If you want anything else, you will have to visit the nearby local Lidl Supermarket. Don't forget our meeting at 2pm." Jack smiled to himself.

For the next hour Jack cooked and ate a light breakfast, unpacked his suite case and sports bag, and then headed for the bathroom for a shave and shower. After changing into a white Nike sports top and matching shorts he went out onto the balcony. The weather was perfect, warm with not the hint of a breeze and the manicured gardens looked magnificent. The water in the heart shaped swimming pool looked like a sheet of glass. He intended to taka a dip after he returned from the Med Club. There was not a sole around; probably most of the occupants of the Marbella Beach Complex were still in bed recovering from their previous night out. His apartment was very modern and tastefully decorated. Two good sized bedrooms, one which had a king size bed and a small balcony, also a fully equipped open plan kitchen, with a large glass and stainless steel table with six black leather chairs. The set up was most impressive but then it should be for three million Euros. Even so, he still preferred his pad in London at the Thames Plaza, which cost far less.

Time was flying by, it was already leaving eleven-thirty, but there was enough time for a walk round the complex gardens and then a quick trip to the nearby convenience store to stock up with some provisions. Jack's intention was to have breakfast in the apartment and then dine out for lunch and his evening meal. He had never been a good cook, but instead bought pre- packed frozen meals or dined out; he could see no reason to change now. Youssef was on reception from the night before and there was no one else around.

"Good morning Mr Sinclair, I trust you slept well?"

"Very well, thank you for asking Youssef. What time do you go off duty?"

The young security glanced at his watch. "In fifteen minutes and then I have a few days off. I am going to visit my family in Tunisia."

"Enjoy your break."

Slipping on his dark shades, Jack went outside into the gardens. The sun's strong rays were blazing down and it was extremely warm. Walking over to the swimming pool he put his hand in the still water, it was cold, even so he still intended to take a swim later when he returned from the Med Club. Jack then noticed a stunning looking young women with long dark hair in a tiny white bikini lying on her stomach sunbathing. The briefs she wore were more like a G-string and disappeared between the cheeks of her lovely shaped bottom. He had difficulty keeping his eyes off her. As he turned away from the pool, there was a splash behind him. Turning round he could see the girl swimming effortlessly through the cool water. Once she had reached the far end she turned and swam back towards him. As she started to climb out of the pool by the white marble steps she looked up at Jack.

"Well, are you not going to pass me my towel instead of running your eyes over my body from behind your dark shades? She then laughed out loud.

Jack immediately passed her one of the soft white cotton towels from the sun bed she had been lying on. She certainly was stunning. As the girl rose out of the pool, water ran from her body exposing her large soft breasts in the tiny bikini top. She had the perfect feminine figure. Holding the towel to her body she started to dry herself, before lying face down again on the sun bed.

"Jack, would you please dry my back for me?" Her accent was very broken but he felt she may be Russian.

Enjoying every moment of the invitation, he gently started to dry the contours of her body. Then it suddenly dawned on him, how on earth did she know his name?

"How did you know my name?"

"I saw you when you arrived last night and asked Roberto who you were. He told me your name and that you will be appearing at the Med Club as DJ Ramos."

Jack broke into a smile but did not speak. The girl then turned over and faced him, her breasts were large and inviting, she knew he was looking at her.

"What do I call you?"

"Olga, I am from Russia."

"And what is Olga from Russia doing in Marbella?"

Her accent was very sexy as she spoke. "I am on a working holiday."

"So what Iine of work are you in then?"

Olga then leaned forward and removed Jack's shades.

"You have beautiful eyes Jack. It is a shame to cover them. I am a sexy dancer at Pinks the girlie club in Puerto Banus, you Brits would probably call me a stripper as I take all my clothes off. I will take you there one night and then you can watch me perform."

"I would love to." Olga smiled and then ran her tongue seductively over her top lip. "Perhaps we could have a meal out together and a drink?"

"I would love that Jack."

"You must earn a great deal of money as a dancer to own an apartment in this complex?"

She laughed. "My uncle owns the property, he is a very rich businessman back home in Russia, and said I could use the apartment for the next few months, but he has no idea that I am a dancer."

Jack was enjoying the conversation but he had to move on, there were jobs to do. "Olga, you are going to have to excuse me. I have some shopping to do and then a meeting with the owner of the Med Club at two. Perhaps I can call you when I return?"

"Please do."

"Do you have a mobile?"

"Yes, but you can call round at my apartment, I am staying in number twenty on the floor above you. We can have a glass of wine together."

Ten minutes later Jack found himself walking into the Twenty Four Hour convenience store. Several bottles of still Mountain Spring Water, four bottles of red and white Spanish wine, an assortment of food for breakfast, including fresh fruit, which would last about 10days and a dozen pre-packed frozen meals in case he decided not to dine out. Two large plastic bags just about held everything. On returning to his Marbella Beach apartment he hastily put everything away. Everything looked spotless; it was as though no one lived there. He was now in a bit of a rush, as he always liked to arrive at appointments early, though he knew at one twenty he should arrive with time to spare.

Once out of the complex he turned left down the Esplanade Paseo, he hadn't even noticed who was on reception when he left the foyer. His mind was so focused on arriving on time. Taking his mobile out of his left hand pocket as he walked, he texted Miles Coburn to tell him he had arrived in Marbella safely. Miles immediately texted back. "Best of luck my friend." Jack then put a call through to his brother Lex in Malaga.

"Jack great to hear from you. I am on the training pitch at the moment with my team, it is difficult to speak. Is everything ok?"

"Yes, everything is fine and the Marbella Beach Apartment complex is stunning."

"Jack, I will call you around seven."

"No problem, I will speak to you later."

A minute later he made his second call, his sister Lilly answered the phone. She was overjoyed to hear from him.

"Jack, I got your text last night. How are you darling, have you settled in?"

His sister always called him darling when she was worried. "I am absolutely fine Lilly. The company have put me up in an apartment which is worth several million Euros in a beautiful complex. I am on my way now to a business appointment, so I thought I would give you a quick call to see how you are."

"I certainly feel better than I was. Jack please don't worry about me, I have a wonderful husband who will always take good care of me."

"How are Bret and the children?"

"Everyone is fine. You must promise to call me every week."

"Lilly, you know I will always call you. How can I ever forget such a loving sister," she laughed. Jack could visualise her beautiful smile. A few minutes later their conversation ended.

The sun was starting to get warmer and he felt slightly dehydrated, a cool glass of lager would be perfect, but it would have to wait until he reached his destination. A few hundred metres past the Albatross Bar and Restaurant, which appeared to have a booming lunchtime trade, Jack could see the Med Club in the distance. The large two storey white building and the gardens opposite looked immaculate. To the right of the building, the private car park was full of up market cars and 4x4's, including Pedro Gonzales's hyacinth red metallic C-Class Mercedes. Above the sand stone arched front of the gated entrance, the name Med Beach Club had been painted in black and gold lettering. The whole area was protected by CCTV cameras.

There were a number people, several with young families impatiently waiting to enter, as the two security guards, an older man and a girl in her early twenties thoroughly checked everyone before allowing them in.

Once inside, you would have thought you were in the reception of a luxury hotel, here you could purchase your entry ticket to a world of luxury and glamour.

"My name is Jack Sinclair and I have an appointment with Mr Gonzales at two."

"One moment Mr Sinclair," replied the girl who was smartly dressed in a black and gold T-shirt with white shorts and a matching baseball cap on her head and gold coloured trainers, then turned away as she spoke into a small receiver which was attached to her left wrist. She then turned to Jack. "I will take you through to Mr Gonzales; he will be with you in a moment."

Once through the security door, it was like going into another world.

There were about twenty five people in the white marble room queuing to buy entrance tickets. There were no windows, only artificial lighting and there was no sign of Pedro.

Jack turned to the female security guard. "Are you English?"

"The girl smiled. "Yes, is my accent still so obvious?"Jack smiled. "I came to Spain with my parents twenty years ago, I think of myself as being Spanish as I have never even been back to the UK." She was very friendly and constantly smiled. "I normally work on the beach or in the swimming pool area, but as we are short staffed today I am on the main entrance."

"What is your name?"

"Kelly."

As they made small talk, a light oak door to the right of the reception desk opened and the owner Pedro Gonzales walked out.

"Mr Gonzales"

Pedro somehow heard Kelly speaking over the chatter of noisy holiday makers and walked over to them; he smiled at Kelly and then warmly embraced Jack, before turning to Kelly again. "I would like you to meet Jack Sinclair otherwise known as DJ Ramos." The girl's eyes lit up. "Jack will be joining us at the Med Club in the next few days."

"How long will you be here for Jack?"

"More than likely for three months, unless the boss decides to fire me." Pedro and Kelly laughed.

Pedro then turned to Jack. "From next week Kelly will become our assistant manager. She will work closely with Matias Lopez, who is also the bar and club manager, he is my second in command. This young lady is a girl in a million, there is nothing she will not turn her hand to." Kelly smiled.

"Right Jack if you will follow me into my office, I will then show you around the complex."

Kelly then disappeared back to the main entrance as they entered Pedro's office. Like the reception room, the large office was built mainly of white marble, with a light grey tiled floor. There were two light oak office desks with modern telephones, both had computers and the desk which faced the large glass sliding window, also had a laptop which was switched on. Four red and black soft leather stainless steel chairs, were positioned neatly along one wall next to a low glass coffee table. In the centre of the table was a beautifully decorated large blue and white vase full of exotic flowers, which gave off a lingering scent. Built in filing cabinets along a second wall were hidden from view by sliding doors. The third wall to the left of the window had ten CCTV screens positioned side by side; this enabled the whole complex to be monitored twenty four hours a day.

"Jack, take a look out of the office window, no one can see you with it being one way glass."

"The view is unbelievable, absolutely stunning." Jack stood there in amazement; there must have been five or six hundred people in the complex. Below him was an Olympic sized heart shaped swimming pool with white marble steps leading down into the pool, and few metres to the right a much smaller children's pool of similar design, also had steps leading down into a shallow pool. There were several water shoots into the adult pool, as well as an open air stage on the left for live entertainment. A hundred metres in front of the pool complex, was the golden beach with two rows of luxury white reclining beach loungers, which must have held close to a hundred sun bathers. In front of the bathers was the inviting Mediterranean Sea. The entire complex was edged with palm trees, which had been flown in from North Africa and numerous giant rustic Terracotta urns full of exotic flowers. Never in his life had Jack seen such luxury but Marbella was the place to be if you had the money and the Med Club was certainly the place to visit.

"You must be very proud of what you and Nada have achieved here?"

"We most certainly are but without Nada's father's financial backing it would still have been a dream."

"How do you operate the complex, I can see there are dozens of families, couples and single people here enjoying themselves."

"The complex is open seven days a week in the daytime from ten in the morning until six in the evening, as a beach and swimming club. Admission is by ticket only, daily or weekly. There is a special price for families. We are also very strict on who we let in, no wild stag parties, they are banned. As you can see there are many gorgeous girls sunbathing and we don't want them to feel threatened. No one is allowed to bathe topless, even on the beach as there are too many couples with young children present in the complex. Let me now show you the rest of the Med Club."

Walking back into the reception area, they entered the indoor section of the complex through double light oak doors, which automatically opened as they approached them. The sign above the doors in black and gold said Night Club, Restaurant and Spa and Beauty Lounge. After walking forty metres along a glass corridor, they entered the club itself, which was the ultimate in luxury and glamour, the very epitome of what a beach club should be in Marbella. The room, which had a long black and gold circular bar, held about six hundred on two levels and faced a large semicircle stage and dance floor, which had a spectacular lighting system and a raised DJ stand. As they walked around, Jack noticed several female staff busy putting the finishing touches to the tables, in preparation for the forthcoming evening.

"We have live entertainment two nights a week, usually Spanish or European singers but none from the UK, they are far too expensive. Our two resident DJ's Jose and Selena cover seven days a week. Outside in the pool area we have a very busy children's club run by an in house entertainment team. The kids who are members of the club get free drinks and food. Cold drinking water is also free from dispensers throughout the complex for everyone."

After leaving the night club, Petro took Jack to have a look at the one hundred and fifty cover restaurant. It was trendy, modern and chic in design, with a partly covered al fresco area to cater for clientele who wished to feel a cool refreshing sea breeze on a hot summer's evening. The Spa and the Beauty Lounge were not Jack's scene, but he had to admit that they would turn the head of any female with their opulence.

Jack turned to Pedro. "You have one hell of a set-up. Your father- in-law must be very impressed."

"He is and visits us several times a year, in fact two of Nada's brothers, who are not married, do so as well. They always stay in the Penthouse above the club."

"How many brothers does Nada have?"

"Six, Nada is the only daughter and youngest child; her father has been married twice. The Sheikh has come to the conclusion that he is not compatible with females apart from having sex with them."

"Tell me how is it that the Sheikh allowed Nada to marry and live abroad. I was always under the impression, that the Arabs are very strict with their daughters, and tell them where they have to live and who they marry?"

"They normally are, but the Sheikh immediately took a liking to me, probably as he found it impossible to control Nada who rarely took any notice of him, he said he was delighted that she had fallen in love with me."

Pedro then went over to a water dispenser and poured himself a glass of water. "Would you care for a glass?"

"If you would, thank you."

"Have you eaten Jack?"

"No not since breakfast."

"Would you care to join me for a light lunch and then we can discuss when you will be performing at the Med Club?"

"I would love to."

"We have a café bar by the swimming pool where I normally eat in the daytime."

The two men then went outside and made their way to the café bar. By the look of the clientele there was a great deal of money floating around in Marbella. Good looking guys with stunning looking girls in skimpy bikinis were everywhere. Many of the girls who appeared to be single smiled at Jack as he passed by, probably wondering who he was and whether he was loaded. The café bar was extremely busy, but they managed to find a couple of vacant seats under one of the large multi-coloured umbrellas. Pedro ordered the same as Jack, a plain omelette with soft bread rolls and a bottle of Estrella lager beer. Less than fifteen minutes later a young Spanish waiter, who did not appear to recognise his boss, brought the food and drink to their table.

"Tell me, why do you close at six?"

Pedro smiled. To allow a small army of cleaners in, we then re-open at seven for restaurant reservations. The night club opens at nine with music, and if we have a programme of live entertainment it will commence at ten. We will finally close our doors at 3am. The beach area like the swimming pools is closed in the evening, unless we are having one of our famous Costa del Sol beach parties, which are mainly in July and August. The punters who come in the evening are much younger and frequently single. We like to think we cater for the Marbella Jet set that is young, glamorous and wealthy. Many girls from all over Europe flock to Marbella and Puerto Banus in the summer months looking for excitement and sex. Many are rich and bored, with daddy footing their bills. Is there anything else you want to know?"

"No, I was just being inquisitive." Pedro laughed. "When do you want me on stage?"

"Every Tuesday evening from next week. You must arrive at the club by nine. The resident DJ's will open up and you will then take over at eleven until one. If you call round tomorrow afternoon at four, I will arrange for one of the DJ's to show you the gear you will be using and how everything works. I have purposely kept away from using you at the weekend to allow you to visit other clubs and bars where the Chechens and Russians hang out. I will give you a list of these venues tomorrow." Pedro then passed Jack a plastic card from the left hand pocket of his shorts. "This will give you free access to the Med Club at any time; just show your VIP pass to the security staff. You will have the opportunity to mingle with the punters both in the daytime and evening without being checked in. You never know you may recognise someone we are looking for. May I suggest that you familiarize yourself with all the photos of the Chechens, which were loaded onto your laptop? When you come in tomorrow, don't forget to bring your laptop, you will need to run through the material you will be playing." Pedro then took a white cotton handkerchief from his pocket and whipped his brow. "Christ! it's hot today, then glanced at his watch. "Jack, you are going to have to excuse me, I have work to do."

"How much do I owe you for the food and drink?"

Pedro waved his hands. "This is on the house my friend."

The two men then got up and walked towards the exit. "I will see you tomorrow at four, my wife normally comes in on a Friday and Saturday, so I will introduce you to her. You take care Jack."

Minutes later Jack was walking along the Esplanade Paseo, Pedro was right it was bloody hot. The sea looked so inviting, memories flooded back of the many happy family holidays he had shared with his brother, sister and parents. Often they would all go into the sea together. As he approached the Marbella Beach Apartments he glanced at his watch, it was almost four thirty. He needed to send a couple of text messages, one to his former boss at Franks, Jim Richardson, and the other to his current boss at MI6 Miles Coburn. Both messages were identical. "Arrived safely last night, accommodation excellent, weather very warm." Now for a quick dip in the pool. Once he had returned to his apartment, he quickly changed and then headed downstairs to the foyer. Roberto was on duty, he didn't speak but smiled and raised his arm, as he was in deep conversation with some Middle Eastern looking guy. There was no one about as Jack walked along the winding crazy paving path towards the pool.

"High, Jack." It was the Russian girl Olga who he met earlier; she looked stunning in her tiny white bikini.

He immediately went over to her. "I will join you in a minute after I have a quick dip to cool down."

"I will be here waiting for you."

Without another word Jack dived into the deep end of the pool. He had always been a strong swimmer, after ten lengths he walked out of the pool up the white marble steps. His body glistened in the bright sunlight as water ran from his hair down his face and body. He had a great physique and he intended to stay that way, which was one of the reasons he was always very careful with his diet, and had spent many hours in the gym whilst he lived in the UK. From the way Olga was looking at him, he knew she was running her eyes over his body from behind her dark designer shades. "Come and sit next to me darling whilst you dry off."

She then passed Jack the white soft cotton towel he had brought down from his apartment. Slipping on his dark shades again he lay down on the sun lounger next to her. He couldn't keep his eyes off her body, her large breasts were incredible. Without any explanation she leaned over on her side facing him, she knew exactly what she was doing. "Darling would you like to fuck me?" Jack didn't answer. "Well, do you want to fuck me or not?"

10

Moscow - Russia

Several months earlier, Colonel Alexander Stepanov had just returned from seeing his daughter Sasha and her family, who lived in Tbilisi, Georgia. It had been quite an eventful trip not quite what he had expected. Having confided in his son- in-law Christian, a heart surgeon, whose father was the President of Georgia, about the hijacked Russian cargo plane in Siberia, he persuaded Christian to ask his father if there were any rumours about the hijack filtering through. The President said he personally had heard nothing, but to be certain he would speak to his Head of National Security, if anyone knew he would and then report back to Christian in the next few days. Whilst in the city of Tbilisi with Christian, they visited the Colonel's former wife's Aunty Sarina. She had brought up their son Sergei, who he had not seen for almost twenty eight years, when his wife Alina walked out on him and took their son with her. Sarina was shocked to discover who he was but later admitted that she had been expecting something like this to happen one day. The shock was even greater, when she was told that Sergei had a sister Sasha, who was married to his doctor friend Christian, who Sarina also knew. Sarina said that when Sergei was away on one of his many trips abroad he never failed to make a weekly telephone call to her. Next time he called, she promised to tell him about his father and sister Sasha.

Colonel Stepanov always one for keeping active, had decided to go for a walk after he returned home from a busy day at the Moscow Aviation and Aircraft Engineering Academy. It was a warm summer's evening in Moscow and he always enjoyed a stroll along the banks of the Moscow River. Alexander had a great deal to think about, if he moved to Tbilisi, Georgia to be near his daughter, he would certainly miss his walks by the river, and the lunch times and evenings he often spent with old friends knocking back a few beers, vodkas and whisky. When he called in at his favourite café bar, which was opposite his apartment, none of his friends were about but he still decided to stay and ordered sweet tea. Just as the barman brought him the sweet tea his mobile in his pocket rang, it was his daughter Sasha in Tbilisi, Georgia. Whenever he heard his daughter's voice it always acted like an adrenalin rush to him.

After enquiring how her father was and telling him how much his grandchildren would love him to move to Tbilisi, Sasha said her husband Christian wanted a few words with him.

"Alexander, Christian here, my father called me earlier today. He spoke to his Head of National Security but he is unable to throw any light on the hijacking. The problem is that since Georgia started doing trade with the European Union against the wishes of the Kremlin, all usual lines of communication have been closed. However my father's Security Chief is flying to Grozny in Chechnya tomorrow for a regional security conference. He will keep his ears close to the ground whilst he is there. I am sorry at the moment that I am unable to be of more help, but I do have some news about your son Sergei. I called in to see Aunty Sarina yesterday at her home; I was concerned about how she had taken the news about you and Sasha."

"How was she?"

"She was absolutely fine. She is a tough old bird. It appears she spoke to Sergei about you and Sasha. He was quite overwhelmed with the news. When his contract is up, he intends to return home to Georgia. He wants the three of you to meet up and get to know each other; he said he would love to be part of the family again."

"Thank you Christian, I appreciate what you have done." "No problem, if I have any more news I will call you." The line then went dead. Raising a glass of sweet tea to his lips, the Colonel took a long slow refreshing drink. Tomorrow he would call Major Ivan Pavlov of the FSB and see if there were any further developments.

The following day during his lunch break at the Academy, Colonel Stepanov telephoned FSB chief Major Pavlov at the Kremlin and told him about the meeting with Aunty Sarina in Tbilisi, Georgia.

"You say she has no idea where he is?"

"That is what she said."

"Do you believe her?"

"Absolutely, I have no reason to doubt her. He could be anywhere."

"No not anywhere. He has been seen on the Costa del Sol in Spain. We have people out there trying to find him but he appears to have disappeared again. Colonel, if you have any information about the whereabouts of Sergei you would be advised to inform us. Now if you will excuse me, I must press on as I have a very busy schedule today."

Without another word passing between the two men, the conversation ended.

The Colonel had the distinct feeling that he had wasted his time calling Major Pavlov. Firstly, the Major did not appear as friendly as before and the Colonel felt that their conversation had been rushed. Secondly, the Major admitted that the FSB already had operatives in Spain looking for his son Sergei, and no doubt they were also tracking the eight Chechens, who were on their wanted list.

Unknown to Colonel Stepanov, pressure was being put on Major Pavlov from the very top at the Kremlin. The President was getting very impatient and wanted immediate action. This embarrassing blip as he called the hijack had to be obliterated once and for all. The criminals brought to justice or exterminated and the diamonds and other precious gems recovered, no way could the Russian Government be held responsible for a crash in the world market. The Colonel's unexpected call was adding to the FSB chief's anxiety. He was a man who liked to do things his way and in his own time. His position of power at the FSB was on a knife edge and he knew it, so now action was needed before heads started to fall.

Major Pavlov rose from his stainless steel red and black leather chair, as the stunning looking girl with long dark hair was shown into his office. Walking over to her, he greeted her most warmly with a kiss on either side of her face.

"I love your perfume Olga, it is beautiful."

"Olga laughed; it is actually called beautiful by Estee Lauder, it was given to me by the man I eliminated."

"Your trip to Rumania with your sister went well. The Rumanian President was delighted with your success."

"It was all down to you Major. The new nerve agent PV44 I injected took just over an hour to act before the victim died in agony. I was having great sex with this guy, who was an outspoken opposition MP on the Government death list. When I injected him in his arse as he was screwing me, he didn't even feel the needle he was so excited, it was no more than a pin prick. One hour later after he left my hotel room, he dropped down dead in the street on his way home to his wife and three children. The local hospital pathologist, who carried out an autopsy, said he died from a massive heart attack probably due to a blood clot.

"Poor guy,"

"You should not feel sorry for him Major; I gave him a really good time."

"Has your sister Tanya settled in Marbella, Spain?"

"Yes, and she has followed your instructions perfectly. She made a point of getting to know Costa Security boss Roberto Sanchez. She said he can't keep his hands off her and wants sex with her every day. Tanya said fortunately he is a good looking guy and very well endowed so she did not mind. He is so besotted with her, that he is trying to persuade her to move in with him permanently rather than stay odd nights at his villa. She has no intention of doing so, as it would cramp her style and handicap the real reason for her being in Marbella, which is to hunt down the Chechens and dispose of them. Major, I need to get to Marbella as soon as possible or I will miss all the fun."

The Major then re-adjusted his gold framed glasses which were slipping down his nose, before taking out a white cotton handkerchief from his right trouser pocket and wiped his brow.

"You look warm Major?"

"I am." The Major looked slightly embarrassed. "When you came to my office door I did not recognise you at first I am so used to seeing you blonde, your dark hair suits you. It was a good idea to change the colour of your hair, we don't want anybody suggesting that you and Tanya are sisters if you are ever in the same room together."

Olga had always been a problem to the Major, he was convinced that she was over sexed and got a kick out of teasing him. She would always sit opposite him in a very short skirt, crossing her long slender legs. If he looked hard enough he could see her white knickers, today he could not, and he was convinced she was not wearing any.

"Ivan, you are the only man I know who has never tried to proposition me. Darling it is never too late."

The perspiration on the Major's forehead was increasing.

"I find you most attractive. Tell your secretary in the outer room that you do not want to be disturbed for an hour, I promise I will give you a good time."

The Major was certainly tempted, he would have loved to explore her naked body but the risk of discovery was far too great.

"What are you worried about Ivan, that I will whisper your name in the President's ear as we make love."

"You haven't have you Olga?"

"That is my little secret Ivan, you will never know." She then started to laugh. "When do I fly to Spain?"

"In two days. You will be staying in the Marbella Beach Apartments. British MI6 agent Jack Sinclair, who is helping the Russian Government track down the hijackers at our request, is also staying there. Get to know him well but under no circumstances must he be harmed in any way. Do I make myself clear?" Olga smiled and nodded her head. "Do not tell him that you have a sister or you are with the FBS, please remind Tanya. Should anyone quiz you about the ownership of the apartment you are staying at, tell them your uncle, who is a very wealthy businessman in Russia, owns it. You have borrowed it for a few months to have a holiday and a good time in Marbella." The Major then paused for a moment. "Would you care for a drink Olga?"

"A glass of still orange if I may."

The Major then picked up the internal phone. "Natasha when you have a moment two glasses of still orange if you would."

Before the Major was able to continue with his conversation, there was a knock on the door and Natasha entered with two glasses of still orange. Placing the drinks on the office table she smiled at the Major, completely ignoring Olga and then left the room.

"Your sister Tanya, is she happy with the hotel accommodation we have arranged for her?"

"Yes, she said though it is a small hotel it is spotlessly clean, and the Russian couple who own it are very friendly."

The Major then passed Olga a medium sized brown envelope. "Inside you will find photographs of the eight Chechens you and your sister have to eliminate. There is also a current photo of Sergei Aslanov, he has not to be harmed at the moment, but we shall require immediate information about his movements once you have made contact with him. Finally, there is a photo of Jack Sinclair in the envelope and a one-way flight ticket to Malaga International Airport. Once you arrive take a taxi to the Marbella Beach Apartments. The key cards to the complex and your apartment are also in the envelope." Major Pavlov then took a small black and white box out of the left hand drawer of his office desk and placed it in front of Olga. "Open the box I have a gift for you."

Leaning forward, Olga then removed the lid. Inside were twelve lipsticks of various colours, she then looked up at the Major as though waiting for an explanation.

Getting up from his chair he walked round to the front of the desk and took a red lipstick out of the box. "Please take careful note of what I do." The Major proceeded to slowly unscrew the lipstick into two halves. The top half containing the lipstick was gold, the bottom half was a small black plastic file. "If you gently press the base of the file a hypodermic needle as small as a pin head pops out and automatically injects the victim. When the file is empty the needle retracts." The Major held it up in his right hand. "This is our new version of PV 44, instead of one hour it will now be two hours before the victim dies."

"Are you certain?"

"Absolutely, the nerve agent has been tried out on several prisoners serving life sentences. My colleague, who carried out the experiment, said it worked to perfection after the injection, and the pathologist who carried out the post-mortems afterwards, said he could not detect any trace of any nerve agent in their bodies. The nerve agent is absorbed into the blood stream, causing a minute blood clot in the body which then travels to the brain and heart, detection is virtually impossible, unless you know what you are looking for. PV44 is one of the world's most deadly toxins with no antidote. If it even touches your skin you are on a one-way ticket to the mortuary."

"How long does the precipitant take to die?"

"Once the victim has been injected it takes about an hour before there are drastic changes to the body. Acute tiredness is the first sign, after half an hour sharp pains to the upper half of the body, followed by stabbing chest pains. The victim's brain is now in turmoil, breathing becomes difficult, they also feel as though they are being choked to death, near the end they normally stand up screaming in agony before falling to the floor dead."

Olga's eyes were glued to the Major in excitement. "Excellent Ivan, I shall look forward to using the new PV44."

The Major then took two mobile phones out of the still open drawer and passed then to Olga. "Give one to your sister Tanya when you see her, they are untraceable and must only be used to call me in Moscow or our Embassy in Madrid. The phone numbers to be used are already in the mobiles. Olga you have a great trip, the Motherland is depending on you and your sister to put the hijacking in Siberia to bed once and for all. Remember no one is to be eliminated until I give the order. Do I make myself absolutely clear? When you meet up with your sister Tanya, please remind her. We do not what a diplomatic incident, our President would not be happy."

As the Major leaned over and embraced her again, Olga ran her hand slowly down his inside leg and pressed his groin hard. "When I return Ivan we must get together, next time I will not take no for an answer." Without another word Olga blew a kiss to the Major as she left the room and gave his personal assistant Natasha a filthy look as she passed through the outer office.

11

Costa del Sol - Spain

Some weeks later, before Jack Sinclair arrived in Marbella, female Russian assassins Tanya and Olga had already settled into a Jet Set life style. Tanya had snared security boss Roberto Sanchez with her stunning beauty and sexual charms, but poor Olga was frustrated. Every day the two girls met at a beach bar for lunch.

"I have been here for almost two weeks and no guy has shagged me. You arrived two weeks before me, tracked your man down and now he shags you every day. It is not fair; my guy does not even arrive from the UK until next week."

The look on her sister Tanya's face said everything. "You can always play with yourself."

"I do every night but there is nothing like running your hands over a well contoured male body and arousing him."

Tanya started to laugh. "When your guy arrives next week, you can make up for it."

"I certainly intend to."

Over the next few days Olga went through all the detailed information which Major Pavlov had passed on to her. Copies of all the photos were taken, so Tanya would be aware of who they were looking for, they could not afford a mistake like what happened in Egypt, when they accidently assassinated the wrong guy.

"Tanya, tomorrow I am going to Pinks in Puerto Banus for an interview as a dancer like you. It is just a formality. The guy, who owns the club, is a sleazy Russian from Moscow with known Mafia connections. He may in some way be involved in the Siberian cargo plane hijack; with a bit of luck and keeping my ears open I should be able to find out some information."

"Be careful, I don't want you ending up dead in the marina."

Rather than bring the box of PV44 lipsticks to the beach bar, Olga took her sister back to her Marbella Beach apartment and explained how the new nerve agent worked and how affective it was.

Tanya looked at her sister. "I can't wait to try it out. Just think you could be miles away from the victim when the poor bastard kicks the bucket." Both the girls started to laugh at the thought of their victim dying in agony. "You had better keep the box of lipsticks hidden in your apartment; no one will come in here without your invitation. If we divide them and I keep half in my hotel room, there is a chance that the housemaid or even the owners may noisy around when they clean the room and could find them. I know so little about the Russian owners of the hotel. They may even be in league with the Mafia."

"Most unlikely, otherwise Major Pavlov would never have booked you in at their hotel. They most probably work for the FSB."

"I hope you are right Olga."

Seven days later Jack Sinclair arrived in Marbella from the UK. After a business meeting over a late lunch with Pedro Gonzales the owner of the Med Club, Jack returned to the Marbella Beach Apartments. Quickly changing into his dark blue swimming shorts, which had yellow stripes down both sides, he headed for the swimming pool. The stunning looking Russian girl Olga was still there sunbathing. After ten quick lengths Jack climbed out of the cold water, slipped on his dark shades and sat down beside her.

"Darling, you are back sooner than I expected, I am just about to go to my apartment and have a glass of wine outside on the balcony. Do you want to join me?" Olga looked at him. Her large blue eyes were inviting and full of excitement just like the rest of her body.

"Would you like to fuck me Jack?" He did not answer.

"Well Jack, do you want to fuck me or not?"

"Of course I would love to but we hardly know each other."

Olga burst out laughing. "We certainly will when I have finished with you."

"What was your apartment number again?"

"Twenty, on the third floor."

"I will walk with you into the foyer and then go and get changed, I will see you in about ten minutes."

Olga took the elevator whilst Jack walked up the white marble staircase to his apartment. After changing into his favourite dark grey shorts and black T-shirt, he headed up another flight of stairs to find Olga's apartment.

When Olga opened the door to apartment twenty, she was dressed in a soft cotton white robe. Her long dark hair flowed over her shoulders and her feet were bare.

"I thought you had chickened out and were going to let me down."

"Sorry, my brother Lex called my mobile just as I was about to leave the apartment. Lex and his family live on the coast near Malaga. They have invited me to their villa on Sunday as Malaga FC has no match."

"What does your brother do in Spain?"

"He is the head coach and manager of Malaga Football Club. Lex used to be a famous footballer; he was an Australian International who also played in the Premier League in the UK and the La Liga in Spain."

Olga then smiled. "He sounds very famous but I am not into football." She turned to Jack. "What would you like to drink?"

"A large glass of Spanish red wine with ice,"

"I am drinking the same as you darling, I love my men to be red blooded." Jack loved her sexy Russian accent.

As he followed Olga out onto the balcony, he could not help noticing that the layout of the apartment was identical to his, though the furniture was very different. It was still very warm outside, and the balcony was very private. After pouring Jack a large glass of red wine, he sat down on one of the soft grey basket chairs. Olga then slipped off her white robe and stood naked in front of him, before straggling him on the chair. She sat up in front of him with her hands on her hips, her breasts were large and soft and in his face. Jack placed his warm hands on her shoulders, before running his fingers slowly down her back and then griping her buttocks firmly.

"Babe, do you want to have sex with me on the balcony or in the bedroom?"

"Wherever you want too,"

"I would prefer the bedroom, I am feeling very horny and I often make a great deal of noise, it may disturb the neighbours."

Though Jack was good looking and well spoken, the type of guy who many women would find attractive, he had never been one for sleeping around until now. To be honest he had never met a girl like Olga before, who was offering sex on a plate so to speak. At five, five she was a stunning looking girl with an incredible figure, in fact the type of girl he had been dreaming about all his life. Jack always prided himself in being a good judge of character but he felt that there was something about Olga which wasn't quite right. She said she had come from Russia to have a good time whilst she was on holiday. The apartment she was staying in she said was owned by her uncle a wealthy businessman from Moscow, but was it? If she came from a wealthy family, why take a job as a stripper at Pinks in Porto Banus unless she was actually a hooker looking for upmarket customers. Another thought crossed his mind. What if she was an operative with the Russian FSB looking for the same Chechen hijackers? Perhaps she already knew who he was and what he was doing in Marbella. She did hitch on to him very quickly, perhaps she was instructed to, but it could be to his own advantage. He was going to visit several night clubs and restaurants in Marbella in the next few weeks, in an attempt to discover the whereabouts of the Chechens and Sergei Aslanov, to have a glamorous girl on his arm would make him less conspicuous. At the moment he had more important things on his mind. Lifting Olga up naked in his arms, Jack carried her into the main bedroom placing her gently on the king size bed. He could already feel himself getting aroused as he slipped out of his clothes and joined Olga on the bed. She appeared to suddenly come to life as she ran her eyes slowly over his body. For the first time in his life he was having sex with a woman who wanted to completely dominate him. For the next hour and a half the extreme pleasure he experienced was out of this world, Olga was a girl who insisted on everything to fulfil her erotic desires. One thing Jack did observe, Olga was not a natural dark haired girl, she had blue eyes which were normally associated with blondes. He also noticed she had shaved her pubic hairs. Why would she dye her hair unless she had something to hide? Blondes are also stunning and as many girls say have all the fun.

"Well darling have you enjoyed yourself."

"You were incredible Olga; you certainly know how to satisfy a guy, I am exhausted with the heat."

"I was born with a gift darling." She then burst out laughing. "Are you going to take me out for dinner this evening?"

"You have taken the words out of my mouth."

"Of course I am. Can you be ready for eight? I thought we might go to the Albatross Bar and Restaurant on the Esplanade Paseo, unless you would rather go somewhere else."

"I am easy darling, whatever you say. Since I arrived in Marbella three weeks ago, I have never been out for a meal. I have been eating pre-packed frozen meals from the local supermarket. It is very lonely at night being a single girl in this city. That was the reason why I took the dancer's job at Pinks in Puerto Banus. I normally work there Saturday, Sunday and Monday and even Friday occasionally, from seven in the evening until four in the morning."

"Were you a stripper in Russia?"

"Yes, for several years in Moscow, so I am used to taking my clothes off." Olga's eyes started to sparkle. "Tell me Jack did you enjoy looking at my naked body?" She then leaned over and whispered in his ear. "Darling, tell me the truth, did you feel excited looking at me?"

"You know I did?"

She then started to laugh. "I need sex every day to feel happy, so make certain you are always available for me, I don't want to have to find someone else. Olga then slipped on her white robe again, before leaving the bedroom and walking out onto the balcony. Jack followed her. It was still warm outside. Picking up the half empty bottle of red wine which was on the balcony table, she poured out two glasses, passing one to Jack. They both took a long drink.

"When will you come to see me dancing at Pinks?"

"On Sunday evening, I am visiting my brother Lex and his family in the afternoon. I shall arrive at the club before eleven."

"I shall look forward to seeing you, I will leave your name as my guest on the door but in any case, I will see you before then. Won't I darling?"

"Of course you will. Olga I need to leave and get changed. I will pick you up at eight."

Olga then put her arms around Jack's neck and kissed him, her lips were warm and soft. "Would you like another session with me before we get changed?"

"Maybe later or tomorrow, I need to recover, you are a wild girl."

"Olga laughed. Perhaps Russian girls have a stronger sex drive than girls from the UK."

"You could be right, I will see you later." Without another word Jack left the apartment and headed down a floor to apartment eighteen. It was almost twenty to seven. After a shave and a refreshing shower he changed into a white short sleeved cotton shirt, dark blue Brutus jeans with a black leather belt and his favourite dark blue and white Reebok trainers. Sitting down on one of the soft cushioned chairs in the lounge he switched on the flat screen TV and flicked the channel to Sky News. As there was very little of real interest to him, his mind switched to Olga. She certainly was some girl with a huge appetite for sex. When he thought of her, the hit song Man-Eater by American pop stars Daryl Hall and John Oates came to mind. He would certainly meet her again for sex, but he had no intention of getting romantically involved with her. Firstly, he did not know who she really was and secondly, he could never trust a girl like Olga to be faithful to him.

Security boss Roberto Sanchez was on duty when Jack and Olga walked into the foyer. Olga looked stunning in the thin white boob top and her black and white short skirt. The matching white three inch heel shoes she wore showed off her slender tanned legs which gave her a touch of elegance. She wore no jewellery apart from a large designer gold watch on her left wrist. Roberto appeared to follow Olga's every movement, at the same time he continued to glance at the CCTV screen in front of him, but he never spoke to her and just smiled.

"Are you heading anywhere exciting Jack?"

"We are visiting the Albatross for a meal."

"A good choice the food there is excellent, that is why it is always very busy. Have a good evening."

Once outside the Marbella Beach Complex they made their way down the Esplanade Paseo towards the Albatross. It was a beautiful evening and still very warm, though the light was starting to fade as the bright gold and yellow sun slowly dropped below the sky line, in another thirty minutes it would be dark. The lights down the Esplanade suddenly flickered on as they approached the Albatross. As usual the bar and restaurant was extremely busy. Jack looked around for the owner Roscoe Rodriguez or his daughter Valentina, maybe they would find them a vacant table; in future he would make a reservation.

"Can I help you Jack?" It was Valentina the boss's very attractive daughter.

"We are looking for a table for two but you appear to be very busy."

"Valentina gave Jack a sexy look. "If you and your girlfriend would care to follow me, I will find you a table inside."

"By the way Olga is not my girlfriend. She is a friend. We are both staying in the same apartment complex and just decided to dine out together. Olga this is Valentina the owner's daughter."

"Lovely to meet you Valentina," then held out her hand which Valentina took hold of and smiled.

Olga turned to Jack. "I think she fancies you. I will have to keep an eye on you otherwise you will be shagging both of us."

Jack laughed but he knew Olga was serious. As they walked into the bar restaurant, many diners glanced up at them. They were a handsome couple who stood out from the crowd, more like TV celebrities or film stars.

"Is your father not in tonight?"

"No, Thursday is his night off."

"Would this table be alright for you Jack?"

"Yes it will be fine, thank you."

"I will send a table waiter over to you shortly." Valentina smiled and then went back outside.

"She is a pretty young girl." Jack smiled but didn't answer, fortunately the waiter turned up at their table. After looking through the menu they both decided on fried sea bass with corn, beans, and a Greek salad topped with a lemon Basil dressing. Jack also ordered a bottle of red Spanish wine and two Americanos with milk. After their meal, which was excellent, Jack and Olga spent the evening drinking by the lounge bar until one in the morning, both had consumed far too much alcohol. Jack told himself that this would not happen again, he had come to Marbella to work and had no intention of returning to the UK an alcoholic. The crickets were back in force as they slowly made their way back to the Marbella Beach Apartments. It was a warm evening with no wind and the sea was very calm.

"I would ask you in Jack but I will be of no use to you, I am so tired with the heat and the booze. I also need a good night's sleep, as I am working at Pinks tomorrow evening until four in the morning." Jack smiled.

Youssef Beji was on duty when they entered the reception area. He acknowledged both of them with a smile but did not speak. After taking the elevator to the third floor, they walked down the corridor to apartment twenty. Olga was unsteady and could hardly stand up as she slipped her key card into the door.

"Jack, I will see you tomorrow around one. I need to get into my apartment, I feel as though I am about to throw up." Without another word she kissed Jack on the right side of his face and then went into the apartment closing the door behind her.

Back in his own apartment, Jack slipped off his clothes and then dropped naked onto the king size bed. The room felt like an oven, with great effort he got up and opened the balcony window a few inches. Within seconds, cool air started to drift into the bedroom and circulate around the apartment. That was the last thing Jack remembered until he woke up at ten on Friday morning.

When he got up he felt good and not having a hangover was an added bonus. Walking into the lounge he opened the balcony doors wide, it was another beautiful day warm and sunny. After a light breakfast and a warm shower, he slipped on his dark grey shorts and black t-shirt before connecting his Apple laptop via a USB cable to his mobile phone. Within seconds, he had transferred all the photos of the eight Chechen hijack suspects and Sergei Aslanov onto his mobile. He was pleased with the result, at least now he had the means to identify possible suspects immediately. A quick glance at his watch showed it was just leaving eleven thirty, time for a quick swim in the pool before visiting Olga. The water had a mid September chill but it was refreshing, after twenty lengths he hauled himself out of the swimming pool, slipped on his dark shades and lay back on a poolside sun lounger to dry off. There was not another sole around so far apart from Olga, he had never seen nor met any of the other occupants of the complex. The warm atmosphere relaxed his body and without knowing he actually dozed off. Fortunately he had not burnt in the sun's strong rays. His body was already quite naturally tanned, just like his late mother who always looked like she had been on holiday to a warm climate. Jack glanced at his gold Gucci watch; it was almost ten to one. After rolling up his white towel he made his way up to apartment twenty on the third floor. He only pressed the door buzzer once and it opened. Olga was stood there in her short white bath robe, as usual she looked stunning.

"Come in darling." She then ran the fingers of both her hands through the dark hair on Jack's chest, before standing on her toes and giving him a warm kiss on his lips. Walking slowly in front of him as she crossed the light grey tiled floor of the lounge towards the bedroom, she allowed the bath robe to slip to the floor leaving her naked in front of him. She turned slightly wiggling her bottom at him and said something but he couldn't make out what she said, his eyes were glued to her body, especially the beautiful shape of her bottom.

"Jack, instead of standing there letting your imagination run away with you, I need you in the bedroom to make love to me."

Jack couldn't help but laugh as he picked up the robe from the floor. He was now Olga's personal stud, perhaps he should start charging her for his services. Two hours later he left apartment twenty. Olga was an incredible woman, whether she took some drug to enhance her sex drive or she was naturally like that he had no idea, but he certainly was not complaining. Apart from going to watch her at Pinks on Sunday evening, she informed him that she would not be about until Tuesday afternoon, as she always stopped at her girlfriend's apartment over the weekend in Porto Banus, her English friend Emma was also a stripper. As soon as she arrived back she would contact him.

Once he had returned to his own apartment, he changed into something more suitable; a short sleeved white Adidas top and matching shorts, along with his favourite Reebok trainers. With his laptop case firmly in his left hand, he slipped on his dark shades and headed down the Esplanade Paseo in the direction of the Med Club. On the way, as he had not eaten since breakfast, he called in at a café bar, bought a roast ham sandwich and sat outside on the low sea wall looking at the sea whilst he ate it. He was enjoying his life in Marbella, at the moment it was more like a holiday, but he had the feeling sooner or later the situation would change.

As usual the Med Club was extremely busy. Kelly the new assistant manager was on door duty, when he passed her his security pass she recognised him immediately.

"Great to see you again Jack, or perhaps I should I say DJ Ramos?"

Jack laughed. He liked Kelly she was a fun loving girl.

"Mr Gonzales and his wife are expecting you; they are in the lounge bar."

"Thank you."

Once in the foyer, he turned right and proceeded down the glass connecting corridor to the lounge. Pedro was by the bar, sat on a black leather high back stool next to an extremely attractive dark haired girl in her early thirties.

"Jack it is good to see you again." Pedro immediately got off his stool and embraced him. "This is my wife Nada."

Jack shook her hand and then kissed her on both cheeks.

"It is a pleasure to meet you Jack. I have heard so much about you from my husband, he speaks very highly of you."

Pedro's wife was certainly glamorous, with her long dark hair tied back in a ponytail, she was dressed in white shorts, with a pink top and gold sandals. She was about five six in height and very slim with long slender legs. Apart from her olive complexion and her accent, you would never have known that she was born in the United Emirate States, as she spoke perfect English.

Jack turned to Pedro. "The complex appears to be very busy."

"We are extremely busy. We shall be like this until November when the weather starts to change." He then turned to the decanter of fresh orange juice on the bar.

"Jack can I offer you a glass?"

"I would love one, thank you."

Nada then leaned over to the bar, lifted up the decanter of fresh orange with her right hand and poured the contents into three tall glasses. After dropping some ice cubes in from the ice bucket on the bar, she then passed one of the glasses to him.

Pedro glanced at his watch. "Jack, if you will excuse me for a moment, I am just going to pop into the night club and see if our DJ's have turned up."

As Pedro walked away Nada turned to Jack. "Are you married or do you have a partner?"

"I am afraid not perhaps I am too fussy, in any case I am happy being single at the moment."

"You never know whilst you are living in Marbella, you may meet a beautiful Spanish girl who fulfils all your dreams."

Jack laughed. "You never know maybe. My brother Lex is married to a lovely Spanish girl. They have just had their first child. The two of them met when he came to play football for Malaga FC. Unfortunately he had to retire due to injury, but he is now head coach and manager of the club he used to play for."

"Your brother is very famous?"

"Yes he is. He played in over fifty International matches for Australia due to our late mother being born there. Lex also played in the English Premier League for several years before finishing his career here in the La Liga in Spain." "Were you never interested in football?"

"I was but I never had my brother's talent and dedication. Instead I went to university and qualified as a gemmologist. In the evening being single, I spent most of my time learning my trade as a DJ and now I am here at the Marbella Med Beach Club."

Nada laughed, she had a beautiful smile which showed off her perfect teeth. "Can I top your glass up for you?"

"If you would, the orange juice is excellent."

"Ah! Pedro is back." He smiled as he approached them. "Our two DJ's Jose and Selena have just arrived. By the way they are brother and sister."

"Excellent, how old are they?"

"Selena is twenty-five and Jose is twenty-six, both are Spanish but speak excellent English, they have been with us for the last five years. I will take you through to meet them." Pedro then turned to his wife. "I will be back in ten minutes." Nada smiled.

As they walked through to the empty night club, Pedro passed Jack a slim white envelope. "I have given you a list of night clubs, bars and restaurants where the Chechens and Sergei Aslanov may possibly hang out. If you identify any of them you must immediately inform Miles Coburn, you have his emergency mobile number and you must also let me know."

"I understand." Pedro smiled.

Though the night club was in semi darkness the DJ stand by the large semi-circular stage was illuminated. Jack could see two figures by the stand. As they walked closer their faces became visible.

"Jose and Selena, I would like you to meet our new DJ from England Jack Sinclair."

It was easy to see that they were brother and sister, both were good-looking, slim and had the same facial features and olive skin. Jose stood about six foot, Selena around five-five. They both had a good head of dark hair, Selena's was shoulder length where as Jose's hair, which was also quite long, was tied back in a ponytail, he also had a gold earring in his left ear and a couple of gold rings on his fingers.

They both greeted him very warmly. Jose shook his hand and embraced him as did his sister. Jack kissed her on both cheeks. He was acutely aware that she wore a very distinct perfume but he had no idea what brand it was.

"Jack will be with us every Tuesday evening from eleven to one in the morning for the next few months, performing house and electronic dance music.

Would you two guys please show him how the DJ deck works and everything else he needs to know including the lighting system? Now if you will excuse me I must get back to my wife. Jack I will call you later." Jack acknowledged Pedro with a smile as he left the night club.

For the next half hour after connecting Jack's laptop to the House PA system, and adjusting the quality of the sound, they ran through a selection of his house and dance music.

"Your music is incredible Jack, we have never had a DJ in Marbella playing this music, it is a completely new concept for us and the punters will love it. DJ Ramos will soon be a star at the Med Club and take Marbella by storm."

"Jose, thank you for your kind words but you are a great talker, at the moment I am not convinced, after the first night is over I will tell you what I think."

Selena who had never said a word burst out laughing. Jack liked the brother and sister DJ's, they were easy to get on with and had no airs and graces. He had a feeling that the three of them were going to get on well together. Jack was looking forward to his opening night next Tuesday. It had been several months since he was last on stage, but he knew that once he hit the music decks the adrenalin would flow as usual, he was a born showman when on stage.

12

When Jack arrived back at his apartment, the first thing he did was to open the envelope Pedro had passed to him at the Med Club. It contained a hand written list of eight night clubs and nine restaurants to visit. Several of the venues like Olivia Valere, Pangea and the Aqwa Mist were already known to him.

Pedro said that Miles Coburn had already told him, that the Russians had received information, that the Chechens were frequenting these establishments. What they wanted from Jack was concrete evidence. Mobile phone photos and if possible any recorded conversations between the Chechens, which could be sent to Coburn at the MI6 Headquarters. He would then pass on the information to his Russian counterpart Major Pavlov at the FSB, who would then take the appropriate action. Jack glanced at his watch it was just leaving six-fifteen, he needed to speak to Olga, he had promised to take her out to a restaurant this evening. Olga took ages to answer the door of her apartment. When she finally did she was wearing her white bath robe and appeared unsteady.

"Are you ok?"

"Of course I am darling. I didn't hear you, I was on the balcony sunbathing and had a few glasses of red wine. I must have dozed off, just too much sun and booze. Please come in."

Jack kissed her as he entered the apartment.

"How did your meeting go at the Med Club?"

"Very well, I am looking forward to next Tuesday's opening night."

"My girlfriend Emma and I will be coming along." "Fantastic, remember I will be on stage at eleven."

Olga then slipped her left arm around Jack's waist. "I get very lonely by myself during the daytime; I could do with seeing you more. We could go down to the beach together and sunbathe and have some fun. In the evening if we are both not working, we could visit some of the night clubs in Marbella."

Jack then put his arms around Olga and pulled her towards him as he kissed her soft lips. There was a sparkle in her eyes. "I completely agree with you." He then undid her bath robe which fell to the tiled floor and ran his fingers down her back before taking hold of her warm bottom with both hands. Olga then kissed him passionately again pressing her tongue into his mouth. Without another word Jack picked her up into in his broad arms and carried her naked into the bedroom. For an hour they made love before Jack reminded Olga that he was taking her out to a restaurant for a meal.

"Can you be ready for eight-thirty?"

"Yes no problem. Thank you for calling round I feel much better now."

Jack could not help but laugh. Kneeling up on the bed Olga pressed her large soft breasts against his face. "What about another half hour darling or are you not up to it?"

Olga who was now by his side naked, pulled herself towards him, she then stood on her tip toes and kissed him. "Darling do I satisfy you?"

"Of course you do, you are incredible."

"Next time Jack I will have a surprise for you."

"Really"

"You will have to wait and see."

Without another word he got dressed and walked towards the exit door. "I will see you at eight-thirty."

Once back in his own apartment, he had a shave and shower. With twenty minutes to spare before he was due to return to Olga's pad, Jack ran through the photos of the Chechens on his mobile phone. He needed to familiarise himself more with their faces. The Gastro Bar Pikaro, where he and Olga were intending to dine at this evening, was the sort of European restaurant the Chechens would hang out at.

Olga looked gorgeous when he arrived at her apartment and looked more like a model or celebrity than a normal Russian girl on holiday. The weather was perfect as they walked into Marbella, which only took twenty five minutes to reach the harbour and marina.

"Where are you taking me to Jack?"

"The Gastro Bar Pikaro restaurant by the harbour, it has stunning views and the food is excellent. Pedro Gonzales who owns the Med Club recommended it."

By Marbella standards the restaurant was quite small, even so it was very attractive, when full it probably did not hold more than sixty. As the weather was warm and there was hardly any sea breeze they decided to dine outside. The only vacant table was close to one with four young guys. Jack noticed that Olga looked at them several times as they sat down. Perhaps she knew them; maybe they had seen her at Pinks in Puerto Banus. They certainly looked pleasant enough and were causing no problems. Jack glanced across to their table, they were already halfway through their meal, though he was not sure what they were eating, he did notice that they were all drinking bottles of local lager beer and spoke together in a language, which was not familiar to him.

Without any prompting Olga leaned over the table and whispered. "They are Chechens, I hate them. They have murdered hundreds of my country men with their useless war of independence." Olga then smiled. "Now I have got that off my chest, what should we order darling?"

Jack smiled. "What about a medium rare steak, fried onions and octopus, with fresh tomatoes and a green salad. Not forgetting a bottle of red wine."

"It sounds delicious darling."

A few minutes later, a small balding middle aged male waiter arrived at the table and took their order. Shortly afterwards he returned with a bottle of red wine, which he proceeded to pure into two long crystal glasses.

Olga immediately took a long drink from the glass. "I am sorry I went on one earlier, but there were many terrible atrocities on both sides during the war, which has created a great deal of hatred in both Russia and Chechen. On the border of the two countries, a school was attacked by the Chechens and over three hundred innocent children and teachers were massacred. It was terrible." There were tears in Olga's eyes as she spoke. "I hate any form of violence."

Jack touched her soft right hand. "Try and forget about the past and enjoy your evening with me." Olga smiled.

Half an hour later their meal arrived. The food was excellent. Shortly after finishing their meal, Jack excused himself and visited the washroom. As soon as he had locked the toilet door, he took out his mobile and checked the photos of the wanted Chechens. All four were on the Russian wanted list. One thing puzzled him, why was Olga so upset about the Chechens; after all she was only a young child when the first war between the two countries took place? Maybe a family member or a close relative died in the conflict? When he returned to the restaurant the four Chechens had departed.

"I see the Chechens have left."

"They left by taxi only a minute ago."

"Do you fancy calling in at the Albatross on the way back to our apartments?"

"Yes why not, it is a lovely bar and restaurant." After settling the bill which was very reasonable, they walked along the Esplanade Paseo passing the Med Club which was very busy. Gorgeous young females many of them scantily dressed, rushed passed in excitement to join the queue of punters waiting to go into the club.

Assistant Manager Kelly was on the door and recognised Jack as he passed by calling to him. "Jack, are you not coming in tonight?"

"No tomorrow night Kelly."

"Great, I will see you tomorrow Jack."

Another three days and he would be starting his residency. He could already feel the excitement as heavy disco music pounded out from inside the complex.

As they continued to walk along the Esplanade Paseo, a warm breeze started to blow in from North Africa across the Mediterranean Sea.

Olga slipped her arm around his waist and looked up at him. "Darling, why don't you stay the night with me?"

Jack looked at her and smiled. "I just might do that." He then leaned over and kissed her forehead.

The Albatross as expected was extremely busy. Walking through the restaurant they made their way into the lounge bar, there were no vacant seats so they stood by the bar whilst Jack ordered.

"What can I get you Sir?" Jack smiled at the barmaid; she was an attractive girl, slim with long blond hair, probably no more than twenty five and spoke perfect English with no accent.

"A large glass of Spanish red wine and a Budweiser,"

"Jack, come and join us,"

He immediately turned round from the bar.

"Come and join us my friend."

The man who spoke had now stood up and was smiling at him. It was Roscoe Rodriguez the owner of the Albatross; he was with Aslan Maskhadov who owned the Cobra Jewellery chain and his friend George. Jack acknowledged both of them with a smile and a wave of his hand. Once the barmaid had served their drinks Jack and Olga went over to them. Both the men glanced at each other but did not speak. Roscoe and Aslan greeted Jack warmly. George never smiled or moved. Jack then slipped his left arm around Olga's waist. "Guys, I would like you to meet my close friend Olga. We are both staying in the same apartment complex." Jack then turned to Olga. "Olga, this is Roscoe Rodriguez who owns this fabulous restaurant." Roscoe then kissed Olga. Jack turned to Aslan. "This other handsome man is Aslan Maskhadov who owns the Cobra Jewellery chain on the Costa del Sol." Aslan also kissed Olga.

Roscoe then stood up and beckoned to a waiter to bring over two extra chairs to their table. This was the second time Jack had met George, as before he appeared to be on another planet. Jack could not help but notice how Aslan watched Olga intently. If George was his boyfriend, perhaps he was bisexual and fancied her but then most normal men would, or more than likely it was because he realised she was Russian and he was Chechen.

Aslan then turned to Olga. "Are you on holiday in Marbella?"

"Yes, I am staying at the Marbella Beach Complex, my uncle owns the apartment. He said that I could borrow it for two or three months."

Roscoe then spoke. "What nationality are you Olga?"

"I am from Moscow Russia."

"I believe Moscow is full of beautiful women like you."

"Thank you Roscoe for those kind words. You are quite right, my sister and I have our mother's genes."

This was the first time Olga had mentioned that she had a sister; perhaps her slip of the tongue was unintentional.

"Jack, have you been dining out this evening?"

"Yes, at the Gastro Bar Pikaro on the harbour front."

"I know it very well, it is an attractive restaurant. How was the food, good?"

"Excellent, we enjoyed our meal and will certainly be revisiting the restaurant."

As the evening progressed, Roscoe ordered several more rounds of alcohol. Jack noticed that Aslan never once dipped into his own pocket, also George, who at times appeared to be nodding off, never entered into any conversation. Rather be branded a sponger Jack bought the next round. Olga had her usual red wine, her sixth glass of the evening. By now the alcohol, too much sun, and the heat were starting to affect her. She looked tired and her speech was becoming slightly slurred, though her Russian accent made it sound far worse than it really was, goodness knows what she would be like when she eventually stood up.

"We should leave soon; you have had far too much to drink." He said whispering in her ear. There was no response from her so he repeated the suggestion again. This time he got a reaction but not quite what he wanted.

"I am fine, one more drink darling and then you can take me back to my apartment."

"We should go now as it is leaving twelve-thirty." Jack then took hold of Olga's hand and helped her to get up from the soft brown leather chair, but she almost fell over.

Both Roscoe and Aslan smiled. "Perhaps we will see you tomorrow Jack?"

"More than likely guys, thank you for your company and sorry about my friend."

As they walked up the Esplanade Paseo, there was a refreshing cool breeze starting to blow in from the Mediterranean Sea. Olga appeared to sober up quickly.

"Sorry about tonight darling, I have made a fool of myself."

"We all drink too much at times."

"Darling, it was not just the booze. That man Aslan, I recognised him. Do you know who he is?" Jack shook his head but he did know MI6 Chief Miles Coburn had already put him in the picture.

"Who is he?"

"Aslan Maskhadov was a Chechen Separatist war leader. My country would have executed him if they could have extradited him from Spain, but the Spanish gave him citizenship and now he is a multi-millionaire businessman. I hate him for all the death and suffering he has brought to my people. His boyfriend George is no better, he is another shitty Chechen. I would not be surprised if Russia has still not got an International arrest warrant out for him, otherwise why does he never leave Spain?"

The penny then dropped, Jack had the feeling he had seen George before. He was one of the Chechens whose photo was on his mobile phone. His dark shoulder length hair had been cut short in a very modern style, which now appeared to give him a new identity. Tomorrow he would inform Miles Coburn of his results so far. Five Chechens out of eight already identified.

Olga looked at Jack. Even in the dimmed lights her eyes appeared glazed. "Are you going to stay with me tonight?"

"I think it would be better if you got a good night's sleep. "If you like I will call round to your apartment about 2pm on Saturday afternoon."

At first Olga did not answer. "Perhaps you are right Jack." Her voice stuttered. "As I said earlier I have a surprise for you and I shall need a clear head."

Once having gained entrance to the Marbella Beach Complex, they made the short walk through the garden to the foyer entrance. The crickets and fire flies were out in force. Jack pressed the illuminated foyer intercom. Costa Security boss Roberto Sanchez, who was on reception duty, recognized them and immediately opened the automatic glass doors. He smiled as they walked in.

"You two look as though you have had a good night out."

"We certainly have but if you will excuse us, I need to get someone to her apartment before she throws up." Roberto half laughed, "I will speak to you again. By the way I will be calling in at the Med Club next Tuesday for your opening night."

"Great, I look forward to seeing you."

After taking the elevator to the third floor, Olga eventually found her key card and gained entrance to the apartment. As she walked towards the main bedroom her legs suddenly buckled, luckily Jack caught her in his arms. After making certain she was ok, he laid her on the bed to sleep off the effects of the alcohol and headed to his own apartment. Stripping off his clothes he threw himself naked onto the king size bed, within minutes he had fallen into a deep sleep.

The strong warm rays of the sun woke Jack shortly before ten on Saturday morning. The bedroom was like an oven. Jumping off the bed he opened the windows wide allowing the fresh air to circulate. When he returned to his apartment in the early hours of the morning, he was so exhausted that he completely forgot to close the window blinds. After breakfast and a shower, he slipped on a white T-shirt, a clean pair of light brown shorts, his Nikki black and white trainers and then headed downstairs to the foyer. There was no one on duty. Once outside Jack slipped on his dark shades and left the complex turning right along the Esplanade Paseo. It was his intention to walk along the shore of the Mediterranean for forty-five minutes and explore the area, and at the same time look out for a mini market to stock up with a few essential breakfast items. Jack's walk of exploration was not quite like he expected. There were no bars or restaurants, just several luxury apartment complexes and a couple of upmarket hotels. The weather was perfect around 24c with no sea breeze, a lovely coast line with very few people about. Sitting down on the low stone sea wall, he took the mobile phone out of his pocket. He needed to call his MI6 boss Miles Coburn about the Chechens, who he saw in Gastro Bar Pikaro. He presumed spies worked seven days a week.

"Miles it is Jack."

"Good to hear from you Jack. Pedro tells me you have settled in well and got yourself a beautiful looking Russian girlfriend."

"The girl in question is called Olga but she is only a friend. Can you run a check on her?"

"You have doubts about her?"

"Yes, there is something about her which is not right."

"Can you email her photograph to me?"

"Yes, you will see that she has dark hair but I would not be surprised to find that her natural colour is blonde. I believe she may also have a sister, she let it slip out in a conversation when we dined out, whilst she was talking to the restaurant owner." Jack then told Coburn about the four Chechens in the Gastro Bar Pikaro. "I have identified them from your photos, but I also managed to take a photograph of them with my mobile, and record a few minutes of conversation without their knowledge. I have not got a clue what they are talking about, as they were speaking in their own language."

"Good work, just email everything to me."

"The guy who owns the Cobra Jewellery chain Aslan Maskhadov, he has a friend called George, who is also Chechen. He is on your list but he has drastically changed his appearance. His long hair has gone and he now has a short modern hair style. If my Russian friend Olga had not told me he was Chechen I would never have guessed or suspected him."

"Excellent work Jack."

"Miles, I will also email you photos of the five Chechen guys I have so far identified."

"Jack, don't forget to inform Pedro of any developments, he needs to be kept in the picture."

"I will speak to him later."

"Is there no sign of Sergei Aslanov?"

"None what so ever, Pedro is convinced that he is away on a business trip and sooner or later he will turn up." "What is your plan for today?"

"This evening I shall be visiting several night clubs and tomorrow I will be meeting my brother Lex and his family at their villa."

"Jack, just one final point before I go, you must be very careful what you say to the Russian girl, she may be a FSB operative on the same mission as you."

"Thanks for the advice, please let me know if you have any information about her."

A couple of minutes later they ended their conversation. Jack glanced at his gold Gucci watch; it was just leaving mid-day or eleven in the UK. He missed his frequent conversations with his sister Lilly. There was no time like the present to speak to her.

"Sis, it is me Jack."

"Jack, I was just thinking about you."

"I'm alright sis don't worry. Where are you now?"

"In the busy Tesco Supermarket in Ludlow, with Bret and the children."

"Please say hello to everyone."

"I will."

"Where are you?"

"In sunny Marbella sat on the sea wall overlooking the Mediterranean Sea." Lilly laughed. "How are you feeling at the moment?"

"Much better, the medication that I am now taking is helping me. Losing mum and dad and you going away was just too much to cope with.

"I do understand but the main thing is that you are now feeling better."

For the next fifteen minutes Jack and Lilly spoke about many things, there had always been a close bond between them, never once even as children had there been a cross word between them.

"Jack, when you see Lex on Sunday would you please give him my love, and tell him that I am always thinking of him and his family."

"Of course I will."

Lilly as usual, never failed to tell Jack how much she loved him whenever they met or spoke over the telephone. Those three little words meant the world to Jack. She was an incredible sister who he adored.

Making his way down an overgrown pathway which was full of wild flowers in bloom, he passed several private apartments and small villas. Eventually he came to the main road which was always congested with fast flowing traffic. This road was the longest and most dangerous in Europe, meandering along the Mediterranean coast from the start of the Costa de Almeria over two hundred miles away. After calling in at a Lidl super market, he dropped in at a café bar for a light lunch and then headed back to his apartment and changed into his dark blue and yellow swimming shorts. There was nothing like a refreshing dip in the pool and a few lengths to invigorate your body after a long walk in the warm sun. For once he was not alone. There was a French couple with two young children, a girl aged about seven and a boy about ten. The only other guests were an elderly couple in their seventies. They were a handsome couple and both wore very expensive looking jewellery. From the look of their well-toned bodies, they must be professional sun bathers. As he entered the pool everyone stopped what they were doing and looked. Jack was a great swimmer and always had admiring glances as his body elegantly cut through the water with ease. After ten minutes he got out of the pool slipped on his dark shades and lay down on a vacant sun bed to dry off. Several times he glanced over at the elderly couple who were now drinking white wine and wondered what nationality they were. One thing was certain they were not British.

At around one-thirty Jack decided to return to his apartment, he needed to put a call through to Pedro Gonzales and put him in the picture about the Chechen guys.

Pedro answered his mobile almost immediately. "What can I do for you Jack?"

"Miles Coburn asked me to call you and put you in the picture about five of the eight Chechen guys." For the next ten minutes Jack told him everything in detail.

"Most interesting you have done well. Aslan Maskhadov will be aware what is going on. No doubt his friend George has told him everything but that does not make him guilty of being involved in the hijack. It is quite possible, that he has bought large quantities of raw diamonds and other precious gems in good faith from Gem Stone International. He is an astute businessman and if he can see a bargain he will jump in and make a killing. It will be extremely hard to link him with anything illegal. He can't afford to fall fowl of the law in Spain and have his citizenship revoked. The Russians would extradite him, put him on trial for war crimes, find him guilty and then execute him. No, Aslan is far too clever for that, I am convinced there is someone else who is a Mister Big over here, most probably a Russian running the show for the Moscow Mafia." Pedro paused for a second. "I would not be surprised if those four young Chechens you saw in the restaurant are not employed by Aslan in the workshop at his head office. For the last two years he has also been producing his own self styled jewellery and selling it overseas, mainly in the Middle East and Africa. From all accounts he is doing very well." Pedro paused again. "Over this weekend I will plant a bug in his car and see what we can pick up. The problem is with him being Chechen I do not understand him unless he speaks in Spanish. I will record whatever conversations I can and email them to Miles Coburn for translation."

"Good idea."

"Jack, will I see you over the weekend?"

"Yes, later this evening after I have checked out a couple of other venues in Marbella. I am hoping I will come across Sergei Aslanov."

"You will sooner or later. At the moment he is probably out of the country. Jack, thanks again for calling me, I will see you later."

Before Jack switched off his mobile, he took the opportunity to familiarize himself once again with the wanted Chechens. Shortly before two he left his apartment and slipped upstairs to visit Olga.

13

Olga was still in her white bath robe when she invited Jack into her apartment. He greeted her with a lingering kiss and pulled her close to him. Her body was soft and warm and even though she wore no makeup or perfume she still looked beautiful and exciting.

"You look incredible considering how you were last night." "Thank you darling, I have great powers of recovery. In any case I can't let you down, as I have a surprise for you. Please follow me darling."

Her eyes sparkled with excitement as she spoke. As they walked into the main bedroom, she turned round and dropped her bath robe to the tiled floor. She stood there facing him, she looked stunning.

"Well darling slip your clothes off and then we can enjoy ourselves for the next hour. I have to be at Pinks in Puerto Banus by seven. You are still coming to watch me on Sunday?"

"Of course I am."

"Lie on the bed and close your eyes, I have a surprise for you, I will be back in a moment."

Jack like an obedient dog did as he was told. His imagination started to run away with him as he felt his body being aroused.

"Well, what do you think darling?"

Jack opened his eyes. Olga was stood legs apart on the bed dressed in a black and red basque, suspenders, and fishnet tights, with a black leather whip in one hand and a pair of handcuffs in the other.

"Lie back darling whilst I fasten you to the bed."

"You must be joking, not on your life I am not into bondage." He did not trust Olga one inch.

"Don't be shy darling let's have some fun."

"Sorry but no way."

Why don't I fasten you up?" Jack already knew what her reaction would be.

"Sorry darling but I am the madam. My girlfriend Emma at Pinks told me that all Englishmen love bondage and the women is always in charge."

"I am afraid your friend forgot to ask me."

For a moment Olga looked most disappointed. Suddenly she burst into laughter and started to remove her sexy lingerie, before diving on top of him. For the next hour perspiration ran from their naked bodies, as their sexual fantasies took complete control.

Jack returned to his own apartment almost two hours later. In many ways he was relieved that Olga would not be around for a few days and he would have a break from her insatiable sex appetite. Sex with this beautiful Russian girl was incredible, but he needed to be focused on what he was in Marbella for.

After a warm shower, Jack switched on the television in the lounge and tuned into the BBC for the football results. The UK was one hour behind Spain. At around four forty-five the English Premier Football results started to come through. Chelsea the team he had supported since he was a child were still top of the Premier League and undefeated, but there was a long way to go. His brother Lex who used to play for them, still watched most of their matches on his laptop, no doubt he was aware about their great start to the season. After half an hour he switched off the television and walked out onto the balcony, sitting down on one of the whitish grey wicker chairs. The sun was still strong and it was very warm, so as he was dressed in his black and yellow underpants he decided to take the opportunity and sunbath. As he sat there with his eyes closed his mind drifted to Olga. She was a one off with her stunning looks, fabulous body and her incredible desire for sex. Why was a young woman with all these attributes not married or living with a partner? She was certainly not a lesbian. Why go on holiday alone to Marbella? Perhaps she was a high class call girl looking for rich pickings. Marbella was certainly the city for that. Maybe she was none of these, but instead worked for the FSB as one of their operatives. With a little luck Miles Coburn would have an answer in a few days. For the next three days he would take a break from sex, until Olga made contact with him the following Tuesday afternoon. Jack glanced at his watch, almost twenty minutes past seven, time to get dressed. He intended to walk into Marbella, have a meal and then later visit the Olivia Valere night club, before finishing the night off at the Med Club. Jack would be visiting an exclusive night spot, full of beautiful women and handsome men, so he needed to dress the part. After slipping on a pair of dark trousers, a white silk shirt and light brown shoes with a matching cream jacket, he was ready to hit the road. Before he left the bedroom, he looked into the long mirror on the wall. He was more than happy with his appearance.

Costa Security Chief Roberto Sanchez was on reception when Jack walked down the white marble staircase into the foyer. They acknowledged each other with a smile before Roberto turned to Jack.

"I see you are on your own tonight Jack, has that beautiful young lady I saw you with last night let you down?"

Jack half laughed as he spoke. "No, she is staying with a girlfriend in Puerto Banus for a few days. She intends to do some serious sunbathing. I am all alone, so perhaps you could recommend a small restaurant for me to dine at this evening?"

Roberto thought for a moment. "The Picasso Café Bar, they only hold about thirty. The bar is very plain but the food is excellent and very reasonably priced. You will find the bar on the left, just before the Albatross, close to the ornamental fountain."

"Let us hope I can get a table with it being a Saturday evening."

"You should do, most of their trade is in the daytime. Apart from the bar area the restaurant is normally quiet in the evenings."

Jack had no problem finding the Picasso Café Bar and a vacant table. It was not the type of restaurant he would normally take Olga to, she was far too sophisticated to be seen in such an establishment. The seafood Paella which he ordered was incredible, the finest he had ever eaten. The elderly Spanish couple who owned the bar made him very welcome. After a couple of Budweiser's, Jack left the Picasso Café Bar and continued walking along the Esplanade Paseo, which was also known as the Golden Mile. It was now completely dark but everywhere was illuminated with the street lights, it looked quite spectacular. Still very warm with hardly a breeze Jack had underestimated the distance, and was desperate for a cold glass of beer.

Once past the Med Club and the harbour, which was full of multi-million dollar ocean going cruisers and yachts, he walked past numerous bars and restaurants which flanked the pavements, all were very busy. Eventually he came to the district of Carretera de Istan, where the Olivia Valere night club was situated on the Istan road near the Marbella Mosque, above the Golden Mile.

Olivia Valere is the epitome of a glamorous and luxury club experience. You can party in spectacular settings on open-air patios, housed in hybrid replicas of the Alhambra Palace and Mezquita. This is the place where celebrities go to get photographed partying. Probably the most prestigious club in Marbella, where you can drink, dance and be seen with society's elite.

When Jack arrived outside there was a long queue of punters waiting to gain entrance, he had no option but to join them if he wanted to get in. He had been in the queue with some very glamorous noisy individuals for less than ten minutes, when someone behind him tapped him on the left shoulder.

"Jack, would you care to join us."

It was George the young Chechen guy, Aslan Maskhadov's friend. He appeared quite normal, not under the influence of drugs or booze like the last time he saw him at the Albatross, and he even spoke good English.

"Aslan knows the owner he is a close friend, we have a table booked here tonight. Come and join us. Aslan is sat in the back of the black and gold Bentley Continental GT Convertible over there." He then pointed to the parking bay, Jack looked across. He could faintly see Aslan in the back of the limousine even though the cream roof hood was closed. Aslan raised his hand when he saw Jack walking towards him with George and lowered the car window down.

"Please join us Jack at our table, we have a VIP pass which enables us to take in two guests, there is no point in you queuing for half an hour."

"Thank you, I would appreciate that."

"Where is Olga tonight?"

"She is staying with a girlfriend in Puerto Banus for the weekend."

The chauffeur then jumped out of the Bentley Convertible and opened the rear door allowing Aslan to get out. "Thank you Freddie, perhaps you will pick us up at three."

"Certainly Mr Maskhadov he replied."

"Freddie, make certain you don't go cruising in the Bentley. Last time the police contacted me."

"You can trust me Sir it will not happen again."

"Good man."

Jack looked at Freddie, he thought he recognized him; he was another of the Chechens on the wanted list.

"Jack, if you would follow George and me, we will enter by the VIP entrance."

A couple of minutes later the three of them were stood facing a gold and black door. Aslan pressed the intercom buzzer on the right hand side of the door.

There was an immediate response. "Would you please hold up your VIP pass close to the screen above the intercom?" There was a slight pause. "Welcome to Olivia Valere Mr Maskhadov, would you and your guests care to enter into our world of fantasy?"

After entering, they were greeted by a very attractive dark haired Spanish girl dressed in white top hat and tails. She was stood next to a handsome black guy who must have been all of six four in his late forties. Broad shouldered and slim, smooth shaven with very short black curly hair. He was immaculately dressed in a black dinner suit with a white bow tie and matching white silk shirt. His black patent leather shoes were so highly polished that you could see your face in them. Aslan and the black guy obviously knew each other extremely well as they greeted each other with a warm embrace. After they all signed the club register, Aslan turned to Jack.

"Jack, can I introduce you to my very good friend Leroy Cardoso. Leroy is one of the owners of this incredible venue."

Jack held his hand out. Leroy immediately took hold, his grip was very firm. "Don't tell me Aslan, this handsome young man is Jack Sinclair, otherwise known as DJ Ramos." Jack smiled. "Your posters are all over the Costa del Sol about your forthcoming gig at The Med Club. We shall be there rooting for you on your opening night." Leroy then leaned over and said something to his beautiful assistant.

"Gentlemen, would you care to follow me?"

"Aslan, we have had to move you from your usual table. International recording star George Michael is celebrating his 47thbirthday with us this evening with forty guests. Your table was right in the middle of the area where they are seated, so I took the liberty of moving you to the front row on the balcony. You will have a spectacular view of the entire club from there."

"Thank you my friend, as usual you always look after us." "What are friends for if we can't help each other?" remarked Leroy with a broad smile, which exposed his white teeth. "Now gentlemen, if you will now excuse me I must do some socializing as we have several famous guests in the Olivia Valere this evening."

Their table was perfect, in fact far better than where Aslan and George normally sat. Aslan was obviously very well known and many of the clientele acknowledged him with smiles or blew kisses. Even his friend George had got in on the act and acknowledged many of the glamorous females and handsome guys with a smile. You would have thought Jack was in the company of a couple of A-List celebrities. It was obvious that both Aslan and George loved the adoration they were getting.

Once they had settled down at their table, a young immaculately dressed drink's waiter came over to them. "Good evening Mr Maskhadov welcome once again to Olivia Valere."

"Good evening to you Roger."

"Thank you Sir. Should I bring you a bottle of your usual wine?"

"If you would please but make it two bottles with plenty ice."

Roger then left their table, within minutes he had returned with two bottles of Sicilian red in a gold ice bucket and three Chrystal wine glasses.

"Jack a glass of red?" Jack nodded his head and smiled. "Your friend Olga would have loved this wine."

"I am certain she would, perhaps too much."

"Aslan smiled. I understand she is Russian?"

"I believe so but I know very little about her."

"She does not like me Jack."

"What makes you think that?"

"I am Chechen, most Russians don't like us Chechens because of the war between our two countries. I can always tell when there is bad blood."

Jack then changed the conversation. "Do they have much live entertainment here?"

George now got a word in. "Very rarely, it is mainly the resident DJ with four dancers, one of which is a good looking Spanish guy who also sings. They are very good Jack."

Aslan then checked his gold Rolex Oyster watch. "Ten minutes and the dancers will be on. Are you staying here all night Jack?"

"I am afraid not. I shall be leaving shortly after one; I have arranged to meet Pedro Gonzales at the Med Club at one thirty."

Aslan suddenly stood up and waved his hand in the air, there was a broad smile on his face. Jack glanced in the direction he was waving, instantly recognizing the man he was waving to. It was none other than the flamboyant pop star Boy George. On seeing Aslan waving to him, he made his way over to our table. The two men embraced passionately like two lovers. Aslan's friend George gave Boy George a strange look but never spoke to him.

"Jack, I would like you to meet my very good friend Boy George."

Jack shook his hand but it was quite limp. "Jack otherwise known as DJ Ramos starts a residency at the Med Club next Tuesday. He will be bringing House Music to Marbella for the first time."

"Fantastic Jack I love the music. Aslan will you be going to Jack's opening night?"

"I most certainly will."

"Then perhaps I can join you."

"We would love you to come with us, wouldn't we George? He did not answer. From the look on his face he obviously thought that Aslan and Boy George were too close for comfort. "I will give you a call tomorrow and make the arrangements."

"Guys, I am going to have to leave you now as I am a guest at George Michael's birthday party. I will speak to you tomorrow Aslan, it has been a pleasure to meet you Jack." Without another word he went and joined in the birthday party celebrations.

Aslan then turned to Jack again. "Boy George and George Michael have been friends for years. Boy George spends a great deal of time in Marbella; whilst he is here he rents an apartment from me which I own. Every other week during the season, he appears three nights a week at the Ocean Club in Puerto Banus as a vocalist and DJ. I have seen him perform many times he is very good."

The dancers were brilliant and put on a spectacular show which they repeated three times during the evening. The Spanish compere, who was also the resident DJ, was no youngster. He was a very handsome guy with thick black hair which was swept back. The music he played was perfect for Marbella's most sophisticated night spot.

Jack turned to Aslan. "Your friend Leroy, how long has he owned the club?"

Aslan leaned over and spoke in a low voice. "He does not actually own the club. I understand that he has two wealthy silent partners. Leroy is a man who loves being in the limelight, so his partners suggested that he ran and fronted the club and he is still here twelve years later."

"I presume he comes from Africa?"

"Yes, he was born in Angola. His parents were both medical doctors and Leroy was their only child. He was sent to Lisbon, Portugal to be educated and ended up studying to be a business lawyer at the University of Lisbon.

After returning to Luanda Angola, he fought for the Government in the civil war against the communist backed rebel insurgents, rising to the rank of Major. Two years later, the twenty seven year war was over after a peace treaty was signed between the two warring factions. There was no conclusive winner and thousands on either side lay dead. Leroy and his parents could see no future in Angola and decided to move to Lisbon in Portugal. Both his parents, who were also surgeons, had no problems finding work in local hospitals. Leroy went to work for a well known legal company in Lisbon, but found the work boring. A couple of years later he went to Marbella on holiday. The city excited him, it was glamorous and exciting. He knew this was the place where he wanted to put his roots down. But there was one problem, he could not speak the language and he had no job. Once he returned to Lisbon from his vocation, he set about learning to speak Spanish; in less than two years studying he was fluent in the language. After moving to

Marbella, he went to work for one of Spain's premier legal companies. The chairman of the company introduced him to two of their clients who owned the Olivia Valere club. The venue needed further investment to make it the top venue for the super rich and celebrities. Where Leroy obtained the money from we will never know, but he paid eight million Euros into the company to become the third partner. There were unconfirmed rumours, that his parents had received millions of dollars worth of raw diamonds from the Angola rebels in return for giving medical aid to many of their injured soldiers. Not everyone liked President Jose Eduardo dos Santos, who was in power for almost four decades, and became known as the man who ended the civil war. He left behind a legacy of corruption and human rights violations, which made him many enemies, many of who sympathized with the rebels."

"I presume Leroy's parents still live in Portugal."

"They do but on their retirement they moved from Lisbon to Albufeira on the Mediterranean, where they bought a three bedroom apartment, in a gated complex on the coast. They are now only two hundred and sixty miles from Marbella or a four hour forty minute car journey, which allows them to see their son more frequently."

George then picked up the bottle of red wine from the table. "Can I top up your glass Jack?"

"Thank you George."

Jack then took a long drink. "This Sicilian red is superb wine." He then turned to Aslan. "Tell me is Leroy married, he is such a handsome guy?"

Aslan then went very quiet, his voice became almost a whisper as he spoke. "My friend Leroy is still a grieving widower."

Jack looked at Aslan with a blank expression on his face. "Leroy did not get married until his mid-thirties. His wife Adelino was a beautiful young woman some eight years younger. She was the youngest daughter of a former Minister in the Angola Government, who fell out with the President over human rights. Her father fled the country in fear of his life to Portugal, where he and his wife and three daughters built a new life.

Leroy's parents, who knew the former minister and his wife, often socialized with them. Leroy was immediately attracted to their youngest daughter Adelino. They fell in love got married and had two beautiful daughters, Emily the eldest and three years later Celma. The family had an incredible life style in Marbella. A magnificent villa on the coast not far from Puerto Banus and both drove top of the range cars, a black and white Range Rover Sport and a white C-class Mercedes.

Also being the man everyone knew as the boss at Marbella's most prestigious club Olivia Valere, allowed Leroy and Adelino to mix with the rich and famous and become celebrities in their own right. They were a glamorous looking couple, always immaculately dressed and were perfect hosts, who loved to socialize. Seven years ago the family had been invited to a friend's wedding. Three weeks before the big day, Adelino and their youngest daughter Celma decided to drive to Malaga in the Mercedes, some forty miles away on a shopping expedition. Like all women she wanted something very special to wear for the wedding. The weather in Spain in February is often unpredictable, one minute brilliant sunshine, an hour later it can be very wet and windy with a month's rain falling in one hour, even fierce electrical storms can strike at this time of the year with little warning." Aslan then poured himself and George another glass of wine, Jack shook his head. He then continued with the conversation. "From all accounts Adelino and their daughter had a lovely day shopping in Malaga. Just before they hit the motorway Adelino rang Leroy on the hands free mobile in the Mercedes to say they would be home in just over the hour. As they spoke it started to rain heavy with thunder and lightning. His wife and daughter said they were frightened and wished he was with them. Leroy told Adelino to drive slowly on the motorway. He told them he loved them both dearly, both the girls responded by shouting into the phone how much they loved him. He never spoke to them again. An hour later he was contacted by the police, who told him that his wife and daughter had been involved in terrible accident. Both Adelino and Celma had died instantly, when a heavy goods vehicle crashed into the rear of their stationary Mercedes, pushing them forward into another vehicle. Leroy and his elder daughter Emily were devastated. Hundreds turned up at the funeral for Adelino and Celma, the whole of the Costa del Sol were in shock. The days and weeks which followed the tragedy were heartbreaking. Leroy knew he had to carry on for the sake of his fifteen-year-old daughter, she idolized her father. Emily was the double of her mother in every aspect. That was seven years ago."

"What has happened to Emily since?"

"She went to Malaga University to study law just like her father, next year she will get her degree, and she will be twenty three then. Most weekends she helps her father in the club. The beautiful young lady dressed in top hat and tails at the VIP entrance was Emily."

"Leroy has a beautiful daughter. Do you think she will eventually come into the business?"

"I have my doubts. She has a steady boyfriend Phillip who I can see her getting married to. Emily will almost certainly work as a lawyer but more than likely help her father in the club at the weekends. It is possible he may even take her boyfriend into the business, though there are problems on the horizon. His partners want to sell out to him, as there are big bucks at stake here, he would have to borrow a great deal of money from the bank. At the age of fifty-two he is not certain he wants the responsibility of running the Olivia Valere by himself."

"You appear to know Leroy extremely well."

Aslan smiled. "He is my closest friend. We have known each other for many years and he is always there for me and I for him."

Jack was beginning to like Aslan; he appeared to be a very genuine guy even though he had a dubious past. He was now even seeing George in a completely different light.

"What is your feeling, do you think he will buy the club?" "No, I am convinced the club will be put up for sale. There are several wealthy Arabs living on the Costa del Sol who would love to own the Olivia Valere. They would probably keep Leroy on to front the business for them, that way the general public would be none the wiser. Aslan then leaned forward and lifted the half full glass of red wine to his lips, before taking a long drink. He then continued with the conversation. "There is no doubt in my mind that Leroy would buy his partners out if his wife was still alive. Since the death of Adelino and his daughter Celma, his life has fallen apart. If it was not for Emily, who he dotes on, he would probably have returned to Portugal to be close to his elderly parents. He wants to see Emily make her name as a lawyer and also be happily married with a family." "What does Phillip do for a living?"

"He is an accountant in the family business." Aslan then completely changed the conversation. "Jack, I understand you will be appearing at the Med Club every Tuesday.

"To begin with yes, but Pedro has already told me it could possibly end up with a Thursday night as well."

"I understand that you were a gemmologist at Franks in Hatton Garden London until you arrived in Marbella and a very good one by all accounts." Jack replied yes and smiled. "My current gemmologist is talking about returning home to Georgia. At the moment he is overseas on business, when he returns I will introduce you to him. If you fancy working for Cobra Jewellery let me know, I shall certainly be in the market for a replacement if he leaves, even if he doesn't, we could offer you a part-time position.

"Aslan I appreciate your offer, I will certainly give it some thought." Jack then glanced at his watch. "It is amazing how time flies, it is just leaving one. Guys, if you will excuse me, I need to head to the Med Club, Pedro is expecting me."

"It has been good to see you again Jack, don't forget my offer."

"I most certainly will not." He then drank the last of his wine before leaving the club which was now extremely busy. He had enjoyed the company of Aslan and George. Punters were still coming into the club as he jumped into a waiting taxi. He had not got the energy to make the twenty five minute walk to the Med Club; also he was concerned about the possibility of being mugged. Even in Marbella it was becoming a problem, probably due to the number of wealthy people who walked the streets late at night.

The Med Beach Club like the Olivia Valere was a hive of activity outside. Dozens of young punters were still queuing to gain admittance. The clientele at the Med Club was mainly under thirty-five, very different than the Olivia Valere, where the famous celebrities and the social elite of Marbella, could be found. After gaining entry with his VIP pass via the staff entrance, Jack made his way to the night club. There must have been between six and seven hundred punters in the room. The music was pounding out with the latest European chart hits. Brother and sister DJ'S Jose and Selena were having a fantastic time. He looked around for Pedro and his wife Nada, but he was fighting a losing battle with the room being so busy. This was Saturday night, when the glamorous and sexy young girls of Marbella wanted to be seen. Jack had never seen so many beautiful young women in one room at the same time. Their sunburned bodies full of perspiration from the heat glistened in the strobe lighting, as they gyrated to the rhythm of the music. Young handsome bucks were trying to entice many of the girls to join them, many did. Walking over to the DJ stand he called out to Jose and Selena. Somehow they managed to hear him over the music and turned towards him.

"Hi Jack, good to see you." Selena was a lovely girl. Her brother Jose raised his arm in acknowledgement and beckoned to him to join them, which he did. Selena immediately welcomed him with a kiss. Jose then shook his hand warmly. "Good to see you my friend."

"Guys, it is very warm in here tonight, it is fortunate that you have the cool air fan turned on. At least it is a great deal cooler up here than down on the dance floor."

Selena slipped on another couple of discs on the twin deck turntable. One of them was the massive George Michael hit 'Freak.' It was a great pity no one had introduced him to George whilst he was at the Olivia Valere, but then again there was always next time as George was a frequent visitor to the club.

Jose leaned closer to Jack as he spoke. "In a moment we will introduce you to the punters. We have been plugging your opening gig for next Tuesday all night."

"Thank you Jose, I appreciate what you both are doing."

Minutes later Selena turned the music down and Jose went on the microphone, "Guys and dolls, if I may have your attention for one moment, the Med Club from next Tuesday are bringing you House Music every week. We will be the only club in Marbella to perform this great music. Tonight, I would like you to meet the guy who will be bringing this unique sound to you. Will you please give him a great Marbella welcome, direct from London, England the one and only DJ Ramos?"

Jack stepped forward and waved to the crowd. The response was incredible, he now felt like a celebrity. The girls were going crazy shouting his name. Jose went on the microphone again. "Guys, remember DJ Ramos is on stage between eleven and one in the morning, afterwards Selena and I will continue until three."

As the music started to blare out again Jack turned to Jose. "If you will excuse me now, I must go and find the boss."

Jose stuttered slightly as he replied. "Sorry, I should have told you earlier. Pedro and his wife went home shortly before you arrived. His mother, who lives with them, called to say that their daughter was ill and was asking for her mother. Pedro told me to tell you that he would be returning later and not to hang around, as he would call you tomorrow. Sorry again for not letting you know."

"No problem, forget about it you are a very busy guy."

Thirty minutes later he left the club and made his way along the Esplanade Paseo in the direction of the Marbella Beach Apartments. It was still quite warm with a gentle breeze blowing in from the Mediterranean. There was an older man in his sixties on security duty at the reception. When he saw Jack walk in he smiled and nodded his head, he had never seen the guy before. Once in his apartment he stripped off and walked naked onto the balcony. He loved this time of the night it was so peaceful, even the crickets and fire flies had turned in for the night. The gardens looked beautiful in the glare of the security lights. His visit to Olivia Valere had put some doubts in his mind. Cobra Jewellery owner Aslan Maskhadov had told him that Leroy Cardoso, one of the owners of Olivia Valere, was his closest friend. Could he be one of the conspirators with Aslan in the Russian cargo plane hijack of the Siberian diamonds? On Monday, he would call Miles Coburn at MI6 and discuss his thoughts with him, but for now he wanted some shut eye. Tomorrow he would have a relaxing day and meet up with his brother Lex and family, and in the evening he would visit Pinks in Puerto Banus to watch his friend Olga perform her exotic show.

14

Jack's mobile alarm woke him at eight-thirty on Sunday morning. Surprisingly he did not feel tired considering he did not get to sleep until well after three am, his decision to be extremely careful with the amount of alcohol he consumed had been right. After opening the balcony doors, he had a light breakfast of mixed fruit and Greek yogurt, then a quick shower and shave, before heading downstairs to the swimming pool. Though it was only a few minutes after ten, it was quite warm outside, as the sun had already broken through the hazy clouds. As usual the pool was deserted, he looked across at the apartment complex, with the exception of his, every balcony door and window blind were still closed. People staying at the Marbella Beach Apartment often frequented the night clubs and casino and then normally slept in late. The water in the pool was fairly cool, and he shivered as he immersed himself in the clear water, even so he swam twenty lengths before lying on a sun bed to dry off. It was just leaving eleven when he left the pool area and walked back through the garden to the apartment complex; flowers everywhere were in full bloom the scent they gave off filled the warm air. Jack was about to walk into the foyer when his mobile rang, it was Pedro.

"Hi Jack, sorry I missed you last night, I presume Jose gave you my message."

"Yes he did. How is your little one?"

"Olivia is much better now thanks, her tummy trouble and the sickness have now cleared up." Pedro paused for a second. "Jose told me he introduced you to the punters." "Yes. I was delighted with the response."

"Are you ready for your opening night?"

"Absolutely, the adrenaline is already building up for the big night." Pedro laughed.

"Have you managed to find out the whereabouts of any of the Chechens?"

"I certainly have. Last night I went to the Olivia Valere club as Aslan Maskhadov's guest. His chauffeur Freddie and close friend George, who are Chechens, are also on the Russian wanted list. So far I have identified six Chechens on the list. Aslan has also offered me a job as a gemmologist with his Cobra Jewellery Company. His current gemmologist is considering moving back home to Georgia. He did not mention the guy's name but it is quite possibly Sergei Aslanov. Aslan mentioned that his gemmologist was out of the country on business until next week, when he returns he will arrange for me to meet him."

"Good work Jack, you need to accept Aslan's offer but only on a part-time basis."

"I fully agree with you. Tomorrow I intend to call Miles Coburn and put him in the picture."

Jack then glanced at his watch, time was flying by and Lex would soon be arriving. Walking into the foyer he made his way up the white marble staircase to his apartment, at the same time carrying on a conversation with Pedro.

"What are you doing today?"

"My brother Lex is picking me up at eleven forty-five. We are then going to his villa for a barbecue which I am looking forward to. Later in the evening I shall be visiting Pinks in Puerto Banus, I believe some Russian guy with Mafia links owns the club."

"Jack, be careful at Pinks, the Russian guy has a bad reputation for violence."

"Thanks for the warning. Pedro I am going to have to go, my brother will be with me shortly."

"I will see you on Tuesday evening at nine, have a good day."

Once inside his apartment, Jack quickly changed. As he was closing the balcony doors his mobile on the kitchen table rang. It was his brother Lex.

"Jack it's Lex. Are you ok?"

"Yes, everything is fine."

"I am parked in my Range Rover Sport on the side road close to the entrance to the Marbella Beach Apartments."

"I will be with you in five minutes."

On leaving the foyer Jack slipped on his dark shades and made his way out of the complex. He soon spotted the 4x4 parked on the right hand side a hundred metres away. Lex must have seen him approaching through his interior mirror as he jumped out of the vehicle and walked towards him.

"Good to see you little brother, you look well."

"So do you big brother."

They laughed and smiled at each other, the two brothers then embraced warmly. It was obvious to anyone that they enjoyed each other's company. Jack then climbed into the passenger seat and fastened his safety belt. Within minutes they were leaving Marbella and heading towards the A7, the new Mediterranean Motorway. Once on the motorway Lex opened up the Range Rover Sport's powerful 4 litre engine.

"We should be at our villa in about fifty minutes unless we are delayed with heavy traffic."

It was an uneventful journey. Jack enquired how Lex's family were and how he was looking forward to seeing them again. Lex on the other hand was desperate to know how his brother's investigation was proceeding. Though Jack trusted his brother completely he still had to be very careful what he divulged, after all he was now an MI6 operative, and was covered by the official secrets act.

As they approached Malaga the motorway became busier with coaches carrying tourists to the Malaga International Airport. After leaving the motorway at the Torremolinos exit, they headed along the coast road to Malaga for about four miles before pulling up at a gated complex, which was surrounded by a six foot high stone wall topped with razor wire. Lex picked up a small black remote control from on top of the Range Rover's dash board and pointed it at the dark wooden double gate, it immediately swung open allowing them to drive in. It was like being transported to another world. Lush green foliage and flowers native only to the Mediterranean were in abundance. There were even several small palm trees. The white two storey five bedroom villa, which was less than fifty metres away, looked stunning. As they pulled up in the parking bay, Lex's wife Maria opened the front door and came over to them holding their young son David in her arms. There was a lovely smile on her beautiful face as she greeted Jack affectionately. Lex was a lucky guy to have such a glamorous looking wife.

"Good to see Jack, you look very well and I love your hair now it is a little longer. With your lovely tan I could now take you to be a Spaniard." Jack laughed.

"Your English is very good Maria."

"Thank you Jack, I thought with my husband speaking fluent Spanish, I should learn to speak English; I go for lessons three times a week."

Lex then turned to his brother. "Jack, please come inside the villa and we will show you around, since you were last here, we have given it a makeover and redecorated."

Their villa inside was as breathtaking as the outside, the builders were master craftsmen. The floors of the split level property were covered in light grey Italian tiles. The walls throughout were painted white with expensive glass fittings, light oak and black leather furniture adorned all the rooms. The huge lounge had black patio doors which opened at the touch of a switch. Outside in front of the lounge, was an Indian slate patio, which overlooked a heart shaped swimming pool, immaculate manicured gardens circled the whole property. The kitchen area was extremely modern 21stcentury; it looked stunning in white and grey with the white and brown floor tiles.

"You have a villa to be proud of and have been blessed with a beautiful baby son who looks just like his mother."

"We are very lucky aren't we Maria?"

Maria slid her arm around her husband's waist. "I have a wonderful husband." Lex leaned over and kissed the side of her face.

"Jack, let us go outside and get the barbecue going whilst Maria changes David."

"Have Malaga no match today?"

"No, it is an International break. We play again next Sunday at home against Real Madrid."

"It should be quite a game."

"I'm sure it will be, you must come to the match, it is a mid-day kick off."

"I would love to."

"Good, I will make arrangements for you to be admitted to the stadium and I will text the details to you later in the week."

"I see Malaga is still top of the La Liga."

"Yes, by three points. We have had a great start to the season and luckily due to the way the fixtures have fallen, we have avoided possibly the four most successful clubs in the league until now. Unfortunately I will not be able to pick you up."

"No problem, I will either hire a car or travel by bus or train." Jack then took in a deep breath. "The food on the barbecue you are cooking smells delicious."

Grey smoke from the barbecue started to curl upwards, slowly disintegrating as it drifted over the garden. Whilst Lex was cooking the food, Jack walked to the edge of the patio and looked across the garden, less than four hundred metres away he could see the blue Mediterranean. It looked stunning as the sun's rays bounced off the tranquil sea. Lex and Maria had everything, a beautiful villa, a lovely baby son and most of all they loved each other. His thoughts drifted to his sister Lilly back home in the UK, a wonderful husband and two adorable children, she had also found happiness. For the first time in his life he felt envious of them both. It was about time he found a wife and settled down. His new Russian girlfriend was not the one for him, she was stunningly beautiful but over sexed. If he married a girl like her, he would be worried in case she was shagging around. He knew eventually he would meet the right girl.

"You like our home Jack?" Maria's voice startled him, he was miles away.

"You and Lex have a beautiful villa and an incredible life style here in Spain."

Maria smiled. "We are very lucky Jack. I just hope it lasts for many years, when your husband is a football manager, if you have a poor season you can be out of a job the following year." Jack smiled, he knew what she had just said was quite true.

The barbecue was excellent; Jack noticed that his brother, apart from one glass of red wine, never drank any alcohol. "I remember brother when you used to enjoy a few beers and a glass a two of wine."

"I still do in moderation but I can't afford to be pulled up by the police when I drive you to Marbella."

"Lex, I will take a taxi to the airport and pick up a coach to Marbella. There is no point going by train as they only run as far as Fuengirola, I would then have to take a taxi or coach as Marbella is another twenty miles south along the Costa del Sol."

Lex looked at his brother. "Are you certain you don't mind?"

"No, not at all, at least now you can enjoy a few drinks."

The afternoon flew by quickly. Shortly before seven, Lex accompanied Jack to the entrance of the villa, when the taxi he had arranged earlier had just arrived to take Jack to the airport so he could catch a direct coach to Marbella.

"Don't forget our home match with Real Madrid a week on Sunday, as I said earlier I will let you have more match details during the week."

"I will probably hire a car; I need to get about more." "Good idea."

"You take care Jack, and please keep in touch; you know you are always welcome here," the two brothers warmly embraced.

The taxi to Malaga International Airport coach terminal took about twenty five minutes. The coach to Marbella left on time at seven thirty, the thirty four mile journey took about fifty minutes, by nine Jack was back in his apartment at the Marbella Beach Complex. The evening was still warm with no wind but by now it was almost completely dark. So far his day out had been most enjoyable, whether his visit later to Pinks would be the same, he would have to wait and see.

At ten thirty Jack called Benny's taxi, twenty minutes later his mobile rang to say that the taxi was parked outside the complex by the main entrance. Whoever the guy was on reception he had never seen him before. As he walked through the foyer, the security office looked up and smiled but never spoke. The taxi driver was not Benny but a girl in her late twenties. She had quite a husky voice as she spoke. "Anywhere in particular you want me to drop you in Puerto Banus?"

"Yes, close to the La Victoria Statue by the roundabout in the Avenida de Nacionalas Unidas"

"No problem."

The journey took less than twenty minutes. Once out of the taxi Jack headed for the harbour. The port was alive with a mixture of tourists, locals and couples looking for an evening of excitement, after dining in one of the exclusive restaurants. All the bars which hugged the sides of the harbour were busy. It was Christmas here all year round. Coloured lights ran around the perimeter of the harbour and marina illuminating the multi-million dollar cruisers and yachts bobbing about to the movement of the sea swell. Like Marbella, Puerto Banus attracted the young, glamorous and wealthy, as well as an older clientele of rich men and women looking for young men and girls for sexual activity. In Puerto Banus that was no problem, if you had the money there was nothing you could not buy to feed your sexual desires. After walking as far as the Moorish harbour tower, Jack checked his watch it was a couple of minutes past eleven-thirty, time to find Pinks lap dancing club. Olga had told him it was to be found in the side street, which ran parallel to the harbour close to Lineker's Bar, which is run and owned by Wayne the brother of former International footballer turned TV sports presenter Gary Lineker. He had no problem finding Linekers, the largest and busiest bar in Puerto Banus. Another hundred meters along the street he found Pinks, and just further along he could see the Ocean Club. This was the highly successful venue Pedro Gonzales and his wife Nada had based the Med Club on, when they first opened. Taking out his mobile phone, Jack brought up the photos of the two wanted Chechens he had so far not identified. It was quite possible they could be employed at Pinks.

There were two broad shouldered and tough looking doormen on duty at Pinks, one black the other white with a deep tan. As he approached the entrance, two of the four skimpily dressed young women they had been talking to came over to him. Both were English, slim and attractive with very short low-cut dresses.

"Hi handsome my name is Katie my friend is called Charlie. Why don't you come inside the club and watch us take our clothes off? You will be surprised what we girls get up to."

"I was about to come in, my friend Olga works here."

Both the girls looked at each other and smiled. "A very sexy Russian girl," remarked Charlie sarcastically.

Without another word Jack walked up to the doormen. "My friend Olga, one of your dancers should have spoken to you about me, my name is Jack Sinclair."

The black guy spoke first. “Olga spoke to me about you Jack there is no problem, so please go inside.”

Leaving the busy street outside the club was like travelling into a different world. Like most of the establishments in Puerto Banus, the club was very opulent inside and had a lighting system, which gave off a pinkish glow. There must have been at least sixty or seventy men of all ages with a few women friends sat on the dark blue leather sofas and chairs, or congregating in front of the long circular bar. There were eight stainless steel poles placed in various spots around the club. The closer Jack got to the bar the more congested it became. Though he could feel the cool air conditioning it was still warm, in fact almost as warm as outside. Eventually he struggled to the bar. There were five people serving, these included three young very attractive long haired girls dressed in pink boob tops, tight white shorts and pink trainers. It wasn’t the girls’ eye popping figures which had grabbed his attention, but the two male barmen. There was no need to check his mobile phone; these guys were the two missing Chechens. He had identified all eight now, just one to go Sergei Aslanov. Or had he, they looked familiar to him and then it dawned on him. When he was dining with Olga at the Gastro Bar Pikaro restaurant in Marbella, these two guys behind the bar were sat at the table next to him with two fellow Chechens. As he was about to buy a bottle of Budweiser the music and the lights changed. From a door behind the stage eight beautiful looking girls completely naked swung into action on the stainless steel poles. Nothing was left to the imagination as the girls slowly gyrated up and down the poles, after ten minutes the girls disappeared and another eight took their place. Jack immediately recognized Olga; she looked incredible with her large breasts thrusting out. Again after ten minutes the girls disappeared, only to return again dressed in very short identical black strapless dresses. All the girls looked stunning; his eyes were glued to them.

“Hi handsome did you enjoy my show.”

Jack lowered the bottle of Budweiser he had been drinking and turned round.

“Hi darling what do you think?”

Jack looked at Olga. Her boobs were almost hanging out of her dress but he had to admit that she looked incredible.

"If you pay me forty Euros, I will give you a private dance behind one of the screens at the far end of the room. I will be completely naked, you can look but you must not touch me."

Jack laughed. "I will wait until Tuesday."

Olga then leaned over and whispered in his ear. I am pleased you said that, it will be far more exciting having sex with you on Tuesday, knowing you are desperate for me. If you will excuse me, I am going to have to circulate and earn some money otherwise the boss will be on to me."

"Perhaps before I leave you will introduce me to him as DJ Ramos?"

"Of course I will darling, I will see you later." Without another word she moved on. The next time he saw her, she was with a balding middle aged guy, who followed her behind the curtain.

Every thirty minutes the girls returned to the poles, including the girls who were at the entrance to the club when he arrived. Jack enjoyed his evening, by one thirty he decided to leave even though he never got tired of running his eyes over the naked girls. Olga was by the bar chatting potential customers up, she saw him and came over.

"Are you leaving Jack?"

"Yes, after you have introduced me to your boss."

"I will find him for you now."

"By the way, which is the English girl you stay with when you are in Puerto Banus, you said she was also a dancer." "She is not working tonight, she is not well. There is the boss Boris." They then walked towards a tall bald headed clean shaven guy who looked to be in his mid forties. "Boris."

The man turned and faced them. As they got closer he spoke to Olga in Russian. She laughed and said something back to him.

Olga turned to Jack. "He said my boobs look magnificent." "They are."

"He has been making suggestive remarks to me ever since I started working here. I know that he is dying to shag me but I am not interested in him." Jack could not help but laugh.

"What can I do for you Olga?"

"Boris, I would like you to meet my friend Jack otherwise known as DJ

Ramos. Jack starts his House Music gig at the Med Club this coming Tuesday."

"Good to meet you Jack, I will certainly be at your opening night." Jack could not help but notice how strong his Russian accent was.

"Boris, you have a fantastic club here and your girls are something else."

"I am pleased you enjoyed your night, come back anytime you want."

"I most certainly will, good to meet you, I will see you next Tuesday."

Jack then excused himself and left the club which was still heaving with punters. The streets outside were just as busy with the occasional drunken tourist throwing up. The night temperature had dropped considerably but it was still very mild and thankfully there was no wind. Once Jack had made his way back to the La Victoria Statue, he was luckily enough to be invited to join a party of girls on board a mini bus taxi heading back to Marbella. As he climbed aboard, one of the girls who was Spanish but spoke good English, called out to her friends that DJ Ramos was joining them in the taxi. From that moment on it was sheer bedlam for the rest of the journey. All six girls said that they would be at the Med Club on Tuesday.

"If you guys have any requests on the night just head up to the DJ Stand and tell me, and don't forget to remind me where we met."

After posing for a selfie with each of the girls on their mobiles and kissing each one of them good night, Jack left the minibus and made the short walk to the Marbella Beach Apartments. The elderly guy who was on duty the previous night was there again. As before he looked up, nodded his head and half smiled, but never spoke. Once in his apartment Jack made himself an Americano coffee and went outside onto the lounge balcony, he glanced at his watch it was almost two-thirty. It was still warm and the garden looked beautiful in the glare of the security lights. The silence was only broken by the sea crashing onto the shale and sand beach immediately opposite the complex. Tomorrow he had to call Miles Coburn in London, and bring him up to date about everything he had so far discovered. The Russian guy who ran Pinks in Puerto Banus was now a strong suspect for involvement in the Siberian cargo plane hijack. He very much doubted that Boris Sokolov owned the club; he was more than likely fronting for the Russian Mafia. The more he thought about it, the more he was convinced of his involvement. Anyway it was for Miles Coburn and Major Pavlov of the FSB to decide. Also Miles had not come back to him with information on Olga, tomorrow he would take it up with him. Closing the balcony doors Jack went into the master bedroom and opened a window to allow the air to circulate before stripping off his clothes and lying naked on the bed, within minutes he was asleep.

15

Jack woke around ten-thirty, for once there was no alarm to disturb him and there was no Olga around today to distract him. After he had called Coburn, he would have a lazy day, go for a swim and sun bath by the pool. By the time he had his breakfast, showered and shaved it was leaving eleven-thirty.

Miles was delighted to hear from him, especially when he rolled off all the information he had gathered over the last few days.

"Now you have identified the Chechens and who employs some of them, all we have to do is find out where they all live. You have done incredibly well in such a short time." Miles paused for a second. "You mentioned last time we spoke, correct me if I am wrong, that you would probably be meeting Sergei Aslanov in the near future."

"I was hoping to this weekend but I now understand, that he will not be returning to Spain until sometime during the following week." Jack then changed the conversation. "Have you managed to find out anything about the Russian girl Olga?"

"Yes I have, we have quite a file on Olga and her sister Tanya. They both work for the Russian FSB as assassins and have one hell of a reputation of getting the job done. They both were born in Moscow. Their father was a Colonel in the old KGB until he took early retirement. It would appear that their father was a career officer, who never married until one day he met the beautiful Kristina Petrova. Kristina was Russia's most famous circus trapeze artiste, though there was a twenty year age gap they fell in love and got married. Twelve months later Kristina gave birth to identical twin girls. A couple of years later, her husband the Colonel, resigned his commission and with the help of his famous wife they formed the most successful touring circus in Russia. Further information about them is a little hazy at the moment but I understand the girls have worked for the FSB for the last eight years. They are both twenty seven and are identical twins."

"What is their hair colour?"

"Blonde. I will email you a recent photograph of them which was taken in Moscow three months ago. Why do you ask about their hair colour?"

"Only that the girl I know as Olga has long dark hair."

"She must have dyed it."

"I am certain she has."

"Another thing Jack, both the girls are psychopaths and take a pleasure in killing someone. In the last eight years they must have assassinated at least fifty men and women. Be very careful, I am told they are both very beautiful women who use men to get what they want."

"Miles thanks for the information and warning about them."

"A couple of minutes later their conversation ended and Jack headed for the swimming pool. Just as he was about to dive into the cool water his mobile rang, it was Pedro Gonzales.

"Jack, sorry again for not being about on Saturday evening when you called. You wanted to speak to me?"

"Yes I did." Jack then gave Pedro a download on the recent information he had discovered about the Chechens.

"You have done well Jack, Miles Coburn should be impressed. I have never met the Russian who runs Pinks but from all accounts I am told he is hard man who does not shy away from violence."

"I believe so." Pedro had previously warned him about the guy last time they spoke. "I spoke to Miles earlier this morning, now he has definite information about the Chechens he intends to email the Russian FSB with details." Jack then told Pedro, what Miles Coburn had told him about the two Russian sisters Olga and Tanya.

"Be careful my friend, we don't want to find you in the harbour with your hands tied and a plastic bag over your head." From the tone of Pedro's voice he knew he was deadly serious."

"Thanks for the warning, I shall be extremely careful." Jack, I will see you on Tuesday evening, the demand for tickets to your show has been incredible, and we will have a full house."

"That is great. I will be in by nine."

As soon as his conversation with Pedro was over, Jack immediately dived into the pool and swam ten lengths, before hauling himself out and lying on one of the sun beds, to dry off in the warm sun. As usual as there was no one else around, even the resident cat which could usually be seen wandering around the complex had disappeared. At one Jack nipped upstairs to his apartment, after changing into a pair of white shorts and a light blue sports top he then left the complex for a bite to eat. Once on the Esplanade Paseo he headed for the Picasso Café Bar, where he had eaten before. As he walked down the busy Esplanade he recalled the paella he had eaten that day, it was delicious.

Again the elderly Spanish couple who owned the bar made him very welcome. Today he did not want a heavy meal for lunch but instead ordered a roast ham sandwich with a pint of local beer. By three, having consumed a further two pints, Jack left the Picasso Café Bar and sat on the sea wall overlooking the Mediterranean. The weather was perfect, slipping on his dark shades he closed his eyes and relaxed in the warmth of the sun's rays. His mind drifted back to his parents and how much he missed them. Especially his mother, in many ways they were so much alike and over the years they had many wonderful conversations. Living with his parents at their Thames side apartment, he saw far more of them than his sister Lilly and brother Lex. There was never any jealousy between the three siblings, as they knew their parents loved them all equally. As he thought of them, their vivid images flickered before him and tears began to form in his eyes.

"Jack, are you ok?" He felt a gentle hand touch his shoulder.

"Valentina," he looked straight at her beautiful face, at first she appeared most concerned and then a smile crossed her face. "Thank you for disturbing me, I was on the verge of falling asleep, I would probably have ended up with sunburn and a headache."

She then sat on the sea wall next to him.

"I thought you were at college in the daytime."

"I am, but I finished early today. You were lucky I called in at my father's restaurant on my way home, otherwise I would never have seen you. Jack you appeared troubled when I first saw you."

"I was thinking about my parents who died in a helicopter crash in Australia last year."

"Oh how terrible, you must miss them."

"I do terribly."

Valentina then touched his arm. "I am certain the pain will go easier as time goes by."

"I hope you are right." Jack then smiled at her. Valentina was a lovely girl, it was a great pity she was only seventeen otherwise she would have made the perfect girlfriend. Are you coming to my show at the Med Club tomorrow evening?"

"Yes, there are about twenty five of us from the college coming to the show; it should be a fantastic night."

"Don't forget to come up to the DJ Stand if you or any of your friends want a particular song playing.

"Will your Russian girlfriend be with you?"

"I presume you mean Olga. She is certainly not my girlfriend, we both just happen to be staying in the Marbella Beach Apartment Complex and have met up for a few meals."

"I can see from your reaction that you do not like Olga."

"Is it so obvious?" Jack smiled.

"She may be a very beautiful woman but I do not trust her, neither does my father. Even Aslan Maskhadov has doubts about her; he thinks the Russian Government have sent her to Spain to spy on him."

"He may be right."

"Jack, many beautiful women use their looks to get what they want."

"Really, then I shall have to keep an eye on you." Valentine blushed but then leaned forward and kissed Jack on the side of his face. "You are a lovely man Jack Sinclair"

"Would you care for a drink?"

"No, but could we walk down the Esplanade to the ice cream parlour I do love ice cream?"

"So do I,"

Jack enjoyed his hour with Valentina, he was very careful not to give her the wrong sort of vibes, the last thing he wanted was any confrontation with her father Roscoe Rodriguez.

After arriving back at the Marbella Beach Apartments shortly before five thirty, Jack went for a quick swim in the pool. The water was considerably warmer than when he took his morning dip. Once he had completed twenty lengths, he got out of the pool and sat on one of the sunbeds to dry himself. There was not a sole around but numerous swallows were putting on a majestic aerial show for him, darting back and forth showing off their incredible aerobatic skills, every time he stood up they swooped down towards him in a kamikaze dive, only to pull away at the very last moment. As he walked back towards the complex the house cat reappeared and bounded over to him, leaning down he ran his right hand down the animals back and stroked its tail as she purred loudly and rubbed her head against his bare leg. There was no one on reception as he entered the reception area. Once he had made his way up the white marble staircase, he then used his key card to gain access to his apartment. Once inside he opened the balcony windows to allow fresh air to circulate around the apartment, before he switched on the television and relaxed watching Sky News for the next half hour. The situation in Iraq was not improving and hundreds of innocent men, women and children were being murdered daily in secretarial car bomb explosions in Baghdad.

Removing President Saddam Hussein had been a grave error and now the country was destabilized. At seven thirty after a quick shower and change of clothes, Jack left the complex and headed down the Esplanade Paseo in the direction of the Albatross Bar and Restaurant. As usual the restaurant was extremely busy. Making his way into the lounge and bar area, he found a vacant table near the back of the room. Almost immediately a young male waiter came over to him and took his order of sliced water melon followed by a chicken omelette with a green salad and a pint of cool Budweiser.

"Your meal will be with you in about twenty minutes. Should I bring you your drink whilst you wait Sir?"

"Yes, if you would."

As soon as the waiter returned with the glass of Budweiser, Jack took a long slow drink allowing the cool liquid to trickle down his throat. It was another warm evening and the cool drink worked wonders. Whist waiting for his meal, he checked his mobile. There was a text message from his sister Lilly, checking to make certain he was alright. He replied back saying everything was fine and he would call her on Tuesday evening before he left to perform his DJ gig at the Med Club. There was also a recent text from Miles Coburn who confirmed, that he had updated FSB chief Major Pavlov with all the recent information about the Chechens, which he had passed onto him.

"Jack, be prepared for repercussions, once the Major has spoken to his operatives Olga and Tanya he may tell them to eliminate the Chechens." After reading the message for a second time he switched off his mobile.

"Good to see you again my friend." It was the owner of the Albatross, Roscoe Rodriguez.

"Jack immediately stood up and the two men embraced. "Have you ordered?"

"Yes, my meal should be with me in about ten minutes." "May I join you until it arrives?"

"Of course, be my guest. Can I get you a drink?"

"No thanks, I am on duty this evening. I never drink alcohol whilst I am working. I would like a quick word with you." The smile on Jack's face disappeared and he had a serious look.

Roscoe laughed. "There is nothing to worry about my friend."

"What can I do for you?"

"You were speaking to my daughter earlier." Jack nodded his head. "She tells me everything. Valentina likes you Jack, in fact I think she is becoming infatuated with you. Please don't encourage her, we want our daughter to go to Malaga University and study to become a teacher. We want her to fulfil her dreams.

Jack lowered his voice and then spoke in Spanish. "I would never do anything to offend you or your family."

"I had completely forgotten that you spoke our language." Jack smiled.

"I now feel most embarrassed; I should not have mentioned it."

"You have every right to, after all she is your daughter and you want to protect her against older guys like me." Roscoe laughed out loud, several customers dining at nearby tables turned and looked.

"Valentina is the double of my wife Sofia who is ten years younger than me. She was only twenty when we got married, so I have no objection to Valentina dating an older guy providing he treats her well."

"I completely understand your concern about your daughter but I have no romantic interest in her, in any case as soon as my contract is up at the Med Club, I will be heading back to the UK."

"Jack, please don't be offended but I had to speak my mind."

"I am certainly not offended. Am I still allowed to buy Valentina an ice cream?" The two men laughed and embraced. "Before I forget, Valentina was asking me about my friend Olga, she said that like you and Aslan she did not trust her."

"Do you Jack?"

"No. I think there is a great deal more to her than we know."

"We feel the same." Roscoe then almost spoke in a whisper. "Aslan told me that he has recently received information via an email from a close friend, stating that the Russian Government have accused Chechen Separatists of being involved in the hijack of a cargo plane in Siberia, which was carrying a vast quantity of diamonds and precious gems. He is convinced that Olga is a FSB agent who has been sent to Spain by the Russians to assassinate him."

"I can understand Aslan's concern, if I was in his situation I would probably feel the same. He needs to step up his personal security."

"I understand that he has recently spoken to Roberto Sanchez of Costa Security."

As they were speaking, the waiter arrived with Jack's meal.

"I will leave you now my friend to enjoy your meal."

Jack did enjoy his meal. Afterwards for the next couple of hours he sat alone by the bar drinking, occasionally talking to Roscoe, who was busy serving behind the bar. One of his bar staff had phoned in on the last moment ill. There was no sign of Aslan Maskhadov and his friend George; it was a pity as he was starting to enjoy their company. Around ten-thirty, Jack left the Albatross and made his way along the Esplanade Paseo towards the Marbella Beach Apartments. It was a beautiful evening warm with no wind. Crickets were out in large numbers, as were the Fire Flies who were darting about in the lush foliage. Once inside the foyer he noticed Youssef Beji was back on reception. There was little chance of speaking to him as he was in conversation with a well-dressed couple, who looked more Middle Eastern than European. Youssef saw him and acknowledged him with a smile. The couple then turned slightly and looked.

An early night was on the cards for Jack; by eleven fifteen he had hit the sack and was asleep in minutes.

His bedroom was like an oven when he awoke a few minutes before nine. He had forgotten to leave the windows open. Going into the lounge he opened the balcony doors, immediately the fresh air rushed in. Standing on the balcony he gazed across the lush gardens. It was slightly cooler and everywhere looked so refreshed probably due to the water sprinkler system, then he noticed the odd pools of water on the paths, there had obviously been a heavy shower of rain during the night. By ten-thirty he had his breakfast, shaved and showered and tidied up the apartment. Thirty minutes later Jack was powering his way through thirty lengths in the swimming pool. By the time he walked out of the pool and dried himself, the air temperature had crept up to 24c. The Costa del Sol was in for another warm day. Rather than take to a poolside sun lounger to top up his already excellent tan, Jack walked back to his apartment and made himself a coffee, before relaxing on one of the whitish grey wicker chairs on the balcony. Flicking through his mobile phone he brought up current photos of the wanted Chechens as well as photo of Sergei Aslanov. As he was familiarising himself with them, an email came through from Miles Coburn.

"Good morning Jack, I thought you might like to see the latest photos of identical twins Olga and Tanya, which one of our operatives has discovered."

Jack's eyes lingered over the photos, it was impossible to say who was who. Their identical looks were quite uncanny. In the photos both the girls had blonde hair so at least he had been right about Olga. He then sent his MI6 boss a text reply. "Thanks for the photos Miles most interesting." Jack then added their photos to the mobile's picture gallery.

The apartment's buzzer rang. Walking across the cool tiled floor to the door in his bare feet, he glanced at the small security screen on the wall, it was Olga. Opening the door Olga came in, she looked stunning in a short black and white floral dress which had a deep V at the front exposing her breasts, and she was also shoeless. Immediately she threw her arms around his neck and pulled him towards her, kissing him passionately. "I have missed you Jack, I am so used to you being about."

Jack ran his fingers through her long dark hair and kissed her neck and shoulders. He could feel the softness and warmth of her body as he held her close.

"Make love to me Jack. I need you."

Lifting her in his arms he carried Olga into his bedroom and gently laid her on the king size bed.

"Did you enjoy my show when you came Sunday?"

"Yes, you were amazing and looked stunning."

"Thank you darling, I always try to please."

Without another word Jack slowly removed her soft cotton dress and white G-string leaving her naked on the bed. As he removed his last item of clothing Olga suddenly without any warning climbed on top of him. For the next hour Jack enjoyed the pleasures of sex which he had only dreamt of in the past.

After leaving the bedroom, Jack went into the kitchen and poured out two large glasses of red wine whilst Olga walked out onto the balcony. It was very warm and the sun's rays were very strong so they both sat under the multi-coloured umbrella as they relaxed and drank wine.

"When we called in at the Albatross the other evening you mentioned that you had a sister."

Olga smiled as she answered yes.

"Is she younger or older than you?"

"I am twelve months older."

"I am surprised that she has not joined you on holiday.""My sister and I have a great deal in common, but going away on holidays together is not one of them. It is quite possible she may join me for a couple of weeks. I really hope she does as I do miss her." Olga then took a long drink of red wine, half emptying her glass. "Darling I am starving, do you think we could go for something to eat, I am always hungry after sex." Jack could not help but laugh.

"I will take you to the Picasso Café Bar on the Esplanade Paseo, it is small and not posh but the food is excellent, we can be there in ten minutes."

"Great let's go then. On second thoughts, I shall need to call into my apartment first and pick up a pair of sandals." Twenty minutes later they arrived at the Picasso Café Bar. After finding a vacant table under one of the large orange and yellow umbrellas, they ordered two roast ham and cheese sandwiches with a large glass of red wine and a pint of local beer. Both Olga and Jack felt very relaxed in each other's company, maybe it was the alcohol or the stunning views across the Mediterranean Sea, but for the next two hours they just laughed and talked. To an observant passerby you would have thought that they were a young couple in love. If Jack was honest, he had to admit that he was attracted to Olga, what normal man would not be. Beautiful, a gorgeous figure with a lovely personality, who loved having sex but there was something about her which put doubts in his mind; she was too good to be true.

"Darling, if you were thinking of taking me out for a meal this evening before you head to the Med Club for your gig, I will not be available."

"You took the words out of my mouth. I was about to ask you to dine with me this evening."

Jack slipped off his dark shades and looked at Olga as she was not forthcoming with an explanation.

"Sorry darling, my girlfriend Emma from Pinks wants to come along to the Med Club this evening to watch you. We have arranged to meet in Marbella at seven-thirty, have a meal and a few drinks, and then make our way to the Med Club by ten-thirty. Jack everyone is talking about you, you are already famous before you have even appeared on stage."

"Will you be staying all night?"

"No, when you have finished your gig, we intend to take a taxi to the Ocean Club in Puerto Banus. I will be staying the night at my friend's apartment. If you like you could join us and even stay the night at my friend's pad. Olga then started to laugh. "Three in a bed would be great fun."

"If your friend is anything like you, I would never be able to cope with you both."

Olga laughed again. "Practice that is all you need darling." Ten minutes later they left the bar and slowly made their way to the Marbella Beach Apartments.

As they were walking, Olga linked Jack's left arm tightly and then turned to him. "We have known each other for less than a week but it feels like I have known you for years. You and I get on so well together Jack."

"We certainly do." He said with a smile.

"I saw you this morning swimming in the pool, you look extremely fit."

"I have to be with a girlfriend like you."

Olga looked up at Jack, her eyelashes fluttered. "Would you like to come back to my apartment for another session?"

"I would love to but I have to work out my programme for this evening, call my sister Lilly, have a lie down and relax and then get a bite to eat before arriving at the Med Club at nine. What about tomorrow afternoon."

"That sounds fantastic darling, I will be back around mid-day so I will call round to your pad. Sex on your king size bed is incredible." Jack had to laugh.

After escorting Olga to her apartment door, he slowly slid his arms around her waist; they then kissed passionately before he left. Once in his own apartment he opened the balcony doors to allow the warm air in the room to drift out. Opening up his laptop, he carefully selected the music he intended to perform during tonight's two hour performance at the Med Club. Forty minutes later he walked into the main bedroom and picked up his Sony mobile from the bedside table and called his sister Lilly. As usual Lilly was delighted to hear from him.

"How are you Jack?"

"Absolutely fine, working hard but I am still finding time to get a great sun tan. The weather is perfect here. What about you Lilly, how are you feeling on your new medication?"

"Incredible, I feel like a new person. I am lucky that I have such an understanding husband, I must have been very hard to live with. I love hearing from you Jack, wherever you are, you must always find time to call me."

"You know I will."

For the next twenty minutes they talked about many things including their brother Lex and his stunning villa on the coast near Malaga.

Lex has invited me to Malaga's home match against Real Madrid this coming Sunday, it should be a great match." "Do you think Malaga will win?"

"Maybe, they are playing very well at the moment." Jack paused for a moment. "You and Bret and the children should come out here for a few days, we could all get together."

What a good idea, I will speak to Bret first and then call you."

"Sis, you are now going to have to excuse me, it is the opening night of my DJ show at the Med Club and I have a lot to do."

"Jack, you have a great night, I completely forgot it was your opening gig tonight. I love you darling, you take care."

"I love you too Lilly."

Every time Jack came off the phone to his sister he always had the same feeling. Complete loneliness. He missed her immensely, Lilly reminded him so much of their mother, the resemblance to each other and the way they spoke was uncanny. At times like now, he wanted to give his mother a hug and look into her eyes and know that she loved him. Fortunately this feeling of loneliness always disappeared.

16

At six forty five with his Apple laptop case hanging from his left shoulder and a medium sized dark blue sports bag, which contained his stage clothes in his right hand, Jack left his apartment and headed out of the Marbella Beach Apartments. There was no one on duty on reception and the foyer electric doors were wide open, which was most unusual in the evening. After a brisk walk down the Esplanade Paseo in the direction of the Med Club, Jack called in at the Picasso Café Bar for a bite to eat. The elderly owners immediately recognised him from the afternoon. The husband who was also the chef came over to him.

"What has happened to that beautiful young lady you were with earlier?"

"Unfortunately, I am working at the Med Club this evening. My friend Olga is meeting a girlfriend in Marbella for a meal and a few drinks, and then they are coming along to the club to watch me."

"You are a singer?"

"No a DJ, I appear under the name of DJ Ramos."

A smile came across the old man's weathered face. "Your posters are everywhere, see we have one on the door. "What do I call you my friend?"

"My name is Jack and the young lady I was with is Olga, and you are?"

"I am Alberto." He then beckoned to his wife who was behind the bar. She immediately came over to them. "Jack, this lovely lady is my wife Gabriela. We have owned this bar for almost fifty years. We intend to retire in two years, we will both be seventy five then so we think it is long enough to work."

"Will your children be taking over the business?" "Unfortunately the good Lord did not bless my wife and I with children, we will have to sell the Picasso Café Bar. Perhaps you and Olga will buy it?"

Jack smiled. "You never know."

Gabriela then turned to Jack as her husband returned to the kitchen. "What can I get you to eat?"

"A ham and tomato omelette with a sprinkling of Andalusian white cheese on top and a latte coffee."

"No alcohol tonight?"

"When I am working I am teetotal, I need a clear head."

"Thank you Jack, your food will be with you in fifteen minutes, I will bring you your coffee." Gabriela then leaned forward. "Neither of us wants to leave this bar but time has eventually caught up with us, if someone made us a reasonable offer now, we would probably sell. We want to enjoy our remaining years together; we have a lovely villa along the coast near Fuengirola. She then went back behind the bar. By the time Jack had finished his meal which as usual was excellent the Picasso Café Bar was very busy. Just after eight thirty he left the bar and made his way down the Esplanade to the Med Club. It was now completely dark apart from the street lights, there was no refreshing wind blowing in from the Mediterranean, it was very still and extremely warm. He hoped the air conditioning was switched on at the Med Club but he doubted it, all the management had to do was to open the large glass doors at the far end of the night club and the cool air would circulate in the room. That was the theory, but in practice it was of little use as the night club was a large room holding well over six hundred punters when full. He would have to make do with the cold air fan by the DJ Stand otherwise it was going to be a very warm night. Using his VIP security pass, he entered the premises by the staff entrance, and made his way to the night club which was already busy and it was only five to nine. Behind the tinted glass divider he could see the owner Pedro Gonzales and his wife Nada dining with some guests in the restaurant. He needed to speak to Pedro, but that would have to wait until later in the evening. As he made his way to the DJ Stand several members of staff spoke to him including assistant manager Kelly.

"We will be all routing for you tonight Jack, the boss is expecting a full house."

"Fantastic, that is just what we want. Can you give me any advice?"

Kelly laughed. "Jack; you are the DJ, I really have not got a clue apart." She then hesitated; there was a look of embarrassment on her attractive face.

"Go on. What were you going to say?"

"Keep the music loud and play mainly dance House Music; there will be hundreds of young punters in the Med Club tonight who will want to dance nonstop."

Jack smiled. "Is there anything else?"

"Yes, make sure you always close your show with the Ibiza dance classic Titanium by French DJ David Guetta, it will bring the house down."

Jack burst out laughing. "We think alike, I was actually going to do that."

Kelly now looked more embarrassed than ever.

Jack then placed his hand on her shoulder and kissed her on the side of her face. "Sorry to embarrass you, it was not intentional, but I had to talk to someone about my opening gig and you originally come from the UK."

"I forgive you." Kelly then put her left hand to the small receiver in her ear. "Will you please excuse me? I am needed at the main entrance I will see you later Jack."

Resident brother and sister DJ's Selena and Jose were already in action. Many punters who had dined early were drifting into the room, by the time he hit the twin decks and audio mixer on the DJ Stand at eleven the club would be heaving. As usual both Selena and Jose greeted him most warmly.

"Jack, with it being your first night, Selena and I will support you in the box with the sound system."

"Thank you Jose, I do appreciate your offer."

Once Jack had ran through his programme of music with Jose and linked up his laptop to the audio mixer and the decks, he was more or less set up.

"I have brought a change of clothes; do you have a dressing room?"

Selena pointed to a door close to the stand. "That is the artiste's changing room. I have the key, for security reasons we always keep the door locked."

"Before I forget Jack, Mr Gonzales would like to see you in his office he has just called me on the house phone." "Selena, if you will escort me to the artiste's changing room I will hang up my clothes and then go and visit the boss in his office."

Ten minutes later Jack pressed the intercom button on the boss's office door which said General Manager.

"Come in Jack." Pedro was stood by the large picture window looking out over the complex. "Good to see you my friend." The two men greeted each other warmly. "I love this time of the year, it is so romantic, the nights are drawing in but it is still warm. Just look at that view it really is stunning with all the lights on. I remember as a child in Buenos Aires Argentina, the Christmas lights use to look like that."

"You have an incredible club Pedro, you and your wife must be very proud of what you have achieved?"

"We are Jack, extremely proud." He then walked over to the red and black soft leather chairs. "Take a seat Jack we need to talk I won't keep you long, I know you need to prepare for your show. It is going to be heaving tonight, every ticket has been sold." Jack smiled. "When you first arrived in Marbella, we talked about a Tuesday and Thursday residency for you. After Miles Coburn called me yesterday, that has all changed. Tuesday will be your big night here. Thursday was only an afterthought. Miles confirmed to me what you told me, about having tracked down all the wanted Chechen. I gather Sergei Aslanov has not turned up yet."

"No, he has not but Aslan Maskhadov did tell me there had been a delay in his return, he now expects him back by mid-week."

"Miles is convinced there is another reason concerning your friend Olga and her identical twin sister Tanya. He told me that they are both assassins working for the Russian FSB. Miles believes it is quite possible someone has tipped Sergei off and told him to keep away from Marbella."

"Miles's theory may well be right but is there any proof?"

"Miles wants you to contact Aslan and take up his offer as a gemmologist but only on a part-time basis. That is the real reason I have not given you a Thursday residency, If Aslan takes you on, he may want you to do some business trips for him."

"Do you believe he is involved in the Russian diamond hijack?"

Pedro laughed. "No way, he loves his life in Spain too much to risk deportation to Russia and certain death. He is an astute businessman. It is quite possible that he has already bought a quantity of cheap diamonds and gems from someone."

"Have you any ideas?"

"It could be that Russian Boris who runs Pinks in Puerto Banus. Once Cobra Jewellery has taken you on, it will be up to you to find out whom, but you are going to have to be quick."

Jack looked at Pedro. "What is the urgency?"

"We know Olga is in Marbella and if her sister is here as well, there can be only one reason. Miles believes that Major Pavlov of the FSB could give the go ahead for the assassination of the Chechens at anytime. The last thing the British Government wants is Marbella to be turned into a killing field. The media and press would crucify the UK Government for working with the Russians if the story was ever leaked out."

"What is your view about the situation?"

Pedro hesitated for a moment before speaking. "Obviously the UK, who are big players in the world diamond market do not want the market to crash. It is in their interest to get this problem sorted out quickly and recover the diamonds. I honestly believe the Russians are using us at MI6 to find the hijackers, they will then send in assassins to eliminate them. It is more than likely, Sergei Aslanov and a few top Russian Mafia bosses are the only people who know where the diamonds are. We have to find Sergei and try to persuade him to come over to our side before he too is eliminated. Miles Coburn also tells me that the Russian Police and Special Forces are making raids all over Moscow, which have resulted in many shootouts and deaths."

"You give me the impression that the Russians have only one objective, if they are unable to recover the diamonds they will assassinate all the hijackers."

Pedro nodded his head. "MI6 have now come to the same conclusion."

Jack glanced at his watch. "Ten fifteen, if you will excuse me I need to return to the Night Club, I am on stage at eleven."

"I won't keep you any longer, we will speak later."

The night club was full to capacity; this was certainly going to be an opening night to remember. By sheer luck he managed to slip into the artiste's changing room undetected. After changing into his black and gold stage gear, Jack took a bottle of cool spring water from the small fridge in the room and drank half the contents, before sitting down on one of the soft black leather chairs. It was now ten forty-five, the door leading to the night club suddenly opened.

"Hi Jack, fifteen minutes to go before DJ Ramos hits the big time on the Costa del Sol." Jack smiled at Jose. "I will introduce you as London's top House Music DJ, and the soundof the opening music will become louder as you hit the DJ Stand. Then you will take over. Selena and I will be close by if you need any assistance with the audio decks."

"Fantastic. One final point, when you present me to the punters would you introduce me in both Spanish and English. I speak fluent Spanish so my show will be in both languages."

"I had no idea Jack that you spoke Spanish, Pedro never mentioned it."

"It probably slipped his mind. I am a man of mystery as I am sure you will discover."

Jose laughed as he went back into the night club, the sound of music was deafening as he opened the door. To say Jack was not nervous would have been a lie, as it was almost eight months since his last major gig, but he had confidence in his ability. The time on his wrist watch was creeping towards eleven when Selena entered the room.

"Are you ready Jack?" He smiled and nodded his head; she then kissed him on the right side of his face. "Best of luck, remember if you need any help with the gear just ask us."

"I certainly will thank you again."

As they spoke the disco music dropped down a few decimals and the house lights dimmed as Jose started to introduce DJ Ramos both in Spanish and English. Jack's opening number Right Here Right Now, by Norman Cook better known as Fat Boy Slim hit the audio decks, at the same time the two giant video screens in the club came to life and the lighting system went into overdrive. DJ Ramos then bounded up to the DJ Stand with incredible energy. His music and patter in both Spanish and English had the punters spellbound. Everybody who was anybody in Marbella had come to watch him. Aslan Maskhadov and his friend George were stood next to Roscoe Rodriguez and his attractive wife

Sofia. Their daughter Valentina along with a number of her college friends, were having the time of their lives dancing to the hypnotic sound of the music. Leroy Cardoso and his beautiful daughter Celma were by the bar talking to Pedro Gonzales and his wife Nada, and several other well healed punters including Costa Security boss Roberto Sanchez. Later in the evening from where he was standing, he could see Valentina and a couple of her girlfriends making their way towards him. She saw him look and waved. Leaving the music in the hands of DJ's Jose and Selena, he turned to Valentina who was stood almost behind him.

"Jack, I would like you to meet my best friends, we think you and your music are fantastic."

"Thank you girls I appreciate your comments." He then kissed them all in turn. "If you have any requests please let me know."

"Jack; we need you up here." Jose and Selena were trying to attract his attention.

"Excuse me girls I must get back to my music, I will see you later. Valentina it has been lovely to meet your friends." Jack always knew what to say to a girl to make her happy, Valentina was no exception.

Perspiration was now running from his sunburned face. The room felt like a furnace with over six hundred punters inside, even with all the doors open and the cool air fan swishing away behind him, the heat was getting to him. Taking a bottle of spring water out of a cool bag, which was on the floor, he immediately downed the contents. As the cool refreshing liquid ran down the back of his throat Jack could feel his body slowly start to recover. He was on the verge of dehydration and it had never occurred to him, he had been so carried away with the music.

It was now twelve fifteen and well over halfway through the show, the atmosphere in the room was electrifying. One person Jack had not seen in the audience was Olga and her girlfriend Emma from Pinks. Maybe they had changed their mind and gone to the Ocean Club at Puerto Banus.

DJ Selena touched his right shoulder. "There is a lovely young lady wanting to speak to you. Can you spare her a minute?"

Jack glanced behind him and laughed. "For that lady I most certainly can." Jumping down from the DJ Stand Jack walked over to the girl and kissed her on the side of her face. His hands held her bare shoulders, she felt very warm and he loved the Gucci perfume she wore.

"Jack, this is my gorgeous girlfriend Emma."

Like Olga, she was stunning with an incredible figure which she amply showed off in the short strapless black dress she wore. Olga's hair was dark but Emma's was silky blonde. Jack kissed her; she too was wearing Gucci perfume.

"Darling your music is incredible. You are a natural DJ and entertainer."

"Thank you. I thought you were not coming to see me tonight."

"We would never miss your show, Emma and I have been at the far end of the bar talking to our sleaze bag of a boss Boris from Pinks."

"Where is he now?"

"He has returned to Pinks. Boris is not a fan of your music but he thinks you are one hell of a DJ." Jack smiled.

"What about you Emma, do you like House Music?"

"Absolutely, I love your music Jack."

Her accent was very good but Emma was certainly no English girl. This stunning looking girl was Tanya, Olga's twin sister. The photograph which Miles Coburn had recently emailed had left him in no doubt. Also when you observed her closely, apart from the two girls having different coloured her there was certainly an uncanny resemblance.

"Girls, you are going to have to excuse me, I need to get back to the decks." As he spoke he leaned over and kissed both the girls.

Olga whispered in his ear. "Darling, I will be back in my apartment at one tomorrow, I will call round and see you."

"I shall look forward to seeing you." He then kissed her again. Take care if you are heading to the Ocean Club, two beautiful girls alone can be tempting to guys on the prowl for sex."

"We will darling, don't worry Emma and I can look after ourselves"

As the clock crept towards one in the morning, the show was gradually drawing to a close, but surprisingly punters were still rolling in to catch the end of DJ Ramos's spectacular gig. Both the resident DJs Jose and Selena were frequently on the mic reminding the punters that Tuesday night was DJ Ramos's night. "Guys and girls if you don't want to be disappointed get your tickets early for next week's gig. Remember DJ Ramos will hit his decks at eleven. Jack then took over the mic again and thanked the punters for an incredible night. Now it was time to finish the night on a high with David Guetta's Titanium. Assistant manager Kelly was right, the track widely accepted as the disco anthem for the holiday island of Ibiza, raised the roof.

Back in the artiste's changing room Jack sank into one of the soft black leather chairs, he felt exhausted. The sound of the ecstatic audience was still ringing in his ears, there was a gentle knock on the door and Selena walked in.

"Great show DJ Ramos I am most impressed." Jack laughed and then took a long drink of spring water from the bottle Selena had passed him. She also passed him his laptop.

"When you have recovered Pedro would like to see you. He is at the end of the main bar with his wife and a couple of friends who would like to meet you."

"Thank you Selena I will be with them in five minutes."

"I will let him know." She then left the room.

Jack closed his eyes for a few moments; he was pleased there was no Thursday gig at the Med Club, tonight's show had taken more out of him than he imagined. In any case he was not in Marbella for a holiday he was now on the payroll of MI6. The sooner he got a part-time job as a gemmologist with Cobra Jewellery, which would allow him to come into contact with Sergei Aslanov, the better. It was only a matter of time before the Russian girls were told by their masters to assassinate the Chechens.

DJ's Selena and Jose were blasting out the latest European chart hits, as he made his way to greet Pedro and his friends.

"An incredible opening night my friend we have never had so many VIP's, club and restaurant owners here on one night."

"I thought you were fantastic Jack, I love your music."

Jack smiled. "Thank you Nada, I appreciate all comments good or bad."

"Jack, there are a couple of friends who want to meet you; I believe you know one of them, they are in the Neptune Bar. We will take you through."

As soon as they walked into the small side bar Jack recognised them instantly. Boy George was with his friend George Michael. Both the stars greeted him most warmly. "Both George and I think you are one hell of DJ and we love your music." Coming from George Michael, who was a known perfectionist, this was a complement.

After Pedro and his wife returned to the main room, Jack sat down talking over a bottle of red wine with the two Georges for the next hour.

"Do you write your own music and songs Jack?" He looked at Boy George and shook his head. "We are going to write you one, a real epic. We will both be on the vocal track but you will make the music."

"I like what I am hearing."

"When you return to London we will get together, go into the studio and record the number." The three of them then exchanged their mobile numbers.

Shortly before three Jack called a taxi. After dropping George Michael off at the 5-star Nobu Hotel Marbella and Jack at the Marbella Beach Apartments, Boy George headed to his own apartment in Puerto Banus.

It was few minutes after five on Thursday evening, when Jack's brother Lex called him and gave him the details for the Spanish La Liga Premier League football match between Malaga and Real Madrid.

"I am sorry Maria and I could not get to the Med Club on Tuesday for your opening night. Being a football manager frequently gets in the way of family functions. At the first opportunity we will come to one of your gigs."

"No problem Lex don't worry about it."

"Did your opening gig go well?"

"Brilliantly, far better than I had expected and the night was a sell-out."

"You got a great revue in the press." Jack laughed.

"The match kicks off at mid-day, if you arrive at the player's and staff entrance no later than eleven, you will be escorted to your seat in the VIP area. After the match you will be taken downstairs to the player's lounge. I will meet you there and introduce you to a few of the stars. Did you hire a car?"

"Yes, a blue three series BMW which I have hired it for a few days; I intend to have a look around the Costa del Sol." "When you arrive at the stadium you will notice that there are several car parks. Head for the VIP car park on the left hand side of the main entrance, I will arrange a pass for you."

"Do you think you will win?"

"I hope so, we are playing very well at the moment but Real Madrid are a very hard team to beat, I would be happy with a draw."

After a brief conversation about Lex's family and their sister Lilly, they parted company.

When Jack left Marbella for Malaga the weather conditions were perfect, warm with no wind, surprisingly the motorway was quiet and he arrived at the La Rosaleda Stadium by ten forty-five. There was no problem finding the VIP car park, by eleven fifteen he was in the VIP lounge having a complimentary drink of Spanish champagne. After leaving the lounge Jack went outside and relaxed in a soft red leather chair overlooking the 30,000 seated stadium, by eleven- forty the stadium was virtually full. The noise and the razzmatazz from both sections of supporters was a spectacle to be seen and heard.

The match certainly lived up to the pre-match hype. Malaga's magnificent defence hung out, until Real's global superstar Cristiano Ronaldo scored in the forty- forth minute with a stunning header from a corner kick. As an attacking football team Real were far superior to Malaga, but the home team had a great defence. Real Madrid attacked continually, then in the eighty-ninth minute they were caught out by the counter attack with a long ball to their star forward Sergio Sanchez, who ran halfway down the pitch and chipped the ball over the head of Real's Spanish International goalkeeper Iker Casillas. Real's manager-coach the self-proclaimed special one Jose Mourinho was livid with the draw, but then again that was football. The Malaga supporters were ecstatic with the result which still left them at the top of the table.

Shortly after the match was over Jack's brother Lex called him on his mobile to invite him to the players'

Lounge; Lex introduced his brother to the players and told them that he worked as DJ Ramos at the Med Club in Marbella. It appeared that several of the Malaga team had attended the opening night and remarked how impressed they were with Jack's performance.

Jack enjoyed his day out at Malaga's La Rosaleda Stadium and meeting the players afterwards including Real Madrid's manager Jose Mourinho and Cristiano Ronaldo, a player who he had always admired.

Whether Malaga FC could win the La Liga was doubtful but for his brother's sake he hoped their brilliant start to the season continued.

For the next three days he spent time in his hire car. After visiting the southern seaside resort of Estepona with its palm lined promenade and magnificent beach, he and Olga drove inland from Marbella into Andalusia's Sierra Blanca Mountain Range. The spectacular scenery and the picture postcard whitewash villages they visited were stunning. On their way back, Jack pulled the BMW into a secluded parking area from which you could see the Mediterranean Sea in the distance some twenty miles away. The view was incredible.

"Darling, do you realize with have not had sex since last Friday?" Jack looked at her and smiled.

"Why don't you make love to me now, there is no one around?" Without another word she slipped off her clothes and stood naked in front of him. "Come on darling you are not shy are you?"

Jack did not need any further encouragement. Before slipping off his dark shades, he ran his eyes over Olga's sumptuous body allowing his mind to run away with his desires. For the next hour they had sex. For Jack, this was a first for him outside in the open and he felt a little nervous. Olga on the other hand appeared to revel in the situation; he had never seen her get so sexually excited.

The days were flying by; it was just over two weeks since Jack had arrived in Marbella. His relationship with Olga had not changed, sex every day apart from the weekends when she worked at Pinks in Puerto Banus and stayed over at her friend Emma's apartment. He had still not made contact with Sergei Aslanov and there was no sign of him in Marbella. He had either returned and was keeping a low profile or was still out of the country. Maybe one of his contacts had tipped him off about the Russian girls and a possible assassination attempt. Jack had to make contact with Aslan Maskhadov of the Cobra Jewellery chain, and take him up on his offer as a gemmologist with his company. The problem was making contact with him, when he telephoned Aslan's office, the girl on reception said he was away for a few days, but she would let him know when he returned, that he had called. Jack was getting impatient; Miles Coburn had called him several times about the whereabouts of Sergei Aslanov, MI6 urgently needed to make contact with him.

"Jack, you are the guy out there so get that job with Cobra Jewellery and talk to Sergei before the Spanish police find him dead with a bullet in his head or his throat cut. Getting this job at Cobra Jewellery is a priority, not fucking around with Olga or as a House Music DJ at the Med Club."

Someone at the top was putting pressure on Miles normally he was far more friendly and relaxed.

"Miles take it easy; I will call you in a couple of days."

"Sorry Jack I'm just pissed off today."

It was now early October and the weather was changing. Though still very warm in the daytime, it was now dark by seven and the temperature often dropped by fifteen degrees, but he still took his daily swim in the complex pool to keep fit. Olga frequently joined him but she never once took a dip, she would lie there in her skimpy white bikini on one of the poolside sun beds, revelling in the warm sunshine toping up her already glorious tan.

"Darling, where are you taking me this evening for our evening meal?"

Jack had no hesitation. "The Albatross the food is excellent." He also knew that there was a fairly good chance that Aslan Maskhadov and his friend George would be dinning there.

"Darling, what time should I be ready for?"

"Is eight ok with you?"

"Absolutely fine, at least we will have time for another session before we leave."

Jack laughed but did not speak. "Darling, don't tell me you are tired and can't cope with me."

Olga was now sat up on the sun bed. Jack stood up in front of her and then gently lifted her up in his arms before kissing her passionately; he could feel himself getting aroused as he looked down at her large soft breasts. "Let's go back to your room."

"Darling, I knew you could not resist me," she replied laughing and fluttering her long eyelashes.

The Albatross as usual was extremely busy when they arrived but due to a sudden drop in the evening temperature everyone had moved inside. Thankfully Jack had taken the insight to reserve a table. As they waited for a table waiter to escort them to their table the owner Roscoe Rodriguez came up to them.

"Good to see you both, he then embraced both Jack and Olga. Jack your show was brilliant on Tuesday evening, just my kind of music."

"Thank you."

"The gentleman over there would like you and Olga to join his table."

Jack turned round. The man and his young companion raised their hands. There was no mistaking Aslan Maskhadov and George. Jack acknowledged them both with a gesture and smile.

"Come and join us Jack, we have not eaten yet." Aslan and George stood up and greeted Olga and Jack most warmly. After sitting down Aslan poured each of them a glass of red wine. He then raised a half full glass of wine. "Good health to both of you."

"Thank you Aslan, the same to you and George."

Olga then turned to George. "I am extremely sorry I was so rude to you when we last met, there was no excuse. The war between our two countries was not our fault. We were both very young then, please forgive me you are an extremely charming man." She then leaned over and kissed him on the side of his face.

Though George appeared slightly embarrassed, he managed to raise a broad smile, to his relief the table waiter arrived just in time.

"Have you two guys ordered?"

"Yes about ten minutes ago."

Olga ran her eyes over the menu. "I would like Sea Bass and mixed vegetables."

The waiter then turned to Jack. "The same for me please and another bottle of red wine." Olga smiled.

Aslan then turned to Jack. "I am sorry that I did not return your call, George and I went away for a few days break. What can I do for you my friend?"

"Your offer of a job, I would like to take you up on it." "Excellent, give me a call on Monday around mid-day and we will sort out the days you can work over lunch." Aslan then slipped his hand inside his light blue jacket and passed Jack a white business card. That is my private line and mobile number.

"I may need a full time gemmologist, the guy who works for me at the present has still not returned to Spain from the Middle East."

Whether this was true Jack had not got a clue. It was highly possible that Sergei had already returned and was in hiding at Aslan's secluded villa. With a little bit of luck, if he joined Cobra Jewellery, he would soon find out.

Shortly before one, Olga and Jack left the Albatross and slowly made their way along the Esplanade Paseo to the Marbella Beach Apartments. The young Tunisian guy Youssef Beji was on reception duty.

"Good to see you again Youssef, I will speak to you tomorrow if you are still on duty." Youssef nodded his head.

"Good to see you again Jack." Youssef smiled and winked at him, there was no more to be said.

Taking the elevator to the third floor, they then walked down the light grey tiled corridor to Olga's apartment. As they stood talking, Jack slipped his arm around her slender waist and pulled her close to him before kissing her passionately. Olga looked up at him, her eyes full of excitement. She then tenderly touched the side of his face. "Come and sleep with me tonight."

17

Cobra Jewellery boss Aslan Maskhadov answered his mobile immediately, when Jack called at mid-day on Monday.

"Where are you Jack?"

"Relaxing in the garden at the Marbella Beach Apartments,"

"I will pick you up in twenty minutes then we can discuss my job offer over a bite to eat. I will be in my red and black BMW Mini Cooper."

Jack glanced at his watch and smiled it was twelve twenty. Aslan was certainly a man of his word when it came to business.

"Jump in Jack, I know a small bar ten minutes away who make delicious food."

"What has happened to your Bentley?"

"I never use it in the daytime, unless I have a long journey planned. It is too conspicuous and hard to park in Marbella."

The traffic was heavy but eventually they arrived at Jan's Café Bar.

"My business Head Quarters and workshop is five minutes away from the next roundabout on the left."

The café bar which held no more than forty people when full was busy. The buxom blonde behind the bar waved to Aslan as they walked in and pointed out a vacant table for two, at the back of the room. Aslan smiled and waved back and then blew her a kiss. A few minutes later the blonde woman, who Aslan said was called Jan, came over to them. They greeted each other extremely warmly as Aslan kissed both sides of her face.

"Jan, I would like you to meet my good friend Jack who comes from England. He is also known as DJ Ramos and has a House Music show at the Med Club every Tuesday night."

Jan's eyes came to life. "I have heard all about you from the girls who work here, they said you were fantastic." Jack smiled. "Thank you Jan, it is lovely to hear such a compliment." Jan smiled, she had beautiful white teeth.

Jan was a lovely looking woman. Long blonde hair tied back in a ponytail, about five three in height, medium build with large breasts, he judged her age to be about forty five. She was Spanish but spoke English perfectly.

"Now guys what would you like to eat?"

Aslan looked at Jack. "I am not a big eater at lunch time, so a roast ham sandwich with Spanish mustard would be fine and a pot of tea."

"Aslan, what can we get you?"

"I will have the same Jan."

"Thank you guys, your food will be with you in about fifteen minutes."

"I thought George would have been with you."

"Aslan laughed. "George may be my close friend but he has to make a living. In the daytime, he and my chauffeur Freddie are working their butts off designing unique pieces of jewellery for my company. They are both very talented designers." Aslan then changed the subject. "I gather from our brief conversation at the Albatross that you would like to join my company as a gemmologist?"

"I would love to and have heard great reports about your Cobra Jewellery Company. My boss at the Med Club, Pedro Gonzales, has now worked out my work schedule. I will only be resident at the club on a Tuesday evening and when the summer season finishes, I will move to a Thursday evening. If it is acceptable by you, I will be available all week apart from Wednesday morning, when I shall need to recover from my Tuesday night gig. I shall also need to finish work early prior to my gig to prepare."

Aslan was just about to say something when one of the young waitresses appeared at the table with their order.

After she left Aslan continued. "So you will be available at the weekends."

"Most certainly, if you require me to visit any of your clients at the weekend I shall be available."

"Excellent, the job is yours on a part-time basis, but there is a possibility that it could become full time in the near future. As I said before, our current gemmologist Sergei is considering returning home to Georgia for family reasons. When he arrives back in Marbella in the next few days, he will have made a decision about his future." Aslan then took a bite of his sandwich. "Delicious, as soon as we leave here I will take you to our head office and let you look at the set up. You will be impressed. We can sort out a financial package for you once we get there."

Aslan was right, the food was excellent and the Lipton's tea was perfect, just as good as any cuppa he had drank in the UK.

Fifty minutes later after Aslan settled the bill, they left Jan's Café Bar and drove to the Cobra Jewellery Head Quarters. A modern glass fronted building set back a few hundred metres from the main roundabout, off the coastal motorway. The building, which had a workshop at the rear, overlooked an immaculately maintained garden and a small car park. The workshop was partly screened on either side by small palm trees and shrubs. Jack was most impressed with the set up. Aslan's office was equipped with a contemporary black wood and glass stainless steel desk, a silver laptop and two computers, as well as two matching filing cabinets and four cream soft leather chairs, not forgetting the two telephones on his desk, one white the other dark green. The walls were painted white and the floor covered in light grey tiles. From inside the office, Aslan could observe the interior of the building including the workshop and reception on two large monitor screens, which were positioned on the wall opposite his desk. Jack also noticed that the outside of the building was covered by CCTV cameras and that the Hi-Tec security system was also linked up to the same monitors. Frankly it was virtually impossible to gain entrance to the building or exit, without having to pass through the security scanner.

Jack was more than happy with the financial package which Aslan offered him. In return he was to use his expertise as a gemmologist, in grading diamonds and other precious gems bought by the Cobra Jewellery Company. He would also be expected to sell the company's exclusively designed jewellery to clients in Spain and other European countries, a job which he had already done for Franks of Hatton Garden, London with considerable success.

Aslan turned to Jack with his right hand outstretched. "Welcome to Cobra Jewellery."

"When would you like me to start?"

"This Thursday, sooner the better and then I can introduce you to everyone. With a bit of luck my gemmologist Sergei will have returned to Marbella, you two will need to get together."

"Aslan, I hope there will be no ill feeling with Sergei, I would not like him to think that I was pushing him out."

Aslan laughed. "No way, take it from me Sergei is an easy going guy. In any case as I said before, there is a distinct possibility that he may be leaving Cobra Jewellery and returning to Georgia. Now if you will excuse me Jack, I have an appointment at five thirty with my manager at our new store in Nerja. I need to get a move on or I will be late. I will see you on Thursday morning at nine. I will get one of the staff to run you back to your apartment." "Thank you."

Thirty minutes later Jack was in the garden of the Marbella Beach Apartments. He could see Olga in her skimpy white bikini, lying on one of the sun loungers by the swimming pool. Quickly going upstairs to his apartment he changed into his bathing shorts. Picking up a pink bath towel, which was on the back of a kitchen chair drying, he made his way down stairs again to the swimming pool. Olga was still sun bathing. Kneeling down quietly, he gently kissed her warm stomach twice and then her lips.

Taking off her dark shades she smiled and then kissed him. "I fell asleep waiting for you, it is lovely and warm out here."

"I had a business meeting with Aslan Maskhadov, if you recall I arranged it with him when we met at the Albatross the other evening. I have decided to take a part-time job as a gemmologist with his company. With the Med Club only using me one night a week I need the money."

"I remember you talking to Aslan. You poor darling, you are now going to have to work for a living." Jack laughed. "How are you going to fit in having sex with me, perhaps I should look around for another lover?" Jack gave her a dirty look. "I am only jesting darling."

Without another word Jack kicked off his flip flops and slipped into the pool. The water was far warmer than when he normally took a dip in midmorning. After twenty lengths he got out, dried himself off with his pink towel and then sat down beside Olga, who was relaxing in the warmth of the late afternoon sun. Half an hour later they both left the pool area and went up to Olga's apartment.Jack's first day at Cobra Jewellery was most interesting, there were eight Spanish staff, five men and three women, five of which were professional gem cutters. They were making very attractive costume jewellery in the workshop, which had been designed by Chechens George and Freddie. Compared with the jewellery he used to sell for Franks of Hatton Garden, London, the quality was very poor. Low grade diamonds and gems were being used. If the finished articles were inspected under a magnifying glass, any reputable gemmologist would soon see the imperfections. Even so Cobra Jewellery was building up a good customer base across Europe and the Middle East. The price was right and Jack had to admit that most of the jewellery did look very impressive. He could understand stores in Europe, who sold cheap jewellery, buying from Cobra Jewellery but not those in the Middle East, where they wanted high quality merchandise only. Sergei Aslanov must have had other reasons for visiting Egypt and the Gulf States. Jack also noticed that none of the cheap costume jewellery was sold in any of the Cobra Jewellery shops on the Costa del Sol. Owner Aslan Maskhadov bought most of his jewellery from reputable dealers in Amsterdam and London, with Franks of Hatton Garden being his main supplier. Over the next few days at Aslan's suggestion, Jack spent time visiting all the Cobra Jewellery Stores on the Costa del Sol using the company's red Audi A4. Being new to the company, Aslan wanted the managers and staff to get to know him.

There was also another reason. "Jack, whilst you are in the stores would you check the quality of the diamond rings and bracelets we have for sale? Several of my managers have heard customers say they are overpriced."

"No problem, but I thought that was Sergei's responsibility?"

"It is, but now we have two gemmologists working for the company I just want a second opinion, we can all make mistakes."

When deliveries of precious gems were made to the Head Office from European suppliers, it was now Jack's job to grade them. He also noticed that Cobra bought substantial quantities of cheap low grade uncut diamonds and other gems from De Beers in Johannesburg, South Africa, which were used in the making of their own costume jewellery. Aslan was very open and answered any questions he asked without hesitation.

Jack never failed to call his sister Lilly in Ludlow twice a week; she was always in his thoughts. He was delighted to hear, that her health had improved considerably since her husband Bret had decided to cut back to a four day week in his Investment Company in Kidderminster, where he was a partner. Brother Lex was always a busy man and in frequent demand by the media as manager of high flying football club Malaga FC. There was hardly a day, when he did not see Lex being interviewed on television or a report in the newspaper about him. He was a great sporting celebrity in Spain, where people remembered him as an outstanding footballer and now as a successful manager at unfashionable Malaga FC, who were flying high at the top of La Liga. At the moment it was difficult for them to meet but they did speak several times a week. Olga on the other hand was not a happy girl, especially when he told her he would be away on a business trip to Madrid for a couple of days.

"Darling, it is bad enough you working in the daytime but being away for a few days is playing havoc with my sex life. How am I going to manage without you?"

Jack took her in his arms and kissed her soft lips. "We still have sex every day, when I return I will make it up to you."

"You can start now by making love to me before we go out for a meal."

Later in the week on the morning Jack left for Malaga to catch the Madrid bound train, Aslan asked him to call in at the Cobra Jewellery headquarters as he wanted to speak to him about his business trip and run through a few details.

"Freddie will drive you to Malaga Railway Station for the eleven thirty train and pick you up there when you return on Friday evening. There is little point in leaving the company car parked overnight on the long stay car park."

Aslan glanced at his gold Rolex Oyster watch as he spoke; it was a few minutes past nine. My secretary Martina has booked you a return rail ticket and overnight accommodation at the Double Tree Hilton Hotel in the city centre. It is very close to the railway station. I have arranged for you to meet our client Marc Fernandez at his office in the city at ten on Friday morning. Marc has a chain of twenty Fernandez Jewellery Stores, which sell large quantities of attractive costume jewellery. He has become an important customer and would like to see our new designs. Take him out for lunch, let him choose the restaurant but you pay the bill. By the way, your train leaves Madrid at five for your return journey to Malaga." Aslan then passed Jack a sheet of white paper. "That is Marc's office address in the city, it is only ten minutes by taxi from the Hilton. One final point, don't lose your black leather sample case, it contains jewellery worth over seventy thousand Euro, then opened the case to show Jack. The samples which were neatly set out looked quite impressive. Afterwards he picked up the white internal telephone. "Freddie, Jack is ready to leave for Malaga we will meet you in the car park."

As the two men walked towards the office door Jack turned to Aslan.

"Have you heard from Sergei?"

"No, not a word, I am becoming very concerned, he is ten days overdue and his mobile appears to be switched off. Maybe I will hear from him by the weekend."

"Is it possible for some reason he has returned to Georgia?"

"I doubt it. I owe him several thousand Euros in commission. Knowing Sergei, he would want to sort everything out before he returned home. No, there must be another reason."

Freddie was in the corridor waiting.

"Have a good trip Jack, if you need to speak to me, call my mobile."

The two men shook hands, Jack then followed Freddie into the car park and got into the red Audi A4. In just over an hour Jack had got out of the car and was making his way to platform one to catch the superfast train to Madrid, a journey of 363 miles, which normally took just under three hours.

Jack had visited Madrid on many occasions to see clients when he worked for Franks of London. The city still had the same excitement. Madrid, Spain's Central Capital was a large city with a population of almost three and a half million inhabitants, which made it the country's most populous city. With elegant boulevards and numerous manicured parks such as the Buen Retiro, the city was breathtaking when the evening lights were switched on. It was also a city of great culture and was renowned for its rich repositories of European Art in the Prado Museum, where paintings by such masters as Goya, Velazquez, Picasso, Dali and Zurbaran were on display. If you wanted to eat fine cuisine then there was no better place than in the heart of old Hapsburg

Madrid in the portico lined Plaza Major, here you could fine great restaurants of all nationalities.

After leaving Madrid's majestic Atacha Railway Station, Jack decided to walk to the boutique styled Double Tree Hilton Hotel five minutes away. It was still very mild and dry but not as warm as Marbella, which was further south on the Mediterranean. Once he had checked into his very modern bedroom, which was on the second floor, he took his mobile phone out of his left jacket pocket and put a call through to Miles Coburn in London.

Coburn immediately answered. "Jack, where the hell have you been, we agreed that you would call me every three or four days?"

"Sorry boss." Jack then told Miles about landing his job at Cobra Jewellery. "As far as I am concerned Aslan Maskhadov is as clean as a whistle. I have done a great deal of snooping around since I joined him. It is quite possible, that he has already handled some of the hijacked diamonds and gems in the past but not now. Most of his cheap uncut diamonds and gems come from De Beers in South Africa and everything is legit. He even buys gems from Franks in London."

"Where are you now Jack?"

"I have just arrived in Madrid to sell a new range of jewellery to one of Cobra's main clients, I shall be back in Marbella late on Friday evening. By the way, have you any more information about the Russian twins Olga and Tanya?"

"No, I have not heard a word."

"Have you heard anything from FSB boss Major Ivan Pavlov?"

"Nothing not a whisper, not even an email asking us to update him on the situation in Marbella. I am concerned that sooner or later he will activate the girls. Then the killing will start. You have done well Jack, so keep the good work up. Have you spoken to Pedro Gonzales?"

"Yes, I have put him in the picture."

"Good. Don't forget to call me every three or four days, even if you have nothing to report."

"I will." Their conversation then ended.

After a warm shower and placing the black case containing the jewellery under the bed mattress Jack left the Double Tree Hilton

Hotel to find a restaurant and something to eat. The young guy on the hotel reception had recommended a small Spanish Restaurant just a few minutes away. He and his girlfriend often dined there. The chicken pasta he ordered was excellent. After downing a couple of pints of local lager beer Jack headed back to the Hilton and an early night.

The following morning he took a taxi for the ten minute drive to jeweller Marc Fernandez's Head Office. Marc was a good looking guy about fifty, clean shaven, slim and about six foot with a full head of dark hair, which was slightly streaked with grey. His English was not good so they carried out their conversation in Spanish. It appeared that Marc ran the business with his wife Carla, who would be joining them in about twenty minutes. Their twelve stores sold both high class and costume jewellery. Marc bought much of their quality stock from Franks of London and the costume jewellery from Cobra. His wife Carla was in charge of that department. Just as his secretary brought in two cups of Brazilian coffee, Carla walked in. She was a stunning looking Spanish woman, about five four, elegantly dressed in her early forties with a lovely smile, long black hair with a great figure. Marc said they had two children, who worked in the business. They were a genuine hard working couple who appeared to run a clean business which was expanding. The new range of Cobra costume jewellery impressed them both, in the end they purchased almost half a million Euros of stock. Later the three of them dined out for lunch at Cobra Jewellery's expense. At around three they parted company. Jack took a leisurely walk back to the Hilton Hotel, where he had left his overnight bag. By the time he arrived at the Atache Railway Station, he had about fifty minutes to spare before the arrival of his 5pm train. Always enjoying a latte coffee he called in at Starbucks, as usual the café was packed with travellers; many of them waiting for the superfast train to Malaga. In the end he stood outside the café bar drinking his coffee. He was certainly relieved that Aslan's secretary Martina had booked a return ticket for him in advance; at least he was guaranteed a seat.

Freddie a man of his word was waiting for him in the red Audi A4 in the short stay car park at Malaga Railway Station, when the train pulled in at eight. Darkness had started to creep in by seven thirty, now it was completely dark. There was a slight chill in the air. The sky was cloudless with thousands of twinkling stars looking down from the universe. The weather was more like spring in London than what he had been used to on the Mediterranean. Once they had left the busy city centre traffic behind, they hit the coastal motorway within twenty minutes. Freddie did not say much at first as he was concentrating on his driving in the fast flowing traffic.

"It going to rain in the next hour, let us hope we can get to Marbella before the heavens open. At this time of the year you can get violent tropical downpours."

"How can you be certain?"

"Since I have lived on the Costa del Sol I take notice of the weather patterns. Mid October can be very unpredictable and the rain normally falls at night." Freddie then went quiet for a few moments before continuing with the conversation. "Mr Maskhadov asked me to remind you about your meeting with him at the Cobra Jewellery Head Office tomorrow morning, he will be there by eleven. Oh! and he said don't forget to bring with you the black jewellery case."

Jack laughed. "Don't worry I won't abscond with it."

"I said it would rain, look at the car window now."

It suddenly started to rain quite heavily and the road in front of them started to flood slowing the traffic down to a crawl.

"Jack, where are you staying at?"

"The Marbella Beach Apartments on the Esplanade Paseo,"

"I know the area well. I will drop you off by the main entrance."

Five minutes later they left the motorway. Once Freddie had dropped him off outside the apartments, he used his key card to gain admission to the complex. Youssef Beji was on reception duty, when he saw Jack outside the foyer he immediately opened the automatic glass doors.

"Good to see you Youssef."

"You too Jack,"

"You look tired?"

"I have just arrived back from a business trip to Madrid, I am shattered."

"I intend to come to your gig at the Med Club next Tuesday, I have heard rave reports."

"That would be great so please make yourself known to me then we can have a drink together after my show. Now if you will excuse me I must head upstairs to my apartment, I need a bite to eat, a shower and some sleep."

The following morning after a goodnight's sleep, Jack arrived at the Cobra Jewellery Head Office by Benny's taxi at ten forty-five. There was only one car on the car park which was Aslan's red and black Mini Cooper. It was hard to believe there had been a violent rain storm during the night. Everything was now perfectly dry, the sun was quite warm and there was no wind, another beautiful day. Walking over to the intercom at the main entrance he pressed the buzzer. Aslan answered immediately. "Please come in Jack I am in my office, just pass through the security scanner."

After knocking on the boss's office door Jack entered. They greeted each other warmly. Jack then passed him the black leather costume jewellery sample case, which he placed on the top of his desk without opening.

"I gather you have had a good trip." Jack stared at Aslan but did not answer. Aslan smiled. "I was certainly not checking up on you but Marc Fernandez called me yesterday. He was most complementary about you and our new range of costume jewellery."

"Have you dealt with him long?"

"Yes, ever since I set up our costume jewellery business. Marc and Carla were my first customers. They have been very loyal to us, which is why I always give them a great deal. Normally I always go and see them myself but I trust you implicitly Jack."

"Thank you Aslan, I appreciate the faith you have in me." Aslan smiled.

Jack then passed the order form of what the Fernandez had bought across the office desk to Aslan. After running his eyes quickly over the order he turned to Jack.

"You have done extremely well Jack, well done." He then completely changed the subject. "Two weeks this Sunday I have my annual charity function to raise money for Marbella's new children's hospice, which is due to be built next year, I would like to invite you and Olga to my event."

Jack didn't hesitate for a moment. "We would love to come. Where do you hold it and what time does it start?"

"At my villa, we put up a couple of large marquees on the patio in front of my pad. There will be free alcohol and soft drinks all night plus a live band and disco. Tickets are 200 Euros per person or 300 Euros for a couple with free entrance into the draw for a new C-Class white Mercedes.

The car has been donated free of charge to the charity by Mercedes. There will also be a glass of Champagne on arrival. All the money raised on the night goes to the charity. Anybody who means anything in Marbella will be there. Even the local chief of police and mayor and their wives will attend. Jack, I need a big favour from you. My usual DJ Bono broke his leg last week in a car accident. Would you stand in for him?"

"Of course I will."

"We will provide the PA system; all you will need is your laptop. Perhaps you will perform music to suit everyone's taste."

Jack laughed. "There will be no House Music until the last half hour of the evening. I can promise you that. Do we get complementary tickets?"

"Of course you do."

"How many guests are you expecting?"

"Over the evening normally around four hundred guests, most of the tickets have already been sold."

"That is fantastic; I shall look forward to the event. Thank you for asking me. What time do you start and finish?"

"We run between nine in the evening and one the following morning when the police say we have to kill the music, you will need to arrive by six to sort out the sound system. There will be food available to all staff from the mobile food van on the private car park between six and seven thirty. I will speak to you next week and give you more information."

"Is there no one else on duty here today?"

"No, only myself, I am not concerned as it gives me the opportunity to check what my staff have been doing during the week." Jack smiled.

Ten minutes later Jack called a taxi and returned to the Marbella Beach Apartments. After changing into his swimming gear he headed for the pool and a dip. Once he had completed twenty lengths, he climbed out and lay down on one of the poolside sun beds to dry off. As usual there was no one else about. The sun was warm with a temperature of around 25c, so he lay there for forty five minutes topping up his tan before heading down the Esplanade Paseo for a light lunch and a couple of beers at the Picasso Café Bar.

18

FSB Head Quarters the Kremlin Moscow Russia

"Good of you to see me at such short notice Major Pavlov."

"I would never refuse you minister."

The two men shook hands and embraced warmly.

"I was just about to call my secretary Natasha for a coffee. Would you care to join me?"

"I would love to, milk with no sugar."

The Major then picked up the white internal phone on his desk and called his secretary. "Natasha, when you have a moment would you please bring in two coffees for Minister Greshnov and me? We both take milk but no sugar."

"Certainly Major,"

After replacing the phone Major Pavlov turned to the Minister. "What brings you here so urgently on this bitterly cold morning?"

"You are right about the weather Major. I could feel a flurry of snow in the air, as I crossed the courtyard to your head quarters." He then paused for a second, just as Natasha knocked at the door and entered with two cups of coffee. When she left the room he continued with his conversation. "Yesterday I had a meeting with our President. We had a long conversation about the Siberian cargo plane hijack and the missing billion Euros of diamonds and gems. He is not happy with the progress so far and that Major is your responsibility."

The Major then took a drink of coffee and was starting to feel a little annoyed. "Minister Greshnov we have done everything we can at the FSB. We have raided numerous clubs, restaurants, bars and homes owned by the Mafia without any success. A considerable number of the Mafia and several police officers have died in these operations. I personally do not believe the diamonds and gems are in Moscow."

"Where do you think they are then?"

"Possibly somewhere in the Ural Mountains,"

"In fact they could be anywhere, there are literally dozens of small landing strips in that region, which have become abandoned since the Soviet Union broke up."

"That is your problem Alexei as you are the Minister for Homeland Security."

The Minister looked straight at the Major and then removed his gold rimmed spectacles. "We have one hell of a fucking problem Ivan. The President wants this incident, as he calls it, sorting out once and for all. He says we have had over twelve months to discover the whereabouts of the diamonds and gems, and that is long enough. Sooner or later the media will hear about the hijacking and then all hell will break out, the diamond markets worldwide will collapse." The Minister then lowered his voice. "The President is adamant that if we are unable to discover the whereabouts of the diamonds and gems, then the Chechens involved in the hijack must be taken out."

"What about Sergei Aslanov the son of Russian war hero Colonel Alexander Stepanov?"

"Under no circumstances must he be harmed, personally we would like him to return to Russia on his own accord, but if not, then with the help of the FSB. Along with the Russian Mafia, he appears to be the leading man in this saga. I am certain he knows where the diamonds and gems are. If he co-operates fully and because of who his father is, he will be immune from prosecution."

"Are you giving me the go ahead for me to instruct my agents to assassinate the Chechens in Marbella?"

"Are your guys in the field good?"

"They are my two top operatives Olga and Tanya."

"Female assassins?" There was a sense of disbelief in the Minister's voice.

"Yes, they are young women, identical twins, age twenty six, they are stunning looking and are ruthless killers, they love their job. So far they have taken out almost fifty victims in Europe, the Middle East and Africa."

"Where are the girls now?"

"In Marbella, where they have been for the last six weeks," "Ivan, what is your latest update on the Chechens and Sergei Aslanov? I need to know before I make my final decision about what course of action to take."

The Major drank the last of his coffee as did the Minister. "As you know we are working with the British MI6, one of their agents Jack Sinclair has uncovered a great deal about them. We now know where the Chechens work and live, there would be no problem taking them out. Sergei Aslanov is a very different proposition, at the moment we have not got a clue where he is."

"Have you any idea who he is working with."

"At first we thought it was the former Chechen Separatist leader Aslan Maskhadov, who owns the very successful Cobra Jewellery Company on the Costa del Sol. Sergei Aslanov is employed by him as a gemmologist. If you recall Maskhadov is a wanted man in Russia because of his war crimes against our country, but Spain granted him citizenship to annoy us. MI6 Agent Sinclair is convinced that Cobra Jewellery is a legitimate company and Sergei Aslanov may be actually working for Boris Sokolov, who is part of the Russian Mafia. Working for Cobra Jewellery is a cover, which gives him an excuse to visit Middle East and African countries that would buy high grade raw diamonds and gems from him for cash, with no questions asked."

"What does this guy Boris Sokolov actually do for a living?"

"He runs the lap dancing club Pinks in Puerto Banus, both my girls work for him as dancers, it is an excellent cover for them."

"Have you any proof that Boris is definitely involved in the distribution of the missing hijacked diamonds and precious gems?"

"No not at the moment."

The Minister thought for a moment. "Ivan, give your girls the go ahead to take the Chechens out but that does not include the Russian Boris. Remember Sergei Aslanov must also not be harmed in any way; you must await my instructions for what we have in store for him. Tell your girls to use the PV44 nerve agent wherever possible and to take their time with the assassinations, we don't want the Spanish Police getting involved."

"Alexei, may I offer you another coffee?"

"I would love one Ivan but I must get back to my office, I have a heavy schedule today, but rather than speak to you over the telephone I had to see you in person, we need to work very closely together."

"Thank you my friend I appreciate your visit." The two men embraced before the Minister departed, the flurry of snow in the air had turned to a thin layer on the courtyard as he made his way back to his office.

Olga was not happy with Jack working part-time. It had interfered with her sex life, which she always had to be in control of. Secretly she had never met a man like Jack with whom she was so compatible, she could have looked around for a new partner to satisfy her insatiable demands, but she knew in her own mind, that could take weeks and she had not got the time. Instead she adjusted her own working life and returned from Puerto Banus to the Marbella Beach Apartments by mid-day on Mondays allowing her to have sex with Jack in the evening. When she thought about her life, she soon realized they still had sex five days a week.

"Olga, we have been invited to Aslan Maskhadov's annual fundraising party for the new children's hospice, at his villa. It will be held outside in a large marquee and I will be the DJ. It should be an incredible evening."

"What date is it?"

"Sunday the 30th October."

"Fantastic I will change my night at Pinks. I love parties and dressing up." She then leaned over and kissed Jack passionately. "Come and make love to me darling."

Major Pavlov's phone call completely took her by surprise. "You and your sister Tanya have been on holiday long enough, now it is time for you both to get to work. Listen to me very carefully Olga, you and Tanya must use the PV44 nerve agent wherever you can, it is virtually untraceable. Under no circumstances must Sergei Aslanov be harmed unless I give you the order. Do you understand what I am saying?"

"Of course I do darling."

"Two further points, the British agent Jack Sinclair must not be harmed; we are working very closely with MI6. The Russian Boris Sokolov who runs Pinks can be taken out when I give you the order, but only after we discover who he is working with."

When Olga replaced her mobile phone on the kitchen table, she could feel the adrenaline running through her body. She could not wait to get started. She enjoyed taking the life of a fellow human being just as much as having sex, especially if she had sex with her prey beforehand. Her parent's genes which had given sister Tanya and her identical looks had also given them identical psychopathic brains.

Within minutes of speaking to Major Pavlov, Olga was on her mobile to her sister Tanya in Puerto Banus. "Tanya I need to speak to you urgently, Major Pavlov has just called me."

"What has he got to say?"

"A great deal but I need to see you at once, it is far too sensitive to discuss over the phone what he said to me. I will call a taxi and be at your apartment in the next hour."

"Ok sis I will see you shortly."

For once Olga was pleased that Jack was at work, she did not fancy bumping into him. The taxi she called made good time even though the main highway was extremely busy. After being dropped off by the La Victoria Statue in the Avenida Nacionalas Unidas at Puerto Banus, Olga made her way towards the harbour. Half way along the narrow street, which separated the numerous bars from the harbour, she turned right down a side street passing Lineker's Bar and Pinks, on her way to Tanya's apartment two blocks away. It was still very warm and the resort was full of holiday makers from all over Europe, all hoping to see some famous celebrities drinking in one of the bars or relaxing on one of the many Ocean going boats moored at the harbour.

Olga pressed the intercom on the wall by the dark oak door. Tanya responded immediately. "Come up stairs darling."

Olga quickly climbed the white marble staircase to the light grey tiled landing of the white two storey apartment block. Tanya was waiting by the open door of her apartment. The two sisters warmly embraced before going inside. Olga's apartment like all the others in the complex had been completely refurnished and modernised three years ago. There were two bedrooms, a kitchen come lounge, a shower room, and a medium sized balcony with two white wicker chairs, but no table. Down below was a paved court yard which had a dozen large rustic urns full of flowers in bloom, the colours were mesmerizing. There were also several hanging baskets full of jasmine hanging from the walls on black metal hooks. You could clearly smell the aroma they gave off from Olga's top floor apartment.

"Is something wrong darling?"

"Our boss from the FSB Major Pavlov called me just over an hour ago." The smile on Olga's beautiful face suddenly disappeared, she looked most serious. "He has given us the go ahead to take out the Chechens. Aslan Maskhadov who owns Cobra Jewellery must not be harmed and neither must Sergei Aslanov or MI6 Agent Jack Sinclair. We can however assassinate Boris Sokolov who runs Pinks, when we have the proof that he is part of the Russian Mafia, but not until the Major gives us the all clear."

Tanya turned to her sister. "I will make certain he has a good send off."

"Darling Major Pavlov said, only when we have definite proof and then we will do it together when he says so. I have an idea which you will love, but we must keep our hands off him until we are ready to leave Marbella for Russia."

"Coffee or tea darling or perhaps a glass of red wine?"

"Coffee will be fine."

"Jack and I have been invited to Aslan Maskhadov's charity fund raising garden party on the 30th October."

"Lucky girl, I wish I was going with you it should be great fun."

"Perhaps your boyfriend Roberto Sanchez will be invited and take you along with him."

"I am certain he will be invited but he will not be taking me, we are no longer an item. We now only see each other once a week, occasionally twice and then it is only for sex."

"What has happened, I thought you liked the guy?"

"I did but he was getting too possessive. I told him that I will be returning back home to Latvia in a few weeks."

"You don't look that bothered."

Tanya laughed, her eyes started to sparkle. "I have got myself another boyfriend a younger model."

"Is he good at sex?"

"He is getting there. I have taught him a lot."

"Where did you meet him?"

"He has been in Pinks several times and we got talking. His name is Youssef Beji, he is from Tunisia. He works for Roberto Sanchez's company Costa Security as a security officer."

"I know who he is. I have seen him on reception at the Marbella Beach Apartments. He is a good looking guy and nice to talk to. Roberto will not be happy, if he finds out that you are shagging one of his staff as well as him."

Tanya laughed out loud. "Roberto also lends Youssef his ocean going speed boat the Black Prince whenever he goes out sea fishing, he frequently takes me with him. We speed out into the Mediterranean from Puerto Banus for about twelve miles, stop the boat's engines and then have sex on the open deck in the middle of the sea miles from land, with only dolphins or the occasional sharks for company. After we usually sunbath naked and drink a bottle of Chardonnay. Youssef has even taught me how to drive the boat."

"He must trust you."

"He does, he is a lovely guy." Tanya then laughed as she spoke. "It is fantastic having sex on the boat, the rocking motion of the sea makes it more exciting. You should try it darling."

Olga stared at her sister before speaking. "You must have another reason for going on the boat with him?"

"I have, no secrets from you darling, you can always tell when I am not telling you everything." Tanya then took a drink of her coffee, Olga did likewise. "I heard a rumour before I got involved with Youssef, that he was using the Black Prince to smuggle drugs into the country. I have watched him for some time when he visits Pinks and have noticed how friendly he is with Boris. When you told me that Boris was suspected of being involved with the Siberian cargo plane diamond hijack, I put two and two together and wondered if Youssef was bringing the diamonds into the country for him. It is far easier to smuggle diamonds into the country than plastic bags of cocaine." Olga smiled but made no comment.

"I have noticed, that recently you have spent more time in your apartment here than in the Seacrest Hotel in Marbella. Is there a reason for that?"

"Yes, I don't trust the Russian couple who own the hotel. I am convinced they work for the FSB and are snooping on me. I know they often go into my room when I am not about, I am just not happy staying there any longer, so I paid my bill, packed my bags, and moved out."

"Did they not ask you where you were going to?"

"Yes, I told them I was returning to Latvia."

"Tanya next time I see you, I am going to give you four of the PV44 lipsticks. You must store them in this apartment very carefully. We will work out a schedule for taking out the Chechens which will not draw any police attention. Remember once the victim receives a pin prick, the nerve agent then takes two hours to bring death."

Tanya looked at her sister and smiled. "I can't wait to use one of the lipsticks on my first victim."

"I just feel the same darling."

The days were ticking by to Aslan Maskhadov's annual charity fund raising garden party, the weather was still glorious. Jack's sister Lilly had told him the previous evening when they spoke over the phone, that the UK was experiencing heavy rain and strong winds with below average temperatures for the time of the year. He was glad he was living in Marbella. Jack's House Music DJ residency at the Med Club was sold out every Tuesday evening. The owner Pedro Gonzales, who was also MI6's man in Spain, had insisted that he and Jack should meet every Wednesday in his private office at the Med Club to discuss any updates on the Siberian diamond plane hijack and the Chechen suspects, who were living in Marbella.

"Jack, sorry to ruin your lie in after your late Tuesday night gig but it was Miles Coburn's idea; he felt we should have more contact. He wants us to plant a couple of bugs. One at Aslan's villa whilst we attend his garden party, I will need your help as it will have to be inside, preferably in the lounge or kitchen area. MI6 have developed a new listening device." Pedro then reached inside the left hand drawer of his office desk, and took out a slim white plastic container, which was no more than one and a half inches long and half an inch wide with a magnetic base. After placing it on the desk in front of him he looked up at Jack smiling.

"That my friend is 21st technology. Once in position you can listen to any conversation perfectly through walls a few inches thick. It also has a radius of ten metres. By using this highly modified Sony mobile phone and a special code you can automatically tune into the electronic single the bug transmits once it is activated. This mobile can then be linked up to my laptop. Whizz kids at MI6 have recently developed a sophisticated new programme, which allows them to tap into my laptop and listen to the device transmitting, whist still in London. One of their trusted interpreters, who used to work for the Chechen Secret Service as a double agent but who has now defected to our side and is fluent in both languages, will listen in and record any conversations made in Aslan's villa. We will then know for certain if he has any connection with the hijack. Coburn also wants you to place one of the bugs in Olga's apartment."

"I don't see how I can, I have never once been alone there."

"You can place the bug on her balcony whilst she is staying in Puerto Banus. On second thoughts forget the balcony; the outside walls are probably too thick to allow the single to be activated and received properly. Pedro then placed his hand in the office drawer again and took out two odd looking long keys made of stainless steel and passed them to Jack. "These will let you gain access to Olga's apartment through the balcony door. Do not try the corridor door as it can only be opened with an electronic key card. Once the bug is placed and activated, a Russian interpreter will listen in and record everything from London. We have to know what Olga and her sister Tanya are up to. Miles Coburn is convinced they will be given the go ahead in the next few days, that is if they haven't already, to begin exterminating the Chechens and anybody else the Russians want removing and that could possibly include Aslan Maskhadov."

"I will get it sorted out. Olga is working this Friday and Saturday in Puerto Banus."

"Have you any news about Sergei Aslanov?"

"No not at the moment absolutely nothing,"

There was a knock on the door and one of the female bar staff walked in with two Pepperoni Pizzas and a couple of mugs of white coffee. "Jack, I hope this food is to your liking."

"It looks delicious, I slept in so late this morning that I had no time for breakfast."

Pedro picked up a slice of the pizza and then continued to speak. "I would not be surprised if Sergei has not already returned to Spain and is in hiding."

"You really think so."

"Yes I do, he could be hiding away in Aslan's villa. It is very secluded and secure and full of the latest high tech security. There are several rooms at the rear which are only accessible from the front entrance, Sergei could be holding up there."

"You appear to be well informed about his villa."

"I am. My wife and I have been guests there many times. He has a stunning property. Due to my involvement with MI6, I keep a great deal of information up here." He then tapped the side of his head. "Once I have placed the bug in position, we should know if anyone else, apart from Aslan, George and Freddie live in or visit the villa."

"Are you returning to work tomorrow Jack?"

"Yes, I am going to Almeria on business for Cobra Jewellery for a couple of days. I shall be using one of their company cars to drive there, I should cover the 125mile journey in just over two hours. On the way back I have a new client to visit in Roquetas de Mar and later make a social visit to Cobra's new store in Nerja. I should be back in Marbella around seven."

"Jack you have a safe journey."

"I will and thanks for the pizza and coffee, it was excellent. I will see you at the garden party on Sunday evening. By the way I have been roped into being the DJ."

"I know it was my idea, I told Aslan to ask you." Jack laughed as he left the office.

Twenty minutes later after a brisk walk along the Esplanade Paseo, which was almost deserted, he arrived back at the Marbella Beach Apartments. After nipping upstairs to his apartment, he changed into his swimming shorts and then headed to the pool for a swim. Olga was by the pool sunbathing in the warm sun. She looked up at him as he approached.

"Darling, I was wondering where you were, there was no reply from your apartment."

"I received an early morning call from Pedro Gonzales who owns the Med Club; he wanted to see me about possibly working an extra night." Olga appeared satisfied with the explanation.

After throwing his light blue towel down on the vacant sun bed next to Olga, Jack slipped into the swimming pool. The water was warmer than he had expected but then again it had been quite a warm day. Twenty lengths later he walked up the low white marble steps out of the pool, dried most of the water off his body and then sat down besides Olga on a sun bed.

"You haven't forgotten that I am away on business tomorrow and Friday for Cobra Jewellery?"

"I had darling, it is a good job you have reminded me. As I am working at Pinks Friday and Saturday, with you being away, I will stay with my girlfriend Emma in Puerto Banus, I shall be back by mid-day on Sunday. Whilst I am there, I intend to visit the chic boutiques in the port and see if I can find a glamorous outfit for Aslan's garden party."

Jack smiled. "I shall look forward to seeing you in your new dress."

Olga then leaned over and ran her right hand slowly over his hairy chest and stomach. "Darling, let's go up to my apartment then you can make love to me, and afterwards you can take me out for an early evening meal, as I have not eaten since breakfast."

Jack was never one to refuse a lady.

19

Jack arrived shortly before eight thirty at the Cobra Jewellery Head Quarters. All his working life he had been punctual today was no exception. In his mind, there was nothing worse than setting off late on a long drive then ending up watching the clock. His appointment in Almeria was at twelve thirty. After Malaga the road ahead was unfamiliar to him but Aslan said it was a busy fast coastal highway to his destination. If he was honest, he was looking forward to the drive and visiting an area which he had heard a great deal about, but never visited. With his black leather jewellery case and overnight bag in the car boot of the company's red Audi A4 he joined the motorway on the outskirts of Marbella. It was another gloriously warm day and perfect for driving apart from the strong sunlight, so he slipped on his Gucci shades. Relaxing in the Audi's black leather driver's seat, he concentrated on the road ahead and watched the miles flash by.

With Jack being away on business, Olga decided to have a lie in, and then have a late lunch with her sister Tanya in Puerto Banus.

"Darling, I have brought you four lipsticks. You must be very careful how you handle them. There is no antidote for the PV44 Nerve Agent. One simple scratch on your skin and you will die an agonising death."

"I will keep them in my bedroom drawer under my knickers." Olga laughed.

"Would you like me to show you again how to use the lipsticks?"

"Of course you can darling."

"When you have removed the gold top of the lipstick all you have to do is press the base, the tiny pin head will come out. Once the Nerve Agent is used it will automatically retract. You must then screw the lipstick head back onto the base and dispose of it in a refuge waist bin, which must be some distance from the victim. By the way, if possible we must always wear these very thin but extremely strong transparent disposable gloves for protection. Also you must never carry more than one lipstick with you when you are on a mission to take out a victim."

"Olga, when can we start?"

"This Sunday at Aslan's garden party. There will be several Chechens there but I still have to decide who will be the first to die." Olga could feel herself getting excited with the thought of what she was going to do. "Come on darling, let us go and get a bite to eat and a drink. You can then come shopping with me for a new party dress, I want something special."

Jack's business trip for Cobra Jewellery to Almeria and Roquetas de Mar proved to be highly successful. As usual when he returned the company car to Cobra's Head Quarters on Saturday morning, he met up with the owner Aslan and give him a run down on the business he had brought in on the two day trip.

"Jack I value your opinion. "What do you think of the manager and our store in Nerja?"

"The store is beautiful and is a credit to you. Your manager is young and good looking. He has a great deal to learn but he is very loyal to you. He appears to be very popular with the female staff, providing he can keep his hands off them and his trousers zipped up, he will be an asset to you."

Aslan laughed and then changed the conversation. "Are you organised for your DJ gig at my fund raising event on Sunday?"

"Most certainly, the music will be spot on and you will have a great evening."

"I am certain we will Jack, I will see you on Sunday at six. Rather than take a taxi back to the Marbella Beach Apartments Jack decided to walk. It was a fairly warm day though the late morning sun had still not broken through the heavy cloud cover. Rain was not forecast but you could never be certain in late October. He prayed it would keep away and Aslan's garden party would be a great success. As he walked through the city centre he stopped to talk to a group of young Spanish girls, who were sat outside a pavement café bar. Several of them had been at the Med Club on Tuesday night and recognised him.

"We shall all be there to see you next Tuesday Jack." Jack smiled and blew them a kiss as he left.

Once he had made his way to the Esplanade Paseo he called in at the Picasso Café Bar. After a roast ham sandwich and a cold beer, he continued to the Marbella Beach Apartments. When he arrived there was no one on duty at reception to stop and talk to, so he headed straight up the white marble staircase to his own apartment.

There was no time like the present for slipping the electronic bug into Olga's apartment. Fortunately many of the holiday apartments now had their shutters closed for the winter months, including those on either side of Olga's pad. Luckily for Jack, Olga's apartment was immediately above his on the third floor. As he climbed onto his own apartment's balcony wall, he made certain the garden below was deserted. With comparative ease he managed to lift himself up to the balcony above. There was nobody about not even the gardener, or a stray cat, even the pigeons which frequented the garden had disappeared. The situation was perfect. Taking the stainless steel key out of his black track suit pocket, he gently slipped it into the locked balcony door pushing the interior key out. There was a slight click and the door unlocked, he breathed a sigh of relief. Closing the balcony door behind him, he just stood there gazing around the apartment. Everything was perfectly quiet. Pedro had warned him to check very carefully, in case Olga had been watching James Bond movies and she had placed a string of light cotton between two chairs. If someone had disturbed the cotton, then the room had been entered. The room appeared completely clean. He had no intention of placing the bug in Olga's bedroom, he did not want to become a celebrity in London with his intimate conversations with Olga being overheard. The lounge or the open plan kitchen was the obvious choice but where? It was impossible to place a bug on any of the walls; the tables were of glass and the sofa and chairs made of mahogany and dark blue leather upholstery. The open plan kitchen was the only choice, the balcony would be no problem but the outside walls were probably too thick to pick up a conversation. It had to be the open plan kitchen. There was a cupboard door just below the stainless steel sink which contained washing up liquid, cloths and pans etc. Between the double sink and the inside wooden frame was a two inch gap. Taking the bug out of his left pocket, he removed the magnetic safety cover, and placed it in the gap allowing it to grip the wooden frame securely. Once he was happy with its position, he took the Sony mobile phone which Pedro had given him out of his other pocket and keyed in a five digit security number. Within seconds a blue light flashed several times and then stayed on permanently. The phone had picked up the bug's electronic single. There was no way anyone would discover the device, unless they were looking for it and then you would have to be aware of what you were looking for.

Once back on the balcony, Jack closed the door and relocked it from the outside with the key already in position. After making certain there was no one around, he gently slipped over the wall onto his own apartment balcony. The whole operation had taken less than thirty minutes. Picking up his mobile phone he called Pedro Gonzales. Pedro answered immediately.

"Pedro it is Jack, everything is completed."

"Good man, I shall be leaving for the club in fifteen minutes, I will call round to the Marbella Beach Apartments and collect the Sony mobile from you. If you wait outside the main entrance to the complex, I will meet you there."

"No problem."

Twenty five minutes later Pedro drew up in his Hyacinth Red Metallic C-Class Mercedes. "Sorry to keep you waiting Jack, I should have remembered the traffic is always bad on a Saturday afternoon."

Jack smiled and immediately passed him the Sony mobile phone which he then placed on the black leather passenger seat next to him.

"As soon as I am in my office at the Med Club I will connect it up to a spare laptop and then call Miles Coburn, he will do the rest. We can't be certain your operation has been successful until Olga returns to her apartment and makes a phone call or carries on a live conversation with someone."

"Leave it to me, as soon as she returns I will call round and see her, I promised to take her out for lunch. Perhaps you will make certain that Coburn knows the guy in her apartment talking to her is me."

Pedro laughed. "Don't worry I will."

Olga arrived back at the Marbella Beach Apartments shortly before mid-day on Sunday. Rather than call in at the Picasso Café Bar for their usual lunchtime break they decided to visit the Albatross. For once the bar and restaurant were quiet and they had a choice of tables. The weather was still fairly mild with strong sunshine, but there was a nip in the air when you stood and faced the Mediterranean Sea. Jack hoped and prayed that the weather would hold out for the next twenty four hours at least. He also noticed that neither owner Roscoe Rodriguez nor his daughter Valentina were on duty. After sitting down at an inside table by the window they decided on a typical English meal

'Sunday Lunch' with roast beef. This was something completely new to Olga who had never even heard of 'Sunday Lunch' but to be honest she loved the food, especially with a couple of large glasses of red wine.

By the time they had arrived back at the Marbella Beach Apartments it was almost two thirty.

"Well darling, my apartment or yours?"

Jack thought quickly, he was almost caught unaware. "We have to be at Aslan Maskhadov's villa by six, I don't want to be late."

"You mean to say you can't spare me an hour?"

"Of course I can, please don't be offended. He then placed his arms around Olga's waist pulled her towards him and kissed her neck. Let us go to my apartment for a change.

"She looked up into his eyes. I missed you last Thursday I love having sex with you."

"So do I, you are an incredible girl."

"Thank you darling."

"Your boss at Pinks, Boris the Russian, is he still trying to get inside your knickers."

"Yes, every day. When I am dancing he stands there staring at me getting himself excited. Mind you that never bothers me, but I don't like the suggestive comments he continually makes to me. You know he even spies on me when I dance privately for a customer. My English girlfriend Emma says that he also comes on to her. The problem is we are the only two girls in the club he has never shagged."

Jack really felt sorry for her but there was nothing he could do, it was either a question of putting up with the situation or leaving Pinks.

"Fuck him." She cried out. Next minute Olga was on top of him naked. Jack was relieved they had not gone back to her apartment; Miles Coburn would have had a field day in London.

After a warm shower, Jack changed into his black and gold stage gear including a new pair of black and yellow Reebok trainers, which he had recently bought. He had arranged for Benny's taxi to pick him and Olga up at five forty. At five thirty with his Apple Laptop programmed and safely in its dark blue case, he made his way up the white marble staircase to Olga's apartment. After pressing the intercom the door opened. Olga was stood there looking absolutely stunning in her black and yellow off the shoulder short dress, and flowing dark hair. On her feet she wore a pair of cream three inch high heel shoes, her legs like the rest of her body were deeply tanned, so there was no need for stockings. Apart from her usual Gucci designer watch and matching earrings she wore no other jewellery.

"What do you think darling?"

"You look breathtaking but then again you always do." "Thank you darling."

Jack then kissed her on the side of her face. "I love your perfume." He whispered.

"It is Gucci like my jewellery. I took my girlfriend Emma with me shopping, she has impeccable taste."

Jack glanced at his black Sekonda Sports Watch which he always wore on DJ gigs. "Our taxi will be here in five minutes, I have arranged with the driver to meet us at the main entrance."

"I am ready when you are darling." Olga then picked up her clutch handbag which was the same colour as her dress, off a nearby chair.

The taxi only took ten minutes to arrive at Aslan Maskhadov's magnificent villa, which was situated some five hundred meters to the right off the main highway halfway between Marbella and Puerto Banus. The spacious white marble five bedroom glass fronted property and heart shaped swimming pool had been built on one level and was surrounded by half an acre of manicured gardens. To the right side of the villa there was a four car garage and a car park which held twelve cars. In front of the main entrance and sliding glass windows was a huge Roman stone patio, where two large marquees had been erected. These contained a stage area and a well stocked pop-up bar. Both marquees had heater blowers in case the evening temperature dropped dramatically. Several very modern ladies and gents powder rooms were discretely situated by the car park, along with a power generator, which would supply electricity independently to the event. The perimeter of the complex was surrounded by a seven foot stone wall topped with razor wire. There was only one entrance to the villa, a double gated dark wood and metal automatically controlled gate, which like the rest of the complex was covered by CCTV cameras. Two smartly dressed security staff carefully checked all the guests entering the complex. Aslan had thought of everything.

Aslan's Chechen friend George, who was obviously in charge, ushered them into the main marquee after greeting them both affectionately.

"What a beautiful marquee George, it looks stunning." "Thank you Olga. By the way, I love your dress you look sensational."

"Thank you George."

"Jack, our live band for the evening Funk have set up earlier and they are on stage at ten thirty."

"I shall look forward to seeing them, I have heard a great deal about them."

"They are a seven piece band with several brass instruments and have a great black male vocalist called Marvin. Most of the band is based on the Costa del Sol and last year they had a number one hit record in Spain and most of Europe. Even though they are now famous, they always do this gig free of charge, to support Aslan's children's charity."

"That is fantastic."

Fifty minutes later after a band call and with expert advice from the guy who had installed the event PA system, Jack was ready to commence his show.

"Jack, can I get you and Olga a drink?"

Jack turned to Olga. "Coffee darling," she said with a smile.

"Two Americano coffees if you would George."

"Coming up shortly, I will get you a couple from the bar."

"What are you going to do all night?"

"Socialize in between talking to you and other guests; I have never been to a garden party like this. Have you?"

"No never, but I gather rich people and celebrities frequently hold them." Olga laughed.

"You do look very sexy this evening. It could be the beautiful dress you are wearing."

Olga looked up, her mouth was slightly open, and her eyes fluttered with excitement. "Unfortunately we will have to wait until tomorrow and then you can." She never got to finish the sentence as George returned with the two Americano coffees.

"You and George appear to be much closer than you used to be."

"We are, I never hold grudges darling. The Russian Chechen war was not his fault. He is a good guy."

George certainly had two sides to his personality, Jack had seen both and he did not like the Chechen when he was high on drugs or booze, but when he was clean he was as Olga put it a good guy.

Darkness had closed in quickly but with the lighting system switched on, it looked more like Christmas in Oxford Street, London with all the multi-coloured lights illuminating the garden. The weather had changed and the slight wind had disappeared, in fact it was a fairly warm evening for the time of the year.

By eight thirty, cars and guests started to arrive. Fortunately there was plenty room on the vacant land opposite the villa to park the Porches, Mercedes, BMW, Lamborghinis, Ferraris and Audis, which arrived in great numbers. Several of Aslan's employees were acting as parking attendants and taking care of the security of the high roller luxury cars. Jack had never seen so many attractive women dripping with expensive jewellery at one event.

By nine thirty the event was in full swing. Jack recognised many of the faces from his gig at the Med Club. Anyone who was anybody on the Costa del Sol was there including several A-list film celebrities and pop singers. Shortly after nine thirty Aslan Maskhadov made his first appearance of the evening, to hold his now famous charity auction. His company Cobra Jewellery had donated a stunning 22 carat ruby and diamond necklace to the auction. This unique piece of jewellery was eventually bought by a wealthy middle aged Spanish property developer for his beautiful young wife for 50,000 Euros. Jack could not help wonder if the necklace was made from gems which came from the Siberian cargo plane hijack.

Leroy Cardoso, the owner of Marbella's most exclusive night spot Olivia Valere and his beautiful daughter Emily came up to the DJ stand to speak to Jack. After introducing Olga to them, she excused herself and disappeared. Jack always knew that like many women, she hated competition from another beautiful woman. Albatross bar and restaurant owner Roscoe Rodriguez along with his charming wife Sofia and daughter Valentina also took time to speak to him. As they were leaving, Valentina whispered in his ear. "Where is your Russian girlfriend?"

"She is a friend like you, not my girlfriend."

"I still don't trust her Jack, please be careful." She then kissed him on the cheek.

Jack liked Valentina; he just wished she was a little older. If she was, he would certainly be dating her. Where the hell was Olga, he hadn't seen her for half an hour. Slightly behind schedule at ten thirty-five, he introduced the band Funk. They were sensational, a mixture of classic pop, soul and blues. Why their hit record and album was not released in the UK was a complete mystery.

Pedro Gonzales and his attractive wife Nada arrived whilst the band were on stage. Their villa was less than ten minutes' walk from Aslan's. Pedro, who was in conversation with Costa Security boss Roberto Sanchez, acknowledged Jack with a wave of his right arm. Roberto turned and looked and did likewise. The young woman he was with glanced and smiled, he had never seen her before and it certainly was not Olga's sister Tanya. Just as the band had finished their encore Olga returned. She came up to him and gave him a kiss. "Did you wonder where I was darling?"

"As a matter of fact I did but I was unable to come and look for you." Olga then gave him a sexy look and then smiled. "I know you are dying to tell me where you have been"

"Aslan asked me if I would like a tour around his villa."

"You are very privileged, I work for him and have never been invited."

"George and Freddie showed me around. It is a magnificent property both inside and out. They have some beautiful furniture. It must have cost a fortune to buy and furnish the villa."

"Aslan probably got no change out of three or four million Euros when he bought the villa." Olga looked quite shocked. "Property prices are sky high in Marbella."

She then changed the conversation. "Would you like a glass of Champagne?"

"Yes I would, thank you."

"Right darling I shall go and join the queue." She then leaned forward exposing her revealing cleavage. "When we get back to the Marbella Beach Apartments you can stay the night with me, I need a really good session to keep me going."

"You can't complain, we had sex for over an hour before we came here tonight."

Olga laughed. "That was earlier darling, this will be later, so don't drink too much alcohol, I always like a guy who can rise to the occasion." She then made her way to the bar in the larger marquee.

Olga had only been gone a couple of minutes when Pedro Gonzales came over to talk to Jack at the DJ stand.

"I received a phone call earlier this evening from Miles Coburn, the bug you placed in Olga's apartment is activated. She made a mobile call to someone and asked to meet them urgently. We gather from her conversation, the person she was speaking to will call her back tomorrow. Who it was we have no idea but it certainly was not her sister."

"Maybe it was someone from the Russian Embassy in Madrid."

"Miles said exactly the same."

"Pedro please bear with me for a moment whilst I programme in a medley of songs, then we can speak."

"Jack, I somehow need to place a bug in Aslan's villa. The only problem are the CCTV cameras, they will more than likely pick me up entering the property unless I can put them out of action for a while." He then put his hand inside his left trouser pocket and took out a small black remote control, no more than two inches long. "This little gadget is quite incredible, it can link into any CCTV system via radio waves and put it out of action for as long as you want, but at the press of a button it can reactivate it." "Amazing, what about an alarm system?"

"It can do the same." Pedro hesitated. "Firstly I have to get into Aslan's villa without being seen. All the doors will be locked for security, though it is highly unlikely that the alarm system will be switched on. I need you to keep an eye out for Aslan, George and Freddie; they are the only people likely to go inside the villa. We can communicate via our mobile phones."

"You still have to find somewhere secure to hide the bug." "Fortunately I know Aslan's villa well. Living close by each other, we often visit each other's homes socially in the winter months. Luckily I know the ideal spot to place the bug." Pedro glanced around and then lowered his voice. "In the foyer of the villa, is a small memorial in memory of his family, who died in the Russian-Chechen war. The base of the memorial is covered with small coloured stones, I will place it there. When I re-join my wife, I will excuse myself after a few minutes to visit the gentlemen's loo, providing Aslan and his two Chechen friends are still socializing, I can gain access to the villa by the kitchen door. If you are unable to see them, you must call my mobile phone immediately."

"I understand."

"Don't look now but if you glance up after I depart, you will see a faint red light flashing below all the CCTV cameras. When this light goes out, you will know that I have entered the villa. Jack I am going to leave you now." "Be careful." Pedro smiled and nodded his head.

Five minutes later Olga returned with George and Freddie who were carrying several Chrystal glasses between them.

"Darling, George and Freddie are joining us."

"Sit down guys if you can find a seat."

Freddie then produced a bottle of Dom Perignon Champagne, which had already been uncorked, then poured out four glasses.

"Good health guys."

"Thank you Freddie."

"Help yourself when you want a refill, a local brewery gave us twenty five bottles. The boss won't miss one bottle."

"Where is Aslan tonight, apart from the Charity Auction he appears to be keeping a low profile?"

George laughed as he spoke. "He is propping the bar up with his friends Roscoe Rodriguez and Roberto Sanchez."

Jack noticed Pedro was no longer in the presence of his wife Nada, who was talking to Roscoe's wife and Roberto's female friend. He automatically glanced up at a nearby CCTV camera and the faint red light was out. He had not seen Pedro leave the marquee. As he programmed a change of music into the laptop, he anxiously kept glancing at the CCTV cameras; they were still closed down, until all of a sudden they came back to life.

"Guys, could you keep an eye on the music whilst I take a leek?"

"No problem Jack," replied Freddie.

As soon as he was in the car park he called Pedro on the mobile. "Is everything ok?"

"Absolutely, I am now by the bar having a drink with Aslan and a couple of our friends, I will see you shortly." The line immediately went dead. Pedro had real guts to do what he had just accomplished.

The night was flying by quickly and by all accounts Aslan's fun raising event had been a great success. Whether or not four hundred guests had actually passed through security he had not the foggiest idea, even so, there was one hell of a lot of people about. Alcohol was flowing fast and free and everyone looked so happy. Even the Chechens and Olga were now on the same wave length and all animosity had been cast adrift, as the three of them joined other revellers on the dance floor. Occasionally Jack joined Olga for a dance. It had been a long and most eventful evening. To get away from being the DJ if only for ten minutes brought a sense of relaxation. Tiredness was creeping in. As much as he enjoyed having sex with Olga he badly needed a good night's sleep to recover, preferably alone in his own apartment. Another hour and the night would be over but not without a blast of Electronic Dance Music, so for the last thirty minutes Jack became DJ Ramos and let the music rip. Eventually the evening was brought to an incredible climax with David Guetta's Ibiza disco anthem Titanium. As Jack was otherwise engaged Olga, who had become an addicted House Music fan, dragged George onto the crowded dance floor for the final number to the amusement of Aslan and several of his friends. Tonight was certainly a night everyone would remember.

Jack and Olga left the villa by taxi for the Marbella Beach Apartments shortly before two. His head was spinning and he felt like shit, had he not known what the problem was he would have suspected that someone had spiked his drink. Until this evening, never once in the last ten years whilst performing as a DJ had he gigged on an empty stomach and consumed alcohol, even though it was Dom Perignon Champagne. The beef burger he tried at seven almost caused him to throw up and tasted more like horse meat, which it probably was being in Spain. After two mouthfuls he called it a day and never ate anything all night. Olga on the other hand used her feminine charms to persuade George to concoct a dish of chicken pasta. Jack also noticed for once Olga drank no red wine on the night only champagne. No wonder she was wide awake, normally he would have to support her to walk. Tiredness was now creeping over his body; he now regretted visiting the Ocean Club in Puerto Banus on Saturday evening when he should have been catching up on his sleep, after a busy week. The Ocean Club had style, luxury and glamorous indulgence, the very epitome of what today's beach club should be, with fantastic views across the Mediterranean Sea and only a short stroll away from all the designer boutiques. In the end his visit proved to be a bit of a wasted journey. His friend pop star Boy George had finished his summer season as a DJ and returned to London. Jack felt guilty that he had not visited the club earlier to see George perform. Rather than tell him the truth, he sent him a text whilst he was at the Ocean Club, with the excuse that he thought that this Saturday was George's closing night. George immediately replied, saying not to worry as they were both busy guys and would meet up when he returned to the UK. Jack could not help but smile to himself when he noticed the cross at the end of the text. Even if you were not gay, you could not help but like George, he was such a pleasant guy. Jack's main objective for visiting the club was not to see George, but to check and see if any of the suspected Chechen hijackers frequented the venue. There was certainly no sign of them on Saturday but then again, they could have chosen another night or be working.

Just as Olga and Jack were about to get into a waiting white Mercedes taxi, a smiling George came over to them.

"Jack, Aslan offers his thanks to you for a wonderful evening, he would have thanked you personally but he is lying down, I think he has consumed far too much champagne."

Olga laughed and then gave George an affectionate embrace as she spoke. "You take care and we will see you soon."

Ten minutes later their taxi arrived outside the entrance to the Marbella Beach Apartments. Once Jack had used his key card to gain entrance to the complex, they walked slowly along the illuminated drive to the apartment foyer entrance. Before entering, Jack paused and cast his eyes over the gardens.

"I love this time of the day, it is so peaceful."

Olga did not smile or answer but held his arm tightly and snuggled up to him for warmth, there was now a distinct chill in the air.

"Darling let's go inside, I am starting to feel cold."

The middle aged grey haired security officer, who had been on duty for the last three nights, was sat behind the reception desk reading a newspaper, looked up and smiled but never spoke as they passed through the foyer.

The elevator silently glided them up from the ground floor to the third. Jack's head was starting to throb and he was now having difficulty focusing his eyes.

"You don't look very well darling you should go straight to bed, I will see you early tomorrow afternoon." Olga then placed her arms gently around his neck and gave him a passionate kiss. "Would you like me to walk you down to your apartment?"

Jack laughed as he replied. "No need to, I am not asleep yet."

Five minutes later after returning to his own apartment, Jack switched off his mobile phone and then collapsed fully clothed onto the king size bed in his bedroom, oblivious to what was happing elsewhere in Marbella.

20

The warm rays of the autumn sun creeping through the partly closed bedroom window blinds caused Jack to awaken suddenly from his deep sleep. Leaning over to his left he picked up his gold Gucci watch from the low cream bedside table. Eventually focusing his eyes, he stirred at the watch face. "Christ it was eleven thirty-five, half the day had already gone." Picking up his Sonny mobile phone which was next to his watch, he switched it on. Whatever had been wrong with him last night had cleared up, he felt quite normal. There were five messages from Pedro Gonzales. The first one was left at seven fifteen, and they all said the same, "Jack, pick up your mobile and call me back urgently." Alarm bells started to ring in his head something was wrong.

Jack put a call through to Pedro who immediately answered. "I have been trying to contact you for several hours."

"Sorry my phone was switched off, as I was trying to catch up on my sleep after Aslan's fund raising party."

"Jack, I have some terrible news." Pedro came straight out with it. "Aslan's friend George was found dead in the villa's swimming pool in the early hours of this morning." Jack never answered, he was shell shocked beyond belief. "Are you still there Jack?"

Jack stuttered as he spoke. "Yes, I am stuck for words. I find it hard to believe. What an earth has happened?"

"I received an emotional phone call from Aslan shortly before five thirty, asking me to come round to his villa. I went round immediately, as our two villas are only a few hundred metres apart, I quickly threw on some clothes and was there in less than ten minutes. George was floating face down in the swimming pool. He was wearing the light grey shorts he normally sleeps in. Aslan is unable to swim due to a serious war injury to his leg so I dived into the water and brought George to the side of the pool, where we both pulled him out. There was no sign of life. It was obvious to us that the poor guy was already dead. We immediately called the ambulance service and police who both arrived within minutes, even with their medical expertise and equipment, the paramedics could not detect any sign of life. They reckon that George had been in the water for at least an hour before he was found.

"How did Aslan react?"

"He was heartbroken. Aslan had gone to bed well before the party finished, leaving George in charge as he felt unwell. He actually never saw him alive again."

Jack then told Pedro about George waving goodbye to him and Olga at the end of the evening and apologizing for Aslan's absence.

"To be honest with you, the last hour was very strange. Aslan was in bed ill and I was heading the same way. I was having difficulty keeping awake and felt as though I had consumed far too much alcohol."

"Had you drank too much?"

"No way, I am always very careful when I gig."

"Perhaps someone spiked yours and Aslan's drinks."

"What are you saying?"

"There is the possibility that poor George was assassinated by the Russians."

"You really think so?"

"I am only guessing at the moment but it may be coincidence that you and Aslan both became ill at the same time. George would be alone and you would be preoccupied with your stage show and your deteriorating health. We know from Miles Coburn that Olga is a Kremlin assassin. Did you see her twin sister Tanya at the party?" "No, but I did look out for her."

"At the moment we have no proof, we shall have to wait and see what the post mortem results are before we make any judgement. The Police Inspector I spoke to said they would have the post mortem results within three days." Pedro paused for a moment. "Where is Olga now?"

"I presume she is in her apartment, she said she would call me early afternoon."

"Should you visit her apartment be very careful what you say as Ml6 are monitoring all conversations. Coburn is convinced she is up to something. Shortly after you placed the bug in her apartment she was on her mobile to some Russian speaking guy. Though we are unable to bug her mobile, our guys got the impression even with a broken conversation that she was after an explosive device and a couple of hand guns."

"Who would she be calling?"

"Most probably the Russian Embassy in Madrid. Coburn said that she has arranged to meet some guy on Wednesday. Where and what time we have no idea at the moment."

Jack thought for a moment. "It is a long hike from Madrid to Marbella, about 362 miles, a five and a half hour journey by car unless you are driving a high powered motor bike, and then you could knock an hour off the time. My guess would be, that the guy from Madrid would arrive around mid-afternoon in the Puerto Banus area, possibly San Pedro and stay the night at Tanya's apartment."

"Jack, you could well be right. We shall need to keep a close watch on her apartment."

"No problem I will check it out from mid-day."

"Pedro do you have Aslan's private mobile number, I need to give the poor guy a call?"

"I have but when you call him, please tell him that I have passed it on to you, he likes to keep it private."

"Of course I will."

"Jack, as soon as I have any more news I will call you, otherwise I will see you at the Med Club as usual on Tuesday evening. Before I forget, when I was placing the bug in Aslan's villa, I snooped around the property as I have been in the villa on many occasions. At the rear of the villa there is what you Brits would call a Granny Flat. There is someone living in it, I could see a faint light and the flashing of a television screen. It is highly possible that Sergei Aslanov has returned from his overseas business trip and is in hiding out at the villa. We need to investigate and find out who is actually living at the villa."

"Maybe the bug you have planted will offer an explanation."

As soon as Jack put his mobile down his mind drifted back to Sunday evening. With the sudden death of George, he was now more than ever convinced that someone had spiked his Champagne. Olga was the number one suspect, but then again George may have died from natural causes, if this was the case Olga would be in the clear. Aslan appreciated Jack's phone call, he was clearly in a very distressed state.

"If there is anything I can do for you please tell me."

"At the moment Jack I am in complete shock. The medics suspect George may have had a major heart attack due to the bluish tinge of his lips, and then stumbled into the swimming pool and drowned. I find it hard to believe, he was such a fit young man." Aslan then fell silent. "Can I confine in you Jack?"

"George and I were not lovers, neither of us are gay, I was like a father to him. He is the youngest son of my sister Mia, she sent him here for his safety because the Russian FSB were after him. How do I tell my sister that her loving son my nephew is dead, I was supposed to be protecting him."

"Are you by yourself in your villa?"

"Yes."

"Would you like some company?"

"Thank you Jack, I would appreciate that."

"I will be with you in about an hour."

After a quick shave and shower, Jack opened the balcony doors to freshen up the apartment whilst he sat in the kitchen drinking an Americano coffee. The weather was overcast with no sun and there had been a sudden drop in temperature. Slipping on his black leather zip jacket, he closed the open balcony doors and headed upstairs to Olga's apartment. When she opened the door she appeared surprised to see him.

"Darling, I thought you would have been having a lie in after last night." She then put both her arms around his neck and kissed him with her soft lips.

"I feel more or less normal but thanks for asking." He then placed both his hands on her slim waist. "I have some really tragic news for you." Olga looked into his eyes but did not say anything. "Aslan Maskhadov's friend George has been found dead in the early hours of this morning in the villa's swimming pool. Pedro Gonzales the boss of the Med Club rang with the news. I immediately telephoned Aslan and offered to call round to see him. We have got to know each other very well since I have been working for him."

Olga still didn't say anything, suddenly tears started to run from her eyes. "How terrible, the poor man must be heartbroken to lose his boyfriend." Jack then took a white handkerchief out of his left trouser pocket and whipped Olga's face dry, accidently smudging her black eye makeup.

"George is not Aslan's boyfriend, neither of them are gay." Olga looked quite shocked. "George is Aslan's nephew."

There was a look of genuine shock on her face. "How terrible to lose a family member so tragically and so young. Do you know what happened?"

"Not really. I gather Aslan found him in the swimming pool around five in the morning. He immediately telephoned Pedro Gonzales who lives close by; the police and ambulance service were then called. We should know more after a post mortem." Jack then took hold of Olga's hands. "I am sorry I am unable to take you out for lunch but I shall be back in a couple of hours, perhaps then we can dine out."

The lovely smile on Olga's face suddenly disappeared. "Darling, I was looking forward to spending time with you today, making love and then going out to a posh restaurant."

"No problem, when I return we will do that."

The smile on her face quickly returned. "I shall look forward to seeing you later. On second thoughts, would you like me to come with you?"

"On this occasion I don't think it would be wise but I will certainly tell Aslan you are thinking of him."

"Thank you darling."

"Now if you will excuse me. I must get a taxi and head over to Aslan's villa, he is expecting me within the hour." Once he had walked down the white marble staircase to the foyer, Jack called a local taxi that arrived at the main entrance within minutes. Twenty minutes later Jack was sat in the modern but extremely elegant lounge of Aslan Maskhadov's stunning villa.

"I appreciate you calling round Jack. It is good to have a friend to talk to." Jack smiled. "George's death has shocked me, I find it so hard to believe that he could have died from natural causes. His mother Mia will be heartbroken when I finally pick up the courage to call her; she lives in Grozny, Chechnya."

Jack smiled as he spoke. "You must call her as soon as possible and tell her the truth, you have done nothing wrong. The post mortem may show that George had a problem which he was not aware of."

"You are quite right Jack, I will call her later." Aslan then stood up and walked over to the closed patio windows and looked out over the gardens before turning round and sitting down again. "Jack, I am delighted that you decided to come and work for Cobra Jewellery. May I say that I find you very easy to get on with and talk to, you are the perfect employee?" Jack smiled but didn't say anything. "Can I offer you a glass of wine or a coffee?"

"A coffee would be most welcome."

Aslan then got up from the soft white leather chair he was sat in and walked towards the kitchen. Jack followed him. "You have a stunning kitchen Aslan, in fact you have a stunning villa."

"Thank you, the kitchen is German. I am extremely fussy I only like quality."

"I am not being noisy but what was your profession before you came to Marbella?"

"I was in the jewellery business in Grozny, Chechnya with my late wife and we had a very successful store."

Aslan then passed Jack a glass beaker of warm coffee. "Milk with no sugar, is that correct?"

Jack smiled as he spoke. "You have a good memory." Aslan smiled again, he was a good looking guy.

"Why did you leave Grozny?"

Jack could swear there were tears in Aslan's eyes as he spoke. "I never wanted to leave Chechnya but life can be so bloody cruel. The Chechen–Russian war had broken out with frequent bombing raids on Grozny. There had been a lull in the fighting for a few days. I was very busy in the store, so my wife and our only daughter and her husband, with their six-year-old daughter Gabrielle, went for a walk in the local park. It was a beautiful summer's day, the swallows were darting back and forth and there was a smell of jasmine in the air. In the middle of the park is a very old and quaint café, which is very popular with the locals. My family were sat outside enjoying the sunshine, when a Russian MiG-29 fighter jet flew over the city, for some reason which has never been explained, the pilot sprayed the café in the park with gun fire. There were about forty four people sat outside including my family, everyone died. There was no need for this attack; it was nothing but fucking murder. We Chechens have carried out atrocities but nothing like this. I will never forgive the Kremlin for taking my loving family away from me, my life was in shreds. I immediately sold my business and with the help of a banker friend, transferred my financial assists, which were quite considerable, to Malta. After much thought I joined the Chechen Separatist Movement and became one of their top commanders. When the war came to its inevitable conclusion, the Kremlin gave the order to assassinate all Chechen leaders including myself. I fled to Spain where I was granted asylum and Spanish citizenship. Once I had settled into my new way of life, I learnt Spanish as I knew very little of the language and had to get by on speaking broken English. Later I transferred a large part of my financial assets from Malta to Spain and set up business in Marbella and along the Costa del Sol."

"What an incredible story. Do you think you will ever return to Chechnya?"

"Most unlikely, apart from my sister all my family are dead. In any case if I returned home, the Russians would send someone to assassinate me. I admit that I do miss my sister, but fortunately she and her family fly out to Spain twice a year to see me and stay in the villa as my guests."

"Tell me, why were the Russians after George?"

Aslan then drank the remainder of his coffee before continuing with the conversation. "About fifteen months ago a Russian Cargo plane carrying over a billion Euros of diamonds and precious gems was hijacked whilst returning from Siberia. The two pilots on board were murdered but the diamonds never found. The Russian Government have a list of eight Chechens who all studied at the Aircraft and Engineering Academy in Moscow, and believe they all had an involvement in the hijack. My nephew George was on that list. I was also informed a week ago by one of my old Chechen contacts that the Russians have sent a hit man to assassinate any of the wanted Chechens, who may have moved to the Costa del Sol for safety. The Russians have a policy, return the diamonds and gems or be exterminated."

"George and Freddie, were they the only two Chechens on the hit list employed by you?"

"Yes. I do employ Sergei Aslanov but he is Georgian."

"Do you think he is involved?"

"He could be but I have no proof."

"What about the other Chechens on the list, are they living on the Costa del Sol?"

"I believe they are. Freddie tells me that two of them work at Pinks and the others are employed at bars in Puerto Banus."

"Have you heard anything from Sergei?"

"Yes, he will be back here in the next couple of days. I will then introduce you to him."

The external buzzer to the villa rang just as Aslan was about to say something else. He immediately pressed a switch by the door and the CCTV screen flickered to life.

"The Event Company is here to remove the marquees and equipment, then tidy up and remove all the rubbish. The police said the area was a crime scene until they gave the ok shortly before you arrived, otherwise everything would have been back to normal by now."

"Would you like me to speak to the marquee guys for you?"

"I would appreciate that Jack. Perhaps you would offer my apologies to them for not being around. Would you also thank them for supplying all the equipment and making it another fantastic fund raising event?"

"No problem, just leave everything to me."

Three hours later the villa was back to normal, looking across the perfectly manicured garden towards the swimming pool, it was hard to believe what had happened just a few hours earlier.

"Jack, thank you for your help, I will see you in the office on Thursday."

"A pleasure, if I can be of any assistance before then please do not hesitate to call me." Aslan smiled and nodded his head.

"Will you be ok by yourself here? It is not the ideal situation to be alone at this moment."

"Thank you for your concern Jack but Freddie will be around."

"Good, I had better get back to the Marbella Beach Apartments. I promised to take Olga out for a meal this evening."

"Jack don't trust her she is Russian. She may be a stunning looking girl, but there is something about her which rings alarm bells in my head."

"Thanks for the warning, at times I have the same feeling."

After calling a taxi, Jack embraced Aslan and then made his way out the villa complex just as the taxi arrived. Fifteen minutes later he was inside the Marbella Beach Apartments complex making his way through the gardens to the foyer.

"Hi darling," Jack glanced to his right. Olga was walking towards him, dressed in a pretty black and white off the shoulder sun dress. I have been enjoying the sunshine whilst waiting for you."

"You look lovely."

"Thank you Jack," Olga's smile looked beautiful and there was a hint of excitement in her eyes as she removed her designer shades. "How was Aslan?"

"Devastated especially with George being his nephew.

"George was his sister Mia's only son."

"Poor man, how terribly sad." Jack then noticed how quickly Olga changed the conversation; she certainly showed very little compassion.

"What is it to be darling? Your apartment or mine before you take me out for a meal."

Jack slipped his arm around Olga's slim waist and then whispered in her ear. "My apartment, by the way where would you like to dine this evening?"

Olga did not even hesitate. "The Albatross, it is a lovely venue and the food is always excellent."

"The Albatross it is then."

Jack had his hour of passion before Olga went upstairs to her apartment to get changed into something warmer. There had been a sudden drop in the temperature and the forecast was rain. Luckily they managed to get to Albatross before the heavy downpour came. Despite the change in the weather the restaurant was still very busy. After dining they sat by the bar for the next two hours and consumed a bottle of Spanish red wine, whilst talking to the owner Roscoe Rodriguez, in between him serving customers behind the bar. Roscoe said the whole of the Marbella community were shocked with the sudden death of George. "The young Chechen was a very popular guy and everyone felt for Aslan. We all pray it is natural causes and there is nothing sinister in his death."

As they were about to leave the Albatross and make their way along the Esplanade Paseo to the Marbella Beach Apartments, the rain started to fall quite heavily.

"Let me call you a taxi, there is no point in walking and getting wet through." Roscoe then opened the double glass door of the restaurant and looked outside. "Mark my words, this rain will freshen everything up and tomorrow will be another beautiful day."

"I hope you are right." The restaurant owner laughed as they walked towards the waiting taxi. Ten minutes later after being dropped off at the main entrance to the Marbella Beach Apartments, they quickly made their way towards the foyer; fortunately the rain had slackened off a little. The young Tunisian guy Youssef Beji was on reception.

Youssef looked up and smiled at they walked in. "Good to see you again Youssef, I have not seen you for a while."

"I have been helping out at a hotel in Malaga where the boss is expanding his business." Youssef then turned to Olga who looked completely bored with the conversation. "I am taking your friend Emma out for a spin in the Black Prince on Thursday, do you fancy coming along?"

Olga shook her head. "No thank you I prefer dry land." Youssef laughed.

"We are having an early night as I will be performing my gig at the Med Club tomorrow evening, and need to be on form." Without another word they made their way across the foyer to the elevator and headed to the third floor.

"Are you certain you won't come in?"

"I would love to but I do need to get some beauty sleep. I will call you around mid-day if you like."

"Good, I thought you had gone off me."

"No way, you are a very sexy lady."

Olga smiled and then kissed him hard on the lips, pressing her warm tongue inside his mouth. Jack then pulled her closer. He could feel the warmth of her soft breasts against his chest. Olga kissed him again.

"Will you be at my gig at the Med Club tomorrow night?" "Of course I will darling, my friend Emma will be coming with me."

"Good, I will see you around mid-day tomorrow."

Olga smiled as she let herself into the apartment. As Jack slowly made his way down the white marble staircase to his second floor apartment, doubts flooded into his mind about Olga. She was extremely affectionate towards him but something told him not to trust her. Miles Coburn had already told him, that she and her twin sister Tanya were Russian assassins. Maybe it was the crocodile tears and the distinct coldness in her reaction to George's sudden death which had triggered alarm bells, from now on he would have to be one step ahead of her.

21

Tuesday was always a busy day at Cobra Jewellery. When Aslan suggested he took a couple of days off to recover from the weekend, Jack did not need any convincing. It had been both a hectic and heartbreaking weekend with the children's' hospice fund raising event at Aslan's villa, and then George's sudden death. There were telephone calls to be made to his boss Miles Coburn and his sister Lilly, which would then be followed by a quick twenty lengths in the swimming pool. In the afternoon after an hour of passion with Olga, he would take her out for a late lunch. Later in the evening, he would head to the Med Beach Club to perform his House Music gig to a capacity audience after an urgent meeting with the club's owner and fellow Ml6 agent Pedro Gonzales.

When the alarm on Jack's mobile woke him at nine, he was thankful for eight and half hours of unbroken sleep. The bedroom and lounge were quite warm so he walked naked into the lounge and opened both the balcony doors. Roscoe had been right with his prediction; it was another beautiful day even after last night's heavy rain storm. After a quick shower and shave and then a light breakfast, he called Miles Coburn in London. Miles was always pleased to hear from him.

"We believe our female assassins are on the move, that is why you and Pedro must monitor Tanya's apartment in Puerto Banus on Wednesday. Tanya and her sister Olga are certainly up to something. Whoever called Olga on her mobile last week has called her again and arranged to meet her on Wednesday at three. Olga's contact said he would call her again when he reached the outskirts of Marbella. We should also hear the results of the post mortem on George in the next couple of days."

"I called round to see Aslan Maskhadov on Sunday and Monday."

"We already know. We monitored your visit via the bug Pedro placed inside the villa. After you left Freddie arrived at the villa, there was a lengthy conversation between the two men, but nothing suspicious. About half an hour later a third male voice was heard in the back ground. This could have been the person who was keeping out of site at the rear of the villa. It could well be Sergei Aslanov but at the moment we have no proof, it will be up to you and Pedro to find out who the guy is. As soon as you do, call me immediately."

Twenty minutes later Jack put a call through to his sister Lilly in Ludlow.

"I was expecting your call today. It is good to hear from you Jack." Lilly paused for a second. "When will you be coming home?"

"Hopefully in the next few weeks, how are you?"

"I am fine, my medication has kicked in and I can now lead a normal life. The children are at school and Bret is at work."

"Give my love to them."

"I will."

After another twenty minutes their call ended.

"Jack don't forget I love you." Lilly always ended their conversation the same way. He missed his loving sister immensely. Tomorrow he would call his brother Lex in Malaga and arrange to see him. Though they spoke frequently, Jack had only visited his brother and his family twice since moving to Spain. It was about time he changed all this so tomorrow he would get the ball rolling.

After completing twenty lengths in a swimming pool, which was colder than usual, Jack was glad to get out and dry off in the sun. Twenty five minutes later, he walked through the still flowering garden to the apartment block foyer. As he was about to climb the white marble staircase to his second floor apartment, he felt a gentle hand on his right shoulder.

"Darling, I was just coming to find you."

Jack smiled and slid his arm around Olga's waist and then kissed her.

"I need to get changed. My swimming shorts are still very damp."

Once in his apartment, he went through to his bedroom and slipped out of his wet shorts. Olga whistled as he stood there naked with his back to her. Picking up a soft white cotton bath towel which was lying on a nearby chair, she wiped his body dry and then pushed him backwards onto the king size bed. Even though her eyes were glued to his body, she still managed to slip out of her clothes and climb on top of him, and then gyrate until she was completely satisfied. An hour and twenty minutes later they left the Marbella Beach Complex and walked along the Esplanade Paseo to the Picasso Café Bar for an early evening meal. As they walked hand in hand she whispered in his ear. "Darling, before you go to the Med Club this evening I want you again, we have plenty of time before I take a taxi to Porto Banus to meet my friend Emma."

Jack arrived at the Med Club shortly before nine. Once he had set up his laptop he made his way to Pedro's office.

"Good to see you Jack." The two men embraced. "I gather you have been speaking to Miles Coburn."

"Yes I have, Miles appears very concerned about the two Russian girls."

"I think we should be because they are up to something. I will pick you up at the Marbella Beach Apartment at ten tomorrow morning, we can both keep an eye on Tanya's apartment and we will also have my car available should we have to follow them."

DJ Ramos and his House Music were once again the stars of the night. A capacity audience full of local celebrities helped to create another incredible night to remember. Olga and her friend Emma came up to the DJ stand and Olga whispered in his ear. "Darling, you are a brilliant DJ and an incredible lover, thank you for a great day I will see you tomorrow." She then gave him a sexy kiss. Emma gave her a dirty look and said something to her; fortunately the microphone was switched off. As soon as his gig finished at one, the Med Club's resident DJs Jose and Selena took over for the rest of the evening and Jack got a taxi back to the Marbella Beach Apartments. Youssef was on reception duty, after a brief conversation Jack made an excuse and headed upstairs to his apartment and bed.

A few minutes before ten on Wednesday morning Jack's mobile rang. "It is me Pedro I am outside the main entrance."

"I will be with you very shortly."

The weather was still quite warm with no breeze and a clear sky but even so he had decided to wear his black leather zip jacket. Pedro was sat in his Hyacinth Red Metallic C-Class Mercedes with the radio on.

"Good morning my friend, jump in and we will be on our way."

As the Mercedes slipped onto the main coastal highway, Pedro switched the radio off.

"Rain is expected by mid-afternoon so let us hope the forecast is wrong. I am going to park on the main car park, from there it is less than a five minute walk to Tanya's apartment. It is in an area where there are many bars and shops. The tourists are still flooding in so we won't be conspicuous.

The highway was busy with traffic but they still managed to make the four mile journey in less than twenty minutes. After parking the Mercedes, Jack and Pedro made their way along Muelle de Ribero, a narrow street just back a few metres from the harbour. Once past Linekers, the largest and busiest bar in Puerto Banus, they proceeded down the street which was very quiet, eventually passing Pinks girlie club, which only opened around six in the evening. Almost at the end of the street Pedro pointed to a white painted alleyway.

"That is where Tanya has her apartment. There are five others in the same block, hers is on the top floor on the right. I would have loved to have placed a bug in her apartment but it proved to be too difficult. Neighbours were always around when I paid her a visit, in the end I gave up." Pedro glanced at his watch. "At eleven fifteen we can visit Pips café bar across the street and order a coffee. If we sit outside we can observe the entrance to the alleyway as there is no rear exit."

"You have done your homework well."

"You have to in this game," said Pedro smiling.

An hour later they left the café bar, separated and each patrolled along the Muelle de Ribera in different directions.

Jack took out his mobile from inside his black leather zip jacket and called Pedro at the far end of the street. "Any sign of the Russian girls?"

"No nothing. We will give it until one and then go for a bite to eat in the café bar. Unfortunately I am going to have to leave you at two. I need to get back to the Med Club as there are two 21st birthday parties booked in this evening. You can keep in touch with me via your mobile."

"Of course I will. I will see you in twenty minutes."

When they arrived at the café bar which had a very busy lunchtime trade, they both ordered a roast ham sandwich and a pint of lager beer.

Jack had liked Pedro from the first day they had met. He was an honest guy who always told you the truth.

"I have an uneasy feeling, that that one of the girls possibly both of them left the apartment before we arrived this morning." Pedro then glanced at his watch. "Unfortunately I am going to have to leave you now." He then drank the remains of the lager in his glass. "Jack thank you for the lunch and do not forget to call me if you need any help."

The two men then got up from their table outside the café bar and walked along the street.

Pedro turned to Jack. "I know it is a bit of a drag, but you need to hang around this end of the street until it starts to get dark. Coburn is convinced something will happen today and he is sold on your motor bike theory."

"Even if nothing happens, I will call you later." The two men then parted company.

The next two hours passed by slowly, the weather was changing and the odd speck of rain started to fall. He was glad he was wearing his black leather zip jacket. Puerto Banus was now getting busier by the hour, more people about made it easier for him to blend in. Around four whilst he was drinking a latte in Pips Cafe Bar, a high powered black and red Ducati Diavel motorbike slowly drifted into the alleyway. The rider was dressed in black leather with dark steel capped boots. As well as a red helmet and black sun visor he wore dark shades and black leather gloves. On his back he had a dark blue rucksack. There was a female pillion passenger sat behind him. She wore tight blue jeans, a high necked black leather jacket, brown boots and gloves, with a red helmet and dark shades. Once the bike came to a standstill they both got off. He then secured the motorbike. Neither of them spoke but the rider who was about six two and broad shouldered, followed the pillion passenger into the apartment block. The girl could easily have been Olga or Tanya but it was impossible to tell for certain, though she was definitely young by the agile way she moved.

Jack then left Pips and walked a few yards to the end of the street, taking his mobile out of his jacket pocket he called Pedro.

"Your theory was right Jack; this guy is here for a particular reason. If you will let me have the registration number of the motorbike, I will do an immediate check on who owns it." The line suddenly went quiet.

"Pedro, are you still there?"

"Sorry, I was just moving around, I am still at the Med Club, the reception is not always good in here."

"What do you think I should do now, it is starting to go dark and I have a feeling it is going to rain.

"Is there any movement in the apartment?"

"No, there is a light on but they have window blinds which are closed, it is impossible to see anything."

"It is a pity that I am not with you, for surveillance like this you need at least two operatives working together. Jack, if you can last out for a couple of more hours these guys will have to eat. When they re-appear, try to get a photo on your mobile of the guy on the motorbike. If you send it to me I will pass it on to Miles Coburn, who might be able to identify him." Pedro paused for a moment. "Then if I was you I would take a taxi back to your apartment, it has been a long day for you."

"The girl on the motorbike concerns me. How did she manage to leave the apartment this morning without us noticing? Are you certain there is no rear entrance?" "Absolutely, Tanya could have stayed in Olga's apartment at the Marbella Beach Apartments last night without your knowledge. After you left there this morning, all she had to do was wait for a mobile call from the guy on the motorbike telling her where to meet him and then take a taxi. You would be none the wiser."

"You are probably right, I had not thought about that." "Jack, call me when you arrive back at your apartment." Their conversation then ended.

At twenty minutes past seven, the lights went out in Tanya's apartment. A few minutes later three people came out of the apartment block into the alleyway. Jack immediately recognised Olga and Tanya but the guy with them was unknown to him. Using his mobile phone camera, Jack managed to take half a dozen clear shots, which included several close ups of the mystery guy. He then forwarded them to Pedro. Jack then ran his eyes over the photos he had just taken. He recognised Olga and Tanya but not the guy. He was a handsome bloke with short blond hair, about six two, very athlete looking and slim, who probably visited the gym most days. After following the three of them to the Port Side Restaurant, he watched them enter and then sit down at a table close to the bar. There was no more Jack could do, so he hailed a taxi and went back to the Marbella Beach Apartments. After a quick shower and a change of clothing, he headed down the Esplanade Paseo for a bite to eat at the Picasso Café Bar.

Olga, Tanya and their mystery male friend left the Port Side Restaurant shortly before ten and walked back to Tanya's apartment. There was a chill in the air but at least the heavy rain expected had kept away.

Once back in the apartment Kazimir, everyone called him Kaz, picked up his black rucksack from behind the window chair and took out a dull plastic container. "When you are ready girls, I will give you both a lesson into how you use this little device."

Both the girls eagerly came over to him just like a teacher with his students. Kaz opened the container and took out one of the two small black plastic objects about the size of a large box of Swan matches, then picked it up in his left hand. "This little gadget can blow this apartment block sky high. What do you girls want it for?"

The twins looked at each other.

"We are on the same side girls, you can tell me."

Olga broke the silence. "We have four Chechens who we wish to take out. They were all involved in the Siberian Cargo plane hijack."

"Why use explosives?"

"Much cleaner and a lot less trouble." said Olga. Both the girls then smiled before Tanya continued.

"The Chechens we want to eliminate all live together in a large rented apartment above an old motor vehicle repair shop on the outskirts of San Pedro. The boys use gas for cooking and heating. The gas boiler for the property is in the old workshop directly beneath the apartment. The building, which is detached, is situated down a rough road off the main coastal highway. We have visited the property several times and gained access to the old garage workshop, it is a real shit hole just waiting for a gas explosion to happen."

"So you girls are waiting for an expert to show you how to do it."

The twins laughed. "Girls, you have come to the right guy. All you have to do is to attach this small box to the boiler where the main gas pipe enters and then press this small switch on the side down, the device is then activated. The base of the box is magnetic so you won't have any problems. May I suggest that you use both of the explosive devices, that way the evidence will be completely obliterated, by the huge fire. There is only one way to set off the explosion, then he took an old Nokia mobile phone from the inside pocket of his black leather bikers jacket. If you tap in 55552 into the mobile, an electronic single will be sent to the explosive devices, which will then detonate them. Providing you do not tap 55552 into this mobile, there is no way the device can be detonated, you can drop it on the floor, throw it up in the air and catch it, but it will still not explode. The only way you can detonate it, is by taping in the code number into this mobile phone, which will then send an electronic single to the detonator. By the way, you must not be more than half a mile away from the explosive device when you detonate, otherwise it may not receive the single.

"What is this explosive?"

"Very similar to the Semtex plastic explosive, but it is ten times as powerful."

Both Olga and Tanya burst out laughing. Kaz looked at them; there was a strange glare in his light blue eyes.

Olga continued to giggle as she spoke. "I bet the Chechen boys never thought they would be attending their own private cremation. Kaz started to laugh as well.

"Kaz, did you bring us two hand guns?"

"Of course girls, I have two Beretta M9 semi-automatic pistols with silencers and several clips of ammunition. Both the pistols are untraceable." He then took them out of his rucksack. "May I suggest after they have been used, that you dispose of them by dropping them both and the ammunition into the harbour?"

Olga picked up one of the pistols and ran her slender fingers over it. "The Beretta is such a deadly and beautiful pistol." She then looked Kaz straight in the eyes. "Would you do us girls a great favour, and come with us now to where the Chechens live. Whilst they are working, you could attach the explosive devices to the pipes leading into the gas boiler, we don't want to make any mistakes. What do you say Kaz?" He did not answer but laughed. "Darling, we will make it worth your while when we return."

"I am sure you will but I never mix business with pleasure. In any case, if I do all the work for you, all the excitement has gone. I am sorry to disappoint you girls but I need to hit the sack as soon as possible, it has been a long day and I need a shower and a good night's sleep. It is a five hour journey back to Madrid, so I intend to be on the road by eight. If you will excuse me now girls I must get some shut eye, I will see you in the morning before I leave." Without another word he left the room.

22

On Thursday morning Jack arrived at the Cobra Jewellery Head Quarters at eight thirty. The owner Aslan Maskhadov's Mini Cooper was on the company car park so to all intent he was already in his office. Once through all the security formalities Jack entered the building.

Aslan was in the entrance hall talking to a staff member. "Good morning Jack, I saw you from my office window." The two men embraced. "Could I have a few words with you in my office?"

"Of course you can. How are you?"

"Still terribly shocked,"

"When do you expect to hear from the police pathologist?"

"There will be a written report by tomorrow." Aslan beckoned to one of the leather chairs, Jack sat down. "I happen to know the pathologist who is carrying out the post-mortem; he called me last night and updated me. He said there was no medical reason why George had a heart attack, he was only twenty six and appeared to be very fit and well. He has taken a sample of his blood from his body, and sent it to the police crime laboratory in Malaga, for a detailed analysis. He should get a result by next Monday."

"How was your sister when you broke the news to her?" "Heartbroken, her husband who was also in shock came on the phone and said they were too upset to speak and would call back later, which they did. It has been a terrible shock for both of them. When George's body is released, they intend to fly over from Chechen and take him back home for burial." Aslan then took a white cotton handkerchief out of his right trouser pocket and gently blew his nose. George was intending to stay permanently in Spain and was in the process of applying for all the necessary documents. It was my intention to eventually take him into the business as my assistant. If I am honest with you Jack, I do need some help in running Cobra Jewellery, but that person has to be completely trustworthy. The company is expanding quickly especially since we started designing and manufacturing our own costume jewellery. Would you be interested in joining me permanently as my assistant?"

Jack was completely taken back; it was the last thing he had expected, a new job offer.

"Obviously your salary will increase."

"What about my DJ gig at the Med Club?"

"That will be no problem, just carry on as normal. After a lie in on Wednesday morning, you could come into the office in the afternoon. You would still carry on your job as a gemmologist, but I would teach you all I know about the other side of jewellery business. If all goes well, I could be in a position to make you the General Manager of Cobra Jewellery in a few months' time. What do you say Jack?"

"Aslan, I am extremely flattered that you trust me so much but I first need to speak to my sister Lilly in the UK, we are very close and she is eventually expecting me to return home. On the other hand my brother Lex, who as you know is the Manager and Head Coach of Malaga F C, will be delighted. Give me twenty four hours and I will give you my answer."

Aslan smiled before he spoke again. "There is no reason why every four or five weeks you can't fly home to see your sister."

Jack smiled. "I will give you my answer by next Monday if that is all right by you." Aslan nodded his head in agreement. "Now if you will excuse me I had better get back to my office, there is a large quantity of precious gems, which need grading." As he got up from his chair Jack turned and faced Aslan again. "How do you know you can trust me?"

"You have to thank your former boss the Chairman of Franks in London, Jim Richardson, who speaks most highly of you. If he trusts you so do I." Jack smiled. He then left Aslan's office, there was a very busy day ahead of him.

The day passed by quickly and later when he arrived back at the Marbella Beach Apartments, he put a call through to his brother Lex and arranged to go to Malaga's Saturday home fixture against Athletic Bilbao.

"I will arrange for you to collect you ticket from the Ticket Reservation Office, it will be under your name. How are you going to get to Malaga?"

"I intend to hire a car for a long weekend."

"Good, after the match you can stay with Maria and me at our villa for the weekend. We can then go out for a meal together. Give me a call when you arrive at the stadium." "Thank you Lex, I shall look forward to this weekend take care brother."

"You too Jack,"

After a couple of quick mobile calls to Miles Coburn in London and his MI6 colleague Pedro Gonzales at the Med Club to put them in the picture about Aslan Maskhadov's business offer, he rang Olga on the internal apartment house phone.

"I am sorry I did not call you earlier but it has been one of those days, I have been extremely busy at work, it was around six thirty when I arrived back at my apartment." "Don't worry darling, which restaurant are you taking me to tonight or would you rather me prepare a meal for us in my apartment. Afterwards you can make love to me; I have missed you this week." Jack went quiet. "Darling are you still there?"

"Sorry, but I did not realise that one of your many talents was cooking."

"You would be very surprised if you knew my entire talents darling."

"Would you rather dine out?" Olga thought for a second. Yes, let's try one of the restaurants in the city centre. We can get a taxi, if we walk down the Esplanade Paseo it will most probably start to rain, there is quite a strong wind blowing in from the sea."

"Do you know the Tempora Restaurant?"

"No."

"Pedro Gonzales, who has the Med Beach Club always dines there with his wife when they go out, he said it is quite upmarket.

"That will be fine by me."

"I will book us a taxi. Can you be ready by eight thirty?" "For you darling, I will make certain I am. As soon as I am ready I will come down to your apartment."

When Olga arrived at his apartment she looked stunning. Jack always felt a million dollars when he walked out with her. Had she not been working for the Russian FSB she would have made a perfect partner, but Jack knew sooner or later their relationship would come to an end. In the meantime he intended to enjoy Olga's company and indulge in her wild fantasies whilst he could.

Friday was another busy day at the Cobra Jewellery Head Office, it was easy to see why Aslan needed an assistant, business was booming. The mobile on his office desk vibrated, he had purposely put it on silent mode. Miles Coburn's number came up.

Jack picked up the phone. "Can you speak Jack?"

"No problem, I am alone in my office at the Cobra Jewellery HQ."

"I am calling about our brief conversation last night. I spoke to Pedro this morning and we discussed the situation. In fact we both came to the same conclusion. If you are offered the position as Aslan's assistant take it. Neither of us is convinced that Aslan is involved in the Siberian cargo plane hijack or even disposing of the stolen diamonds and gems. The bug in his villa has proved most useful. Our expert has identified the voices of two males who are living at the villa, Aslan and Freddie. There is also a third who we suspect is Sergei Aslanov. Once Aslan has gained your confidence, it is possible he may confide in you about who else is staying in the villa."

Jack then gave Miles an update on the pathologist's unofficial report on the death of George.

"I would not be surprised if it is a new Russian nerve agent which creates a heart attack. The British have been trying for years to perfect one at their research centre at Porton Down, Wiltshire. Mind you, so have the Americans and the French and probably the Chinese as well. There have been rumours floating around for a while, that the Russians have finally perfected an untraceable nerve agent, which gives the effect of a major heart attack. Go ahead Jack take the Job offer, the sooner we can wrap up this incident the better. The PM is not happy with us helping the Russians, but he is prepared to put up with the situation, providing we get the right result in the end, best of luck.

The heavy overnight rain on Thursday brought everything back to life. There was freshness in the air and the sun was shining as he made his way to a nearby café bar to get a bite to eat for lunch. Jack glanced at his watch; it was a few minutes past one. The café was fairly busy but eventually he managed to order his usual roast ham sandwich and latte coffee. As there was a lack of room inside, he sat at one of the vacant tables outside. It was a sheltered area and it felt quite warm. Taking his mobile out of the inside pocket of his black leather zip jacket, he called his old boss at Franks in the UK, Jim Richardson.

Jim immediately answered. "Jack, I thought you might call me. How are you my friend?"

"I am very well and enjoying life in Marbella."

"And you?"

Health wise I can't complain but as usual I am overworked."

"My father always said you loved your job." Jim laughed. "By the way thank you for your glowing reference, Aslan was most impressed."

"I meant every word of it. There is every chance that if the promotion works out, he may make you the General Manager of Cobra Jewellery."

"He has already mentioned that."

"Should this happen, Franks would be most interested in linking up with you. We could do with a close permanent contact in Spain; you would make a perfect partner. Cobra Jewellery by all accounts is a very profitable company and with Franks behind them, well Europe is their oyster."

"Do you understand what I am saying?"

"Very clearly,"

"When do you imagine you will be returning to the UK?"

"Possibly in late November or early December but at the moment it is difficult to say."

The two men continued to speak for another ten minutes before their conversation ended.

After returning from his lunch break, Jack had only been back in his office ten minutes when the internal phone on his desk rang. Natalie from reception, the attractive young Spanish girl with the long black hair flowing down her back, was on the other end of the line. She spoke in Spanish. Being fluent in the language he had no problem communicating with her. She said there was someone on the outside line, who wished to speak to him, but the caller would not give her name as it was a private matter.

"Jack Sinclair speaking can I help you?"

"Jack it is Olga, I have a problem. My friend Emma who has an apartment in Puerto Banus and works at Pinks with me is very distressed. That scum bag of a manager Boris, is now threatening to fire her and replace her with another girl, unless she has sex with him. She hates him. It is the way he looks at her every time she is on stage. Emma a wants me to take a taxi to her apartment and work for her tonight, she is going to tell him she is ill. I am sorry to let you down tonight but I must go and see her."

"I understand."

"Thank you darling, I knew you would understand I will make it up to you on Monday evening."

"I shall look forward to that." A few minutes later they finished their conversation.

Jack did not believe her, Olga was more than likely meeting her sister Tanya as something was brewing up.

Around four Jack's mobile rang again, it was Pedro. "Can you speak?"

"Yes, but if someone enters my office, I may have to cut you short."

"I understand."

"Miles Coburn called me about half an hour ago. Ml6 have identified the mystery Russian from your mobile photos, he is on their data base. It is Kazimir Baizhanov. He was born in Moscow, Russia thirty years ago. He is the only child of Askar and Zarina Baizhanov, who fled Kazakhstan more than thirty years ago and gained asylum in Russia. At the time Askar was a young outspoken opposition politician, who received death threats. As a young man Kazimer represented Russia in the Olympic Games at pistol and riffle shooting and won two gold medals. He then disappeared off the radar for four years, only to turn up as an operative for the Russian FSB. We knew that he was a small arms expert but he is also now a highly skilled bomb and explosive expert. Ml6 call him a trouble shooter rather than an assassin. Wherever there is a problem Kazimer always turns up. He is known to have operated in more than twenty countries, including Iraq and Libya."

"What do you think he was up to in Puerto Banus?" More than likely he was delivering explosives and guns to Olga and Tanya. Ml6 inform me that the girls are trained in the use of them. I have a feeling that in the next few days something big is about to happen. By the way his Ducati Diavel motorbike is registered to the Russian Embassy in Madrid" Pedro then coughed a couple of times. "Will we see you this weekend?"

"I am afraid tonight only. Tomorrow I am going to watch Malaga's home match against Athletic Bilbao and then staying over with my brother and family for the weekend."

"I will see you later Jack."

When he left Cobra Jewellery HQ shortly after five thirty Jack went and picked up the white and black Range Rover Sport from the rental company, which he had hired for three days.

As usual Friday evening was very busy at the Med Club. The four guys who made up the local band on stage were excellent, but he could not remember their name. Jack also recognised two of the Chechens who were on the hit list. They were stood by the bar in the night club drinking and eyeing up all the glamorous young girls. After a couple of pints he decided to leave and head back to the Marbella Beach Apartments in the Range Rover Sport. He thought of staying longer, but then he would have had to get a taxi and in the morning to return and pick the Range Rover up. Far too much hassle, when he needed to leave for Malaga by eleven on Saturday morning. He was extremely tired and was glad to hit the sack.

After an unusually early night, Jack was up by eight the following morning. Once he had shaved and showered, he nipped out to the local mini-market and stocked up with a few provisions. Rather than cook a breakfast when he returned, he called in at one of the café bars where he ordered an egg omelette and latte. The rain had held off and it was now quite warm. As he walked towards the reception area in the Marbella Beach Complex he glanced across to the deserted swimming pool. He had not swum for a couple of days but there was nothing like the present. The water proved to be bloody cold but he still did twenty lengths. At ten minutes past eleven he left the apartment complex in the Range Rover Sport, he then joined the busy motorway and headed towards Malaga for a weekend of relaxation.

23

"Darling, what an earth is wrong you sound devastated on the mobile? Has that bastard Boris at Pinks been at you again?"

Tanya laughed. I wish I fancied him, I believe he is built like a donkey"

Olga then burst out laughing. "What is wrong then?"

The look on Tanya's face suddenly changed. "My boyfriend Youssef is dead."

"How do you know?"

"The sharks got him."

"The sharks, what do you mean? you had better explain." The two girls sat down opposite each other. The strong sun was shining through the window into Olga's eyes, so Tanya closed the window blind slightly.

"If you recall, I told you that Youssef was taking me with him on one of his fishing trips in the Black Prince yesterday. He always picks me up at the Puerto Marina in San Pedro."

"Why is that, what is wrong with Puerto Banus?"

"Youssef did not want his boss Roberto Sanchez to know that I was involved with him. The Black Prince is a very conspicuous speed boat easily recognizable, and there are also many CCTV cameras by the harbour and around Puerto Banus. By comparison Puerto Marina is very quiet with very few cameras. I always wait for him in a harbour side café. The weather was good and the forecast great, so we headed out into the Mediterranean. After twenty miles we stopped and had sex on the deck of the boat, it was so exciting both of us naked and miles from anywhere. Out of the blue, Youssef suddenly announced that he was also a part-time smuggler and unofficially worked for Boris, who ran Pinks. He kept glancing at his watch and said at two thirty he was expecting to meet up with a Tunisian fishing trawler. As we were talking I could see a trawler heading towards us from the direction of the North African coast. As the boat drew closer Youssef suggested that I go down below which I did. He did not want the people on board the trawler to see me. As I was below deck I heard the trawler bump against the side of the Black Prince, and the noise of her powerful diesel engine. I have no idea how many men were on board the trawler, their voices were muffled due to the chugging of the trawlers engine. After about twenty minutes, the trawler left and headed back towards the North African coast. Youssef then restarted the engines of the Black Prince and we slowly started to move back towards the Spanish coast, by now I was back on deck. We were both dying for sex again so Youssef stopped the boat and put out a sea anchor. For the next hour we were both in ecstasy.

"What are you smuggling I asked. Not drugs I hope." Youssef laughed, we were both still naked and I could see he was getting aroused again, so I slipped my arms around him and whispered in his ear.

"Please tell me darling what you are smuggling."

He just laughed. "Something worth a great deal more than drugs, uncut diamonds. That wooden box over there contains twenty million Euros of uncut diamonds. Boris pays me ten thousand Euros for every trip I make for him."

"Where do the diamonds come from?" I asked.

"I have no idea and providing I always get paid I am not really interested."

"Look the dolphins are back I cried out."

Youssef immediately climbed onto the stern of the boat whilst still naked and started to stroke the four dolphins, which kept swimming back and forth to him.

"Can I drive the boat back to land?"

"Of course you can, just give me a moment."

I don't know why I did it but I must have misheard him, as I fired the speed boats powerful turbine engine. The sudden forward movement of the boat in the sea swell with the sea anchor still out, must have caused Youssef to lose his balance and fall into the sea. At first I had no idea he had fallen overboard until I turned round to speak to him, then I could not see him on board. After a couple of minutes I realised he must have fallen overboard. Stopping the boat I looked around, I could see him a few hundred meters away bobbing up and down in the swell waving to me. The dolphins, which had been swimming around him, suddenly disappeared and to my horror I could see two Requiem sharks heading towards him. Youssef kept shouting to me to drive the boat closer to him and throw a life buoy into the water.

"Tanya, quickly wind in the sea anchor and then taxi the boat towards me and pick me up."

Youssef had not seen the two sharks which were some twenty metres away; they were now starting to circle him.

All of a sudden he screamed out. "A shark has got hold of my right leg and is going to pull me under, get me out of the water."

"I was now only about six metres from him when the second shark attracted by the blood oozing from Youssef's partly severed leg attacked him. The screams of agony he made were unbearable, so I reached inside my pink rucksack and pulled out the Beretta M9 pistol and fired four bullets into his bare chest. I could not bear to see a close friend and lover die in such a terrible way, there was nothing I could do for him. I feel such terrible guilt, because I know that I caused his death by starting the speedboat's engine and moving before winding in the sea anchor."

"How did you manage to return to Puerto Banus?"

"With a great deal of luck, I am very fortunate that Youssef had taught me how to operate the Black Prince. The weather was still holding out but the light was starting to fade when I arrived back at Puerto Banus, which was to my advantage, as less people would notice the boat slipping in. I carefully parked the speedboat in its usual place and tied up at the quay. I knew the CCTV cameras would be in operation, so in advance to avoid any detection, I put on Youssef's yellow oilskins and peeked cap, the rest of his clothes and fishing tackle went overboard. I left the keys for the boat below deck on one of the chairs. After making certain the boat was secure I headed to my apartment; it was now completely dark apart from harbour security lights. I was so stressed that I went to bed early and then called you when I awoke the following morning."

"What did you do with the oilskins?"

"I put them in a plastic bag and dumped them in a restaurant waste bin in one of the alleyways, where there was no CCTV. Don't worry no one saw me."

"Are you certain?"

"Of course I am." Tanya gave Olga a dirty look. "Youssef meant a great deal to me. He was a lovely gentle person and we had great sex together."

"You will have to find yourself another guy now."

"What about Jack?"

Olga raised her eyes. "Darling, I was only joking."

"You better had, as I am not sharing him with anyone."

"Darling, I feel sad for you but Youssef was helping the people behind the Siberian Cargo plane hijack, we would have eventually had to take him out."

"He had no idea about the hijack; all he was interested in was making money. You may not believe it, but he only recently found out what he was bringing into the country. Yesterday was his sixth trip for Boris."

"Did you throw the diamonds overboard?"

"No, they are in the bedroom cupboard. I will get them." Tanya got up and disappeared into the bedroom. A couple of minutes later, she returned with a dark grey wooden box which was about the size of a large shoe box, she then placed it on the low glass coffee table.

"I have forced the box open as I could not find a key on the boat. Open it darling."

Olga opened the box. She sat there mesmerised. Hundreds of uncut diamonds and precious gems sparkled in front of her like bright stars in the sky. Olga turned to her sister. "Tanya, what are we going to do with the diamonds?"

"We should contact Major Pavlov at the FSB in Moscow, he will probably arrange for Kaz from our Madrid Embassy to collect them."

Olga then smiled at her sister. "You do realize that you and I are the only people who know the location of these diamonds. Boris and the Russian Mafia will be searching for Youssef, who they think has taken a runner with their diamonds."

"We could put them in a bank security box for safety. When the time is right, we can leave the FSB and settle down her in Marbella or in fact anywhere else in the world. We would be made for life. If we both keep our mouths tightly closed no one will ever know.

"Tomorrow if you agree, we can buy a box with a key, transfer the diamonds and gems into it and then visit the Bank of Santander in Marbella, to arrange a safety deposit box. What do you say?"

"Sooner the better darling, it does get so very boring killing people."

"We must now carry on as normal. Tanya, are you working at Pinks tonight?"

"No, I rang in and told them I was ill."

"Good, we can now find a quiet out of town restaurant, order something special, have a couple of drinks and then we can return to your apartment for an early night."

Tanya smiled, she did not know what she would do without her sister Olga, who was the brains and organizer.

Olga then turned to her sister. "The four Chechens, I think we should eliminate them next week, possibly Thursday evening. What do you think?"

"I agree, darling, you have brightened my day and given me something to look forward to." Both the girls then hugged each other in a tight embrace.

Jack's weekend break turned out incredibly well. The weather was warm and dry. Malaga FC won their sell-out match against Athletic Bilbao 3-1, which kept them on top of La Liga by one point from Real Madrid. Staying with his brother Lex and his wife Maria, made him realise how much he was missing out on family life. The way they both doted on their young child David made him feel quite envious. He promised himself that once he returned to the UK, he would find himself the perfect partner, get married and have a family. Though at the moment it was not top of his list, but as soon as the Siberian plane hijack business was sorted out, he would have no excuse.

Jack left his brother's villa by seven thirty on Monday morning and drove directly to the Cobra Jewellery Head Quarters in Marbella. The motorway was extremely busy but he still managed to make good time.

"Have you had a good weekend Mr Sinclair?"

"I most certainly did, thank you for asking me Natalie. I watched Malaga FC beat Athletic Bilbao and then stayed with my brother and his wife at their villa over the weekend."

"The girls in the office tell me you have a famous brother, is that correct?"

"Yes, it is quite correct. My brother Lex used to play for Malaga FC and Australia and is now the manager and head coach of Malaga FC." Natalie smiled. She was a lovely young woman who always looked so happy. "Is Mr Maskhadov in his office?"

"Yes, should I call him for you?"

"Yes, if you would please, I would like to see him if it is possible."

Natalie then picked up the internal phone. "Mr Sinclair is in reception, he would like to see you if it is convenient." She then replaced the phone and turned to Jack. "Mr Maskhadov will see you now, if you would like to go through to his office."

"Thank you Natalie."

"Good morning Jack. Have you had a good weekend?"

"I have actually. I went to watch Malaga FC defeat Athletic Bilbao and then stayed over the weekend with my brother Lex and his family."

"Did you go to the match?"

Aslan shook his head. "I just could not face going alone. When George kept off the booze he was a lovely guy to be with and we enjoyed going to support Malaga."

"What about us going together to the next home match, I believe it is on a Wednesday evening?"

The smile returned to Aslan's face. "Jack, I will take you up on your offer."

"Good, I shall look forward to our evening out."

"I presume you wanted to see me, to give me your answer to my offer last week."

Jack smiled. "I would like to take you up on your offer." "Excellent, I was hoping you would."

"Aslan, there is one proviso, if either of us is not happy with the new situation, we can return as before with no ill feeling."

"No problem my friend," he then shook Jack's hand warmly. "You will spend half your day working with me in my office, the rest of the time carry on your normal job as usual. Also from next week, I would like you to start visiting each of our stores on a weekly basis. I am very happy with all our managers but it does no harm to keep them on their toes." Jack could not have agreed more. "Obviously there is going to be more work for me to do, so what hours do you want me to work?"

"Should we say Monday and Tuesday all day? You can still finish by four on Tuesday due to your gig at the Med Club. Wednesday from mid-day, which will give you chance to recover from your previous night's gig and Thursday and Friday normal hours? Perhaps when you have got used to your new roll, we could both share alternate Saturdays." "Yes, that would be fine with me. When would you like me to start?"

Aslan thought for a moment. "Unless you have made any prior arrangements would you like to start to-day?"

"Yes, that is fine by me."

"Good, if it is all right by you, we can meet later and discuss your salary over lunch?" Jack smiled and nodded his head. "I will call you later Jack."

Ten minutes later Jack left Aslan's office and headed to his own.

At twelve thirty, Aslan called Jack on the internal phone and they left Cobra Jewellery HQ for lunch. After returning the Range Rover Sport to the rental company, they called in at a nearby café bar for a light lunch. Jack was more than happy with the financial package Aslan offered him, he was a generous employer, but there was no doubt in his mind that he would want results.

When Jack arrived back at the Marbella Beach Apartments shortly after six, he found a note pushed under his door.

"Darling, come up to my apartment, I have a surprise for you."

Unable to resist a mystery invitation, he had a quick shower and went upstairs to Olga's apartment. She opened the door almost before the doorbell stopped buzzing, dressed only in white bath towel, which was tightly wrapped round her. As Jack closed the door behind him, Olga put both her arms around his neck. "Darling, where are you taking me to tonight?" As she spoke the bath towel slipped free and fell to the floor. He immediately lifted her up in his arms, her warm breasts pressed against his face.

"I shall be taking you to the Albatross for a meal and a few drinks but first of all what is this big surprise you have for me?"Without another word he carried her into the main bed room, after partly closing the door with his right foot he gently laid her naked on the soft king size bed.

Around eight thirty Olga and Jack left their respective apartments and took the elevator to the ground floor foyer. Costa Security boss Roberto Sanchez was on reception duty, he greeted them both warmly.

"What has happened to Youssef we have not seen him around for a while?"

"You are not the only one asking the same question. I lent him my boat the Black Prince for a fishing trip last Thursday; he has borrowed it several times previously with no problems. It was almost dark when the boat was seen returning to the harbour in Puerto Banus. For some reason he left the keys for the boat below deck on a chair, the boat was not even locked or tied up securely. To be honest with you I am very concerned about young Youssef, he has always been extremely reliable. It is possible that he has got involved with the wrong people. That Russian guy Boris, who owns Pinks girlie bar, called me a couple of hours ago, he was also looking for Youssef."

"Have you reported him missing to the local police?"

"No, but I may do after tomorrow. The Harbour Master, who is a good friend of mine, is going to let me check the CCTV footage. I not convinced that Youssef piloted the Black Prince to her moorings and tied up. He is extremely fussy and has always treated the boat like his own property. He would never in a thousand years have left the boat unlocked or tied her up at the quay like I found her. She could easily have slipped her moorings and drifted out into the Mediterranean Sea. The Black Prince is worth almost half a million Euros, Youssef knew that and always treated her with greatest respect."

"I hope for everyone's sake that he turns up safely."

"So do I, that Russian guy Boris was not a happy man, from all accounts he is not a guy you mess around with." Neither Olga nor Jack made a comment.

"Where are you two heading to this evening?"

"We are dining at the Albatross."

"I won't detain you guys any longer, enjoy yourselves." Once outside the Marbella Beach Complex, they briskly walked down the Esplanade Paseo to the Albatross. It was an exceptionally mild evening for late October; you could even hear the crickets carrying on a conversation in the bushes, as they meandered along the walkway. As usual the Albatross was busy, even though it was a Monday evening. The owner Roscoe Rodriguez saw them walk in, after embracing them both and a brief conversation, he found a secluded table for them a short distance from the bar. After ordering a bottle of Spanish red wine and two Spanish Omelettes, which were made from eggs, potatoes, ham and onions, they sat at their table for almost two hours drinking before they eventually left at eleven thirty. As they returned along the Esplanade Paseo Jack turned to Olga. "Did your friend Emma sort out her problem with the Russian Boris at Pinks?"

"Not really, she is considering giving up her job and returning home to Latvia. She has asked me to cover again for her on Thursday. I will then have Sunday night off."

"Good, I have an invitation to the end of season party at the Olivia Valere Club. Spanish heart throb Enrique Iglesias will be appearing, his even more famous father Julio Iglesias has also promised to be there. It should be an incredible night."

"Darling how fantastic, I will get a new dress and look stunning for you."

"Are you coming to my gig at the Med Club tomorrow evening?"

"Of course darling, I have never missed one yet."

"What about Emma, will she be with you?"

"I won't know until I speak to her tomorrow but I have my doubts."

Roberto Sanchez was still on duty at reception when they arrived back at the Marbella Beach Apartments. He acknowledged them with a weary smile as they walked through the foyer to the elevator. Jack could not help but notice how worried he looked. Something serious was on his mind. "Darling, do you want to come back to my room?"

"I would love to but I have not got your energy, I need a good night's sleep for my gig tomorrow. I will call you about one tomorrow."

Olga laughed and then gave him a passionate kiss, pressing her warm body against him.

The weather was quite warm on Tuesday morning when he finally surfaced after a nine hour sleep. After a quick shave and shower and a light breakfast, he ventured into the swimming pool and swam a leisurely twenty lengths. The water was bloody cold, at one point he was in two minds whether to get out but he had never been a quitter and he had no intention of starting now. Shortly before one, he called Olga on the internal phone and arranged to take her out to lunch to one of their usual haunts, the Picasso Café Bar on the Esplanade Paseo. As usual the food was excellent, the proprietors Gabriella and Alberto always went to a great deal of trouble to make their customers welcome. Both Jack and Olga had got to know the elderly Spanish couple well and enjoyed their company. To Jack, being in their company was like having a conversation with his departed parents.

Jack's gig at the Med Club on Tuesday was incredible, once again he performed to a sell-out crowd. Numbers were down with foreign tourists due to the time of the year, but punters where now travelling to see him from all over the Costa del Sol. Olga and her friend Emma turned up, apart from the occasional wave from the girls in his direction, he saw very little of them. Owner Pedro Gonzales and his wife Nada were conspicuous by their absence. Assistant manager Kelly said their daughter Olivia was ill again. Providing there was no deterioration in her health, Pedro would call in at the club later.

When Jack finally came off stage shortly after one, after closing his set with David Guetta's Titanium, he looked around for Olga and her friend Emma, but both had disappeared. Pedro never made an appearance; he prayed that his friend's daughter would be alright. At the moment, she appeared to be having a few too many health problems for a child of her age. Shortly after two he arrived back by taxi at the Marbella Beach Apartments and headed straight to bed.

The weather was still warm and dry on Wednesday, so Jack decided to walk to the Cobra Jewellery Head Quarters. Luckily he knew a few short cuts which avoided most of the traffic congestion and the city centre, it took him less than twenty five minutes and he arrived by eleven fifty.

Natalie on reception had a message for him. "Mr Sinclair." Jack immediately stopped and turned. "Mr Maskhadov would like you to go through to his office, he is expecting you. Would you like an Americano or latte?"

"I will have the same as Mr Maskhadov, an Americano coffee with milk but no sugar." The girl smiled.

Jack then turned and walked down the grey tiled corridor, before stopping at Aslan's office. He then gently knocked twice on the light oak door.

"Come in." Jack recognised Aslan's deep Chechen accent. "Take a seat my friend. You will be working with me this afternoon but before we get down to work, I want you to read this, I have just received the police pathologist's official report on the cause of George's sudden death." He then passed Jack a red plastic folder. "His three page report is inside the folder with a letter from him."

Jack got up from his chair and walked over to the large office window glanced outside and then opened the folder.

"I will ask Natalie to bring us both a coffee whist you read through the report, a latte for you Jack?"

"No an Americano if you would." Aslan smiled.

"Sorry Aslan, Natalie has already asked me what coffee I wanted before I entered your office." Aslan smiled.

Jack quickly ran his eyes over the official looking report from the Marbella police, which was in Spanish. Everything appeared to be straight forward. Death was due to a massive heart attack. The pathologist was surprised, as George's body and organs were in perfect condition, which they should have been for one so young. He had to conclude that death was due to natural causes as there was nothing to suggest otherwise. The pathologist, who was a personal friend of Aslan, was not happy with the result, so he asked for a second opinion which also came to the same conclusion. In the meantime he sent a blood sample to a doctor friend who was in charge of the Malaga Police Pathology Laboratory. There was a separate private report from him in the folder. The scientist in charge, Dr Mohammed Abadi, a former Iraq exile, who fled the country fearing for his life when Saddam Hussein was President, was convinced that George had been assassinated with a nerve agent. Possibly from a Russian or American, it could even have been the Syrian Government, who were in the early stages of developing them. It appeared that when Dr Abadi lived in Iraq, he was in charge of a laboratory, which was developing nerve agents for the regime. Many of these nerve agents were tested on men and women who were held in prison and classed as enemies of the state. They were all waiting trial and almost certain execution, no one ever survived the experiments and all of them experienced horrific deaths. Their bodies were cremated and their ashes scattered in the desert wind. When blood samples were taken from their bodies immediately after they died and sent to the doctor for analyst, they all had one thing in common. Their white blood cells were not as clear as they should have been. George's white blood cells were the same. None of his staff in the Malaga Police Pathology Laboratory are aware of the difference and he has not put them in the picture, as it meant explaining how he knew and no way did he want his past life becoming public knowledge. He is convinced from his personal experience in Iraq that George has been assassinated with a lethal nerve agent.

Jack fell silent for a moment before turning to look at Aslan who shook his head.

"There is nothing I can do. I will just have to accept the police pathologist's report."

"Why do you think he was murdered?"

Aslan did not even hesitate with his reply. "Because of his involvement in a Russian Siberian Cargo plane hijack which was carrying one billion Euros of diamonds and other precious gems to Moscow. The Russians threatened to take out George and all his Chechen friends who were involved with him in the hijack, unless they returned the diamonds. They are now carrying out their threat, George is the first and his friends will be next."

"Did, you know any of his Chechen friends?"

"No not really apart from Freddie; the only time I have met them has been at my charity fund raising garden party when they worked behind the bars. George always arranged everything."

"I am puzzled, why do the guys not simply tell the Russians where the diamonds are if their lives are in danger?"

"The Russian Mafia are involved and arranged the hijack so they are the only people who know where the diamonds are, apart from." He then stopped abruptly as if he had already said too much.

"Aslan you need to very careful who you associate with, you do not want to put your Spanish citizenship in jeopardy."

"I have already thought about that, I am being most careful."

"Can I ask you something, if you don't want to answer me tell me to mind my own business."

"Go ahead Jack, what is on your mind?"

"Have you ever bought any of the diamonds?"

"Yes, three months after the hijack took place. The Russian guy Boris, who has Pinks in Puerto Banus, offered me thirty five uncut diamonds. He turned up here on a Tuesday morning at my office without an appointment with the diamonds, and I might add most convincingly told me that a Russian friend of his who was living in Portugal had hit hard times. His friend had asked him to try and sell the diamonds for him. They were of a very high quality and when cut and polished, I estimated they would be worth in the region of half a million Euros." "How much did he want for them?"

"Forty thousand Euros, it was the buy of the century. I paid him in cash, which as you say in England came from under the bed; it is my slush fund so the taxman knows nothing about it. Within weeks the diamonds were cut and polished and set in rings and bracelets. The last piece of jewellery containing these diamonds was auctioned at my recent fund raising event. There is no way any of the diamonds from the hijack can ever be traced back to me. It was a one-off deal which will never ever be repeated." Jack then changed the conversation. "Are you going to the end of season party at the Olivia Valere Club on Sunday?" "Because of what has happened to George, I have not really given it much thought. Are you going?"

"Yes, I am taking Olga along as my guest. Would you like to join us?"

"I would love to."

"Excellent."

"I will arrange for Freddie to pick you and Olga up in the Bentley at eight thirty." Aslan then glanced at his gold Rolex Oyster watch. "I need to go through the list of International suppliers with you and then you will know who to contact, you will probably know most of them. Afterwards we can then discuss the Cobra Jewellery emporiums. As I said before, all ten outlets should be visited by one of us every week. At the moment it can often stretch to three or four weeks before I can fit in a visit. You will see from the computer printouts, which I will show you later, that all the outlets are very profitable. However if we started selling our own range of costume jewellery, we could increase our profits by a considerable amount. Once you have read through the printouts tell me what you think. I am always open to any suggestions from you."

The afternoon flew by, Jack arrived back at his Marbella Beach Apartment shortly after six, he felt exhausted but he needed to make an urgent call to Miles Coburn in London.

Coburn was still in his office when he picked up the phone.

"Good to hear from you Jack, I was just about to leave for home." Coburn then came straight to the point. "Have you any news for me?"

Jack then told him in detail about the Marbella police pathologist's report about George, and what the eminent Dr Mohammed Abadi, the former Iraq Government scientist, now in charge of the Malaga Police Pathology Laboratory said about George's blood sample.

Miles listened intently and never interrupted once until Jack had finished.

"Very interesting, it looks as though the girls have taken out their first victim. Be careful Jack not to get in their way, both these girls are psychopaths they will think nothing of eliminating you. How are you doing at Cobra Jewellery?" "Good from what I have seen so far, there is no way Aslan Maskhadov has any connection to the Siberian cargo plane hijack."

"Maybe so but keep digging, if Aslan trusts you he may lead you to the whereabouts of Sergei Aslanov."

"Now if you will excuse me I must catch my train, give me a call if you have any further news."

As soon as the conversation had ended he called Pedro and told him about George.

"I am shocked Jack but not surprised, I was expecting repercussions. Be careful, when you go out at night maybe you should carry a shooter. I will speak to Coburn and see what his views are. Will I see you this weekend?" "Yes, on Friday night. On Sunday I am attending the end of season party at the Olivia Valere Club with Olga and Aslan."

"Excellent, Nada and I will be there. We will join you for a while." Jack could hear children's voices in the back ground. "Sorry Jack family duties. I have to read my kids a story before bedtime. I will see you on Friday, take care my friend."

Jack envied Pedro Gonzales he had everything he dreamt of. A beautiful wife, two lovely children a very successful beach club and a magnificent villa with top of the range vehicles. He had everything but he had certainly worked hard for it. One day he would have the same. After a quick shower and a change of clothes, he called Olga. An hour later they took a taxi into Marbella for a meal and a night out, he would not be seeing Olga again until Saturday.

24

"Darling, we are going to have to be very careful. There could be repercussions over the Black Prince."

Tanya put her cup of coffee down and looked at her sister. The smile on her face had disappeared as though she was in shock.

"What do you mean?"

"Your ex-boyfriend Roberto Sanchez, who owns the Black Prince, is going to check the CCTV cameras at the harbour and marina in Puerto Banus. His friend is the harbourmaster."

"How do you know?"

"Roberto was on reception at the Marbella Beach Apartments the other evening when Jack and I went out for a meal. Jack happened to mention that he had not seen Youssef around for a while. Roberto then said neither had he, that was why he was standing in for him. He also mentioned that a very angry Boris Sokolov had called him, asking if he knew where he was."

"Why should he want to check the CCTV cameras at the harbour?"

"He does not believe Youssef was at the helm of the boat when it was tied up, as it was not secured properly and could have drifted out to sea."

Tanya sighed. "Sorry sis, I have never secured a boat before."

"Also Youssef would never have left a valuable boat like the Black Prince unlocked, with the keys below deck on a chair. Let us hope he does not recognise you from the CCTV."

"Stop worrying sis, after tonight we will soon be on our way home."

"Do you think I should give Roberto a call and meet him"

"Yes, sooner the better darling. Most men tend to talk too much when they are having sex, he may let something slip."

Tanya laughed. "I will suggest Friday afternoon." She then changed the conversation. "Now darling about tonight, what time do you think we should arrive at the Chechen's apartment?"

"They normally arrive home from work between two and three in the morning. We should get there by midnight. It is a three mile walk; we have to avoid at all costs being seen. There should be very few people about at that time of night and the main highway will be fairly quiet. When we have completed our task, we will return by the coastal pathway." Tanya opened her mouth to speak. "Before you ask, we must not travel by taxi."

At eight thirty they walked to a nearby restaurant and ordered a chicken and chorizo paella with rice. Rather than drink wine as both the girls wanted clear heads, they concluded their meal with two Americano coffees. After walking along the harbour front, they slowly made their way back to Tanya's apartment.

"Are you still shagging Jack?"

"Of course, he is a lovely guy but I find it hard to believe he is an MI6 Agent. Do you think it is possible that Major Pavlov has made a mistake about him?"

Tanya started to laugh. "You fancy the guy don't you? You are not in love with him are you?" Olga did not answer. "You are. You are in love with him."

Olga smiled but didn't answer at first. "I like Jack a lot and could settle down with him but I am not in love with him. Darling, I will never leave you alone and my duty to our mother land is too strong a pull. Let us talk about something else."

Half an hour later both the girls changed into identical clothing, tight dark jeans and pink polo neck jumpers with trendy black leather jackets. On their feet the girls wore black Chloe leather boots. Both the girls had fastened their long hair up and covered it with mauve head caps, pulled down to their ears. Olga carried a dark blue rucksack which contained two small high tech bombs and the Nokia mobile phone, which would trigger the explosion.

Tanya, who had been out of the bedroom for a moment, walked back in with a pair of high-tech Spy night goggles and two Beretta M9 pistols in her hands. "We may need these if the Chechens try to escape from the burning building, and here is the torch you asked me to buy."

They were all placed inside the rucksack which Olga fastened and then placed on the bed.

Just before eleven thirty Tanya and Olga left the apartment and made their way out of Puerto Banus, which was still fairly busy even for late October. The weather was dry and mild with no wind. Perfect conditions for what the two girls had in mind. When they arrived at the nearby coastal highway, there was more traffic flashing back and forth than they had expected.

Olga who normally made most of the decisions was the first to speak. "Darling, we need to separate. I will take the footpath on the right side of the road you keep on this side and walk parallel to me. As soon as we reach the gravel road on the right I will wave to you. If the highway is clear and there is no one around walk across to me. We should be there in less than forty minutes."

The two girls then hugged each other before a break in the traffic allowed Olga to quickly walk to the other side of the highway. Both the girls kept close to the trees and foliage as they walked along the highway towards San Pedro, always making certain that they could see each other. After a brisk forty minute walk Olga came to the gravel pot holed lane leading from the highway, she looked for Tanya and then softly whistled to her. The traffic was still quite heavy with late night revellers, taxies, and the odd half empty local coach. Eventually, there was a break which allowed Tanya to run across the highway to her sister. The girls glanced round as they disappeared down the lane. Neither of them spoke until they reached the empty run down garage repair building, which was about three hundred metres from the highway. Putting on their night goggles, they stood back in the bushes for the next five minutes and scanned the area for any movement. Convinced they were alone, they moved towards the building and the weather beaten double wooden door, which barred their entry. "Shine the torch directly on the door whist I open the lock, but first of all we both need to put on our Latex surgical gloves, we don't want any trace of finger prints."

After putting on her surgical gloves, Olga took a thin piece of metal which was more like a long file out of the rucksack, which she used to open the lock. Once inside Tanya closed the door behind them. For a few minutes they stood perfectly still and never spoke a word, listening intently for any possible sound or movement from the Chechen's apartment above the garage. There were none. Tanya shone the torch beam around the interior of the workshop; it was a real junk shop which had not been sorted out for years. There was an old Ford pickup with no engine or wheels propped up on wooden blocks on one side of the workshop. On the other side a long wooden bench was stacked high with empty orange boxes and numerous vehicle spanners. Six large drums of diesel oil and petrol were stacked in one corner, along with Oxy acetylene welding equipment and several Oxygen cylinders. There were also a dozen Calor Gas containers stacked on top of each other close by.

Olga looked at her sister. "This is an accident just waiting to happen." Both the girls giggled.

The dirty oil stained concrete floor was covered in thick dust and cobwebs. The workshop was a shit hole and had not seen any action for many years.

Olga then took out the two small plastic containers containing the high tech bombs from the rucksack, and attached them both to the outside gas pipe, at the point where the rust pitted pipe fed into the heating boiler.

Tanya smiled at her sister. "Are you ready darling, should we activate the bombs together?"

"Of course that is why we are here." The girls then pressed the tiny switches down on the two plastic containers. "All we have to do now is to wait for the Chechens to return to the apartment from their evening jobs and then we can have one hell of a bomb fire." Both the girls started to laugh.

"Let us go outside and find a secluded viewing point where we can see the entrance to the upstairs apartment."

Opening the heavy wooden door about twelve inches they squeezed through. Whilst Olga relocked the door, Tanya scanned the terrain outside through her night vision goggles for any movement. As the bushes and scrubs were overgrown there was no problem finding cover. From this advantage point they could observe the Chechens arriving home.

"Olga, it is highly likely that they will be dropped off by taxi at the entrance to the lane due to all the pot holes, and then they will have to make their own way to the apartment."

Olga turned to her sister. "We will have to speak very quietly otherwise we will not hear anybody arriving. I understand that the two guys who work behind the bars at Pinks always finish at two on a Thursday. The other two are employed in harbour side restaurants in Puerto Banus and finish at one."

Tanya glanced at her watch. "We have about an hour before anyone walks up the lane. Have you noticed the bars on all the windows, no one will be able to get out once the fire takes control?"

Olga smiled. "How disappointing, I was looking forward to taking one of the bastards out with my Beretta pistol." Time was flying by quickly, it was almost one thirty and the night temperature was slowly dropping, but at least there was no wind or rain.

Olga took out a bottle of cool Andalusian Mountain Spring Water from her rucksack. After taking a quick drink she passed it to her sister who did the same, suddenly she held her finger up to her lips. "My night goggles have picked up a movement."

Tanya touched her sister's arm and pointed to her own night goggles and then nodded her head. Coming towards them were two young Chechen men talking and laughing seemingly without a care in the world.

"These are the guys who work in the harbour restaurants." Olga smiled at her sister but never spoke.

One of the Chechens switched on his mobile phone light, whilst the other opened the door to the apartment. As they entered the building the internal lights suddenly came on, including two security lights on the outside wall of the property.

"Tanya, we must be most careful now the security lights are on. It is highly likely every so often they will look out of the apartment's windows now they are home. We don't want them to even see a shadow."

"I understand sis."

"I will be glad when this is all over and then we can go away on holiday and relax; the last week has been more stressful than usual."

Olga looked at her sister and smiled. "I was very sorry to hear about Youssef, he was a lovely guy."

"He was. We had some fantastic times together." Tanya then went extremely quiet. "I hope Roberto does not contact the police?"

"The sooner you contact him the better."

"I intend to, later today."

Tanya was looking at her watch when Olga asked her what time it was.

"There is more movement coming up the lane, I can see them now. The two Chechen barmen who work at Pinks are arriving home."

Like their friends before them, they were laughing and joking with each other. After knocking loudly on the apartment door, one of the occupants' opened it from the inside and let them in. After about twenty minutes the security lights were switched off leaving only the apartments lights switched on. Ten minutes later they went out. Everywhere was in complete darkness; a blanket of low clouds had now drifted across the Moon. Neither of the girls spoke, it was so quiet that they could hear each other breathing. Around three forty-five the girls moved a little further back into the bushes, eliminating any possibility of being seen. They then proceeded to remove the Nokia mobile phone from the rucksack.

"Darling, would you shine the torch on the mobile whilst I tap in the security code. Remember, after the building goes up we head down the lane and across the highway, making our way back to your apartment along the coastal path. If we keep our night goggles on until we reach Puerto Banus it will be easier to see where we are going. Are you ready? Olga then taped in 55552, put your finger on top of mine we will press the enter button together. On the count of three we both press down, one, two, three."

All of a sudden there was a crack like a gun going off and a huge red and yellow fire ball shot high into the air and completely engulfed the whole building, blowing out all the glass windows. The girls could feel the immense heat as the fire ball bellowed outwards towards them.

"Look Olga, there is some guy at the window trying to get out. Should I shoot him and put him out of his misery?"

"No way, let him burn, there is no way he can get out as all the windows have bars across. In any case I hate the Chechens." As she spoke, the faceless man was engulfed in flames.

"It is good job we moved back otherwise we could have been badly burnt. No one can get out of that alive, come on darling let's get out of here before the police and fire service arrive, someone is bound to report a fire like this."

Making certain everything was in the rucksack they left their hideaway and quickly made their way down the lane towards the deserted coastal highway. They were still wearing their night goggles.

Once across the highway they walked down a narrow sandy path, past several apartment blocks and exclusive villas towards the Malaga Coastal Path, which snaked along the edge of the Mediterranean Sea to Puerto Banus, and then on to Marbella. The Coastal Path was not particularly well lit with lights as most of them were switched off after midnight, but using their torches and night goggles they had no problem.

Tanya suddenly touched her sister's arm. "Listen is that the sound of the police and fire engines?"

"Yes." Both the girls turned and looked back, the night sky was full of flashing blue lights. "Let's get out of here, do you fancy jogging for a couple of miles." Olga smiled and nodded her head.

As soon as they were a few hundred metres from Tanya's apartment she went ahead alone. All the street lights were switched on, but by keeping to the side streets and alleyways of the resort and close to the buildings, she avoided any possible CCTV cameras and soon arrived at her apartment. Never once did she see another human being only a lone cat hunting a mouse. Once inside she called her sister Olga on the mobile. "Everything is clear, I will see you in a few minutes, keep to the route we planned.

When Olga finally arrived, the girls hugged each other in jubilation.

Tanya turned to her sister. "Major Pavlov will be so proud of us when he hears of what we have done tonight."

Olga then hugged her sister again. "Darling, let's go to bed I am exhausted, we can sort our clothes out later."

Both the girls slept through until mid-day. Whilst Tanya put all their clothes in the washing machine and cleaned their boots, to remove any evidence which could connect them with the fire, Olga took a walk to the busy harbour. As she was stood by the water's edge, she accidently or so it seemed, dropped the Nokia mobile into the water, within seconds it had sank to a watery grave. On her way back to the apartment, she disposed of the surgical gloves in one of the many overflowing restaurant bins, which were waiting to be emptied.

"What about the night goggles and the Beretta pistols?" "We may need them; they can soon be disposed of when they are not needed. In the meantime we must act normal, tonight and Saturday we go back to work at Pinks, and then on Sunday I must return to the Marbella Beach Apartments. Jack is taking me to the end of season party at the Olivia Valere Club in the evening. Darling don't forget to call Roberto, try to get him to meet you as soon as possible."

"I will give him a call now." She did and arranged to meet him on Sunday afternoon.

Jack was about to leave his apartment for the Cobra Jewellery Head Quarters when his mobile rang, it was Pedro Gonzales.

"Jack it's Pedro, have you heard the news this morning?"

"No, I was just about to leave for work. What has happened?"

"It is all over the local TV and radio. There was a huge fire at an old vehicle repair garage just off the main highway before you get to San Pedro. There was a four bedroom apartment above the workshop, and I am fairly certain that is where the four Chechens who are on the Russians wanted list live. According to reports, the building was completely gutted by fire. The police made a statement saying that no one could have survived such a blaze, but at the moment they are not certain that the apartment was occupied. They are trying to contact the owners of the property, who are believed to live in Malaga. Jack, this could have deep implications if the Chechens were in the apartment and are dead, then the FSB's female assassins are at work. George has been murdered. Youssef who was bringing the diamonds into Spain for Boris has disappeared and is more than likely dead and now these four. Jack I won't keep you any longer, you have a good day, I intent to call Miles Coburn and put him in the picture. At least we now know what Kazimir Baizhanov was doing at Tanya's apartment. If there are any further developments I will call you at Cobra Jewellery."

"It will be interesting to see what Aslan has to say today."

"I agree we will speak later."

Jack arrived at the Cobra Jewellery Head Quarters shortly before ten. The weather was changing, the temperature had dropped by twenty degrees, and it was starting to rain.

Natalie as usual was on reception. "Good morning Mr Sinclair, I have a message for you from Mr Maskhadov." "Good morning Natalie."

"Mr Maskhadov called me at home at seven thirty this morning and asked me to open up the building. Unfortunately he will not be in until around eleven. Some problem has arisen which he needs to sort out. He said you are very welcome to use his office."

"Thank you." Jack then started to walk down the corridor to his office.

"One moment Mr Sinclair," Jack turned round.

"Please call me Jack unless I am with a customer, we have known each other for a while." Natalie smiled.

"You will need the spare key to Mr Maskhadov's office to get in, if you leave it in the left hand drawer of the boss's desk I will put it away for safe keeping, all the office and workshop keys are kept at reception."

"How long have you worked at Cobra Jewellery?"

"Eight years, I love working here. Mr Maskhadov is such a lovely man." Jack smiled and then left the reception area. He spent most of the morning drifting between his and Aslan's office. He was kept extremely busy on the phone, with several customers ringing in with jewellery orders in excess of 100.00Euros. Aslan eventually turned up a little after eleven and came straight into his office.

"Sorry I was not here when you arrived this morning. Have you heard about the dreadful fire?"

"Yes, I saw it earlier on Television, I hope there was no one inside."

"There were four young Chechen guys living there, they were all George's friends and had been involved in the Siberian cargo plane hijack. Someone is killing them; it has to be the Russian FSB on the instructions of the Kremlin. Poor Freddie is terrified that he will be next. He was one of the reasons for my late arrival this morning."

There was a knock at the door and Natalie came in with two Americano coffees.

"Thank you Natalie, would you please put them on my desk." Natalie smiled and then left the office.

"I gather that young lady has been with you for eight years." "She has and she is a very loyal employee."

"Why do you not make her your office manager, she could liaise between you and any other staff including those in the workshop."

"Good idea Jack, I will speak to her later. I could do with someone I can trust to take it in turn with me to open up the building in the morning."

"Are you going to replace George in the workshop?"

"Yes, we have a young but very talented Spanish guy starting next week. We shall need him as our business is increasing, and there is also a possibility, that Freddie may not be with us much longer."

"Why is he going home to Chechnya?"

"After this morning's fire he certainly wants too and who can blame him." Aslan paused for a moment whilst he took a drink of his coffee before continuing. Jack did the same. "Jack, I call you a trusted friend, if it is not inconvenient I would like you to speak to Freddie. Is there any chance you could call round at my villa on Saturday afternoon at two and then you two can meet and talk, you may find what he has to say most interesting and you can also join us for a late lunch."

"Aslan, if I can help in any way I will. You can count on me. I will certainly be at your villa on Saturday."

The rest of the day continued like it had started extremely busy. He was glad Aslan offered to drop him off at the Marbella Beach Apartments in his Mini-Cooper on his way home. The weather was crap, chilly and wet just like the UK in late October. After a shower he sat down in the lounge and watched the evening news. There was extensive coverage about the fire near San Pedro and the police confirmed that the remains of four bodies had been found in the debris. They said that an old suspected gas boiler leak was the possible cause of the explosion. After an evening meal at the Picasso Café Bar, and a couple of beers, Jack walked down the Esplanade Paseo to the Med Beach Club as he needed to speak with Pedro Gonzales. At least the weather was picking up and the rain had disappeared, there was no wind and the temperature had jumped up again, tomorrow he would go for a swim in the complex swimming pool.

25

Jack did manage to get his swim in the Marbella Beach Apartment swimming pool; in fact he did his normal twenty lengths though the water was bloody cold. Luckily for him the cloud cover cleared as he was getting out of the pool and the sun broke through, it then felt quite warm.

Rather than walk to Aslan Maskhadov's villa Jack took a taxi. Once he had gained admittance to the villa complex, he made his way along the drive to the Indian slate patio in front of the main entrance, where Aslan was waiting to greet him.

"Please come in my friend, I am most grateful to see you." Jack followed Aslan into the villa and down the hallway before turning left into the stunning lounge. Freddie was sat on the soft leather cream sofa watching a film on the large screen television, when he saw Jack he immediately stood up, switched off the television with the remote control, and walked towards him. The two men embraced each other.

"How are you Freddie?"

"Worried sick that I will be next, the net is closing in on me."

Aslan suggested that they sit down and talk, whilst he brought in some food and drink, which they had already prepared.

"How many Chechens are there living on the Costa del Sol?"

"I am the only one left alive, originally there were seven of us but three months ago Mikhail got cold feet and fled back to Grozny in Chechnya. Whether he arrived back safely I have no idea, he could be dead as I have had no contact from him."

"Correct me if I am wrong but I understand the FSB are after you, because you did not give the diamonds and other precious gems back to them."

"It was impossible to return them as we had no idea where they were. The Russian Mafia took control, as far as I know only four people actually know where they are hidden."

"Why did you and your friends get involved in the first place?"

"Our patriotism for Chechnya got the better of us. We all dreamt of joining the Chechen Separatist movement and fighting for our country. My friends and I studied at the Aviation and Aircraft Engineering Academy in Moscow. On a night out at a club in Moscow, we were approached by a Chechen, who was now with the Russian Mafia. He offered us five million Euros each to take part in the Siberian cargo plane hijack. Stupidity got the better of us and we joined them. We were under the impression that we would then have the money to buy guns and rocket launchers, and that the Separatist movement would welcome us with open arms. We never got paid, only death threats, and there was nothing we could do."

"Did you not ask for part payment upfront?"

"No, the deal was that we would all be paid once the hijack had taken place. The bastards renegade on the deal and told us to clear off. If anyone opened their mouth we would all be hunted down and executed. The problem was that they hated us because we came from Chechnya. They just used us and we fell for it."

"What about Sergei Aslanov, how does he fit into all this?" Freddie was about to answer when Aslan re-entered the room carrying several plates of food.

"I hope this food is ok for you. Warm meat pie and mixed vegetables. Help yourself guys."

Jack turned to Freddie. "As I was saying before how does Sergei Aslanov fit into all this?"

Freddie looked at Aslan as if asking for help.

Aslan hesitated for a second and then got up. "Will you excuse me for one moment?" He then left the room but returned shortly afterwards. "Jack, there is someone I would like you to meet."

Aslan walked towards the door again and spoke to someone who was in the hallway. Jack blinked. At first he thought his eyes were deceiving him. Had he not known the man so closely when he lived in Johannesburg, South Africa, he would not have recognised him, gone was the long hair and pony tail, to be replaced by short dark hair and a neatly trimmed beard. Sergei Aslanov was a handsome man, six one and slim with broad shoulders. At first the two men did not speak but instead embraced each other warmly.

"Jack, it is over two years since I last saw you, you look incredibly well my friend."

Jack smiled. "So do you, I have heard a great deal about you but I never thought we would meet again especially in Marbella."

"Jack, I have also heard a great deal about you from Aslan."

Sergei joined the three of them for lunch. There was a great deal of reminiscing about their time in Johannesburg. After about twenty minutes Aslan broke into the conversation. "Jack, I asked you here for several reasons. Firstly to meet Sergei, who has been hiding away in my villa for the past three weeks, and secondly as I trust you, I need some advice on security for the villa and also for my friends."

"Aslan I am no expert on security, I personally would speak to Roberto Sanchez from Costa Security; he will give you expert advice. He may recommend that you need armed security at the villa." Jack then turned to Sergei. "I gather from all accounts that you were involved in the hijack." Sergei nodded his head. "Why the hell did you ever get involved? You are a top gemmologist and qualified aircraft pilot, you could always earn a good living as an honest citizen."

Sergei's face went most serious. "There is a great deal you do not know about me my friend. After I qualified as a pilot and gemmologist, I continued my studies working for De Beers in South Africa, that is where I met you in Johannesburg and we became great friends." Jack smiled at his friend who did likewise. "To be perfectly honest with you, when I returned home to Tbilisi in Georgia I became bored with life, as I knew I would never make my fortune in Georgia, so one day I packed my bags and moved to Moscow, Russia. My beloved elderly Aunt who had brought me up was heartbroken, but I always promised to keep in touch with her, which I always have done. Whilst in Moscow, I was approached by a military attaché to fly cargo planes into war torn Damascus in Syria, which I did for twelve months. I was very well paid and loved the danger and excitement. The experience I gained has helped me develop into a first class pilot." Sergei then took a long drink of warm tea before continuing. One day on a night out in Moscow, in fact it was the very same night club my Chechen college friends used to frequent, I was approached by a guy who I found out later was a top man in the Russian Mafia. He said his organisation were looking for a very experienced pilot to help them in the hijack of a cargo plane carrying one billion Euros of raw diamonds and precious gems from Siberia to Moscow. I would actually be involved in the hijack as a navigator and co-pilot, which would involve a MIL Mi-26 Russian Military Helicopter flying the diamonds to a deserted and long forgotten small run down airbase in the Ural Mountains, close to the Kazakhstan border, which was last used in the cold war between the Soviet Union and the West. My job after would be to fly large quantities of diamonds from the airbase via Turkey in a small twin engine plane to a remote desert runway on the Tunisian - Libyan border, some thirty miles inland from the Mediterranean Sea. I would be met there, by a middle aged Russian man and his wife, who live in a nearby farm house. You are probably aware, that there are many Russians living and working in Tunisia. The Russian government are currently investing millions of rubbles in the country building new hotels and roads. By doing this, they believe they will get a foothold in North Africa, which the Chinese are already doing."

"I believe so."

"After leaving the air strip, the diamonds are then driven to the city of Sousse to be transferred to a fishing trawler, which then heads across the Mediterranean Sea to Southern Spain. When about twenty miles from the Spanish coast, the fishing boat arranges to rendezvous with an Ocean going speed boat called the Black Prince."

"I know the Black Prince. She is a magnificent boat, which is owned by Costa Security chief Roberto Sanchez. It is moored in the marina at Puerto Banus. Sergei, no way is Roberto involved in smuggling diamonds and precious gems into the country, he has far too much to lose. Someone else must be using the boat."

"Aslan then got involved in the conversation. "I feel certain that the Russian guy who has Pinks is involved someway. He is a dodgy guy, I just don't like him."

"I could have an explanation as to who was skippering the boat." They all looked at Jack. "Costa Security are in charge of all the security at the Marbella Beach Apartments where I am staying, and that includes the reception desk in the evening. A young Tunisian guy called Youssef Beji is often on reception in the evening. I had not seen him around for a while, and it just so happened when I was on my way out one evening Roberto Sanchez was on duty. I mentioned to Roberto that I had not seen Youssef for a while. He said he was covering for Youssef who had not turned up for work. Roberto then went on to tell me, that he often allowed Youssef, who was an experienced sailor, to take the Black Prince out to sea on his fishing expeditions. The day before he failed to turn in for work, Youssef had been out fishing, he had apparently returned the boat to the marina undamaged, but had left the Black Prince, a very valuable boat, unlocked with the keys left on a chair below deck. He then appears to have disappeared into thin air. A couple of days later Boris the Russian who runs Pinks called him, asking if he knew where Youssef was. He said Boris was very agitated and used a lot of foul language and threats over the phone." Nobody spoke for a moment but looked at each other. "I might add Roberto is convinced that something has happened to Youssef, he could even be dead."

Sergei was the first to speak. "It is quite possible that Youssef is the fishing boat's contact and he also works for Boris."

"Aslan this meat pie is delicious; you must let me know where you bought it from."

"I prepare and cook all my own food. When I lived in Chechnya, my wife prepared all the food but every Sunday I would become chef for the day. I always cooked something very special and all the family came round for a meal. Happy days and memories, if I had not been a jeweller I am certain that I would have been a chef." Jack could swear there were tears in his eyes as he spoke. "My neighbours Pedro and Nada Gonzales, who live close by, always come round for a meal every month, you must join us."

"I would love to."

"Jack, would you like another helping of pie?"

"Yes, I would love one."

"Freddie, Sergei, would you care for a second helping?" Freddie nodded his head.

Aslan got up and went into the kitchen, Jack followed. "How are you coping?"

"Absolutely terrible, losing George was horrendous. He was family being my nephew. When he arrived here he changed my life. I am aware that many people thought he was my boyfriend as I only told a couple of close friends who he actually was. By the way, I received a phone call this morning to say that George's body will be released by the Coroner on Monday. His mother and father will be arriving here on Wednesday to take him back to Chechnya for burial; they will stay with me until they return. Perhaps you could run the office for me?"

"Of course I will."

"Thank you my friend. Can I confide in you?"

"Of course, please do."

"I am a very lonely wealthy man with no one to share my life with."

"Would you like to remarry?" I certainly miss the tenderness of a woman but I adored my wife and cannot imagine being with anyone else."

"Your wife would understand, sometimes you have to let go. You are an excellent catch, handsome, wealthy and a nice guy and still relatively young."

"My wife has a younger sister Gabrielle we all called her Gaby, she is always writing to me."

"Is she married?"

"She was to an ex-army officer who was a real bastard. Drink was his problem. They had no children because he did not want any. After he left the army, he did not know what to do with his life. Every night he went out drinking until late, when he came home he would beat Gaby black and blue if he did not get sex. One night he was out drinking and got into a violent fight, he was a huge man and it took three guys to overpower him. As he fell to the ground his head hit the stone floor causing a brain haemorrhage, he died in hospital three days later. Gaby believe it or not was devastated, she said that when sober he was a gentle man who she loved, but he needed help with his addiction and severe stress, which was caused by the Russian- Chechen war, but there was no one to ask for help. There are many men in Chechnya suffering from depression needing help, which is what war does."

"Why don't you invite her over here for a month or so to see you, you never know what might transpire, you are both very lonely people."

"A good idea Jack, I will call her. Freddie and Sergei will be wondering what we are up to, we had better go back into the lounge."

"Sergei, I need to ask you something?" Jack already knew the answer to his proposed question as Miles Coburn had already told him, but it would be most interesting to hear Sergei's version.

"Go ahead Jack anything you want to know just ask me." "Why did you not turn the Russian Mafia boss down instead of taking the money and getting involved with them?"

"I had no choice because he threatened to have my father killed unless I joined them. I was born in Russia not Georgia as everyone presumes. My parents lived in Moscow and had two children a girl and a boy. Our father Colonel Alexander Stepanov met our mother Alina, who was born in Chechnya, at a military function where he was receiving a medal for outstanding bravery. He is a national hero and has been awarded more medals for bravery than any other living soldier. When war broke out again between Russia and Chechnya, my mother decided to return and fight for her homeland. One day when he was at work my father, who had by now retired from the military to become head of the Moscow Aviation and Aircraft Engineering Academy, discovered that my mother had walked out on him. She left our home, my father and sister, and returned to Chechnya with me. No way could my mother take a young child into a war zone, so she arranged for her widowed aunty, who lived in Georgia and had no children of her own, to bring me up. I was to be known as Sergei Aslanov. Aslanov was my mother's maiden name before she married. I never got to know my mother, as she was killed in a Russian bombing raid on the city of Grozny, but I understand she was a very brave woman. After the war ended the citizens erected a memorial in her honour in the city centre."

Aslan then spoke. "It is a beautiful memorial to your mother Sergei always surrounded by flowers, I have seen it many times and often wondered who she really was. Now I know I am so proud for you."

"Thank you Aslan. My aunty did a wonderful job bringing me up and when I was nineteen I gained a scholarship to the Moscow Aviation and Aircraft Engineering Academy. I was a star pupil and gained a degree in aircraft engineering and also qualified as a pilot. I studied at the Academy for four years, in all that time I had no idea that my father was the principle, and as far as I know he was not aware of me. When I finally left, I furthered my education by studying at Moscow State University to be a gemmologist. I then moved to South Africa for more experience where I met my good friend Jack.

"If I had not joined the Russian Mafia in their venture, they would have certainly killed my father, whether he was a national hero or not.

They knew where he lived and all his movements, and even which café bar he frequented with friends, overlooking the Moscow River.

"What has happened to your sister?"

"Sasha has done very well for herself. She is married to the son of the Georgian President, they have two children. My sister is a doctor and her husband is a heart surgeon at the local hospital. She loves her life in Georgia and will never leave. As for me my life could change, I have illegally lived in Georgia for almost twenty eight years. As I am Russian by birth, the Kremlin may even try to extradite me once I return or more than likely try to assassinate me whilst I am in Spain. Now you all know everything about me, like Freddie here I am fearful for my life."

"Have you spoken to your father?"

"Yes, on several occasions, my sister and her husband have spoken to my aunty who arranged everything."

"Would you like to return to Georgia?"

"Most certainly, I want to meet my sister, find myself a wife and settle down and have a family." Jack smiled. "My father has recently told me, that he would like to leave Russia and move to Georgia to be closer to his family, so that is another reason why I have to return."

"Sergei, I have listened closely to everything you have told us. I don't believe the Russians will ask the Georgian Government to extradite you, if your story came out there would be repercussions for them in the diamond markets, the whole of the industry would be in melt down. There is a very good chance that both you and Freddie are in danger here in Spain; you are both going to have to be very careful when you venture out especially at night." Jack then turned to Freddie. "Would you like to return to Chechnya?"

"Not really, I enjoy my life here and my job with Aslan. Maybe one day I will return or go back for a holiday, you never no."

"For everyone's sake, it is a great pity we are unable to involve the Spanish police." Jack then thought for a moment before turning to Aslan. "I have an idea, my former boss at Franks in London Jim Richardson, has a close friend who is a high ranking intelligence officer with MI6, maybe I should speak to him for advice? It is possible that they may be aware of what is going on in Marbella. What do you think guys? The three men did not answer at first but looked at each other.

"Well, what is it to be, do you want me to speak to Jim Richardson?"

Aslan broke the silence. "Jim is a fine trustworthy man who I have known for many years, Jack please go ahead and speak to him."

"Good, I have his private mobile number so I will speak to him when I return to my apartment and in the meantime you must contact Roberto Sanchez and discuss your security arrangements at the villa with him. Don't be surprised if he recommends an armed guard." Jack then glanced at his watch it was four forty-five. "Guys if you will excuse me I must depart, unless there is something else we need to discuss."

"Jack, thank you for coming, it has been good to talk to someone."

"I hope that I can help in some way, as soon as I speak to Jim Richardson and get some answers I will come back to you. In the meantime don't forget to call Roberto Sanchez, he is an expert on personal protection."

Aslan then walked over to Jack and embraced him, Sergei did the same. "It is good to see you again my friend we must have a drink together and reminisce."

"Should I call you a taxi? No, I am going to walk, it is still light and the weather is mild and dry, the exercise will do me good. Thank you again for the food, it was delicious."

Aslan smiled. "I will see you in the office on Monday morning." He then let him out of the villa complex.

Jack arrived back at the Marbella Beach Apartments at five forty and immediately went up to his apartment. After pouring himself a large glass of cool red wine from the fridge and taking two long drinks, he called Miles Coburn on his private mobile. He did not answer and a recorded message came on.

"Miles, Jack Sinclair here, please call me as soon as you are able too?"

Minutes later he put a call through to Pedro Gonzales, he too was on answer phone. "Hi Pedro it is Jack, I will be calling in at the Med Club this evening, I need to speak to you urgently."

Walking into the lounge he switched on the Television. After flicking through the channels, he brought up Sky News and sat down on the soft leather cream sofa. Just as he was about to take another drink of red wine his mobile rang. It was his boss Miles Coburn.

"How are you Miles?"

"I am fine Jack. I have just returned home from watching the Arsenal-Chelsea match."

"What was the result?"

"A great match but it ended in a 2-2 draw. What can I do for you Jack?"

Jack then proceeded to tell Miles about the meeting he had at Aslan Maskhadov's villa with Freddie and Sergei Aslanov.

"No way am I going to pass this information of their whereabouts onto Major Pavlov, it will sign their death warrant. Sergei needs to get back to Georgia as soon as possible. Once there he can then divulge to the Russians where the diamonds are hidden, they should then let him off the hook, because of who his father is."

"There is only one problem, the Russian Mafia in reprisal for losing the diamonds will probably carry out their threat to kill Sergei's father Colonel Stepanov, unless his father moves to Georgia before we speak to the Russians. This will allow the FSB to strike at the Mafia before they know what is really going on. In any case before I can sanction anything, I need to get everything cleared by the top brass. I will call you on Monday. In the meantime make certain that Aslan Maskhadov calls in Costa Security. You have done well Jack but take care."

Picking up the Television's remote control he switched over to the Spanish News Channel. There was a report about the apartment fire near San Pedro. The local fire chief and a senior police officer were being interviewed. Both said it appeared to be an explosion from a very old and badly maintained gas boiler. The man, who owned the premises, admitted that there had been no maintenance to the boiler since he closed the garage workshop eight years ago. The police chief said that it was too early to say whether any charges would be brought against the property owner, until all investigations had taken place. So far it had been impossible to identify any body remains, but he was lead to believe from information they had received, that four young Chechen men were asleep in the apartment above the garage, when the boiler ignited in a ball of flames.

Resting his head back on the sofa, Jack closed his eyes for a minute as his mind drifted back to his parents, how he missed them, their conversations and the tender love he always received from his mother. Tomorrow he would ring his sister Lilly; he had not spoken to her all week. When he eventually opened his eyes again it was just leaving seven thirty, he must have drifted off. He was not particularly hungry and he didn't fancy going out alone to a restaurant, so he decided to cooked himself a ham and cheese omelette, before finally leaving his apartment for the Med Beach Club. Rather than take a taxi Jack walked down the Esplanade Paseo. The weather was mild but there was a breeze starting to blow in from North Africa across the Mediterranean Sea. As he walked down the Esplanade he could hear the sea crashing onto the rocks below, at least it was not raining. The Picasso Café Bar was deserted apart from three customers standing at the bar drinking, even the Albatross was not as busy as usual for a Saturday evening, and eventually he arrived at the Med Beach Club. The car park was full with a long queue of punters waiting to gain admittance. Assistant manager Kelly was on door duty with a couple of security staff. When she saw Jack she smiled and pointed to the staff entrance. Several of the punters recognized him as DJ Ramos and applauded him as he used his security key card to gain entry. Heading down the glass connecting corridor, he gained entrance to the night club. He was amazed how busy it was so early in the evening. Jose and Selena were taking it in turn to spiel out their patter and play the latest dance music. Jack walked up to the DJ stand and embraced them both.

"Do you happen to know if Pedro is around this evening?"

"Yes, he is in the side bar with his wife Nada."

Selena was a very attractive looking girl with a lovely personality. He found it hard to believe at twenty six she was still single with no regular boyfriend. When Olga and Tanya go back home to Russia, providing he was still living in Spain, he would ask her for a date. She could only say no."

"Thank you." He then kissed her on both sides of her face. She smiled at him.

Jack could see Pedro and Nada stood by the bar with their backs to him. As he walked towards them the barman, who was serving them, must have said something to Pedro as he suddenly turned round.

"Good to see you my friend, come and join us." Jack embraced both Pedro and Nada. "Can I get you a drink?" "A Budweiser if you would."

Pedro turned to Jack whist his wife was talking to the barman. "I gather you want to speak to me urgently?"

"I certainly do."

"Give me about twenty minutes and I will meet you in my office. Are you stopping here all evening?"

"Yes, more than likely."

"You appear to be very busy this evening. I would have thought you would be quieter now that the season is coming to an end."

"We used to be but these days we get many visitors to the Costa del Sol at this time of year. The weather here is certainly much warmer than in the rest of Europe and the UK." Jack smiled.

"If you will excuse me I will leave you with Nada whilst I circulate for a while, I can see someone I know so I will see you in about fifteen minutes." Walking back towards the DJ Stand, he could see Valentina, whose father Roscoe Rodriguez owned the Albatross Bar and Restaurant. She was on a very congested dance floor with a couple of girlfriends. Slowly, he made his way over to her approaching her from behind and gently touched her bare arm, which was warm. At first she was slightly startled and then a beautiful smile spread across her face as she realized who it was. Jack then kissed her on both cheeks.

"You have already met my friends Anna and Luciana before." Jack then embraced both the girls.

"Jack, I was not expecting to see you here tonight."

"I have a meeting with the boss in about fifteen minutes afterwards perhaps I could join you if I may?"

"Of course you can." Valentina then kissed Jack on the side of his face. "It is good to see you again Jack Sinclair; I thought you had forgotten all about me."

"I could never forget you; you are such a lovely girl." Valentina started to blush and then pressed his arm tightly. "When you have finished talking to your boss, you know where to find us."

Knocking on Pedro's office door, he waited for it to open.

"Come in Jack and take a seat." Pedro then went over to the large circular window and closed the blinds slightly giving them more privacy. "What can I do for you my friend?"

Jack then told him what had taken place at Aslan Maskhadov's villa a few hours earlier. Pedro sat there listening to every detail before he spoke.

"Now we know who the other voice belongs to in Aslan's villa, the guy we could not find Sergei Aslanov. Have you spoken to Miles Coburn?"

"Yes, four hours a go."

"What did he have to say?"

"He was delighted that we had found him before the Russians did, otherwise he and the Chechen Freddie would both be on their death list by now. He has no intention of informing the FSB of Sergei's whereabouts."

"You did right in putting Aslan in touch with Roberto Sanchez, he will tighten up security at Aslan's villa and more than likely provide an armed guard."

"I also told them at the meeting, that my former boss Jim Richardson of Franks in London has a close friend who works for the UK security services. If they were in agreement, I would ask Jim to speak to him for advice, they immediately agreed."

"Is Jim aware of what is going on?"

"Yes, he knows all about the Siberian cargo plane hijack, it appears his friend keeps him up to date on the situation."

"Once Miles Coburn comes back to you with information, you will need to have a meeting with Sergei. I can't get involved otherwise my cover will be exposed."

"Miles said he would call me tomorrow, I will let you know what is happening."

Pedro nodded his head and smiled. "Now if you will excuse me, I need to make my nightly calls around the club. Jack if I don't see you later, I will see you at Olivia Valere tomorrow evening."

The two men then parted company. Jack then went back into the night club and joined Valentina and her two girlfriends on the dance floor. After a few dances they slowly made their way to the bar. The girls ordered cocktails whilst he had his usual Budweiser.

Valentina leaned over and whispered in his ear. He could feel the warmth of her breath on his neck. When are you going to ask me out Jack or are you worried in case Olga finds out?" He laughed. "We could go down the coast to Estepona for a couple of days. I know a lovely hotel there. My father would never find out, I will tell him I will be staying with a girlfriend. What do you say Jack?"

Jack smiled. "I don't know whether you are serious or just playing a game with me."

The smile on her face suddenly disappeared. "Am I not attractive enough for you, would you not like to shag me?"

"Of course you are, you are a beautiful looking girl and I would love to have sex with you."

"So what is the problem?"

"Your father is one of the problems. If he found out I would lose his friendship, he is a fine man who I like immensely."

"You said he is one of the problems?"

"You are ten years younger than me."

"Next Thursday I shall be eighteen and nine years younger than you. My dad is ten years older than my mother and the age gap has not been a problem." Valentina then whispered again in his ear. I always thought older men dreamt of having sex with a young girl?" Jack laughed.

"You win I will take you out. Let me have your mobile number and I will give you a call in the next few days." "Would you and Olga like to come to my birthday party next Thursday?"

"We would love too. Where is it being held?"

"At the Albatross, of course. Where else? There will be a disco, live band, and a buffet so be there for eight. Jack if you take me out, I guarantee that I will give you a good time, she then kissed him on the cheek again."

Half an hour later he left the Med Club for the Marbella Beach Apartments by taxi, it was starting to rain. By twelve fifteen he had hit the sack for an early night.

26

At one on Sunday afternoon the door buzzer rang at Jack's apartment. It was Olga; she looked stunning in her figure flattering short white dress and cream high heel shoes, with her long dark hair flowing over her shoulders.

"I have missed you darling, your bed or mine?"

"You are in my apartment so we might as well stay here."

"Would you pour me a glass of red wine whilst I slip out of my clothes?"

Taking a bottle of Spanish red wine out of the fridge, he poured out two glasses and then walked into the main bedroom. Olga was lying on the bed naked; she started to laugh as he walked in. "You should have seen your face darling as I walked in, you looked so surprised. Get your clothes off quickly I am dying for a good session, for the last few days all I have had are men staring at me and no sex, it has been quite frustrating."

Since Jack had arrived in Marbella in September and met Olga, they had made love many times. Today she was extra rampant as though she had taken an aphrodisiac to boost her performance but Jack was not a guy to complain.

An hour later she turned to him. "I am starving darling, where are you taking me out to lunch?"

"You decide."

Olga thought for a moment. "The Picasso Café Bar, the food is excellent and the couple who own it are lovely. Once we have eaten, we can come back here and make love again."

Jack did not answer but if that was the case, he had better be careful what he was going to drink. No way did he want to let her down.

Two hours later after dining at the Picasso Café Bar, they left and then made their way back along the Esplanade Paseo to the Marbella Beach Apartments in between the odd heavy shower of rain. It was not particularly warm outside but Jack certainly was after his second session with Olga.

"What time are we going to Olivia Valere this evening?"

"Aslan is picking us up at eight in his Bentley, Freddie will be our chauffeur."

Olga glanced at her designer watch. "It is only just leaving five thirty darling; we have time for a little more fun." Olga returned to her apartment at six thirty. After a warm shower, Jack changed into a light grey suit with a white shirt and orange tie and black shoes. It was a special night and he wanted to impress. At ten minutes to eight Olga rang his apartment door buzzer. She looked stunning in her low cut, short black dress which exposed her ample cleavage and cream high heels. Her long silky dark hair flowed over her bare shoulders. Around her neck she wore a gold necklace, this was the first time he had seen her wear any jewellery, apart from a designer watch and earrings. In her left hand she carried a small black velvet vanity bag.

"How do I look darling?"

"You look stunning, your dress is beautiful and you look like a star celebrity."

Olga then came closer to Jack and touched his left arm as she kissed his face. He could smell the Channel perfume she wore. "Darling when we return later, I want you to spend the night with me."

Jack leaned over and kissed her neck. "Of course I will." The older security officer was on reception duty as they walked into the foyer, as usual he smiled but never spoke. Jack's mobile rang it was Aslan. "Jack, Freddie and I are in the Bentley outside the main entrance to your complex." "We will see you in five minutes."

When they arrived, Aslan got out of the front passenger seat and greeted them both kissing Olga on both cheeks. Olga smiled as Aslan complemented her on her looks. Twenty minutes later the Bentley pulled into the private parking bay at the Olivia Valere Club, which was already full of other luxury cars.

"Thank you Freddie, I will call you around one and let you know what time we require to be picked up."

Jack and Olga then got out of the car just as Aslan, who was still in the front passenger seat, leaned over and spoke to Freddie in a low voice. "Be careful where you go if you are going for a spin, and whatever you do, don't leave the car and go for a walk alone."

"Boss, I shall be most careful, I intend to drive along the coastal road at Puerto Banus and park by the harbour and marina, later I will return to the villa to watch a movie with Sergei."

"Make certain you park inside the villa complex, there is a possibility the car could be tampered with if you park on the road outside."

"I will." Freddie then let the window down. "Have a great evening folks," he called.

Aslan then got out of the Bentley and joined Jack and Olga as they made their way to the venue VIP entrance. The unpredictable weather had changed again and it was now quite mild with no wind, perfect for an evening out. Once gaining entrance to the club with Aslan's VIP pass, they were met by a security guard dressed in a black suit, white shirt, and dickey bow, along with the gorgeous Emily who was the owner Leroy Cardoso's daughter. After checking their names on the guest list, they followed Emily into the cabaret room where a reserved table had been pre- booked for them on the balcony. Jack glanced around the room, which was full of beautiful women many of them young and elegantly dress in designer dresses. On their fingers they wore expensive rings, whilst their neck and wrists were draped in diamonds and gold.

Aslan turned to Emily. "Thank you, our table is excellent we shall have a great view of the floor show from here."

"I will send the table waiter to you, the buffet is available for invited guests from eight forty-five to nine forty-five in the adjoining function room. Have a lovely evening and enjoy the cabaret."

Olga then whispered in Jack's left ear. "I hate beautiful looking young women like Emily, she is stunning."

Jack laughed. "So are you."

"Thank you darling, I feel much happier now."

Minutes later a young male table waiter arrived. Aslan ordered two bottles of red Sicilian wine and one bottle of Australian Chardonnay, Jack also ordered a Budweiser for himself.

"Good evening, can we join you guys?"

Aslan and Jack looked up, Olga did the same. Pedro and Nada smiled and greeted everyone warmly.

Aslan was the first to speak. "You are more than welcome to join us."

Just as everyone sat down again the table waiter arrived with the drinks.

"What would you and Nada like to drink?"

Pedro turned to his wife. "A Marbella Sunrise cocktail. It is a fantastic drink, you should try it Olga it has an exquisite flavour."

"I will have the same as you Jack, a Budweiser."

The room was now full to capacity. Jack raised his arm several times to both men and women who recognised him from the Med Club. The owner of the club Leroy Cardoso made a brief visit to their table but was called away by the bar manager. The evening was now in full swing, with the resident DJ Mateo blaring out the latest European chart music. When the girls excused themselves and went to visit the Ladies Powder room, Aslan took the opportunity to go into the function room and sample the buffet.

Pedro turned to Jack. "When you look at Olga it is hard to believe that she could be a cold hearted killer, I still keep wondering whether Miles Coburn has not made a mistake about her."

"I know what you are saying and it has crossed my mind several times. If she and her sister Tanya are behind the assassination of the Chechens, then Olga is one very cool lady, she always appears so normal."

"Jack, the girls are returning. When you are ready ladies should we go through to the Function Room and join Aslan at the buffet table?"

The food was excellent but then again for a club with the reputation of the Olivia Valere it was expected to be.

At ten the music changed and DJ Mateo walked to the centre of stage. Jack had always admired Lorenzo Mateo from the first day he had seen him, for his impeccable dress and professionalism on stage. "Ladies and gentlemen, if I may have your attention, would you will please take your seats as international singing sensation Enrique Iglesias with his brilliant band and backing singers will shortly be on stage."

Five minutes later, the velvet burgundy curtains surrounding the semi-circle stage slowly opened and the handsome young Spaniard came on stage to rapturous applause. For the next one hour and twenty minutes he performed all his greatest hits, concluding with perhaps his greatest track 'Hero'. The girls loved Enrique a truly great singer and performer. Just as the audience thought the show was ended, he went on the microphone again.

"Ladies and gents as you know the annual end of season party night at the Olivia Valere club is always very special. Tonight is no exception. I would like you all to meet a man who means the world to me and my family. One of the greatest singers Spain has ever produced, my father Julio Iglesias." The audience all rose as Julio immaculately dressed in a white suit walked onto the stage. The applause was incredible for the star. He has sold over 300 million albums worldwide in fourteen languages and has performed at more than 5,000 concerts. "Tonight as a special request from our close friend Leroy Cardoso, my father will perform one of his greatest hits 'Begin the Beguine'. As Julio started to sing the audience stood up to a true legend. This was a night Jack would never forget.

The room was still buzzing with excitement, when DJ Mateo returned to the stage and upped the music, after the spectacular show came to an end.

Shortly afterwards Emily arrived at their table. "My father would like to invite you to a private party in the Oyster Bar, would you care to follow me?"

The Oyster Bar which Aslan said he had never visited was in the close proximity of the stage. It was not a particularly large room, but it was elegantly decorated and furnished, with a barman and waitress to meet everyone's needs.

Leroy who was with his wife came over to them. "Guys, I would like you to meet some good friends of mine."

Jack had never been overwhelmed meeting famous people, his career as a top DJ had given him many opportunities. When he was introduced to Enrique Iglesias and his partner of many years, the former Russian born International tennis legend Anna Kournikova, he was not particularly moved, but when he met Enrique's father Julio he really did feel like he was meeting a true superstar. As the night progressed he could certainly understand why Leroy Cardoso described the Iglesias's as close friends, they were without doubt three of the most charming celebrities he had ever met. Shortly before they left the Oyster Room to make their departure from the club both Julio and

Enrique spoke to Jack. "

"Leroy tells me you are one of the UK's top House and Dance Music DJ's and you perform every Tuesday evening at the Med Club."

Jack smiled as he replied. "Yes, I have been appearing there ever since I arrived from London seven weeks ago. I shall be there this coming Tuesday, if you are still in Marbella please come along and support me." Jack then glanced to the right a little. "The couple over there with Leroy own the Med Club, it is an incredible club but very different than the Olivia Valere, who cater for a more sophisticated clientele."

"Anna and I have yet to decide when we are leaving Marbella. Once we leave here, we will be staying with my father and his wife at their Madrid home for a week, before flying home to Florida. If we are still here on Tuesday, we will definitely come along see your show at the Med Club."

"Fantastic, I shall hopefully look forward to seeing you both."

Jack turned to Julio. "Perhaps you will join Enrique and Anna."

A broad smile crossed Enrique's face as his father hesitated. "I don't think so, it is not my scene. In any case I have to return to my home in Madrid tomorrow. Jack I wish you well, from what I hear you are quite brilliant at what you do. Being a top DJ is no different than being a successful singer; you have to be passionate at what you do if you want to achieve your ambition. I wish you every success."

He then embraced Jack before leaving to talk to someone else.

Enrique turned to Jack. "Don't be offended, my father comes from an era of ballad singers, he has never been a fan of electric computer enhanced music however good it is."

"I am not offended in the least."

"Jack, if you will now excuse us we need to socialize, it has been great meeting you, we hope to see you on Tuesday." Enrique and Anna then embraced him.

At one thirty Jack, Olga and Aslan left the Olivia Valere, it had been a great night. Aslan had arranged for Freddie to meet them at the main entrance. There was a chill in the air and a light breeze as they got into the Bentley. Freddie their chauffeur for the night was unusually quiet. Aslan said something to him in Chechen before commencing a long conversation with him, in low voices. At times Freddie appeared to be getting quite stressed.

Jack turned to Olga and whispered to her. "Have you any idea what those two are rambling on about?"

"I have not got a clue. I never studied Chechen when I was at college."

Whether she had he would never know. Olga then started to massage the top of his left leg sensually. "Darling, you are still staying with me tonight, aren't you?"

"Of course I am." Sliding his arm around Olga's slender waist he pulled her towards him and kissed her soft lips. His eyes drifted downwards, her large breasts looked magnificent in her low cut dress. Luckily he had been very careful how much alcohol he had consumed, he had no intention of letting Olga down. He knew one day soon she would suddenly disappear and fly back to Moscow.

"Here we are guys the Marbella Beach Apartments."

The Bentley gradually slowed down and stopped by the side of the kerb, about twenty metres from the main entrance to the apartment complex.

"Jack, I will see you tomorrow morning, I have an appointment with the coroner's office tomorrow afternoon about the release of George's body. His parents, who will be arriving late on Monday evening, will be staying with me before returning home on Thursday morning with their son. I will fill you in with a few more details when I see you tomorrow."

As they got out of the car, Jack turned to Aslan. "Thank you for joining us; we have had a great evening."

After gaining admission to the complex, they walked along the short driveway to the foyer. The middle aged security officer, who was on reception duty when they left earlier in the evening saw them, and pressed a switch to allow the automatic doors to swish open. Jack smiled and said thank you. The security officer raised his right hand and nodded his head but again never spoke.

Taking the elevator to level three they entered Olga's apartment. Once she had dimmed the lights as she entered the room, she immediately kicked off her shoes and slid out of her dress, standing naked in front of him apart from a small black G-string.

"Come on darling let us have some fun before you fall asleep. You have to be up early in the morning to meet Aslan at the Cobra Jewellery Head Quarters."

Olga was laughing as she spoke. Jack then picked her up in his arms and carried her into the master bedroom.

When his mobile alarm rang at seven the following morning he immediately sprang out of bed, surprisingly he was not as tired as he expected to be. Olga was lying naked on top of the duvet, she looked stunningly attractive even when she was asleep. Looking at her, he found it hard to believe she was a ruthless killer or had Miles Coburn got his facts wrong and she was just a very sexy and passionate young woman. Picking up her black and gold silk dressing gown from a nearby chair he covered her, and then left for his own apartment. A quick shave and shower certainly brought him back to life. He even found time for a coffee and a light breakfast before he flicked on his mobile and called Benny for a taxi. Ten minutes later, he was sat in the passenger seat of a yellow Seat Ibiza tearing down the narrow streets of Marbella.

The heavy overnight showers had disappeared leaving uncanny stillness in the warm late October air.

"Don't worry Mr Ramos I will get you to the Cobra Jewellery HQ by eight forty-five. I know these streets like the back of my hand."

"You have just gone down a one-way street."

Benny looked horrified. "You are joking Mr Ramos." Jack laughed.

Jack liked Benny the young Spanish taxi driver, he was good at his job, reliable and never took life seriously.

"My girlfriend and I will be going to watch you at the Med Club tomorrow evening. We have never missed one of your shows. Boy George was our favourite English DJ until you arrived in Marbella."

Jack then put his right hand into his jacket pocket and took out two complementary tickets for his show. "Be my guest Benny and by the way call me Jack that is my first name."

"Jack Ramos, I would never have guessed that you had Spanish blood in you." Jack could not help but laugh.

"Here we are Mr Ramos, Cobra Jewellery HQ." The Seat swept into the company's car park.

"Thank you Benny, keep the change. If I need a lift later I will give you a call."

"Thanks Mr Ramos."

As usual, Natalie was on reception duty when he walked into the building.

"Good morning Natalie."

"Good morning Mr Sinclair. Mr Maskhadov is already in his office, he would like to see you when it is convenient. Oh! and thank you for putting a good word in for me with Mr Maskhadov, he has now promoted me to office manager as well as receptionist."

"Excellent, you deserve the promotion. I hope you have received a substantial pay rise."

"I have, more than what I expected."

"I will just nip into my office before I see the boss."

"Would you like me to bring through a couple of Americana coffees?"

"Yes, that would be lovely. In about ten minutes if you would."

Five minutes later Jack knocked on Aslan's office door.

"Come in." There was no mistaking his boss's Chechen accent.

"Good morning."

"Good morning to you Jack, please take a seat; I need to speak to you in confidence." The smile on Aslan's face disappeared. "When Freddie picked us up at Olivia Valere after their end of season party, I sensed there was something wrong with him. This was the reason we both spoke in Chechen. No way did I want Olga listening into our conversation, I just don't trust her. I gambled that she did not understand our language." There was a knock at the door and then Natalie entered with two mugs of Americano coffee. After placing them on the office table she left with a smile.

"Thank you for the coffee Jack, I could just do with this." Aslan then took a long drink, Jack did the same.

"As I was saying Freddie was most stressed. After he dropped us off earlier in the evening, he drove to Puerto Banus, and parked by the harbour overlooking the marina.

He loved sitting there looking at the luxury Yachts and Ocean cruisers dreaming of one day owning one. After slipping on a CD of Chechen pop songs, he rested his head back and reminisced about where he used to live and how much he missed his family. The car park normally held about ten cars, tonight it was empty, apart from a black motor scooter which had recently pulled in about thirty metres away. The rider just sat there looking in his direction without moving. Suddenly the rider, who was dressed all in black with leather boots and a black crash helmet, got off the scooter and started to walk towards him. Freddie immediately felt concerned, so he locked all the Bentley's doors. About three metres from the car the scooter rider stopped and pulled out a Beretta Pistol and pointed it at Freddie, he really thought he was going to die. Fortunately a second car pulled onto the car park and a young courting couple got out and sat on a nearby hardwood bench. This must have distracted the scooter rider, who calmly put the pistol away before returning to the parked scooter, the rider then drove away. Freddie, by his own words, was convinced that he would have been killed had the young couple not come on the scene. Within minutes he had left the harbour and was heading home to my villa. As he drove into the villa complex he looked down the road, some forty metres away he could see the same scooter rider parked, waving what looked like a pistol at arm's length. Unknown to him he must have been followed back to the villa. Once inside the villa he spoke to Sergei about the incident, he was most concerned especially after the recent unexplained deaths of five young Chechens on the Costa del Sol. Sergei told Freddie that one of his contacts believes the Kremlin have already sent two assassins to Marbella, with instructions to eliminate all the Chechens, who were involved in the Siberian Cargo Plane hijack."

Jack was taken aback and did not speak for a moment. After finishing the remains of his coffee he turned to Aslan. "Did Freddie notice anything which would identify the scooter rider?"

"Not really, the lights by the harbour are low apart from the four security lights by the marina, but they did not shine in his direction. One thing Freddie did say was that he thought the shooter was a young guy or maybe a woman. When the shooter closed in on him, the moon broke through the clouds lighting up the rider's body outline, which looked slim and shapely, no more than five, five in height. The more Freddie thinks about it, the more he is convinced the shooter was a young woman."

"Freddie had real guts to pick us up later. He must have been very worried stepping outside the villa."

"He was but he is very resilient, he will be back in the Cobra Jewellery workshop tomorrow, he will be driving my Mini Cooper, as I will not be in until Thursday."

"What has happened to Freddie is very concerning. He must not venture outside your villa complex at night under any circumstances. If you have no objection, I will speak to Freddie tomorrow when he comes into work." "That is absolutely fine by me."

"When I return to my office, I am going to make a call to Jim Richardson in London and see if he has managed to speak to his friend at MI6."

"Jack, please keep me informed. If I have left the building please give me a call on my mobile."

"What time are George's parents arriving?"

"Their plane is due to land at Malaga International Airport from Grozny Chechnya at seven thirty. Sergei and I will be picking them up."

"Aslan be very careful."

"We will, don't worry." Aslan then changed the subject. "We have a new client from Barcelona calling in to see us on Wednesday afternoon; they want to see our latest range of jewellery. Perhaps you would you take care of them, I understand they own six jewellery stores, so they could be a valuable customer."

"No problem."

"Natalie will give you their file, all the information you will need is there. Before I forget, on Friday I would like you to visit our branch in Nerja, all our branches need to get used to visits from head office. You can use the company Audi A4."

"I shall look forward to the drive. I enjoyed my day out last time. Should I email the manager of my intended visit?"

"Yes, if you would."

Aslan appeared a little agitated. "Now if you will excuse me Jack, I need to get to the bank with taking a few days off this week. As I shall be leaving the office early, I will leave you and Natalie to lock up, don't forget to activate the alarm system, Natalie knows the code."

"If you need any help please call me."

Aslan smiled. "I will."

Jack then walked towards the office door. "Jack, thank you for everything you are doing."

Raising his hand he smiled at Aslan. He genuinely felt sorry for Aslan, at times he wished he could come clean and tell him the reason why he was in Marbella, and that he was a MI6 operative. It was becoming increasingly harder to be two faced, especially to a friend.

When Jack eventually arrived back at the Marbella Beach Apartments it was almost six thirty and dark, it had been a hard day. After a quick shower and a change of clothes he called Olga on the house phone, there was no reply, there was a possibility that she would be working at Pinks on Monday evening, it had completely slipped his mind. Jack glanced at his watch. It was just leaving seven fifteen. As it was a dry mild evening, he decided to walk down the Esplanade Paseo to the Picasso Café Bar for a meal and a beer, before returning to his apartment for an early night. Tomorrow Tuesday was going to be one hell of a day. He had an appointment at ten thirty with a new client from Barcelona, who he would probably take out to lunch, if he clinched a deal with them. Then there were calls to be made to several other customers in Spain, regarding the new range of costume jewellery, which Cobra Jewellery were about to launch. Tuesday night was also Jack's big night at the Med Club, he needed to be on top form, every time he went on stage his reputation was at stake, so it was essential he woke up with a completely clear head.

27

It was amazing what a good night's sleep can do for your system. Rather than call Benny for a taxi, Jack decided to walk to work. The temperature was dropping on the Costa del Sol but it was still a hell of a lot warmer than the UK, and in another few days it would be November. It was Tuesday morning and he needed to arrive at the Cobra Jewellery Head Quarters by eight thirty, as the owner Aslan Maskhadov would be off until Thursday. At least by walking there would be no traffic hold ups, Marbella was no different than any other great city during the rush hour. Car horns were screaming and vehicles belching out toxic fumes into the air from their exhausts. Even so he enjoyed the half hour walk. When he arrived at the company's private car park Freddie was just pulling in, he blew the Mini Cooper's horn when he saw Jack. They both greeted each other warmly.

"Aslan needs me in the workshop, I understand it will now be a couple of weeks before George's replacement can start."

"Have George's parents arrived?"

"Yes, early yesterday evening. They are staying at the villa with us."

"Aslan told me what happened after you dropped us off at the Olivia Valere Club on Sunday. A most frightening experience, you must never travel out alone at night until the situation with the Russians is sorted out. Even in the daytime whether you are in a car or walking always keep to the main roads, no side streets. I can see the Mini Cooper has a Cam Recorder, when you are driving always keep it running and your doors securely locked."

Freddie smiled before he spoke. "Thank you for the advice Jack. Can I give you a lift back to your apartment when we close for the day?"

"Thank you, I would appreciate that." Jack then proceeded down the corridor to his own office. Once inside he put a call through to Miles Coburn in London. "Good morning Jack. What can I do for you?"

"Good morning to you Miles." After a few pleasantries about the weather, Jack finally got down to the reason for his early morning call, the line was not particularly clear. "Sorry about the reception Jack, I am on the train heading into the city. All my office calls have been diverted to my mobile."

"I am sorry to call you so early, I had completely forgotten about the one hour time difference."

"No problem."

Jack then told him about what happened to Freddie on Sunday. "What do you think Miles?"

Miles lowered his voice. "Have you spoken to him about security?"

"Yes, and Aslan Maskhadov has brought in an armed guard at the villa where he, Freddie and Sergei Aslanov live." "Good Jack, give me an hour and I will call you back, I will speak to my superior when I get into the office. I have an idea but I need to get his approval. Have you spoken to Pedro about what has happened to Freddie?"

"No, I needed to speak to you first."

"Good man, give him a call now."

The interference grew worse and the call suddenly went dead. After waiting for the call to be reconnected which never came, Jack put a call through to Pedro Gonzales. "Jack, what can I do for you?"

"Sorry to call you so early."

"I was already up and dressed, I have an appointment with the bank this morning."

Jack then told him about what happened to Freddie on Sunday evening.

"Christ man, the situation is getting more serious by the day. Once the sisters have taken out Freddie, there is a very good chance that their next target will be Sergei. We need to get these guys back home to their own country as soon as possible. Have you spoken to Coburn?"

"Yes, I spoke to him earlier, he was on the train travelling into London, I completely forgot about the time difference with the UK. He said he would call me later, after he had spoken to his superior."

"Jack, when you hear from Coburn would you give me a call. If I am on answer phone leave a message and I will call you back, otherwise I will see you this evening."

After placing his mobile on the office desk, he sat down on one of the soft black leather chairs, leaned back and ran his fingers through his dark hair and closed his eyes for a second. He felt certain the bubble was going to burst sooner or later. Perhaps he should be carrying a shooter; he would speak to Miles Coburn when he called back.

At twenty minutes to eleven Natalie called on the internal phone. "Your client Miss Isabella Lopez from Barcelona has just arrived."

"Would you show her through to the showroom, I will be with you in one moment? He then quickly switched his mobile to answer machine and left the office to meet his client. After a gentle tap on the showroom door, he entered the brightly lit room.

"Miss Lopez." An elegantly dressed young woman in a cream suit and matching high heels, who was looking at the display cabinets, turned round.

"I am sorry that I was unable to meet you in the reception but I was on the phone."

"I was early, no need to apologise." They then shook hands.

Isabella Lopez was an extremely attractive young woman with long black hair, slim, about five four or five and aged around twenty six, who had a very soft sexy voice. There was only one way to describe her smile, it was beautiful.

"My name is Jack Sinclair, I am Mr Maskhadov' s right hand man so to speak."

"You are English?"

"Yes, from London."

"Your Spanish is perfect."

"Thank you."

"What is an Englishman doing working in Marbella?"

Jack laughed. "I have a residency as a DJ at the Med Beach Club here in Marbella every Tuesday evening. Mr Maskhadov was looking for a gemmologist to join his company, and as I am qualified in that profession I joined him.

"Would you care for a coffee?"

"I would love one, a latte if I may."

Jack picked up the internal phone. "Natalie two lattes please when it is convenient for you. Mr Maskhadov sends his apologies for not being here, the last two weeks have been terribly distressing for him with the sudden death of his nephew George, who was staying with him."

"How awful for him," Isabella looked most concerned.

"He was over here on holiday from Chechen and was staying with his uncle for a few months. As he was a highly skilled costume jewellery designer, Aslan gave him a job whilst he was here. Mr Maskhadov found him dead in the swimming pool in the early hours of the morning. He apparently died from a massive heart attack. He was only twenty seven and such a lovely guy. His parents flew in from Chechen last night to take their son home for burial. The Coroner only released his body on Monday."

"What a distressing story, he must be devastated."

"He certainly is and I feel so sorry for him."

Natalie then arrived with their coffee.

"You must be tired after your early morning flight from Barcelona?"

Isabella smiled. "Not in the least, I arrived on Sunday for the week. I am staying with my brother Mario and his wife Ellie, who are both doctors at the Hospital Costa del Sol in Marbella."

"You enjoy being in the jewellery business?"

"I do but I have known nothing else since I left High School. My parents just presumed that I would follow my two other brothers into the family business. Mum and Dad are more or less retired from the daily running of the company." Isabella then took a drink of coffee, Jack did the same. "Now Jack, if I may call you by your Christian name. What have you got to show me? Please call me Izzie, everyone does."

Isabella Lopez spent over two hours in the showroom and purchased jewellery worth almost one hundred thousand Euros. Jack thought the least he could do was to offer to take her out to lunch, which she accepted, provided it was a light meal in one of the nearby café bars. After calling a taxi they headed to Aslan's favourite bar for lunch.

Jack enjoyed Izzie's company, she was easy to talk to and quite shy at times. He discovered she was twenty five and single and had never been in a serious relationship.

"If you are not doing anything this evening, perhaps you would care to come to my gig at the Med Club as my guest?"

"Jack, I would love too. I will bring my sister in-law Ellie with me. On second thoughts perhaps I should ask her first." The couple then exchanged mobile phone numbers. "I will call you later, Ellie is off work for a few days from tomorrow, so I don't really see any problems."

Shortly before three they parted company. Isabella decided to walk into the city to visit several of the up market fashion shops. Jack made his way back to the Cobra Jewellery HQ. He had a busy afternoon covering both his own work and Aslan's and was glad when the day ended, and Freddie dropped him off at his apartment on the way home to the villa.

Earlier in the afternoon at Emma's apartment in Puerto Banus the two twin sisters Tanya and Olga were deep in conversation.

"Darling, did you speak to your friend Roberto Sanchez." "Of course darling, he picked me up in his red Ferrari Portofino car and whisked me back to his villa, he could not wait to get my clothes off and luckily he still has the hots for me. For the next two hours we had a hell of a time. I approached him about his Ocean going cruiser the Black Prince. I told him that you had mentioned it to me."

"What did he say?"

"The harbour and marina CCTV did not really throw any light on his suspicion. He did not want the police involved and in any case the boat was in perfect condition. Roberto said he was still very concerned about Youssef as it was completely out of his character. I felt like telling him the truth that Youssef fell overboard and the sharks ripped him to shreds." Tanya started to laugh. "When I close my eyes, I can still see the blood pouring from his body and hear his cries for help."

"You are terrible sis but I love you." She then kissed her soft lips.

Olga's mobile rang, it was Major Pavlov from the FSB.

"How are you Ivan, are you missing me?" She then switched the mobile onto the loud speaker. The Major ignored her question.

"Olga, you and your sister Tanya will be returning to Russia very shortly, but first you must take out the Chechen Freddie. Take your time and make certain it is a perfect killing, us the nerve agent PV 44 if possible. The Russian couple whose hotel you stayed at when you first arrived in Marbella are FSB Agents. They have been based in Spain for many years. The husband works in the daytime at Malaga International Airport in the departure terminal. He has access to who is arriving and flying out of the airport. There is a distinct possibility that Freddie may try to return to Chechen, no way can we allow this to happen. You will have to assassinate him."

"Is there anything else?"

"Yes, you need to move out of the Marbella Beach Apartments as soon as possible. Move in with Tanya."

"I gather you are still very friendly with the MI6 Agent Jack Sinclair."

"I am. He serves a purpose." The Major ignored the remark, Olga started to giggle.

"Are you absolutely certain that Jack Sinclair is an MI6 Agent, he has never once given me any inclination that he is."

"Olga, take it from me that he is. On no account must he be harmed. Tell him that your uncle from Moscow and his wife will shortly be arriving for a holiday."

"What about Sergei Aslanov."

"What about him."

"Do you want us to take him out?"

"Absolutely not and if you do, both you and your sister will suffer severe consequences. If he is to be assassinated, the order will come from our President himself."

"Why is everyone so frightened of touching him?"

"My dear, his father is Colonel Alexander Stepanov. He is a National Hero to the Russian people, so we have to make certain that nothing tarnishes his image. We also believe that the only reason Sergei got involved, was due to the fact the Russian Mafia held a gun to his head. They threatened to kill his father unless he worked for them as a pilot and gemmologist."

"Do you think they would have killed his father?"

"I most certainly do and Sergei as well."

"Olga, I have been on the phone far too long, I am a very busy man."

"Major, I will call in to see you when we return to Moscow. I have a present for you."

Olga switched the mobile off. Tanya turned to her." What is this present you have for the Major?"

"The last time I saw him he could not keep his eyes off me, he was even looking up my skirt. His face was full of perspiration. When I see him again, I will give him a hand job in his leather chair, whilst his shit of a secretary is working in the outer office."

Tanya looked at her sister. "You are a very naughty girl Olga." They both started to laugh.

"What are we going to do about the Russian Boris, should we take him out or teach him a very severe lesson."

Olga looked at her sister. "Teach him a lesson. Before we leave you tell him that we would like a threesome with him, but he will have to book a room in a hotel during the afternoon."

"He will jump at it. Julie one of the English girls at Pinks who shags him every week, says he is sex mad and built like a donkey."

"All the English girls are cock mad. I shall look forward to our session with him." The girls started to giggle again.

Olga was still not around when Jack headed down the Esplanade Paseo to the Picasso Café Bar for a light evening meal before his gig at the Med Beach Club. When he sat down there were only two other couples dinning. An hour later, after a ham omelette and an Americano coffee he got up to leave.

The owner's wife Gabriela came over to him. "Where is your friend Olga tonight?"

"In Puerto Banus, she is staying with a girlfriend. She will be back tomorrow."

"She seems a lovely girl"

"She is."

Without another word, he left with his Apple laptop firmly held in his left hand and started to walk down the Esplanade. Considering it was the first Tuesday in November, he was surprised how mild the weather was. Even the Crickets were chirping and the occasional Fire Fly darted in front of him. The sea was gently lapping against the rocky sea wall as he wondered along the Esplanade, and there was a strong smell of sea salt in the night air. Twenty minutes later, as Jack gained access to the Med Club with his security pass card via the staff entrance, his mobile phone rang.

It was Isabella. "Jack, I shall be coming to the Med Club with my sister in-law Ellie tonight, we will arrive about ten."

"Fantastic, there will be two tickets at reception in your name; I will see you both later."

Before going into the night club, Jack went into the foyer and gave the girl on reception two VIP tickets made out to Isabella Lopez. The club was starting to get busy with a long queue forming at the main entrance. Punters were already starting to drift into the night club as Jack made his way to the DJ Stand. Brother and sister DJ's Jose and Selena, who were on duty, welcomed him warmly.

Jose turned to him. "It looks like we are going to have another very busy Tuesday night."

"I hope so." Jack then told Selena and Jose about the possibility of pop star Enrique Iglesias and his beautiful partner, the former Russian International tennis star Anna Kournikova, visiting the club tonight.

"That would be pure magic if Enrique came, he is so handsome and I have always wanted to meet him." Jose and Jack laughed. "Do you really think they will do?"

"I can see no reason why they should not come, Pedro says he has not heard anything to the contrary and the couple are still in Marbella. Let's keep our fingers crossed."

Shortly after ten Pedro Gonzales, the owner of the Med Club and his attractive wife Nada, walked into the night club and sat on the high stainless steel red leather chairs, at the far end of the long bar. Immediately, one of the young barmen came over to them and they ordered drinks. Pedro looked around the room and then spoke to his wife; she looked at him and said something before continuing to raise the wine glass to her lips. Pedro then noticed Jack at the DJ stand and beckoned him to join them.

"Guys, if you will excuse me for a moment the boss wants to speak to me."

Selena smiled at him. "Would you like us to set your Apple laptop up for your gig?"

"Thank you, I would appreciate that."

Pedro and Nada as usual greeted Jack warmly.

Pedro turned to Jack. "It looks as though we are going to have another very busy night."

"It is possibly busier than usual at this time of night."

"Have you any news, whether or not Enrique Iglesias and his partner Anna Kournikova will be visiting us tonight?" Pedro glanced at his gold Rolex Oyster watch. "They will be with us in five minutes as Kelly has just called me on my earphone. Enrique decided to stay in Marbella until Wednesday and visit us tonight, before flying to his father Julio's home in Madrid."

As they spoke many of the punters suddenly started to cheer and applaud as they recognised the celebrity couple walking in. They certainly looked the part, glamorous and both dressed in matching white suits, apart from Ann's outfit, which had a deep plunging neckline. The couple greeted Pedro, Nada and Jack most warmly.

Whilst they were in deep conversation with the Med Club owners, Kelly came over to Jack and whispered in his ear. "When you go on stage, don't forget to introduce our celebrities to the punters."

Jack smiled. "Thank you for reminding me."

Whilst Pedro opened a bottle of Dom Pedro Champaign for his guests, Jack headed to the artiste's dressing room to get changed. Ten minutes later, he climbed up the steps to the DJ stand for the start of his electrifying show. As the packed room went wild to the opening medley of dance house numbers, Jack asked Jose to invite Enrique and Anna to the DJ stand. The smiling handsome couple could not resist the invitation, and were cheered loudly as they were escorted up the steps. Selena was quite overwhelmed when Enrique gave her a hug and a kiss.

Jack turned the music down. "Guys and dolls may I please have your attention, the Med Club is proud to have two very famous stars here tonight. Spanish super star Enrique Iglesias and his partner Russian tennis star Anna Kournikova. I want you all to give our guests a fantastic Marbella welcome, so on the count of three, one, two three." The punters in the room then erupted as one.

Jack was now on a roll and he loved the excitement and the toxic atmosphere which bounced around the room. Virtually every great house music track he could recall flowed from the turntable.

Halfway into his show Jose leaned over to him. "Jack, there are two gorgeous looking girls asking for you, they are with Selena."

Jack turned and looked. A smile crossed his sunburn face a he recognised Isabella, he presumed the other girl was her sister in-law Ellie. Climbing down from the DJ stand he made his way over to them and greeted Izzie with a kiss on either cheek, she then introduced Ellie to him.

"Jack, both Ellie and I think your show is amazing, thank you for inviting us here tonight, your gig in a fantastic club."

Jack laughed. "You two girls look amazing."

Izzie fluttered her long eye lashes as she looked up at him. "You should be a fulltime DJ; you could tour the world gigging."

"If I did, you and I would never have met and I would also never have met Ellie." Both the girls smiled. Raising his right arm, he attracted the attention of one of the barmen who came over to them. "David, would you be good enough to look after these two lovely ladies at the bar, and whatever they order please add to my drinks tab." "No problem Mr Ramos. Ladies, would you care to follow me?"

"Jack, we need you on the stand, your track is almost ended."

"Izzie as soon as my show has finished I will join you." The night was incredible, even fellow DJ's Jose and Selena stood watching Jack in amazement at the way he worked the audience. His final song David Guetta's Titanium was electrifying. As he left the DJ stand he was mobbed by dozens of young Spanish girls.

Pedro came up to him accompanied by Enrique and Anna. "Jack, thanks for another fantastic show,"

"Thank you." He then turned to Enrique. "When I am performing it is though I am in a different world."

Enrique smiled. "I have exactly the same feeling. You should become a full time DJ and come to Florida. I could have a word with my agent for you."

Jack laughed. "Maybe, two of my showbiz friends Boy George and George Michael are collaborating on a song for me and they will both be on the track. When I return to London, the three of us intend to go into a recording studio and put the track down. Boy George is bringing out a new album, which will involve guest artistes on some of the tracks."

Enrique then turned to Pedro and his wife. "Guys, you are going to have to excuse Anna and myself as we have an early morning flight from Malaga to Madrid tomorrow. It has been great meeting everyone. Pedro you have a fantastic set up here."

"Thank you. You are both always welcome here."

After embracing Jack, Enrique and Anna along with Pedro and Nada made their way to the exit and the waiting taxi. Jack looked around in the packed night club. He needed to find Izzie before she and Ellie left.

"Are you looking for me Jack?"

He knew Izzie's voice immediately and swung round.

"Ellie and I thought you were fantastic. If you continue working here you will become a legend on the Costa del Sol." Jack could not help but laugh.

"Come and join us on the dance floor." She then took hold of his hand.

Both girls were excellent dancers and looked stunning in their off the shoulder figure hugging short white dresses. Izzie was very easy to get on with and he knew he had to see her again. When Ellie was looking elsewhere he whispered in Izzie's ear. "May I call you tomorrow on your mobile?"

"I would love you too."

Shortly before two, the three of them left the Med Club by taxi, after dropping Jack off at the Marbella Beach Apartments, the girls continued to Ellie and her husband's home on the outskirts of Marbella.

Once Jack had entered his apartment complex, he used his security card to gain entrance to the foyer. There appeared to be no one on reception.

"Good evening Sir or perhaps I should say good morning." Jack laughed, it was the first time he had heard the middle aged security guard speak in almost six weeks. "I have just made myself a coffee. Would you like one?"

"Thank you for the offer but I have to be in work tomorrow by eight thirty, I need to get to bed. By the way my name is Jack, what do I call you?"

"Antonio."

"Next time I see you Antonio, we will have a coffee together."

Jack smiled, raised his arm and then slipped into the elevator before heading to the second floor. As he let himself into his apartment, the interior lights automatically came on. There was a slip of white paper on the floor in front of him, he stooped down and picked it up. It was from Olga, she must have slipped it under the door. Jack quickly ran his eyes over the message. "Darling please forgive me for not attending your Tuesday night gig at the Med Club, it is the first one I have missed. I stayed at my friend Emma's apartment on Monday evening and became ill with a stomach bug after we went out for a meal, I then spent most of Tuesday in bed, I felt lousy. Eventually I got a taxi back to the Marbella Beach Apartments and went straight to bed. Perhaps when you arrive home from work on Wednesday we could get together. I will call you later. Olga x"

Whether or not it was true he would never know, but he would give her the benefit of the doubt. Once inside the apartment, Jack opened the balcony doors and walked outside. There was a chill in the air and the temperature had dropped considerably, a breeze was getting up as he leaned over the front of the balcony to admire the garden, and there was even the odd spec of rain in the air. Returning to the lounge he closed the balcony doors, switched off the lights, and headed into the master bedroom.

28

When Benny the taxi driver picked him up at eight thirty the following morning, the odd specks of rain which he felt on the balcony the previous night had turned to a heavy drizzle.

"It looks as though we are in for a miserable day with the weather today Mr Ramos."

"I thought it rarely rains on the Costa del Sol?"

"The weather is very unpredictable at this time of the year; tomorrow you could be sun bathing with temperatures in the mid-seventies. By the way, I thought your show was brilliant at the Med Club last night."

"Thank you Benny, I appreciate your comments."

"You must know many famous pop stars in your line of work."

"I do Benny, most of them are really nice people but the odd few have their heads in the clouds." Benny laughed. A few minutes later the taxi pulled into the Cobra Jewellery Head Quarters. Aslan's Mini Cooper was on the car park, he presumed Freddie was driving it whilst Aslan was off work for a couple of days. When Jack entered the building, Freddie was talking to Natalie on reception. They both turned towards him.

"Good morning guys, what a miserable day let us hope the weather picks up."

"Good morning Jack," came the reply.

Jack had been in his office for about an hour when there was a knock at the door.

"Please enter." It was Freddie.

"Can I have a word with you Jack?"

"Of course you can. What can I do for you?"

"Do you recall our conversation at Aslan's villa, when I said I was undecided about returning to Chechen?" Jack nodded his head. "Obviously I am concerned about my safety in Spain but there is another reason. Natalie on reception and I have become very close, there is a possibility that we may end up together." Jack smiled. "She has also asked me to go with her to the Fuengirola Street Market on Sunday. Do you think I should accept her invitation?"

Jack thought for a moment. "Yes, I would go. Are you travelling by car?"

"No, we intend to take the direct bus link from Marbella to Fuengirola. Natalie does not drive and I am concerned about using Aslan's Mini Cooper, in case the car is known to the Russian assassins. I will feel much safer with members of the public close by." Jack smiled.

"I intend to take a taxi from the villa and meet Natalie at the Marbella Bus Terminal."

"Have you spoken to Natalie about your predicament?" "Yes, and like me she is very concerned, but as she says you can't hide away forever and I agree with her."

"Freddie, you must be very careful and alert, if you need to contact me urgently call my mobile number." He then picked up one of the company's business cards off his office desk and wrote his mobile number on it and passed it to him.

"Have George's parents arrived safely?"

"Yes, Aslan booked them in for three days at the Marbella Coral Beach Hotel, which is very close to where he lives."

"I thought they were going to stay with Aslan?"

"They were, but they changed their minds and asked if they could stay in a hotel, as they are so stressed. Today with Aslan, they are visiting the mortuary and making arrangements for George to be flown back to Grozny Chechnya on the Thursday morning flight from Malaga."

"It is an extremely sad occasion, I feel for them."

"Jack, I will not be in work tomorrow morning, as I shall be driving Aslan and George's parents to the Malaga International Airport. Both Aslan and I will return to work on Thursday afternoon."

"No problem Freddie."

"Now if you will excuse me, I must get back to the workshop we have a couple of big orders to complete."

"Is there any chance of a lift back to the Marbella Beach Apartments when we close this evening?"

"Of course, I will call you when I am leaving."

Jack had to admire his boss Aslan Maskhadov. He had built up an extremely busy and very profitable business from scratch by himself. Today the phone never stopped ringing, work was flowing in, and there were several enquiries from overseas. No wonder Aslan required an experienced second in command.

Jack was relieved to arrive back at his apartment by six fifteen, Freddie's lift had been a godsend. The weather was crap with intermittent showers of rain and the outside temperature according to his mobile phone was 12c. What he needed now, was a warm shower and a change of clothes before he called Olga on the house phone. Just as he was about to slip into the shower, his mobile phone which he had left in the lounge rang. Walking naked into the room, he picked up the phone, it was Olga.

"Hi darling, how are you, have you missed me?"

"I certainly have, give me half an hour. You can then come to my apartment and massage my back; it has been a long day, especially after my gig last night."

Olga laughed. "How did your gig go last night?"

"Fantastic, pop star Enrique Iglesias and his partner the former Russian tennis star Anna Kournikova paid us a visit."

"Olga sighed. "I would love to have met them again but I felt so ill."

"I found your note under the door. How are you now?" "Absolutely fine, I will see you in half an hour. Which restaurant are you taking me to tonight?"

"I thought about the Gastro Bar Pikaro by the harbour, it is a while since we paid them a visit."

"I remember the restaurant very well. Those four Chechen guys who died in that terrible fire were also dining there. I will see you later darling."

As usual Olga was punctual. Once inside the apartment, she slipped her arms around Jack's neck and kissed him passionately. He then placed his hands on her slim waist and looked into her large blue eyes, she looked stunning. It was hard to believe that this beautiful young woman he was about to make love to was a cruel vicious killer, but also the most passionate woman he had ever met. They left his apartment shortly before eight thirty taking the elevator to the foyer. Security officer Antonio was on reception duty.

"Good evening Antonio."

"Good evening Jack." He acknowledged Olga with a smile and a slight nod of the head. "A miserable evening, can I call you a taxi?"

"Thanks for the offer but I have a guy I always call." He then took his Sony mobile out of the inside pocket of his soft black leather zip jacket and called Benny.

By the time they had walked to the main entrance it had stopped raining but it was quite chilly, so Olga placed the black shoal she was carrying, over her bare shoulders. Jack slipped his arm around her waist and kissed the left side of her face. Once out of the complex, Jack saw Benny's white BMW 3-series parked nearby. As they got into the rear of the vehicle, Olga's dress moved up exposing more of her legs. Benny's mouth was wide open, he could not keep his eyes off her slender brown legs. Olga knew he was looking and smiled at him.

"Where can I take you to Mr Ramos?"

"The Gastro Bar Pikaro by the harbour."

"I know it well the food is excellent, my girlfriend and I often eat there."

Twenty minutes later they arrived at the restaurant. "Benny, I will call you later and let you know what time we want you to pick us up."

"No problem Mr Ramos."

As they walked into the restaurant which was quite busy for a Thursday, Olga turned to Jack.

"Why does Benny call you Mr Ramos, he must know your real name?"

Jack laughed. "He does but he feels important having a celebrity using his taxi. There are loads of punters called Jack but there is only one DJ Ramos." Olga burst out laughing.

"Sir and Madam may I show you to your table?"

Jack and Olga followed the young Spanish waiter to a table by the picture window, which overlooked the illuminated harbour and marina.

The view in the darkness was spectacular with dozens of yachts and ocean going cruisers gently bobbing up and down in the water.

"Can I get you a drink?"

"Yes, a glass of Spanish red wine with ice for the lady and a Budweiser for me."

"Certainly Sir, I will leave a menu with you."

When the waiter returned with the drinks they ordered their favourite dish, Paella which contained a variety of sea-foods, white rice, chicken, vegetables and saffron. Whilst they waited for their meal, which would took about half an hour to cook, Olga took hold of Jack's right hand.

"Darling, I have something to tell you." She looked most serious as she spoke.

"You are not pregnant are you?"

Olga laughed as the smile returned to her face. "No darling I am not. My uncle in Moscow who owns the apartment I am staying in has been in touch with me. He wants me to vacate the apartment in the next ten days. He intends to fly over with his wife for a holiday and he wants to stay in the apartment."

"What are you going to do?"

"I have very little choice. I will have to move out. Would you like me to move in with you?" She looked at him smiling; her eyes were full of excitement. "We could then have sex every day, how exciting." Jack did not answer. Don't worry darling, my friend Emma in Puerto Banus has offered to put me up or I could even stay at the Seacrest Hotel, where Emma first stayed when she arrived in Marbella."

"I don't know the hotel."

"Emma said, the Seacrest was a small but very clean bed and breakfast hotel not far from the Motorway Exit, it has been run by husband and wife Russian ex-pats for over twenty years. There is only one problem. They also act as cleaners to keep their expenses down. Emma said the wife was a nosy bitch and often moved things around in her room and opened drawers when she cleaned it. That was the reason why Emma moved to her own apartment in Puerto Banus."

"Look, if you have any problems with accommodation, I truthfully don't mind you staying here."

"Thank you darling, that it is so sweet of you."

Olga was about to say something else when the waiter arrived with their meal.

"Enjoy your meal guys. If you require any more drinks please give me a call." He then left their table.

"You were about to say something."

"Was I? She then paused for a second. "You are quite right I was. I don't know how to break it to you as we have become very close, but I am going to have to return to Russia. My visa runs out in two weeks but I intend to apply for a new visa and then return to Marbella as soon as possible. It is my intention to apply for a resident's permit and live here permanently with you, if you are willing to risk your future with me. Well what do you think darling?"

Jack was taken aback, at first he did not know what to say but he soon recovered his composure. "When my contract is up at the Med Club I may return to the UK permanently."

"Are you not going to take up the job offer which Aslan Maskhadov made to you?"

"You have put me on the spot, I love working for Cobra Jewellery but I am still undecided. Olga you are a lovely girl and I do have feelings for you, in the next couple of weeks I should be able to give you an answer, but not at the moment."

"I understand darling take your time." She then leaned over the table and kissed Jack on the lips."

The food and service was excellent, if Olga had anything on her mind you would never have known. She was her usual vivacious self. After a couple more drinks they decided to leave the restaurant and walk back to the Marbella Beach Apartments.

Once outside they quickly changed their mind. The wind was now whipping up sand from the Sahara Desert and blowing it across the Mediterranean Sea in the direction of the Spanish mainland. It was becoming most unpleasant, with fine sand particles being showered everywhere. Jack immediately called Benny, who picked them up in his taxi ten minutes later.

"Benny, do you often get sandstorms at this time of year?"

"Yes, quite often but the Khamseen as it is called, is normally hot and dusty in September, though it tends to cool down in late October as it passes over the Mediterranean."

As they pulled up outside the Marbella Beach Apartments, Jack arranged for Benny to pick him up at eight thirty on Thursday morning.

"No problem Mr Ramos." Jack then passed Benny a ten euro bill as payment.

Once out of the taxi they quickly gained entrance to the complex and walked up the driveway towards the foyer.

Jack slipped his around Olga's waist. "Did you mean what you said about going back to Moscow and then returning to live in Marbella?"

"Of course I did, I have been thinking about moving to the West for some time, but I will need to apply for a holiday visa before I can leave Russia, that normally takes two or three weeks, but I will return to Spain and then apply for a resident's permit."

As they approached the glass doors to the entrance to the foyer they automatically opened. Antonio was on reception duty.

"Good evening Jack. I saw you approaching."

"May I introduce you to my friend Olga?" Antonio immediately walked from behind the reception and greeted Olga. Olga smiled but never spoke.

"Have you been far this evening?"

"We went for a meal to the Gastro Bar Pikaro, the food was excellent."

"I know it well, my wife's cousin is one of the owners, you could not have chosen a finer restaurant."

"Do you happen to know if Youssef Beji has turned up yet?"

"As far as I am aware no, I am certain Roberto would have told me if he had. For Youssef's sake, he needs to keep a very low profile wherever he is, that Russian guy who runs Pinks is out to get him by all accounts. He is continually visiting hotels and apartment complexes where Costa Security officers are based and asking them if they have any news about the whereabouts of Youssef. He is a real nasty piece of shit; I would not like to cross him."

"So I believe."

Olga still never spoke but from her body reaction he knew she wanted to head upstairs.

"Antonio, thank you for the information about Youssef, I will most probably see you tomorrow if you are on duty."

Without another word, Jack and Olga then took the elevator to the second floor.

"Would you like to stay the night in my apartment?"

"Of course, I would love to darling." She then pressed Jack's hand tightly. "Do you think Youssef is dead?"

"I have no idea but Roberto Sanchez who owns the Ocean going cruiser the Black Prince and Costa Security is convinced that he is. He believes that Youssef died at sea and someone else who had limited experience sailing big boats brought the Black Prince back into the harbour." "Why has he not informed the police about his theory?" "He does not want an investigation which will involve the police asking questions. The Black Prince is undamaged, if Youssef turns up all well and good, but at the moment he does not want to stir up a hornet's nest."

Olga was about to say something but suddenly changed her mind.

"You were going to say something."

"Do you think Youssef was into smuggling?"

"More than likely, he was probably working for that Russian Boris, who is desperate to find him. It is possible that Youssef had a friend on board or an accomplice working with him, they could have fallen out. The accomplice could have killed him or there could simply have been a terrible accident and Youssef may have fallen overboard and was taken by sharks. If Youssef was alive, I am certain he would have piloted the boat back to harbour himself; he is a very experienced sailor.

As I said before, Roberto Sanchez is also convinced that whoever piloted the Black Prince was inexperienced and it was sheer luck they managed to return to Puerto Banus harbour and marina safely. To be honest with you, at the moment no one knows and everything it is just speculation. We will just have to hope and pray that eventually Youssef turns up alive."

As Jack opened the apartment door with his security key card, the internal lights of the lounge automatically came on. No sooner was the door closed when Olga touched his face and kissed him passionately.

"Thank you darling for such a lovely night out."

"My pleasure," he said, kissing her again.

After closing the lounge window blinds he turned to Olga. "Would you like a coffee before we go to bed?"

"I would love one. Jack is it alright if I slip on your bath robe?"

"Of course you can."

Olga then disappeared into the bath room. A few minutes later she returned. Walking bare foot across the light grey tiled kitchen floor, she slipped her arms around Jack's waist and looked alluringly up into his eyes. "Are you going to make love to me again before we get some shut eye or are you too tired?"

Jack laughed. "You know very well that I would never turn you down." Olga smiled and then started to giggle as she started to walk towards the master bedroom. "Bring our cups of coffee with you darling and don't be long." She called out from inside the bedroom.

29

Jack's alarm on his mobile phone woke both him and Olga up at seven fifteen.

"Stay in bed as long as you want, there is food in the kitchen if you want something for breakfast but just make certain the apartment door is closed when you leave."

Olga was half asleep and he doubted whether she heard him, she looked beautiful lying there with her long dark hair flowing over her bare shoulders. After kissing her tenderly he pulled the quilt up on the king size bed and covered her. Fifty minutes later he was heading down the white marble stairs to the foyer; there was no one on duty. As Benny was due to pick him up in ten minutes, he quickly made his way down the driveway firmly holding the laptop case in his left hand. The weather was quite mild, the wind had dropped and the sand which had blown in from the Sahara had almost been washed away with the heavy early morning rain. It was going to be another perfect day on the Costa del Sol.

Natalie was her usual bubbly self when he arrived at the Cobra Jewellery Head Quarters. She was enjoying her recent promotion and the responsibility which went with her new position as office manager-receptionist, and of course the increase in salary certainly helped.

"Mr Maskhadov and Freddie will not be in until 2pm." Jack smiled, he already knew but he did not say anything.

"I shall be working from Mr Maskhadov' s office this morning, perhaps you would bring me a latté coffee about ten."

"Of course I will."

For the next hour the outside phone line never stopped ringing. The more he got involved with the day to day running of Cobra Jewellery, the more his admiration grew for Aslan Maskhadov. To build a business up alone from scratch like Cobra Jewellery took some real skill and guts. When Aslan first arrived in Spain, he could hardly speak the language and got by on English. Fifteen months later he was fluent in Spanish. As soon as he was granted political asylum and citizenship he never looked back, and now controlled a jewellery empire employing sixty full time staff. Jack took his hat off to him. He could now see why Aslan needed a permanent assistant. Jack loved his job as a gemmologist and he was highly skilled, but the problem was he did not need the money due to his inheritance from his late parents. Did he want to make his home in Spain? He was not certain, he missed his sister Lilly and her family who he was very close too, but he also knew that he needed to find himself a wife. If the girl of his dreams was Spanish, he could not expect her to live in the UK where they had more rain than sunshine. Olga could be an option but did he want to be married to a girl who was an assassin and worked for the Russian FSB? Maybe his boss Miles Coburn had got it wrong about her. Valentina was another option but she was too young and he did not want to wait for her until she qualified as a teacher in three years, but he had to admit she was a lovely girl. Emily the daughter of Leroy Cardoso who owned the exclusive Olivia Valere would have been an ideal choice, she was both intelligent and beautiful but she already had a serious boyfriend. Perhaps the young lady from Barcelona Isabella Lopez was now in contention; fate can have a very strange way of working. They were certainly both instantly attracted to each other. The outside phone suddenly rang. Isabella Lopez was on the line. "Jack, you promised to call me yesterday, have you forgotten me already?"

"Izzie, please accept my apologies, I won't embarrass you with an excuse, I really have no excuse for not calling you. May I take you out on Friday or Saturday for a meal before you return home?"

"It will have to be on Friday, my brother Mario and his wife Ellie are taking me out on Saturday evening."

"That will be fine."

"Jack, do you think your boss Mr Maskhadov would like to join us? I would love to meet him."

"I will ask him later, he should be back in his office at 2pm. As soon as I speak to him I will call you."

"By the way, I loved your show on Tuesday and so did Ellie. You are a very talented guy Jack Sinclair or should I call you DJ Ramos, they both laughed."

Shortly after twelve thirty, Jack took a break for lunch and made the short walk to the Tapas Café Bar, which was his usual lunchtime haunt. After ordering a roast ham sandwich with a slice of cheese and for a change a pot of Lipton's English tea, he sat back and checked his mobile phone, there were two text messages. His brother Lex was inviting him to Malaga's next home match against Villarreal, a week on Sunday. He replied. "Thank you for the invitation, I will certainly be there, speak to you soon." The other message was from his sister Lilly, telling him how much she missed him. He replied. "I will return home as soon as possible, I never stop thinking of you and your family, all my love Jack." For a second he was overcome with emotion and closed his eyes.

"Are you alright Sir?" It was the young female waitress with his food order.

"I am ok thank you, I was just daydreaming." The girl looked at him strangely, glancing back as she left the table.

As he ate the food, which was excellent, his thoughts turned to Olga who he had left sleeping alone for the first time in his apartment. No doubt when she got up she would naturally snoop around, but he knew in his own mind she would never find anything to connect him with MI6. His mobile phone, USB stick and laptop never left his side. Most of his money and his passport along with an expensive Gucci designer watch were in the bedroom safe. Every day he conscientiously swept the room for any electronic bugs, Olga could snoop all day but she would discover sweet F-all.

Jack arrived back at Cobra Jewellery shortly before one thirty and went straight to Aslan's office. Natalie had left a message for him to call an important client in Madrid. Whilst they were talking he noticed Freddie drive into the car park. Aslan was sat in the passenger seat. As he got out of the Mini Cooper, he glanced over to his office window and acknowledged Jack. A few minutes later Aslan came through to his office, they greeted each other warmly.

"Thank you for looking after Cobra Jewellery."

"It has been my pleasure." Jack then picked up a sheet of white paper off the desk and passed it to Aslan "I have made a note of all my business phone calls, six orders have come in including a new client from Barcelona."

Aslan smiled as he placed the sheet of paper on the desk, before sitting down on one of the soft red leather chairs.

"You look shattered."

"I am. It has been a very stressful and emotional two weeks. I was very fond of my nephew, his parents are devastated, they can't believe that their son could die so young. Though I have always been close to his parents, I was glad when they flew back home to Chechnya with George, I have never seen two people so distressed. George travelled to Malaga International Airport in a private black hearse. George's parents and Freddie accompanied me in the Bentley."

"I will get you a coffee."

"Thank you my friend."

Jack then picked up the internal phone and spoke to Natalie. A couple of minutes later, she knocked on the office door and entered with two white mugs of Americano coffee. "Who is the new customer Jack?"

"Isabella Lopez, her father owns the Bellaire Jewellery chain in Barcelona. They placed a sizeable order. I intend to take her out for a meal on Friday evening, perhaps you would care to join us, Izzie said she would love to meet you."

"I would love too, after a good night's sleep I am certain that I will feel much better tomorrow."

"Why don't you and Freddie head for home, Natalie and I will shut up shop?"

"Thank you, I will do that."

Once Aslan and Freddie had left the building, Jack made a call to Isabella Lopez.

"Izzie it's Jack Sinclair."

"Hi Jack."

"I have spoken to Mr Maskhadov and he would love to join us for dinner tomorrow evening. We will pick you up at eight. I know the area where you are staying but perhaps you would let me have your address."

"I will text it to you. Jack I am looking forward to seeing you again."

"Me too, Izzie,"

Jack left Cobra Jewellery shortly after six, as arranged Benny and his taxi were waiting in the company car park. "You look as though you have had a hard day today Mr Ramos."

"It has been a hard week Benny, a very hard week."

Once back at his apartment he had a quick shower and a change of clothes. As he was about to walk into the lounge, Olga called on the house phone.

"Hi darling, I hope you did not mind me tidying up your apartment?"

"Not at all, it looks as though no one lives there now, it is so tidy."

"Are we dining out tonight?"

"Of course, where would you like to visit?"

"My friend Emma recommends the Paco Jimenez."

"She has excellent taste, I know the restaurant well. It is a hidden gem in the centre of the historic old town of Marbella. It is situated on the second floor above several shops and overlooks the Orange Square. I will call Benny to pick us up at seven thirty. Fantastic, give me ten minutes and I will be with you."

Paco Jimenez certainly lived up to its reputation with a high standard of cuisine and service. If you wanted excellent food with a wide choice of restaurants, then Marbella was certainly the city for you. Shortly after eleven, Jack called Benny for a taxi back to the Marbella Beach Apartments. Olga again stayed the night in his apartment as it would be Monday before he would see her again or so he thought.

Aslan was already in his office at the Cobra Jewellery Head Quarters when Jack arrived for work the following morning. Before going through to his own office he called into to see his boss.

"How are you today?"

"I am fine, for the first time in my life I was in bed by nine thirty. A good night's sleep has worked wonders for me. Freddie told me about his proposed trip to Fuengirola street market with Natalie on Sunday. If I am honest, I am a little concerned."

Jack turned to Aslan. "You can only do so much for him. Does Freddie want to hide away in your villa for months or even years? I would say no, someone of his age wants a life of his own."

"Now I know the real reason why he did not want to return to

Chechnya, Natalie. I am very happy for him, Natalie is a lovely girl."

"I believe Freddie should be relatively safe in a crowded street market, there will be too many witnesses around if the Russians tried to attack him."

"Let us hope so but I still feel very uneasy about the situation. By the way, thank you once again for running the business whilst I was off."

Jack smiled. "Any time you want a break just let me know. Tonight when we take Isabella Lopez out for a meal, should I book a taxi to pick us up."

"No, I will drive the Bentley, What time did you tell the young lady we would pick her up?"

"At eight, her brother and his wife's apartment is not far from your villa."

"I will meet you up at the main entrance to the Marbella Beach Apartments at seven forty-five. Have you decided which restaurant we are taking Isabella to?"

"I thought about the Albatross, it is an upmarket venue and the food is always excellent."

"Good choice, I will call Roscoe and book a table, would eight thirty be ok?"

"That would be fine." Jack then glanced at his watch. "If you will excuse me I need to make a move, I have arranged to visit our Estepona branch this morning." "Good, perhaps on Monday next week you could visit our branch in Nerja."

"Certainly, I will give them a call. I will see you later." Friday turned out to be a very busy day. In fact every day was busy at Cobra Jewellery and having Aslan back in the office and in charge, was a relief. How he had managed to build up and run such a successful business single-handed, he could not comprehend.

As soon as Jack arrived back at his apartment at ten minutes past six he slipped off his jacket, switched on the Sky News and then lay back on the soft black leather sofa and relaxed for half an hour. With Olga staying with her friend Emma all weekend whilst they worked at Pinks, he intended to have a couple of early nights and catch up on his beauty sleep. Tomorrow, if the weather forecast was correct with the temperature expected to be in the early 70's, he would take a final dip in the swimming pool, before it was closed for maintenance work. At six fifty he took a warm shower and then changed into more casual attire. Darkness had already descended as he opened the balcony doors and walked outside. The neatly manicured gardens below looked stunning under the glare of the security lights, the wind had dropped and it was now quite mild, a perfect evening.

Slipping on his black leather zip jacket he headed down the white marble staircase to the foyer. There was a very attractive blonde haired woman who he never seen before, on reception. Her hair was very short but it suited her, he guessed her age to be in her late thirties. Aslan was about to park his Bentley as Jack arrived at the main entrance and immediately flashed the car headlights, when he saw him. Opening the passenger door he got in. Aslan appeared far more relaxed than when he saw him earlier.

"Jack, I received some very good news as I was about to leave the villa. My sister in-law Gabrielle rang from Grozny, she wants to come and stay with me for a month. If she likes Marbella and feels that she could live here, she intends to move here permanently."

"Perhaps you two will get together."

"Maybe, I have always been very fond of my sister-in-law, she is a very kind and loving woman just like my late wife. We have one thing in common; we are both very lonely people."

Jack smiled. "I hope it works out for you both. If you turn left at the traffic lights, her brother and his wife's apartment is on the right, number fifty four. I said that I would call her mobile when we arrived." Jack then took out his mobile and made the call. "Izzie, we are outside waiting for you."

"This is an expensive apartment block. What does her brother do for a living?"

"He and his wife are both doctors at the main hospital in Marbella."

Minutes later Izzie appeared with Ellie by her side. Her sister-in-law waved. Jack waved back as he got out of the black and gold Bentley to open the rear passenger door for Izzie. Once inside Jack introduced her to Aslan.

"I am sorry to hear about your nephew George, it must have been a terrible shock."

"The stress has been terrible, I don't wish it on anyone." He quickly changed the conversation. "Please accept my apologies for not being available when you called to see us, but I gather Jack has looked after you well."

"He most certainly has. My sister-in-law and I even went to watch his gig at the Med Club. He was fantastic, you are lucky to have him as your assistant, DJ Ramos could easily become a star in his own right if he was a full-time DJ."

Aslan laughed. "So everyone keeps telling me."

Ten minutes later the Bentley pulled into the well lit private car park of the Albatross. As they got out of the car, Aslan went over to Izzie and greeted her again.

"Lovely to meet you Izzie but please call me Aslan. We are dining at the Albatross Bar and Restaurant, a very good friend of mine owns it, the food is first class and the restaurant is exquisite. It is only a short walk to the main entrance."

Jack ran his eyes over Izzie. She looked stunning in her tight figure hugging black jeans, cream jacket and matching high heels. Apart from a thin gold necklace she wore no other jewellery. The nails on her slender hands were painted a deep red to match her lipstick. Izzie was the complete opposite to Olga, who oozed sex appeal before she even spoke. This beautiful girl from Barcelona was elegant and perfectly spoken with a very sexy voice, very similar in many ways to the UK television star actress and former model now turned presenter, Joanna Lumley.

As usual the Albatross was busy; Roscoe Rodriguez the proprietor greeted them most warmly. After a few words of condolence to Aslan about George, he showed them to their reserved table. From where they sat they had a perfect view of the restaurant. Several of the dinners who recognized Aslan and Jack turned and smiled. They had just settled down at their table, when the waiter arrived with a bottle of Dom Perignon Champagne and left them with the food menus.

"A special drink for a very special occasion," Aslan then poured out three glasses of champagne. He then turned to Izzie. "I would like to welcome you and your family to the Cobra Jewellery Organisation, may we have a long and successful business relationship."

Thank you Aslan, I know my parents would love to meet you."

The sea bass with mixed vegetables they ordered was perfectly cooked and presented. A selection of local Andalucian Spanish cheese with biscuits followed, along with three Americano coffees. The evening turned out to be a resounding success. Jack enjoyed Izzie's company, she was intelligent and easy to talk to but then again so was Olga. Even Aslan was taken up with Izzie. Once he had settled the bill they made their way back to the car park, it was still fairly mild for the time of the year. After they dropped Izzie off at her brother's apartment, Aslan half turned to Jack as he drove to the Marbella Beach Apartments.

"Izzie is one hell of a lovely girl, beautiful, elegant and well spoken. Forget the Russian girl Olga, she may have stunning looks, but if I am not wrong that girl has unknown baggage. You could have big trouble with her."

Jack did not answer. "I know you fancy her, most men would, but is she worth the risk. Izzie is Spanish and single, her family are very wealthy and she is attracted to you, don't let her get away from you Jack, she would make you an incredible wife."

"Thank you for your advice, you could well be right." He then got out of the Bentley and started to walk away.

"Jack, have a good weekend and I will see you on Monday." Jack held up his arm and waved. He knew Aslan was right and he had a problem.

Once inside the complex, Jack walked up the driveway to the foyer entrance to the apartment block. He could not help but think what Aslan had just said to him. Approaching the foyer, he could see that the female security officer was still on duty, so he pressed the intercom on the wall by the door to attract her attention.

"Please identify yourself."

"Jack Sinclair, apartment eighteen."

The automatic doors immediately opened. Jack raised his hand in a gesture of thanks and smiled as he passed by the reception desk. The officer looked up and then acknowledged him with a smile. Rather than take the elevator to the second floor, he walked up the stairs to the second floor. Taking the key card out of his black soft leather zip jacket, he gained entrance to his apartment. The room felt cold and lonely, at eleven fifty the lights went out in his bedroom.

30

The strong sunlight breaking through the partly closed blinds in the bedroom woke Jack from a troubled sleep. He had slept for almost nine hours but his mind was in turmoil. He knew in his own mind that Aslan's assessment of Olga was correct, unless Miles Coburn had got his facts wrong about her, which was most unlikely. He needed to find a wife, but he was not certain that he wanted to spend the rest of his life in Spain. His sister Lilly was the main problem, he was drawn to her like a magnet, they had always been close as children, but since his parents' tragic death their relationship was even closer. Whatever happened once his contract was up in Spain, he intended to return to England and visit Lilly. Freddie and Natalie visiting the street market in Fuengirola on Sunday concerned him, perhaps if he advised against the visit everybody would have fallen in line with him. Or would they? Perhaps not but it still troubled him.

By eleven thirty he was in the swimming pool doing his usual twenty lengths, the water was quite cold but the sun at least was warm and there was complete stillness in the air. Whist he dried off on a poolside sun bed, he called his sister Lilly in Ludlow.

As usual she was delighted to hear from him but she did not seem her normal self.

"Are you ok Lilly?"

"Not really, I am having problems with my medication. I am feeling very anxious at the moment."

"Where is Bret?"

"He has gone with the children to Tesco shopping. They will be home in about twenty minutes."

"Good."

"Jack, when will you be returning to the UK?"

"At the moment I am unable to say for certainty, but in the next two to three weeks I will come over and see you and your family for a long weekend."

Lilly's voice suddenly picked up, she was now more like the sister he knew and loved. For the next fifteen minutes they talked about many things.

"Jack, I am going to have to go, I can see Bret and the children have just arrived back. I love you darling I will speak to you soon."

It was Jack's intention to have a lazy day, the long interrupted sleep had done him some good, but he still felt tired. On the spur of the moment whilst walking back through the gardens to the apartment block he decided to call Izzie.

"Izzie it is Jack Sinclair."

"I recognised your voice Jack. So what can I do for you?"

"I called to invite you out for lunch."

"I would love to."

"Great, I will be at your apartment for one. There is a café bar close to the Blue Coral Hotel which does food, I have never been there but I believe it is very good. The bar is less than ten minutes' walk from where you are staying." "Sounds great to me, I will see you at one."

Rather than take a taxi to meet Izzie, Jack took the coastal path which snaked along the Mediterranean coast towards Puerto Banus. It took about twenty minutes and he enjoyed the walk. For early November the weather was perfect, very mild, no wind, and cloudless sky with strong sunshine, very different than what the UK would be at this time of year. Passing the prestigious Blue Coral Hotel, which overlooked the sea, he walked down a private road between several villas until he found the apartment complex where she was staying. Taking the mobile out of his trouser pocket he called Izzie.

"Jack, I can see you outside, I will be with you in five minutes."

Izzie looked amazing when she came out of the apartment complex, with her long dark hair falling loosely over her shoulders; she was dressed casually and wore white Nike trainers and dark designer shades. They greeted each other warmly.

"My brother knows the café bar we are going to, it is owned by the Blue Coral Hotel"

Ten minutes later they arrived at the Corol Café Bar. As it was a beautiful day, they decided to sit outside and enjoy the warm sunshine. In fact there were more customers outside than inside. The waiter took their order, two prawn salads, a glass of white Spanish wine and a Budweiser. For the next couple of hours they just talked, both very relaxed in each other's company. Izzie asked him about his family, he said it was a very emotional subject. She sat there just listening to him as tears formed in his eyes; luckily his designer shades covered any embarrassment. When he had finished she held his hand tightly, "you are a very brave person you deserve some happiness in your life." Jack just smiled.

Shortly before four they left the café bar and slowly made their way back to her brother's apartment stopping several times to sit on the low sea wall. At their last stop Jack took a selfie of him and Izzie, and then sent it to her phone.

As they approached the entrance to her apartment complex she turned to Jack. "I would like us to keep in touch. Perhaps you would even visit me in Barcelona for a long weekend?"

"I would love to."

A smile spread across her face as she moved closer, before kissing him on the side of his face. "I will call you from Malaga International Airport before I fly home on Sunday morning."

"What time is your flight?"

"Ten thirty in the morning,"

"Enjoy your meal tonight."

"I will." She then disappeared into the complex with a wave and a smile.

After returning to the Marbella Beach Apartments, he went for a swim in the pool against his better judgement. The water was bloody cold even after twenty lengths. That would definitely be his last dip of the season. Once back in his apartment he poured himself a glass of red wine and then switched on Sky sports. For the next two hours he sat back and relaxed switching from one channel to another. At seven forty-five, he decided to cook himself a ham omelette rather than dine out alone. This was the first Saturday he had relaxed alone rather than hit the town. There was a good film on Sky about a Russian assassin trying to hunt down the American President. He could not help but laugh maybe he would pick up a couple of tips. By midnight he had consumed the entire bottle of red Spanish wine, he was beginning to nod off in front of the television screen, so he hit the sack.

On Sunday morning at 9am Natalie and Freddie climbed aboard the Marbella to Fuengirola express coach. The coach was packed to capacity with punters going to the Fuengirola Street Market but luckily they found a couple of vacant seats near the rear of the coach on the right hand side. Like any young couple romantically involved they only had eyes for each other. Neither of them noticed the black and white Citroen C3 following them at a discreet distance along the motorway. After a twenty mile drive which took about forty minutes, the coach arrived at Fuengirola's Central Coach Station. The town was already alive with tourists and local shoppers looking for bargains. Dozens of brightly coloured stalls and café bars had been erected along all the side streets leading to the promenade, in all there must have been more than one hundred and fifty stalls. The sound of music filled the air. Freddie looked around in amazement as there was nothing like this back home in Chechnya.

"This is the Costa del Sol's premier street market, my father said it was one of the largest in Southern Spain."

As they mingled with the crowd Freddie held Natalie's warm soft hand and whispered in her ear. "I am glad that I never returned to Chechnya; otherwise I would never have met you."

Natalie smiled and then kissed him. "I am really happy you never returned, I love being with you."

The weather was glorious, warm and dry, a perfect day for meandering around the colourful stalls. Slipping on their dark shades, they walked around for about forty minutes before calling in at a café bar and ordering two glasses of pure orange juice.

"You took a big risk getting involved with me. When we met I only knew a few words of Spanish and because of your help and patience I can now speak the language fluently." Natalie laughed. That is because I fancied you from the first day I met you." Freddie then slipped his arm around her waist and kissed her.

There was a sudden commotion down the street and people started to shout and clap their hands. Several clowns, a juggler and unicyclist, followed by two stilt walkers came along the street. A man dressed in black and red with a top hat who was obviously a circus ring master also walked by, he was carrying a large placard advertising Pepe's

Touring Circus, which was now appearing in Marbella. As they were disappearing further along the street, two female Rollo skaters dressed head to foot in red, wearing dark shades and baseball hats which covered their hair, came into view. The stunts they performed were brilliant and people moved back in amazement to watch. After a few minutes they moved on. Natalie and Freddie decided to leave the café and follow the two Rollo skaters further down the street, so they could watch their performance again. There were more people than ever watching, and the couple had to stand right at the front, a matter of only three metres from the performers. Their finale was when one of the girls spun round at speed with her partner holding her ankles. It proved to be an incredible exhibition and the people around went wild. As the Rollo skaters spin came to a halt, the girl who was being spun stood up, she understandably was a little dizzy and unsteady on her feet. Freddie was close by and offered her some support; she leaned against him smiling before touching his bare left arm but did not speak. Seconds later she and her partner continued their journey and disappeared along the street. For the next hour or so Natalie and Freddie walked up and down the narrow streets in brilliant sunshine, enjoying the atmosphere of the street market. Just after mid day Freddie said he needed to take a break and sit down. He was starting to become tired and had a bad headache. Natalie suggested they walk to the promenade, which was not far away, to find a café where they could have something to eat and drink. Freddie had gone very quiet and was struggling to breath but he still insisted he would be alright. Eventually they found a café where they could sit outside. A female waitress in her late twenties took their order. Freddie ordered a coke with no food, Natalie a cheese sandwich and an Americano coffee with milk. Natalie was now becoming increasingly concerned about Freddie, not only was he breathing heavily, he kept saying he felt as though he was choking and could not breathe and he was now also having difficulty keeping awake. Just as the waitress brought their order, Freddie stood up and clutched his chest as he screamed out in pain, rushing forward he stumbled over one of the white plastic chairs before falling to the ground. Poor Natalie was horrified. She and several other customers went to Freddie's assistance but it was too late, he had already stopped breathing. One of the customers who turned out to be a male nurse tried to resuscitate him but with no success. The bar owner, who had witnessed everything immediately called the Spanish emergency number 112. Within minutes an ambulance with two paramedics a man and a woman arrived. Though they worked frantically their efforts were in vain. Natalie was overcome with grief and screamed out loud. A female police officer, who had also arrived on the scene minutes later, tried to comfort her but to no avail.

"Freddie was my life. We intended to announce our engagement on his birthday in two weeks' time. We intended to get married next year and have a family.

Earlier in the morning around nine forty, Isabella Lopez called Jack from Malaga International Airport.

"I am in the departure lounge waiting for my flight; I said I would call you. It has been a pleasure meeting you Jack."

"It has been lovely meeting you Izzie."

"When we went out for lunch on Saturday afternoon, it was as though we had known each other for years. We must keep in touch."

"I promise you I will. In fact I will call you in a few days."

"Jack, I am sorry but I am going to have to leave you, my flight has just been announced."

"Take care Izzie,"

"And you too Jack."

For the first time in his life, Jack knew this was a girl he had to keep in touch with; there was no way he could let her disappear from his life.

When Pedro Gonzales called Jack on his mobile around one thirty he was horrified to hear about Freddie's sudden death. He immediately thought of poor George and the way he died, the similarities were so similar that they must somehow be connected.

"Pedro, who was it who told you about Freddie?"

"Aslan Maskhadov, his friend is the Chief of Police in Marbella; he called Aslan with the news."

"Where is Natalie now?"

"At home with her parents, she has already made a statement to the police."

Pedro then went on to tell Jack everything he knew about Freddie's death.

"How is Aslan?"

"Mortified, my wife is with him now, we are at his villa."

"Is Sergei Aslanov there?"

"Yes."

"Tell him to keep inside the villa and not venture out into the gardens. It is highly likely someone might try to shoot him. Is the security guard still on duty?"

"Yes, may I suggest that you speak to him about the situation?"

"Leave everything to me." Pedro then paused for a second. "Jack, I think you should call Miles Coburn and put him in the picture, use his emergency mobile number, you will be certain to contact him any time of day."

"Right, I will call him now. I will speak to you later."

Jack then opened the balcony doors and went outside. Placing his hands on the safety railing, he took in a couple of deep breaths before glancing around the garden and then went back inside the apartment and called Miles Coburn on his emergency number 0044 757575.

"Miles it is Jack Sinclair, sorry to disturb you on your day off but it is very urgent."

He then went on to tell Miles about Freddie's death and what he and Natalie were doing in Fuengirola. According to Pedro they were like any other young couple, wandering around the market stalls and watching the street entertainers from Pepe's Touring Circus, which are appearing in Marbella.

"It looks very like the cause of death will be a severe heart attack like his friend George. Once the police pathologist has carried out a post-mortem we shall know more."

"You will need to get Aslan Maskhadov to send a blood sample to his Iraqi scientist friend for testing. We shall know for certain then if Freddie has been assassinated with a nerve agent."

"One thing puzzles both Pedro and I. How did the Russians know that Freddie and Natalie were going to the street market in Fuengirola?"

"I can answer that question for you. The Israelis, who are the world leaders in high tech mobile surveillance equipment, recently developed a bug which can intercept mobile calls and allow whoever placed the bug to listen into the conversation. The Russians must have got hold of it and planted it in Aslan's villa. It is quite possible that Olga placed the bug in the villa, when you both attended the recent charity fund raising event there." Miles paused for a moment. "What is Olga up to at the moment?"

"She is moving out of the Marbella Beach Apartment complex on Wednesday. She tells me that her Uncle and his wife are due over from Russia next week and want to stay there."

"Where is she moving to?"

"Puerto Banus, she intends to stay with her friend Emma. She also told me that she will be returning to Moscow very shortly as her visitor's permit will shortly expire."

"Jack, keep an eye on her and her sister Tanya, it looks to me that they are coming to the end of their assignment. There is a distinct possibility that they may decide to remove Sergei Aslanov before they disappear back to Russia. Also you and Pedro keep your eyes open for Kazimir Baizhanov who may be back on the scene assisting the girls."

"Miles, I am very concerned about Sergei Aslanov, what do you think we should do?"

Coburn thought for a moment before replying. "He should leave Spain as soon as possible and return to Tbilisi, Georgia; he will never be safe in Spain. Once in Georgia he can inform the Russians where the diamonds are hidden in the Ural Mountains. Before he does this, he must make certain his father Colonel Alexander Stepanov is safely in Georgia before he makes any announcement, otherwise the Russian Mafia could very well kill him in revenge. Jack, speak to Sergei first and then check out direct flights to Georgia from Malaga. Let me know as soon as possible what is happening." Then as an afterthought Coburn continued to speak. "In the last few hours I have received more information about Olga and Tanya which may answer a few of your questions. The twins' parents were famous circus owners in Russia. Their circus travelled the country; Olga and Tanya were one of the main attractions with their incredible Rollo Skating show. On their nationwide tour, the circus appeared in the city of Minsk Belarus for five days to capacity audiences. During the early hours of the morning after the final show, their parents touring caravan was set on fire whilst they slept. They both died in the inferno. The twins were overcome with grief at the loss of their beloved parents, and sold the circus to their main competitor, who was based in Moscow. It would appear that the owner of the Moscow Circus had been unsuccessfully trying to buy their parents' circus for the previous two years. At the age of twenty, the twins just disappeared never to be seen again on stage, until possibly today. The State police carried out an investigation but no charges were brought against anyone. However they did say the fire was caused by arson and that the Russian Mafia had been pursuing their father for protection money, which he refused to pay. They also believe that the Mafia are now part owners of the Moscow Circus."

A few minutes later their telephone conversation ended. Jack's head was in a spin, everything was starting to move quickly. Picking up his mobile he called Pedro and told him in detail what Miles Coburn had said and suggested.

"Jack, we also need to speak to Natalie and find out if there were any Rollo Skaters performing at the street market. I will also have a look around the villa and see if I can discover the bug which Olga may have planted. You also need to come over to Aslan's villa as soon as possible and speak to Sergei."

"Do you think I should level with Aslan and Sergei and tell them that I am with MI6?"

"No, if you do, it will ruin your relationship with Aslan. Just act as though you are the middle man between Jim Richardson and his friend who works for MI6."

"Right I will see you in the next hour."

31

After a quick bite to eat, Jack called Benny's taxi, the weather was changing and a light drizzle was falling.

"Where are we going to Mr Ramos?"

"Aslan Maskhadov's villa off the main highway."

"I know his villa well I have been there many times. I will be with you in about twenty minutes."

When Jack arrived at the main entrance, Benny was already waiting in his white Seat Leon.

"Is anything wrong Mr Ramos you don't look your normal self."

"I am very worried Benny. Freddie who works for Mr Maskhadov at Cobra Jewellery and lives at his villa has suddenly died from a possible heart attack."

"When did this happen."

"Earlier today at about one, Freddie was at the street market in Fuengirola with his girlfriend Natalie, who also works for Cobra Jewellery, when he suddenly collapsed with a violent pain in his chest. The paramedics and police arrived within minutes but he was pronounced dead."

"If I am not wrong, didn't Freddie's friend George also die of a heart attack?"

"He did."

"Very strange Mr Ramos, they are both young and come from Chechnya"

Benny then pressed his foot hard down on the Seat's accelerator. "I will have you at Mr Maskhadov's villa in ten minutes."

Benny was a fast driver, luckily the roads were dry as the light shower of rain had passed over and the sun was starting to shine.

"Here we are Mr Ramos, Mr Maskhadov's villa. If you need me later just give me a call."

"I will, thanks again Benny."

Jack quickly jumped out of the Seat, settled his fare with Benny, and then walked towards the villa entrance before pressing the intercom buzzer by the black double gates.

"Can I help you Sir?"

"Jack Sinclair, I'm here to see Mr Maskhadov."

"One moment please Mr Sinclair."

Seconds later the small door by the double gates opened and an armed security guard stepped outside.

"After you Mr Sinclair or is it DJ Ramos." They both laughed. "I presume you know your way to the villa."

"I certainly do no problem."

As he walked towards the front door along the winding garden path, he could see Pedro waiting for him. They greeted each other warmly.

"Aslan and Sergei are in the lounge with my wife if you would like to go through."

Once in the large hallway, they walked past the ornamental garden and into the spacious lounge.

When Aslan saw Jack he got up from the white leather sofa and greeted him. "It is good of you to come Jack, I can't believe what has happened. It is a nightmare."

Jack then turned to Sergei, who was sat at the far end of the long L-shaped sofa, he also stood up and the two of them embraced.

"Good to see you again my friend, I have the distinct feeling that someone is trying to attract our attention."

"You could well be right."

Jack then walked across the room to Pedro's wife Nada who was seated and greeted her. She looked most distressed and tears were in her eyes.

After a few minutes Sergei stood up again. "I will make a cup of tea for everyone. Jack would you mind giving me a hand."

As they walked into the large modern kitchen, Pedro followed them, when the opportunity was right he spoke to Jack in a low voice so

Sergei could not hear.

"I have had a good look around inside but I found nothing. I have removed the surveillance bug I planted; it has served its purpose."

"Maybe the Russian bug is outside."

"I will go and check, if anyone asks where I am, tell them I am outside getting some fresh air."

Sergei looked at Jack. "Pedro is checking in case any bugs have been planted by the Russians." He then changed the conversation. "I spoke to my MI6 contact in London about an hour ago and told them what has happened. He is of the opinion that you should return to Georgia as soon as possible, but you must make absolutely certain your father is in Georgia for his own safety before you leave Spain. Once you have arrived home safely, the co-ordinates of where the diamonds are hidden in the Ural Mountains must be passed onto the Russian Government, I am sure they will lose interest in you then. If your father stays in Moscow, there is a likelihood that the Russian Mafia will take him out in retaliation for losing the diamonds. The question is do you want to return home or not?"

"Of course I do as soon as possible."

"Good, your safety is our priority now. Contact your father but tell him to ring you back on a landline. Give him Aslan's landline number and tell him to call you back on that." According to my MI6 contact, there is a possibility that all mobile calls to and from this villa are being intercepted." Sergei looked shocked.

The kitchen door opened and Pedro walked in. "Jack, can I have a word with you. Would you come outside with me for a moment I want to show you something?"

The two men walked along the side of the villa until they came to the lounge, they could see Aslan and Nada talking through the large double window.

"Run your eyes carefully along the white marble above the window frame from left to right. What do you see?" "Absolutely nothing,"

"Look very carefully above the left hand corner."

"I still can't see anything unusual."

Pedro then climbed up a pair of aluminium ladders which he had got from the nearby garage. Reaching out he removed with a great deal of effort a small white object from the wall. "Have you ever seen one of these before?" In the palm of his hand was a small white dish no more than four inches wide, it could only be described as a micro-satellite dish.

"What the hell is that?"

"That my friend is the latest revolutionary mobile interception bug, which has been developed by Israel for the Jewish States intelligence service Mossad. The dish picks up all the electronic singles coming from the mast by the main highway. These singles are then intercepted by a small decoding device, probably disguised as a laptop. You could then sit in a parked car close by and listen in to all incoming and outgoing mobile calls." "Incredible, the Russians are always one step ahead. I wonder how they got hold of the device."

"They would have known exactly when and what time Freddie and Natalie where going to the street market in Fuengirola."

"One or both the twins obviously understand Spanish, I would never have known, Olga has certainly never given anything away."

"They probably spoke Chechnya as well."

"You appear to be very well informed about this latest device."

"I have heard about it but never seen it. Being an electronic surveillance expert I am intrigued to see new inventions, I am like a child with a new toy." Pedro sighed. "I will contact Coburn and let him know about the bug. Let's go back inside."

Aslan, Nana and Sergei who were drinking cups of Lipton's English tea when they returned to the lounge, looked up at them.

Nana was the first to speak. "Pedro is everything alright?" "Of course it is."

"She stared at her husband before turning to Aslan. "I need to return to our villa, Pedro's mother is looking after the children, but they normally play her up when we are not around."

"I will walk you home."

"There is no need to; we only live a few hundred metres away."

"I insist I walk with you."

Nada then rose from the sofa. Both Aslan and Sergei embraced her.

"Thank you for supporting me Nada, I appreciate everything you have done for me." Nada tried to smile but she looked so dejected.

As they walked out of the lounge, Pedro whispered to Jack who was stood by the door. "I will be back in about twenty minutes." Jack smiled and nodded his head.

Once outside the villa complex Nada turned to her husband as they slowly walked up the tree lined road to their villa. "What is going on Pedro, why were you and Jack outside by the lounge window?"

"You must trust me. I promise I will explain to you later." "Do you think Freddie was murdered like George?"

"More than likely, we will know for certain in a few days." "Are the police involved?"

"Yes, they arrived at the scene with the ambulance. When they discover that Freddie is from Chechnya like George and they knew each other and have both died from heart attacks, I am certain they will be asking some delicate questions." Pedro then gave his wife an assuring hug and a kiss as she entered their villa complex. "I will be back within the hour and explain everything to you."

"That did not take you long my friend." Pedro looked at Aslan and smiled.

"Can I get you something stronger than English tea?"

"A whisky and tonic water if I may?"

"Same for you guys." They both replied yes but with diet coke. "Four whisky's, two with coke and two with tonic water. Sergei, would you mind acting as waiter? There is ice in the freezer."

"Of course I will."

When Sergei left the lounge Aslan turned to Jack and Pedro. "This is a dreadful situation, I just hope and pray that Freddie's cause of death does not turn out to be the same as George."

Jack then told Aslan that he had spoken to Sergei about leaving Spain and returning home to Georgia.

"I could not agree with you more."

As he was speaking Sergei walked back into the room. "Have I missed something, I heard my name mentioned." He then passed the drinks around.

"I was briefly telling Aslan what my MI6 contact in the UK said when I spoke to him earlier today. Don't forget Sergei, as soon as your father arrives safely in Georgia then it is time for you to leave." He then took a drink of his whisky and coke.

Pedro then showed Aslan and Sergei the electronic bug he had discovered on the outside wall of the villa. "This little gadget along with a sophisticated decoder probably disguised as a laptop, would allow whoever placed it to listen in to all mobile calls without the caller knowing." He then downed the last of his drink and stood up.

"Would you like another whisky my friend?"

"Thank you but no, I need to return home, Nada will be wondering where I am." He then glanced at his gold Rolex Oyster watch. "Christ it is almost five, I have to be at the Med Club by seven. Aslan, if you need anything just call me." The two friends then embraced each other.

Jack rose from his chair as Pedro started to leave the lounge. "I will see you out."

As they walked to the main entrance, Pedro held the mini satellite dish which was now in a white plastic bag, up in his raised right hand. "I need to get this little baby to MI6 as soon as possible. Jack I will call you tomorrow after I have spoken to Miles Coburn. You be careful my friend, you never know what Olga or Tanya may have in store for you before they skip the country, if they suspect you are an MI6 operative. But then again they are probably already aware of who you are."

Jack then returned to the villa. Pedro was correct, from now on he had to be most careful.

"Aslan if you like I will run Cobra Jewellery for you tomorrow."

"Thanks for the offer Jack but I feel that I should go in. Natalie will be off for some time and I have to break the news about Freddie's death to the staff, he was a very popular team member. I would appreciate your assistance in this matter as some of the staff will be very upset. If you like, I will pick you up tomorrow at eight fifteen."

"Excellent, I will meet you at the main entrance to the complex, now if you will excuse me I should be going; I need to call my brother Lex and sister Lilly in the UK."

"You are more than welcome to dine with us, Sergei is an excellent chef."

"Thank you for the invitation but I really should be getting back. Sergei, I also need to check on your flight times to Georgia and don't forget to contact your father it is most urgent."

Rather than call a taxi Jack decided to take the coastal path back to his apartment. It was a walk he always enjoyed along the Mediterranean, the scenery was stunning and the weather was fairly mild. To be honest he was looking forward to the stroll which would take about thirty minutes, perhaps it would clear his head. Freddie's death had shocked him, he had grown to like the guy and he felt desperately sorry for Natalie, whose dreams had been so cruelly snatched away.

There was no one about when he entered the Marbella Beach Apartment Complex. The foyer doors were wide open and for once there was no one on reception. Quickly climbing the white marble staircase to the second floor, he used the key card to gain access to his apartment. Walking over to the balcony doors he opened them both wide to allow some fresh air to rush in. Standing on the balcony he looked out over the garden, it still looked immaculate even in the fading light. Seconds later the security lights came on; closing the doors he went back inside the apartment and switched on the television flicking the channel to Sky News. After catching up on the English Premier League football results he started to relax, especially when he realised that Chelsea's away win had moved them to the top of the Premier League by three points. At six thirty he went for a warm shower and change of clothes, before making phone calls to his brother Lex and sister Lilly.

It was now completely dark outside, so after closing all the blinds and switching off the television, he slipped on his black soft leather zip jacket and left the apartment for the Albatross Bar and Restaurant. It was just leaving seven thirty.

After a brisk twenty minute walk down the Esplanade Paseo he arrived at the Albatross. Tonight was the quietest he had seen the restaurant since his arrival in Marbella. The owner Roscoe Rodriguez was behind the bar with his daughter Valentina assisting two of the regular table waiters. When Roscoe saw Jack he immediately came from behind the bar and embraced him.

"I am shocked to hear about Freddie, he was such a lovely guy. Aslan must be devastated."

"He is, especially after the loss of George. It is difficult for him to comprehend."

As they were speaking Valentina came over and joined them touching his arm. "I am so sorry to hear about Freddie, I find it hard to believe that someone who was so young and fit would have a heart attack."

Jack shook his head. "I feel exactly the same as you, I appreciate your kind thoughts, let us hope the post-mortem report will show what caused him to have a heart attack."

"Are you dining with us tonight?"

"I most certainly am."

"Take your pick."

"What about the table in the corner close to the bar? By the way, you look lovely tonight."

Valentina looked up at him. There was a sexy smile and sparkle in her eyes as she replied "Thank you Jack," once he was seated she passed him the menu.

"What do you recommend?"

"The sea bass is fantastic with mixed vegetables."

"Sea bass it is then. You knew it was my favourite." Valentina laughed. "What would you like to drink?"

"A beer if you would."

"I will bring your drink immediately; the meal will take about twenty minutes." She then leaned over the table. "Is there anything else you would like?"

"If I told you, your father would not be very happy with me."

"Why, what would you like," she replied with a mischievous grin on her beautiful face.

Valentina then went behind the bar and pulled a pint of cold beer, a few minutes later she returned with his drink. "Where is your friend

Olga tonight?"

"She has been staying with a girlfriend in Puerto Banus since Friday."

"I hope she does not come back." Jack laughed.

"I gather you do not like her."

"I do not trust her, just call it another women's instinct. "She may have the looks that most women would die for but please be careful Jack."

"You will be pleased to know, that Olga will be returning to Russia before the end of the month, as her visitor's permit expires."

"Good, sooner the better. Will you please excuse me?" She then left to take an order from another table. "See you later Jack." She whispered.

He could not help wondering whether Valentina was jealous of Olga or did she really have bad vibes about her. He would love to get to know Valentina more intimately, but he just wished she was a few years older and then he would have no problem being in a relationship with her. As usual the food was excellent, for the next couple of hours he sat at the bar consuming far too much alcohol, whilst talking to Roscoe and Valentine. Shortly before eleven he got up to leave the Albatross.

"Thanks Roscoe for another excellent meal and your company."

"A pleasure to see you my friend, you take care."

Jack then went outside to the Esplanade Paseo, below the low sea wall he could hear the sea smashing against the rocks in the darkness. There was a wind slowly sweeping in from North Africa.

"Jack, have you got a moment."

Turning towards the sound of the voice, he could see Valentina coming towards him. Her long dark hair was blowing in the wind, she looked stunning. When she got close she touched his arm.

"I am not too young for you, I know you fancy me." She then tiptoed and kissed him on the lips.

Jack placed his hands on her shoulders and looked down into her wide open brown eyes. "Valentina, you are a lovely girl, any guy including myself would be proud to be involved with you. Your age is not the main problem though I admit I would like you to be a few years older. If I am honest, I don't even know if I will still be in Spain in December. If the Med Club do not renew my contract, I may return to the UK."

"I thought you had a good daytime job with Cobra Jewellery."

"I have and I love my life here at the moment. Franks the company I used to work for in London want me to return, they are one of Europe's major gem dealers. I know that I will have to make a decision soon."

"Valentina then kissed him again."

"Getting involved with me would create many problems as you are due to start Malaga University to be a teacher. You must make certain your dream is fulfilled. Don't let yourself or your family down, your heart must not rule your head."

There was sadness in her eyes as she looked up. My mother is ten years younger than my father and they have a wonderful marriage. I know, your father told me that your mother was almost twenty one when they married, but you are only eighteen." Tears started to roll from her eyes staining her cheeks; taking out a white handkerchief from his left pocket he wiped the mascara stains away. "What I want to be, is your very close friend. I do have feelings for you but at the moment I am in limbo. I think you should return to the restaurant before your father comes out to find you. Remember Valentina I think you are a very special girl then kissed her lips softly before leaving.

Twenty minutes later he arrived back at the Marbella Beach Apartments just as the rain was starting to fall.

Once inside his apartment, he set his mobile alarm for seven fifteen and went straight to bed. His head felt in a maze, it had been one hell of a day, one which he hoped would never be repeated.

32

Cobra Jewellery boss Aslan Maskhadov, was already waiting in his Mini Cooper by the Marbella Beach Apartments main entrance, when Jack walked out to meet him at eight-fifteen.

"Good morning Aslan you are very punctual."

"I have always been a good time keeper all my life. To be perfectly honest with you, I woke around six this morning, and as I lay there dozing I realized I had no way of contacting Freddie's family in Chechnya. All I know is that he was born in Grozny and had lived there all his life, until he won a scholarship to the Moscow Aviation and Aircraft Engineering Academy."

"Has Sergei any information about him?"

"I spoke to him this morning. As far as he is aware, his father is a well known lawyer in Grozny."

"You will have to speak to the police. They will contact the Chechnya Embassy in Madrid. They should have no problem tracing his family if his father is a lawyer."

"Once I get into the office I will contact the police."

"How are you today?"

"Still shell shocked and very worried."

The early morning traffic was now building up as they skirted the city centre.

"With Natalie being off for a few days, would you mind covering reception?"

"Of course I will. How has the new jewellery designer settled in?"

"Ricardo, he is going to be an excellent addition to the team, young with some great ideas, he is quite a brilliant designer."

"I am pleased. You made an excellent choice when you took him on straight from college."

Aslan then went quiet for a moment as they drove into the car park at the Cobra Jewellery Head Quarters. Once he had parked the Mini

Cooper he turned to Jack.

"I shall need your help breaking the news to the staff about Freddie's death."

"Don't worry I shall support you."

"Thank you my friend." Jack smiled.

Aslan's concern about his staff was justified, Freddie had been a very popular team member and there were many tears. Monday as usual was a very busy day with endless phone calls and a delivery of precious gems from South Africa. In between grading the gems Jack spent time on his mobile checking out flights between Malaga and Tbilisi, Georgia. The main airline appeared to be Turkish Airlines, who operated daily flights between the two destinations, with a two hour stop at Ankara, Turkey to take on additional passengers and refuel. The flight which was over 2,600 miles would take over ten hours. Sergei had no option, the sooner he booked the flight the sooner he would be safely on his way home.

When Aslan and Jack left Cobra Jewellery shortly before six fifteen in the Mini Cooper, Jack brought up Sergei in conversation.

"Perhaps you would tell Sergei that I will call him around seven."

"If you call my landline, I will make certain that he knows you will be contacting him."

Jack had only been in his apartment ten minutes when the house line rang.

"Darling it is me."

"Hi Olga, have you had a good weekend?"

"Fantastic darling so are you taking me out for a meal tonight or would you like to stay in and I will cook something special for us?"

"I was not aware cooking was one of your many talents?" Olga laughed. "You would be surprised what I can do so is it your apartment or mine?"

"Yours if that is ok and I will bring a bottle of red."

"I will see you at eight darling, don't be late."

Jack needed to visit Olga's apartment and remove the security bug before she moved out. This was an ideal opportunity.

At seven Jack called Sergei, who immediately answered the phone.

"How are you?"

"Still shocked over poor Freddie's death and very worried in case the Russian assassins try to take me out."

"You must continue to keep inside the villa for your own safety."

"I am being extremely careful."

"Have you managed to make contact with your father?" "Yes, I texted him and he said he would call me later this evening."

"I have checked flights to Tbilisi, Georgia from Malaga. Turkish Airlines run a daily service with a two hour fuel and passenger stop at Ankara. It is a good ten hour flight. Remember your father has to be safely in Georgia before you can leave Spain."

"I completely understand what you are saying. As soon as I hear from my father I will call you."

"Aslan has my mobile number. Hopefully Sergei I will speak to you later."

"One minute before you go Jack. Aslan says he will pick you up at eight fifteen tomorrow if that is ok with you"

"Would you tell him that the offer of a lift is appreciated?"

Twenty minutes later he headed upstairs to Olga's apartment. Seconds after pressing the intercom entry buzzer the door opened.

"Come in darling I have missed you."

Olga looked stunning in her long black low cut dress. She wore no shoes and her toe nails were painted red to match her finger nails. Coming up to him, she stood on her tiptoes and pressed her body against him as she put her warm slender arms around his neck, and kissed him passionately.

She then stood back with her arms in the air. "What do you think darling?"

"You are stunning as usual."

"Not me." She then moved to the left.

The black granite kitchen table was laid out for two, appropriately with two red burning candles and a bottle of Spanish champagne in an ice decanter in the middle.

"What is the celebration?"

"It is your birthday?"

"No, not until next month,"

"I have always wanted to cook you a meal. This may be my last opportunity as I move out of my apartment this Wednesday, and tomorrow night you will be gigging at the Med Club."

Jack looked slightly taken aback. "I am sorry I completely forgot about you moving. You look as though you have gone to a great deal of trouble."

"No problem darling, it has been a pleasure preparing the food for you."

Jack then went over to her, slipped his arm around her waist and pulled her close to her. "Thank you," he whispered in her ear before kissing her soft lips. "Can I help you?"

"No thank you, you can open your bottle of red wine, I could do with a glass, our meal will be ready in about fifteen minutes."

"What have you made?"

"My secret, just wait and see."

Fifteen minutes later Olga served the meal, she was already on her second glass of red wine.

"How do you like the Paella darling?"

"Perfect."

"At least I know what your favourite dish is."

"I shall miss you when you leave your apartment."

"We shall carry on as normal. When I am not working at Pinks, I will get a taxi from Puerto Banus and visit you, I could stay overnight if you like."

"I would love that."

Olga then leaned over the table and placed her hands under her breasts. "Do you think my boobs are getting bigger?"

"They look magnificent to me but then again I like large breasts, it is probably due to all the red wine you are consuming." Olga started to laugh.

"Darling, will you open the Champagne whilst I get a couple of glasses from the cupboard?"A minute later she returned with two long crystal glasses.

An hour later the Champagne bottle was empty and Olga was opening a second bottle of red wine. Jack shook his head when she offered him another glass.

"You don't mind if I have another glass?"

"No not at all." Jack knew from experience what was coming next.

"You are going to stop the night darling?"

"I would love to." Olga amazed him; rather than alcohol dulling her sex drive it actually had the opposite effect. She was without any question the most exciting woman he had ever met.

After an hour of pleasure Olga lay back naked on the bed.

"Darling I am completely exhausted."

"I am not surprised with all the alcohol inside your body. I need to set my mobile alarm for seven as Aslan will be picking me up at eight fifteen. Will you be coming to my gig at the Med Club tomorrow evening?"

"I will definitely be there though I can't speak for my friend Emma, as I have not spoken to her yet. I will call you tomorrow on your mobile and let you know."

"Have you any fresh orange juice in the fridge?"

"Yes, there are two containers. Why, do you want a drink now?" Jack laughed.

"No, I always have a glass of orange first thing in the morning."

"Switch the light out darling."

In the darkness he turned over to Olga and slipped his hand around her waist before massaging her soft breasts, within minutes they both drifted off.

When Jack's mobile alarm rang at seven the following morning, it was as though he had only been asleep an hour, he felt tired and weary. Olga was a restless sleeper; her body was partly uncovered so he covered her with the gold coloured bed quilt. Quickly dressing he went into the kitchen, opened the fridge door and poured himself a full glass of orange. After checking that Olga was still asleep, he went over to the sink and opened the cupboard door below. Placing his right hand between the sink and the top of the door frame, he felt for the security bug he had placed in position several weeks before. It was still in place. Quickly removing the bug, Jack checked that Olga was still asleep, before silently returning to his own apartment.

After a shower and shave and a change of clothes which was followed by a light breakfast, Jack left the Marbella Beach Apartments and walked down the short driveway to the main entrance. Aslan was just arriving in his Mini Cooper as he left the complex. When Jack got into the car, Aslan appeared far happier than on Monday.

"Good morning, my friend."

"Good morning to you. How are you today?"

"Slowly coming to terms with Freddie's death."

"Did you contact the police about tracing Freddie's family in Chechnya?"

"Yes, they were extremely helpful and said they would sort it out. I must say that I am very relieved at the outcome. Before I forget, Sergei asked me to tell you that he has spoken briefly to his father. His father said he will call him in the next forty eight hours from a safe landline."
"Good." Jack smiled.

"Have you heard from Natalie?"

"As a matter of fact I have. She wants to return to work on Wednesday; she said being occupied will help keep her mind off what went on at the Fuengirola street market."

"She must be a very strong young woman."

"Natalie is certainly an extremely brave young woman, she has my admiration."

"Would you like me to cover the reception again?"

"Yes, if you don't mind."

"Don't forget I finish at four today due to my gig at the Med Club this evening."

"No problem, just call me when you are leaving and I will take over on reception."

Tuesday proved to be another busy day, in fact every day was busy, but for some reason today time seemed to drag by. When Jack left the Cobra Jewellery Head Quarters at four he was relieved to leave work behind. Rather than call Benny for a taxi, he decided to walk back to the Marbella Beach Apartments, the exercise would do him the world of good and clear his head.

Antonio was on reception duty, as the foyer was empty he stopped and spoke to the security officer for a good fifteen minutes. He was about to ask him if there was any news on the whereabouts of Youssef, when he brought up his name in conversation.

"My boss Roberto Sanchez tells me that Youssef's parents have been in touch with him. It appears that Youssef has not spoken to them for over a month; normally he calls them every week."

"I gather from what you are saying, no one including Boris the Russian has heard anything from him. What does Roberto think?"

"Like Youssef's parents he is convinced something terrible has happened to him. He has now reported Youssef missing to the police, so there is now bound to be a full investigation into his disappearance."

"It does not look good, he was a lovely guy."

"Are you out tonight Mr Sinclair?"

"Yes, I am DJ Ramos at the Med Club this evening." Antonio looked flabbergasted. "I never realized that you were DJ Ramos. You are famous throughout the Costa del Sòl."

"If you ever get a night off on a Tuesday and you would like to come along to the Med Club, give me a call and you can come along as my guest."

"Is my wife included in the invitation?"

"Of course she is"

"Next Tuesday I am not working, so we will come to the Med Club."

Jack then reached into the inside pocket of his grey jacket and took out two complementary tickets. "The night starts at nine with DJ's Jose and Selena, I take over at eleven for two hours. Antonio, make certain you make yourself known to me on the night, you and your good lady are my guests."

"I will, thank you Jack."

As soon as Jack entered his apartment he called Olga on the house line. There was no reply from her apartment, just as he was about to replace the phone his mobile rang, Olga's name came up.

"Hi darling it is me. I am at my friend Emma's apartment in Puerto Banus. She is not well again so she won't be coming to your gig tonight."

"I am disappointed. I was hoping to see you both tonight." "I shall be there darling, I have never missed one of your shows and I certainly will not be missing your gig tonight. I will get a taxi and arrive about ten thirty."

"Give me a call when you arrive outside and I will meet you at the staff entrance."

"Would you mind if I park myself by the DJ stand, I feel uncomfortable being alone?"

"Don't worry I will look after you. Will you be going back to your friend's apartment after my gig?"

"No, I was hoping you would invite me to stay the night with you in your apartment."

"Of course you can, I am not due into Cobra Jewellery until one. By the way, if you need any help moving please let me know." Olga never answered. "Would you like me to ask Benny's taxi to drive you to Puerto Banus?"

"Too late darling, Emma has already made arrangements to have me picked up at three but thank you for offering. I had better go now. It looks as though Emma is going to throw up again."

"You should call a doctor."

"It is entirely her own fault; she has a sensitive stomach, too much rich food and far too much alcohol. I will see you later darling, bye."

Either Emma was generally ill or the two sisters were up to something, if he had to make a guess it was probably the latter.

Rather than dine out, Jack popped a frozen vegetable and chicken curry into the microwave, which he had recently bought at a nearby super market. It was quite tasty but on reflection he wished he had dined out at the Picasso Café Bar. After a shower and a change of clothes he switched on the television and watched the Spanish news for the next half hour. At eight thirty he left his apartment and headed outside into the garden. Apart from the security lights the complex was in darkness. The showers of light rain had drifted away, and it was now considerably milder than it had been for the last few days. Rather than call a taxi he decided to walk down the Esplanade Paseo to the Med Club.

Jose and Selena were already on the DJ stand when Jack walked into the night club at the Med Club. The three of them greeted each other warmly. Once he had linked up his laptop to the house DJ deck and PA system, and ran through a quick sound check, he went over to the bar and ordered a Budweiser. The room was slowly starting to fill up, looking around he could see no sign of his boss Pedro Gonzales, so he took out his mobile phone from his jacket pocket and called him.

"Jack, good to hear from you, where are you?"

"By the bar in the night club, I have just finished setting up."

"I am in my office. Nada is at home tonight, one of the children is poorly."

"Nothing serious I hope."

"No just a minor aliment. This is what you get with young children. What can I do for you?"

"I have a present for you."

"I am intrigued. Why don't you pop into my office now, you can have a coffee with me?"

"I am on my way. I will be with you in five minutes." Downing his half empty glass of Budweiser, Jack made his way to Pedro's office. A few minutes later he was knocking on the light oak office door, which immediately opened.

"Come in my friend," he then embraced Jack and closed the door behind him. "Take a seat," Pedro then walked over to the large picture window and looked out into the darkness, which was illuminated by the security lights. "I always love gazing out over the pool at night, it looks so beautiful. What can I do for you?"

Just as Jack was about to speak, there was a knock on the door and one of the male table waiters from the restaurant walked in with two white mugs of coffee.

"Thank you David, would you please put them on the table."

As soon as David had left the office Pedro turned to Jack. "Now what was it you wanted to see me about?"

Reaching into his jacket pocket, Jack passed to Pedro the security bug from Olga's apartment. Pedro immediately went over to the wall opposite the window and removed a large family photograph from the wall exposing a small safe. Pressing in a security number the safe door opened, allowing him to place the security bug inside. "Better to be safe than sorry, we can't afford anybody getting hold of it, though I have to admit it is nowhere near as effective as the new Israel device the Russians have got their hands on."

After closing the safe door and replacing the photograph back on the wall, he turned towards Jack.

"Did Coburn tell you to remove the bug?"

"No, I have not spoken to him for a few days."

"He will not be happy you have removed it without his authorisation."

"I was given no option. Olga is moving out tomorrow to stay with her friend Emma, who as you know is her sister Tanya. According to Olga, her Aunty and Uncle, who own the property, are flying in from Moscow at the weekend for a holiday. This may be a load of bullshit. It is more than likely that the people who are arriving are FSB agents based at the Russian Embassy in Madrid. If they are, they are bound to do a thorough sweep of the apartment for bugs."

"Good thinking Jack. Would you like me to inform Coburn?"

"Yes, if you don't mind." He then told him about his conversation with Sergei.

Pedro then took a drink of his coffee, Jack did likewise.

"As soon as you have any news about Sergei's father arriving in

Georgia let me know immediately. We don't want the Russians jumping the gun and taking out Sergei because information has not filtered through to them."

Pedro then changed the conversation. "From the second week in December, we only open the Med Club from Thursday to Sunday throughout the winter months. The night club is still busy but the rest of the complex is very quiet apart from the week leading up to Christmas. Would you fancy switching to Thursday if you are still around in Marbella?"

"That would be no problem you are the boss." Pedro smiled.

Jack then got up from his chair. "If you will excuse me," he said glancing at his watch. "I need to get back to the night club as I always like to relax alone for a while in the dressing room, before I go on stage."

"Have a great night; I will speak to you later."

It was just leaving ten fifteen when Jack arrived back in the night club. It was a good house almost full, several of his female fans waved to him as he went into the dressing room. Once he had changed into his flamboyant stage gear, he went into the small fridge and took out bottle of cold Andalusian Spring Water and drank half the contents. He then sat down on one of the soft red leather chairs, and relaxed for a few moments with his eyes closed thinking about tonight's gig. Jack was not a DJ who switched and changed the show round continually. He believed if you had an explosive opening and a great finale to the show, which he certainly had, whatever he played in between would be accepted. What made DJ Ramos unique was his exuberant personality on stage, and the fact that he played House Music from artistes worldwide, some famous, but generally most were unheard of struggling talented musicians.

There was a gentle knock on the dressing room door which suddenly brought him back to reality.

"Please come in."

"Hi darling, "the door opened and Olga walked in. She looked stunning in her short off the shoulder white figure hugging dress. Coming over to Jack she sat on his knee, placed her arms around his neck and kissed him passionately.

"How is your friend Emma?"

"Better than she was but it will happen again, alcohol is her main problem."

"Poor girl, you are very lucky because alcohol improves your sex drive." Olga gave him a sexy smile. "Would you care for a glass of red wine?"

"I would love one."

"I am on stage in ten minutes. If you go and speak to George, he is the guy with the beard and pony tail behind the bar, get whatever you want and put it on my tab."

"Thank you darling I will."

As Jack followed Olga out of the dressing room, he ran his hand over her bottom. She turned round and gave him a very suggestive look before running her tongue along her top lip, and then blowing him a kiss as she walked towards the bar. Five minutes later DJ Ramos hit the decks. For the next two hours, Jack held the punters in the packed night club in the palm of his hands.

Once the gig was over, he mingled with friends and fans for a good hour before calling Benny to pick them up in his taxi at two thirty and run them back to the Marbella Beach Apartments. Though Olga had consumed far too much wine, her powers of recovery were quite remarkable when she slipped onto the king size bed with him.

33

Olga left Jack's apartment shortly before eleven on Wednesday morning. She even refused his offer of breakfast, as she had no idea they had slept in so late.

"I need to return to my apartment, Emma has arranged for a taxi to pick me up at three. I have a great deal to sort out before I leave; I even have to clean the apartment. Darling we should have set your mobile alarm for nine at the latest."

Olga then quickly kissed Jack and headed for the door.

"I will call and see you before I leave for work."

"Ok darling." She then disappeared upstairs to her own apartment.

He still found it hard to believe that Olga was an assassin. To him she was just like any other girl. His assessment of her was completely wrong as Olga was not like any other girl he had met. She was a one off, stunningly beautiful, highly intelligent and always in complete control of her actions, apart from when she had sex.

At twelve fifteen, Jack went up the white marble stairs to the third floor to visit Olga before he set off to work. Pressing the intercom buzzer on her apartment door he stood back.

"Come in darling and close the door. I am in the main bedroom."

Walking through the lounge he entered the bedroom. Olga, who was now dressed in a long pink flowing dressing gown, had her back to him. She turned and smiled when she heard him. "When I first arrived from Moscow I had one large suitcase, now I have had to buy a second due to all the clothes I have bought."

Placing her arms around Jack's neck she kissed him passionately. "I will give you a call on Thursday once I have settled in at Emma's and then we can get together, I am only working at Pink's on Saturday and Sunday this week."

"That is fine. I am going to watch Malaga play Villarreal on Sunday."

Jack then glanced at his watch. "I must fly otherwise I will be late for work. I have decided to walk as the weather has improved. We will speak on Thursday."

"Darling, I will call you on your mobile at mid-day."

Jack raised his right arm in acknowledgement as he left the apartment.

When Jack arrived at the Cobra Jewellery Head Quarters, Natalie was on reception duty. She did not look her normal self, gone was the infectious smile, she looked drawn and sad. When she saw Jack enter the building, she tried her best to smile, but he could see it was an effort. Jack immediately went over to her and gave her a hug. "You are very brave to come to work you should have stayed off all week."

"My parents said the same but I had to do something, I just could not sit around thinking of Freddie all day." Jack smiled. "Would you like me to bring you a coffee through to your office?"

"If you would, say in about half an hour. Have you had your lunch?"

"No, I am not very hungry."

"I bought a couple of pre-packed sandwiches on my way in this morning so, we can share them when you bring me a coffee. Is Mr Maskhadov in his office?"

"No, he has gone into Marbella to visit our two branches." Natalie then passed Jack a sheet of paper. "A couple of customers called earlier wanting to speak to you or Mr Maskhadov, perhaps you would contact them."

"Of course I will."

When Jack went into his office, there was a great deal to do and time flew by quickly. He had completely forgotten about his coffee until Natalie knocked on his office door. "Sorry I am late with your coffee, the phone has never stopped ringing."

"Put the reception answer phone on for twenty minutes, get yourself a coffee and share these chicken sandwiches with me."

"Thank you, I will go and get myself a coffee, I will be back in a few minutes."

Natalie soon returned.

"Did Mr Maskhadov say when he would be back?"

"Yes around four."

"Jack, do you think they will find out why Freddie died of a heart attack?"

"I am certain they will. Once the pathologists report comes through we should have some answers." Jack then took a drink of his coffee, Natalie did the same. "May I ask you a question?"

"Yes go ahead."

"I believe at the Fuengirola street market on Sunday Pepe's Circus had several of their entertainers parading through the streets."

"That is quite right they did. They were all fantastic especially the Rollo skaters who followed the parade later."

"Were they not actually with the circus?"

"I don't think so, they were about ten minutes behind the other entertainers. They performed an incredible display. It was so spectacular that we followed them along the street to watch their performance again. There were so many people watching, that we had to stand right at the front only a few metres from where they performed. The grand finale of their performance was when one of the girls was spun round at great speed only inches from the floor. When they finally stopped, the girl who was being spun round appeared to be quite dizzy and bumped into Freddie. She was very apologetic and kissed him on the cheek."

"Were they both girls?"

"Yes, most certainly, though they were both identically dressed from head to foot in red all in one outfits with dark shades and baseball hats, you could tell from the shape of their bodies that they were both definitely females. And of course one of them kissed Freddie on the cheek."

"When did Freddie start to feel ill?"

"About an hour later, he started to feel very tired. It was strange, because he was absolutely fine when we first arrived at the street market."

Jack then took hold of Natalie's right hand. "I really am very sorry for your loss if there is anything Aslan or I can do please tell us."

"When will the pathologist's report come through?" Probably, in the next couple of days."

Natalie then glanced at her watch. "I had better get back to the reception desk. When Mr Maskhadov returns, he said I could go home. Thank you for the sandwich Jack."

As usual Jack was kept very busy between answering phone calls, paper work, and assessing the valuation of recent deliveries of precious gems, and keeping an eye on the staff in the workshop. When Aslan returned it took a great deal of pressure off him. As soon as Natalie left he took over on reception, then shortly after Aslan appeared from his office.

"How are you my friend?"

"I have had a very busy afternoon since I came in."

"I believe so. Natalie said the phone never stopped ringing."

"I don't know how you managed before I came to work for you?"

"I did but with a great deal of difficulty."

"Has Sergei any more news from his father?"

"He has received a second text, saying he will contact him as soon as possible."

"He is probably having difficulty finding a safe phone." "Sergei said the same."

"How did you enjoy your visit to the Cobra Jewellery stores in Marbella?"

"Very therapeutic, I needed a change of scenery. It gets quite claustrophobic at times working in an office all day." "I agree with you there."

"Perhaps next week you could visit our branches in Malaga and Nerja."

"Would Monday be ok?"

"That would be fine."

"How do you fancy coming with me to watch the Malaga – Villarreal match on Sunday?"

"I would love to. What time is the kick off?"

"At three,"

"Why don't we make a day of it? As you know I have a box there, so we could have lunch and then watch the match. I will pick you up in the Bentley at ten thirty." Aslan then thought for a moment. "Why don't we take Sergei with us, it will probably be our last chance to socialize with him before he returns to Georgia." Jack did not answer at first. "Well, what do you think?"

"You have tinted rear windows in the Bentley?" Aslan nodded his head. "Providing Sergei sits in the rear passenger seat for security I have no objection. If he is in the rear of the car, no one will see him leave your villa. The only person who will be aware that you are carrying a passenger will be your security guard."

The internal telephone then rang in Aslan's office. "Jack will you excuse me?"

The next hour and a half passed by slowly, he was relieved to switch on the reception answer phone as the final member of staff left the building. Aslan offered to drop him off at his apartment on his way home. Jack was grateful for the lift he felt weary, the weather was changing again and there was a cold chill in the air, with light rain starting to fall. Rather than dine out alone, he popped another pre-packed frozen meal into the microwave, this time Chinese. For the next three hours, he relaxed on the sofa in front of the television enjoying his meal and consuming several bottles of Budweiser, whilst he watched Sky News and a feature film, before hitting the sack for an early night.

Thursday proved to be no different, work, work, work. Olga called him at mid-day as promised.

"Have you settled in?"

"I have but there is nothing like having your own space." "How is your friend Emma?"

"She is fine now but it will happen again. What time should I arrive at your apartment tomorrow?"

"By seven, it will give me time to arrive home from Cobra Jewellery, have a shower and change of clothes. I thought I might take you out to the Olivia Valere, they have an excellent restaurant. Put on your glamorous party dress and we will have a great night out."

"Fantastic darling, I shall look forward to our evening out together."

Ten minutes later their conversation ended.

Flicking through the phone numbers in his mobile, he brought up Pedro's and called him.

"Pedro it is Jack."

"I recognised your voice my friend."

"Can you speak?"

"Give me one moment. Right what can I do for you?"

Jack then told him what Natalie had said about the two female Rollo skaters at the Fuengirola Street Market.

"This is too much of a coincidence; it has to be Olga and Tanya. The sister, who stumbled into Freddie, must have injected him with the nerve agent. Leave it to me Jack and I will inform Coburn when I call him later." Pedro paused for a moment. "Has Olga moved out of her apartment?" "Yes, on Wednesday afternoon."

"Keep your eyes open, it is possible our friend Kazimir Baizhanov may move in to give the girls some support." Shortly after six, Aslan dropped Jack off at the Marbella Beach Apartments. It had been a busy day. As soon as he arrived in his apartment, he called his brother Lex in Malaga.

"Once you arrive at your box in the Rosaleda Stadium, give me a call on my mobile and I will come and see you. Once the match is over, I will ask one of the stewards to escort you down to the players' lounge as my guests."

"Are Maria and baby David ok?"

"Yes, they are fine. Jack, you must come and stay with us again."

"I would love to."

"How is your investigation going on?"

"Good, in the next few weeks I have the feeling that everything will come to a head one way or another."

Jack missed seeing his brother Lex more frequently, but they both had extremely busy lives. Once his life had returned to normal, he would make the effort to see him and his family more often.

For the second night running he decided to eat at home. It was a miserable night outside. Heavy rain was falling with a strong wind blowing in from the Mediterranean. Opening the balcony doors he stood outside, it looked quite eerie with the trees swaying in the semi-darkness casting shadows and the rain crashing down. After a couple of minutes he returned inside, closed the balcony doors and pulled down the blinds before switching on the television. He intended to have another early night; tomorrow would be out of question with Olga staying over.

On Friday whilst in Aslan's office at Cobra Jewellery, he asked him again if Sergei had heard anything from his father.

"As far as I know nothing, apart from the two text messages earlier but when I arrive home I will ask him again, if he has I will tell him to call you."

Just as Jack was about to say something Aslan's mobile rang. Picking up his mobile from the office desk, he walked over to the window turning his back on Jack. The conversation did not last long.

"Thank you, I appreciate all your help and I completely understand the situation." He then switched off his phone and turned round; there were tears in his eyes. "The nightmare has returned again, that was my friend the Marbella Chief of Police. He has just heard from Dr Mohammed Abadi who is in charge of the Malaga Pathology Laboratory. Freddie died as we thought from a heart attack, by natural causes just like George. My friend also informed me, that they intend to carry out an investigation into why so many young Chechens have recently died on the Costa del Sol. So Jack if you will excuse me, I need to contact Dr Abadi and see if he has the results of the blood sample from Freddie. As soon as I hear anything I will let you know. Before I forget, can I offer you a lift to your apartment?"

"Thank you I would appreciate that."

Shortly after five thirty Jack left his office and went through to the reception area. Natalie was just leaving. It had been a trying week for her. Minutes later Aslan appeared, he looked quite sombre. As soon as all the staff had left the building, Aslan keyed in the security alarm system code and made the building secure. Once in the car park Aslan turned to Jack as they were about to get into his Mini Cooper.

"My friend Dr Abadi called me shortly before we closed. He confirmed our suspicions about Freddie's blood sample. It was identical to George's blood sample and said there was no question in his mind, that

Freddie was killed with the same nerve agent."

"What has he done with George and Freddie's blood samples."

"He has destroyed them, no way did he want them falling into anyone else's hands."

Jack then placed his arm on Aslan's shoulder. "You have had a hard time recently; let us hope life improves for you." Aslan smiled.

"I truly hope nothing happens to Sergei."

"At the moment, I doubt he is on their hit list because of who his father is."

"Let us hope you are right."

Olga arrived at Jack's apartment shortly before seven. He could not help wondering how she still managed to gain entrance to the complex, if she was no longer a resident. There could only be one explanation, she still had her security key card.

"Hi darling, it is good to see you again. They greeted each other with a passionate embrace. "Are we going to make love before we go to the Olivia Valere?"

"Of course whatever you want. Let me take your dress cover bag into the bedroom. Would you care for a coffee?"

"If you insist but I would rather have a glass of red wine."

"Red wine it is but only one glass before we go out."

Olga laughed. "I will just pop into the bathroom whilst you get our drinks."

A few minutes later Jack returned to the bedroom with a glass of red wine and a coffee, as Olga came out of the bathroom in Jack's white bathrobe. She looked incredibly sexy with her dark hair flowing over her shoulders. Pulling her close to him, he ran his fingers through her soft hair, kissed her neck and soft lips, before gently lifting her up in his arms as he laid her on the king size bed.

An hour later he whispered in Olga's ear. "We should get ourselves ready now, we are dining at nine thirty and Benny will be picking us up at nine."

Half an hour later, Olga had slipped on her new all in one black figure hugging catsuit. She looked simply stunning and she certainly had the figure and looks to carry it off. The high heel cream Jimmy Choo shoes added a touch of elegance to her outfit. Apart from her usual designer watch she wore no jewellery. Jack was dressed casual with dark trousers, a black shirt and cream jacket with dark brown shoes. They were a handsome couple. After slipping his mobile into his pocket, they headed down to the foyer by the elevator. Security guard Antonio was on reception. He raised his hand and wished them a good night out. Jack's mobile suddenly rang, it was Benny waiting outside in his taxi.

"We will be with you in five minutes."

As they walked to the main entrance Olga turned to Jack. "I am glad the rain has stopped because I forgot to bring a jacket with me. At least it is a little warmer."

"Good evening Mr Ramos." Olga could not help but laugh. "Where can I take you to tonight Mr Ramos?"

"To the Olivia Valere club,"

"I will have you there in fifteen minutes."

True to his word Benny pulled up outside the main entrance to the club in fifteen minutes.

"Benny, I will call you later, perhaps you could pick us up." "No problem boss."

As they got out of the taxi many of the punters queuing to get in turned and recognised Jack as D J Ramos and called out his name and waved.

"Darling, do you like being famous?"

Jack laughed. "I really don't mind, it no different than you being admired by the opposite sex because you look beautiful."

A smile crossed Olga's face but she never spoke.

"We need to take the restaurant sign to the right."

Once inside the restaurant, the floor manager took them to their reserved table on the balcony. Minutes later an immaculately dressed table waiter brought them a menu. "If it's alright with you Sir I will return in ten minutes? May I get you and the lady drinks?"

"Yes please. A bottle of Spanish red wine and a Budweiser."

"Thank you Sir."

A few minutes later he returned with their drinks. "I will return shortly Sir for your order."

Just as Jack had poured Olga a glass of red wine the owner of the club Leroy Cardoso came over to their table.

"Jack, it is a pleasure to see you and Olga again." He then embraced both of them. "You are both always welcome here. I saw your names on the restaurant guest list." He then acknowledged several guests at a nearby table. "I was very sad to hear about Freddie's death, a lovely young man. My friend Aslan is mortified, I spoke to him a couple of days ago. First it was his nephew George and now Freddie."

"It is terrible for the poor man," remarked Olga.

"You look lovely tonight Olga."

Thank you she replied with a smile that showed her perfect white teeth.

"Have you any live entertainment on tonight?"

Leroy turned to Jack. "Yes, our resident DJ Mateo and the dancers."

"Leroy then touched Jack's left shoulder. "If you will both excuse me I must circulate, we will speak later."

As Leroy walked away, the table waiter returned and took their order of melon, followed by sea base with mixed vegetables. Both Jack and Olga were surprised how busy the restaurant was. Then again this was the Olivia Valere, who catered for the rich and famous, who had money to burn. The food was excellent but no better than any of the other restaurants they frequented in Marbella. What made it different was the way the meal was presented, and the impeccable attention they received, no wonder the Olivia Valere attracted such an affluent clientele.

At ten DJ Mateo hit the stage. Jack was ardent admirer of the middle aged DJ. He was a good looking guy who always smiled, immaculately dressed and above all played the right music for the venue. The dancers were the same, well rehearsed, glamorous and sexy. Olga was certainly enjoying her night out, she had almost consumed one bottle of red wine, but you would never have known. There were many beautiful looking women in the club but Olga stood out, there was something about her which continually drew admiring glances. Looking at her, he still found it hard to believe that she was an assassin, who killed for pleasure. From where they sat on the restaurant balcony, they had a panoramic view of the club. It had always amazed Jack how many handsome single guys frequented The Olivia Valere until Pedro Gonzales explained why.

"There are many single or divorced women both young and old who live in Marbella; many even come here on holiday. All have one thing in common, they all looking for sexual excitement with a handsome young guy with no strings attached. Every year, dozens of studs arrive in Marbella from all over Europe including the UK for the summer season, many even stay all year. They can make thousands of Euros a week satisfying sex starved wealthy women."

One guy in particular grabbed his attention. He was stood at the far end of the bar. He was a tall guy about six two, athletic build with short blond hair. Every so often, he picked up a small glass off the bar top and took a drink. He reminded him so much of The Russian trouble shooter Kazimir Baizhanov from their embassy in Madrid, who he saw in Puerto Banus with Olga and Tanya. But then again he could not be certain it was him, without checking the mobile photo he took of him on his way to the Harbour Restaurant with the girls.

"You are very quiet tonight Jack."

"Sorry, I was just thinking how much I will miss you when you return home to Moscow. I enjoy our nights out together like tonight."

"Darling how sweet of you to say that then leaned over and kissed him. "Should we join the dancers on the floor?"

"Sure why not."

They then stood up and made their way to the dance floor. Jack slid his left arm around her waist and pulled her closer to him. Olga glanced up and smiled at him. After an energy sapping half hour of dancing to the latest disco sounds, they returned to their table. The mystery guy who was stood at the bar was no longer there. Making an excuse to visit the men's room Jack checked the recent photos in his mobile. He instantly recognised the Russian, there was no mistaking him. What was he doing back in Marbella; he certainly would not be on holiday? Something big must be on the horizon where the twins needed some assistance. He needed to speak to Pedro and Coburn as soon as possible. Bringing up Pedro's name he sent him a text, explaining that he was at the Olivia Valere and had just seen Kazimir Baizhanov.

Almost immediately a reply came back. "Something is in the pipe line, we need to meet tomorrow. Would you call me at mid-day tomorrow and we can arrange a meeting." He replied. "Message received."

As Jack left the men's room and walked back to his table on the balcony, he noticed a guy in his late thirties talking to Olga. As he got closer the guy looked up touching Olga on her right shoulder, they both half glanced towards him, he then said something to her before walking away to mingle in the crowd.

"Hi darling I thought you had got lost."

Jack smiled. "My boss at the Med Club has just called me, he wants to meet me tomorrow afternoon and discuss moving my show to Thursday during the winter nights."

He then took a long drink from the half empty glass of Budweiser.

"Who was the admirer you were talking to?"

"He is a regular every Saturday night at Pinks; he says he only visits the club to watch me. You are not jealous are you darling?" She then leaned over and kissed his lips. "I was only joking. Did you not recognise him?"

"No, but I felt that I had seen him somewhere before."

"It was Boris my boss from Pinks."

"I would have assumed that he would have been working at Pinks on a Friday night."

"He should be but he often goes out leaving his friend the head barman in charge for a few hours."

"Where does he go to?"

"Other clubs and bars where good looking girls hang out, he is a sex mad pervert, so when he gets fed up with the girls at Pinks, he goes out on the prowl and pays girls to come back to Pinks for a session in his office. Emma and I are the only girls he has not shagged at Pinks. That is why at times he treats us both like shit, especially Emma. One day soon his day of reckoning will come." She then changed the conversation. "Darling, are going to make love to me again when we get back to your apartment?" Jack grinned at her but did not answer.

Two hours later after a call from Jack, taxi driver Benny met them outside the main entrance and drove them back to the Marbella Beach Apartments. After his initial glimpse of Kazimir Baizhanov at the bar, Jack never saw head or tail of him again during the evening. As they sat in the back of Benny's taxi a thought crossed his mind. Perhaps Kaz as everyone called him was in the Olivia Valere on a spying mission. Who could he have been sizing up, there could be only one answer to that.

"Have you had a good night Mr Ramos?"

"Fantastic, the Olivia Valere is a fabulous club."

After Benny dropped them off, they walked up the driveway to the foyer entrance before gaining entrance, it felt quite cold though looking at Olga you would never have thought so. Mind you she had drunk almost two bottles of red wine; even so she was still wide awake. Boy this girl could certainly take her booze.

34

When Jack awoke around ten thirty, he went into the kitchen leaving Olga asleep in bed. After a glass of fresh orange juice from the fridge he sent a text to Pedro. "I am unable to call you at the moment in case I am overheard, but could we meet at the Med Club at about four."

Moments later a text came back. "See you at four in my office, take care."

Within the hour Olga was up, showered and dressed and had joined Jack on the balcony for a coffee. Out of the breeze it felt quite warm.

"Have you had any breakfast?"

"No, just a glass of fresh orange, I drank too much red wine last night."

Jack half smiled. "You are just as bad as your friend Emma." He almost said Tanya but corrected himself at the last moment.

"Not quite as bad," she said with a smile. Why don't we go to the Picasso Café Bar for lunch?"

"Good idea, the walk will do us the world of good."

Forty minutes later they left the apartment and made their way down the Esplanade Paseo to the Picasso Café Bar. The bar was not particularly busy but as usual the food was excellent and the elderly owners Alberto and Gabriela were great conversationalists. On their way back, Olga took her mobile out of her white Gucci handbag and called her usual taxi service.

"Would you meet me at three fifteen at the main entrance to the Marbella Beach Apartments?"

"I will give you a break on Monday, perhaps we could meet again on Tuesday and then I could accompany you to the Med Club and then stay the night."

"What about your friend Emma, will she not be coming to the gig?"

"I shall just tell her that I am staying the night with you, she won't bother coming then."

To say that Jack was not concerned about Olga was an understatement. He enjoyed her company immensely but she was a distraction, he was in Marbella on a mission for MI6, which he kept telling himself he must never forget. What was her twin sister Tanya (Emma) up to when Olga was with him?" Was she just as dangerous as Olga? When Olga got into her taxi he immediately felt a sense of relief, he was now once again completely in charge of his own destiny.

Jack decided to walk to the Med Club rather than take a taxi. He felt he needed the exercise now he had stopped using the apartment swimming pool, he was not a wimp but the water was just too bloody cold, in any case it was now closed for maintenance.

After entering the club via the staff and VIP entrance, he made his way towards Pedro's office. The club would not officially be open until six; consequently there were very few people about.

"Hi Jack." He knew the female voice instantly, it was Kelly the assistant manager. She was a lovely girl, slim, and attractive with a warm infectious personality, he could not help wondering why she did not have a partner. Pedro had made a wise decision making her his assistant; she certainly took a great deal of pressure off him. They both greeted each other warmly.

"The boss is in his office, he is expecting you."

"Thank you." As soon as Olga returned to Moscow, he would take the plunge and ask her out.

"Good to see you Jack, take a seat. Since our text conversation last night, I have given the situation a great deal of thought. I am convinced like you that Sergei Aslanov could be the next target. I have spoken to Miles Coburn and he is of the same opinion. He now informs me, that the Russian trouble shooter Kazimir Baizhanov used to be in the Russian Army, he is highly skilled in the use of fire arms."

Jack then told Pedro about the trip to watch Malaga FC tomorrow.

"You are going to have to be very careful."

"We will be in Aslan's Bentley, the rear windows are blacked out. Sergei will be in the back and apart from Aslan and I, the only person who will know about who is in the rear of the car and where we are going, is the security guard at the villa."

"Can you trust him?"

"I spoke to Costa Security boss Roberto Sanchez, the guy at Aslan's villa is Roberto's cousin, he said he would trust him with his life."

"Just be careful Jack, if you need any help call me immediately."

"Thanks I will."

"Coburn thinks you should be armed as Baizhanov is now in the picture."

"What about the Spanish police, if I am stopped and searched I could be in big trouble?"

"The British Foreign Secretary intends to speak to his opposite number in Spain tomorrow, and put him completely in the picture. The UK Government are not happy with the situation since the Russians started assassinating the Chechens. Coburn tells me you have been trained in the use of fire arms."

"Yes."

"Coburn said he will call back as soon as he gets the all clear from the Foreign Secretary." Pedro then rose from his chair. "Jack, you will have to excuse me, we open the restaurant doors in one hour and I need to give Kelly a hand."

"I will see you on Tuesday unless we speak before."

The weather was certainly changing. The evenings were getting colder and the days shorter. For the second consecutive Saturday Jack decided to stay in and cook his own meal rather than dine out which was Chicken Chow Mein with rice, a couple of cans of Budweiser, and an evening watching Television, followed by another early night. Aslan called Jack shortly before ten thirty on Sunday morning. "I am just about to leave the villa. I will be with you in about fifteen minutes."

"Great, I will see you at the main entrance."

Casually dressed, he then slipped on his black soft leather zip jacket, before picking up his mobile phone and dark shades from the kitchen table, then heading down the white marble stairs to the foyer. As there was no one on reception duty to speak to, he walked towards the electric doors which immediately opened, within minutes he was standing outside the complex by the main entrance. Two or three minutes later Aslan's black and gold Bentley convertible drew up at the kerb side. As Aslan raised his hand in acknowledgement, the rear door of the Bentley opened and Sergei got out.

"Good to see you my friend." There was a broad smile on his handsome face as the two men embraced. Sergei then got back inside the rear of the car whilst Jack sat in the front next to Aslan. Twenty minutes later they were on the coastal motorway heading to Malaga. The weather was sunny and mild, ideal conditions for a Spanish La Liga football match. Slipping on his dark shades, Jack settled down in the soft cream leather car seat for the sixty minute drive to the La Rosaleda Stadium, the home of Malaga Football Club.

They had only been on the motorway for twenty minutes when Aslan turned to Jack.

"Sergei has some news for you."

"I spoke to my father last night. We have only very recently been reunited again but I told him everything. He was very sceptical at first until I told him that the Russian Mafia had threatened to kill him, unless I helped them dispose of the diamonds and other precious gems. He has agreed to fly to Tbilisi, Georgia and stay with my sister Sasha and her husband for as long as it takes. Having recently retired as head of the Aviation and Aircraft Engineering Academy in Moscow, long holidays were now no problem for him. To avoid any unnecessary suspicion, he will inform the authorities where he can be contacted if need be. Today he intends to contact my sister with the news, if they agree which he feels certain they will, he will then book a flight to Georgia in the next few days. My father was over the moon, that after so many years we will once again be reunited as a family."

"Sergei, I am so happy for you, as soon as you have any more information please let me know, and then we can make arrangements for your flight to Georgia."

The day proved to be an incredible success, as soon as they arrived at La Rosaleda Stadium they were escorted to Aslan's private box. Jack then called his brother Lex on his mobile, who found time to call in and greet everyone. The pre-match meal was excellent and the final result a 2-1 victory over Villarreal, kept Malaga's great start to the season flying. Meeting Lex and the team in the player's lounge after the match was a great finale to a fabulous day out.

Darkness had descended by the time they arrived back at the Marbella Beach Apartments.

"Thank you guys for a great day out, I have enjoyed your company immensely, we must go out again before you leave for home Sergei." Jack then turned to Aslan. "If I was you I would call your security guard and tell him you will be at the villa in fifteen minutes."

"You are very security minded Jack."

"I always have been, because of my late father's job with the UK Government. It is better to be safe than sorry."

"You are quite right." Aslan then picked up his mobile and called the security guard."

"I will let you guys get off. Aslan I will see you in the office on Monday."

"Do you want a lift in the morning?"

"No, but thanks for the offer I am trying to keep fit so I will walk." Jack then turned to Sergei as he got out of the Bentley. "Sergei don't forget as soon as you have any more information from your father please call me."

Sergei then got out of the car and embraced Jack. "Thank you for everything you are doing for me, you have always been a very good friend Jack Sinclair."

Jack smiled and then started to walk away as Sergei got back inside the Bentley. They then drove off towards the coastal highway and the short drive to the Aslan's villa.

Jack glanced at his watch as he made his way to his apartment; it was just leaving seven thirty. Once inside he texted his brother Lex and thanked him for inviting them to the player's lounge and the hospitality they were shown. Within a few minutes, Lex sent a next back.

"My pleasure, you are always welcome, next time if you are alone you must stay the night with us. Jack you take care."

As he had already eaten in the player's lounge and could see no point of going out just for the sake of it and consuming far too much alcohol, he decided to have another evening in watching television. He was lucky he was fluent in the Spanish language, as there was a very interesting documentary on about UK criminals hiding away in Spain. Most of them were involved in drug dealing and gun running between North Africa and Spain. Many of them had set up a legitimate business as a cover, especially on the Costa del Sol. It certainly gave him food for thought. By eleven he was feeling tired and decided to turn in.

Whilst at work on Monday, Jack received a late afternoon call from Pedro on his mobile.

"Are you able to speak?"

"Yes, I am alone in my office."

"Miles Coburn called me earlier regarding you carrying a fire arm. The UK Foreign Secretary has been vetoed by the Prime Minister. No way does he want the Spanish Government to know about the Siberian diamond cargo plane hijack. If it got out there would be pandemonium worldwide. In any case, he gave the Russian President his word that the details of the Siberian Cargo plane hijack would go no further. Jack, how do you feel about carrying a fire arm unofficially?"

"I am very concerned about being stopped by the police. However, I am prepared to carry a gun whilst escorting Sergei to Malaga International Airport when I get the go ahead to book his flight to Georgia."

"Jack, I will be accompanying you to the airport."

"I am relieved to hear that, if the Russians are going to take him out, it will be on his way there or at the airport." "Have you ever used a Glock 18 hand gun?"

"Yes, I was trained by a fire arms instructor from the SAS in their use. They are a very effective short range weapon."

"I have two in my possession, we will both be armed for our own protection on the day we drive Sergei to the airport."

Jack then updated Pedro on the latest information about Sergei's father. "With a little luck we should have some movement this week."

There is a well-known saying 'Time waits for no man' it was certainly true in Jack's case, the days were flying by at an ever increasing pace. The end of November was in sight with December on the horizon. If anyone had asked him three months ago would he still be on the Costa del Sol in December, he would have answered no. Olga arrived at his apartment early on Tuesday evening, rather than dine out they ate in. She then accompanied him to his gig at the Med Club and stayed the night at his apartment before leaving late morning for Puerto Banus.

They next saw each other again on Thursday evening. After dining out at the Albatross Bar and Restaurant she again stayed overnight. As she was working at Pinks all weekend, they arranged to meet as usual the following Tuesday.

His workload at Cobra Jewellery was increasing by the week. He was staggered at the amount of business the company turned over. On Monday he visited their stores in Malaga and Nerja, whilst his boss Aslan did likewise in Puerto Banus and Estepona. Natalie on reception at Cobra Jewellery was back working full-time, but it was obvious she was struggling, especially when the results of Freddie's post-mortem were published.

"Jack, I can't believe a heart attack killed him, he was such a fit looking guy. He never ever complained of feeling ill. There is something strange going on, his friend George also died of a heart attack, it can't be coincidence that they both come from Chechnya."

Jack felt so sorry for the poor girl that he felt like telling her the truth.

On Saturday afternoon Sergei phoned, he had just spoken to his father at length. His father Colonel Alexander Stepanov, who had recently retired as head of the Aviation and Aircraft Engineering Academy in Moscow, had informed the Russian authorities that he intended to visit his daughter in Georgia for possibly three months. There was no objection and they had wished him well. He has since booked an open end flight return ticket for the following Thursday. As soon as he arrived safely at his daughter and husband's house in Tbilisi he would inform Sergei by text or email of his arrival. Sergei would then call Jack, who will book a one way flight ticket to Georgia for Sergei. Jack also reminded Sergei, that the Russian Government still required the flight co-ordinates of the abandoned air strip in the Ural Mountains, where the hijacked diamonds and gems were hidden. So far he had not been forthcoming, believing that the Russian Mafia would take out his father if he gave the FSB the information, before his father arrived safely in Georgia. Ml6 Commander Miles Coburn had instructed Jack to inform Sergei, that if he renegades on the agreement to pass on the flight co-ordinates to the FSB and returned to Georgia, hoping at some later date to steal the diamonds, there would be serious consequences. As he was born in Russian and still a citizen of that country, they would ask Georgia for his extradition.

"Jack, I will not let you down. I just want to make certain that my father and I are safely in Georgia before I give them the information they require. You will just have to trust me."

"Sergei, I do trust you but the problem is do the FSB trust you?"

"I will not let you down Jack, trust me." Sergei paused for a moment. "I need a favour Jack?"

"Go ahead, if I can help you I will."

"I have never seen your Tuesday night show at the Med Club. I would like to see you in action before I return home, I have heard so much about you."

"If Aslan brings you I can see no reason why you should not come. I personally would love to see you there. If you like I will speak to Aslan and arrange everything."

"Thank you Jack I would appreciate that."

Early on Monday morning Aslan texted Jack, he had only been out of bed ten minutes. "Can I offer you a lift to Cobra Jewellery?"

The weather conditions were awful outside, heavy rain with a light wind. Autumn had now arrived quickly to the Costa del Sol.

"Your offer is greatly accepted." Five minutes later he would have called Benny for a lift.

"Good, I will meet you at the main entrance to the Marbella Beach Apartments at eight fifteen."

When they met, Aslan appeared much happier than he had for some time. "My sister-in-law Gabrielle called me last night, she intends to arrive in Marbella two days before Christmas Eve and stay here for three or four weeks. She will be staying at my villa." He then went quiet for a few minutes as the traffic started to build up. Eventually they started to move again. "It was good news about Sergei's father. Once he arrives in Georgia, Sergei will soon be on his way home."

"That reminds me, when I spoke to Sergei last night he asked me about coming to the Med Club tomorrow night. He wants to see my show before he returns home."

"What was your reaction?"

"Providing he is with you, I can see no problem."

“I agree. We will arrive around ten.”

“I will arrange for you to gain entrance to the club by the staff and VIP entrance. If you call my mobile as soon you arrive in the club car park, I will then meet you.”

Monday being the start of a new week was busy as usual. There were many telephone enquiries from new and existing clients, one of which was from a leading UK jewellery chain, who were very impressed with Cobra’s new catalogue of costume jewellery. So much that their Sales Director arranged a date in early January, when he would be flying over to visit Cobra Jewellery in Marbella. All these calls took up a great deal of time but eventually after returning from a late lunch, Jack managed to call Pedro Gonzales on his mobile.

“I am not happy with the situation but I can understand Sergei’s frustration, after all he has been a prisoner in Aslan’s villa for several weeks.” He then went quiet for a moment. “If Sergei stays with Aslan and does not drift around the club alone, I will agree.”

“Good, I will let Aslan and Sergei know. By the way Sergei spoke to his father yesterday; he will be booking a flight to Georgia in the next few days. He has also informed the Russian authorities, that he will be going to stay with his daughter Sasha and her family for up to three months.”

“What was their reaction?”

“They wished him well and said to have a good holiday.” “Jack, give Miles Coburn a call when you have a minute and put him in the picture.”

“I will. Pedro, I am going to have to leave you now, I am needed in the workshop. I will call you as soon as I have any more news.”

On Tuesday Olga arrived at his apartment at six forty-five. After calling Benny’s taxi they dined early at the Albatross Bar and Restaurant. At eight forty they continued their walk down the Esplanade Paseo to the Med Beach Club, luckily the rain had stopped, there was no wind and it felt quite mild, but the Mediterranean Sea was still very rough with waves crashing continually against the sea wall.

“I love your dress, you look stunning in it, it suites your dark hair.”

“Thank you darling.” She then slid her right arm round his firm waist and kissed him.” I will let you into a secret, it belongs to my friend

Emma, we happen to be both the same size. She was never happy wearing it, her blonde hair never seemed right with the dress, so she gave it to me."

After gaining access to the Med Club via the staff and VIP entrance, they made their way down the glass connecting corridor to the night club. The room was slowly starting to fill up. DJ's Jose and Selena were already set up, in ten minutes their show would begin. The four of them greeted each other warmly.

"Jack, would you like me set your laptop up for you?"

"I would appreciate that, thank you." he replied with a smile. "We are going to the bar for a drink, can we get you anything?"

"We are both ok thanks, we only drink Spring Water when we are on duty."

"You are very wise; alcohol can certainly cloud your judgement."

Jack was the same, always teetotal on a gig. Tonight he had broken his strict rule and had drank one glass of red wine with his meal, now it would be bottled water until the end of his gig, by ten the room was filling up. When he was due to walk out on stage in one hour, there would be over six hundred adrenalin pumping fans raring to go. At ten twenty-five his mobile rang. Olga looked at him as he took out his mobile but never spoke.

"I will be with you in a few minutes. Olga my boss Aslan is coming to the gig tonight with a friend. Would you excuse me for five minutes? I need to sign them in. If you want another drink just get one and add it onto my tab."

When Jack arrived at the staff entrance, Aslan and Sergei were stood outside by the door. They greeted each other warmly.

"Good to see you guys, one moment whilst I sign you in." When all formalities had been completed, they followed Jack into the night club where Aslan greeted Olga with a smile and a kiss. "Olga, let me introduce you to our friend Sergei Aslanov. Sergei is a gemmologist like Jack with Cobra Jewellery."

Sergei then took hold of Olga's hand, whilst he kissed her on the left side of her face.

"Have you worked for Aslan long?"

"For about fifteen months."

"Jack has never mentioned you before."

"I not surprised, I have spent a great deal of time overseas selling Cobra Jewellery products to clients. Jack and I are old friends, aren't we Jack?"

"We certainly are. I first met Sergei in Johannesburg South Africa. We were both working for the diamond mining conglomerate De Beers learning our trade. We became very good friends in the two years we spent working together. Sergei eventually returned home to Georgia, whist I stayed on for a few more months, before returning to the UK. My friend Sergei is a very talented guy, as well as being an excellent gemmologist he is also a very accomplished airline pilot." Jack then glanced at his watch. "You guys are going to have to excuse me; I am due on stage shortly."

Once he had entered the dressing room by the DJ stand, he sat down in one of the soft black leather chairs and relaxed with his eyes closed for a good ten minutes. It was a ritual he never missed for one good reason. It always gave him time to think about his parents and how much he missed them.

Shortly before eleven there was a gentle knock on the door and DJ Selena entered.

"When you are ready Jack, you will be on stage in two minutes."

As his signature tune hit the air waves, DJ Ramos bounded out of the dressing room to face a capacity audience with all his adrenalin flowing and with the charisma of a star. For the next two hours, Jack held the punters in the palm of his hands.

Aslan, who had previously admitted that he was not a House Music fan, was full of praise. Sergei was even more forthcoming, when Jack finally came off stage and made his way over to the bar, he embraced him.

"You were incredible my friend, your show was electrifying, now I know why everyone on the Costa del Sol talks about you."

Olga for once was speechless, she just stood there looking beautiful with a glass of red wine in her right hand and her eyes glued to Sergei as though she had seen a ghost. The rest of the week was more or less a replica of the previous week, with Olga working all weekend at Pinks.

However the phone call Jack had received on Thursday morning whilst working at the Cobra Jewellery Head Quarters was a game changer.

"Jack, I know you are a busy guy but you told me to call you as soon as I had any more information from my father."

"Sergei no need to apologize, I am always available for you."

"My father has booked a flight for next Tuesday to Tbilisi with Georgian Airlines."

"Excellent, as soon as he arrives safely at your sister's house we will book your flight. Are you excited about returning home?"

"To be honest I am, I have enjoyed my stay in Marbella and I am indebted to Aslan for what he has done for me, but the thought of seeing my sister and aunt again and rekindling my life with my father really excites me." Sergei started to sound emotional but then quickly recovered his composer. "Jack, as soon as I have any further information I will call you."

During his lunch break, Jack called both Pedro and Miles Coburn and put them in the picture. Coburn again reminded him that the Russians were still insisting on the flight co-ordinates of the small landing strip in the Ural Mountains, before Sergei returned home.

"I am fully aware that Sergei does not trust the Russians but it is mutual. He has to understand, that the Russians have the upper hand. Whilst the two twin sisters and Kazimir Baizhanov are still in Marbella, it is impossible to guarantee his safety without asking the Spanish authorities for help. Unfortunately this will not happen.

"Miles, I still can't get my head around the situation, there must be more to this scenario than either the Russians or Sergei are telling us."

"At MI6 we are convinced there is and we also have a couple of interesting theories. If you recall Jack, Sergei told you that only three people know the exact location of the diamonds and that included him. Over the last few months, our man in Moscow informs us, that the Russian Police and Military have carried dozens of raids on Mafia controlled businesses and homes of their leading members. The Russian's policy is very different than what would happen in the UK. They go in with guns blazing and then interview any survivors often using extreme methods. We believe, but we are unable to confirm, that Sergei and only one other person know exactly where the diamonds are hidden."

"Why have the Russians not used satellite technology to find the landing site and track any aircraft in the vicinity of the Ural Mountains?"

"They have but the Mafia have been very clever, they have used a single engine light aircraft flying virtually at ground level to avoid any radar or satellite spy cameras. You must also remember in Sergei Aslanov, they have a highly skilled pilot, who thrives on danger. Once he has picked up whatever quantity of diamonds they require and refuelled, the light aircraft flies to its base which is a small airport several hundred miles south in Northern Turkey, close to the Syrian border. Sergei then switches to a twin engine plane and continues with his flight to the remote Tunisian border destination. We believe that Sergei at some later date, maybe not for a couple of years, will fly back to the Ural Mountains to collect whatever quantity of diamonds he requires, and then sell them on the black market to renegade dealers. As you know Sergei is a qualified gemmologist with many contacts worldwide. Jack, we also have a second theory."

"What is that?"

"Once Sergei arrives back in Georgia, he may ask the Russians for a ransom fee to disclose the whereabouts of the diamonds, but in our opinion that could be a very dangerous game to play."

"On the other hand Miles, Sergei may be genuine when he says he does not trust the Russians, but intends to give them the co-ordinates, when he is safely back in Georgia."

"You could well be right Jack, but you still need to speak to him again and try to get him to change his mind before it is too late."

"Very well, I will speak to him again." In his own mind Jack knew Sergei would never change his mind.

35

Four days earlier, around eleven thirty on Sunday evening at Pinks in Puerto Banus, Olga and Emma had just come off stage for a break. As usual the Russian manager Boris had been watching them perform naked on the poles. He watched every girl in the club closely, slowly running his eyes over every inch of their supple bodies. Olga and Emma pissed him off, they were without doubt the fittest looking birds in the club, and he still had not shagged either of them, and time was running out. It was now or never.

"Girls, when you have changed I need to see you both in my office."

"Ok boss," they called out and then started to giggle.

"Unfortunately girls I have a big problem. From the second week in December, Pinks will be closed Monday, Tuesday and Wednesday for the winter months. That means I will have to let several of our girls go. I would love you two girls to stay but as I said before there is a slight problem." The girls looked at each other and smiled. "All the other girls working here are extremely friendly and enjoy a bit of fun with me, but you two are the opposite. You said you were both lesbians, but that was a load of shit and you know it was. You Olga are screwing that English guy at the Med Club, DJ Ramos and you Emma are shagging Costa Security boss Roberto Sanchez. What is wrong with me I own Pinks?"

"Roberto drives round in a red Ferrari, you use a taxi."

Tanya started to giggle. Boris gave her a filthy look.

He then turned to Olga. What is your excuse?"

"He is famous, everyone knows who he is and he spends money on me, and treats me like a princess."

"You are both my top girls, I even managed to get you cheap accommodation in the town centre. I would like you both to stay, but if you are not prepared to cooperate with me you can both leave at the end of next week."

The girls then looked at each other. "I can speak for Emma. We both love working here and do not want to leave. We will both have sex with you on two conditions. Firstly, you will stop treating us like shit and show us more respect and secondly, we will only have sex with you once a week. Do you agree?"

A smile crossed his sunburned face. "I agree, when can we get together girls?"

Emma replied immediately, "what about this Friday afternoon here in Pinks? Then we could use your office." Boris hesitated. "We are worth waiting for; you will have the time of your life."

"Good idea. Now let me get you both a drink at the bar."

Both the girls cheekily smiled at each other as they followed him into the cabaret room.

The following day both girls slept in until after mid-day. They only had one topic of conversation when they got up. What were they going to do with Boris the Russian? All the girls he is shagging at Pinks say he is built like a donkey, so they certainly intended to have some fun with him. But when they had enjoyed themselves, he had to suffer some form of humiliation and pain.

"We could inject him with PV44 or even blow his brains out."

"How could you Tanya when he is Russian. We don't execute our fellow countrymen unless the FSB instruct us to do so."

"You are quite right; we will have to think of something else." A smile crossed her face. "I know what we will do. Do you recall that Iranian Diplomat, we taught him a lesson for being unfaithful to his wife, she was the daughter of the President?"

"You have a good memory Tanya, I remember him well. What we did to him was perfect; if we do the same to Boris he will never forget us."

Both the girls started to laugh and giggle. Olga then took hold of her sister's hand. "Darling, come on, let's go out for lunch."

The week was flying by. Jack spoke to Sergei again, about giving the Russians the information they required, but to no avail. He was now starting to believe what Miles Coburn had said.

Olga was with her sister Tanya, in her Puerto Banus apartment when she made a mobile phone call to Kazimir Baizhanov.

"Darling, we shall need your help on Thursday. Can you pick us up in the car park by the Harbour Tower at three thirty? After Thursday we will no longer be working at Pinks, so we will have to move out of our apartment. We will have two suitcases each."

"No problem. Where are you moving to?"

"The Seacrest Hotel in Marbella.

"That is where I am staying."

"Darling, we are aware of that, would you make arrangements for us to stay there for a few days? We don't mind sharing a room if they have no single rooms spare."

"Leave everything to me. I will make certain you are both accommodated"

"Good, we will see you on Thursday, don't be late."

As usual Olga was delighted to see Jack when she arrived at his apartment early on Tuesday evening. Rather than dine out before going to his gig at the Med Club, they stayed in and ate a readymade mild chicken curry, followed by a couple of Americano and then had sex. Being quite a mild evening they walked to the Med Club along the Esplanade Paseo rather than call a taxi.

Jack had another incredible night, but he was glad when he finally left the stage and headed back to his apartment. The pressure of having two high profile and very demanding jobs was starting to take its toll. Though in his mind, he was fully aware that the situation could get far worse.

Earlier in the day Colonel Alexander Stepanov flew on a Georgian Airline flight from Moscow's Sheremetyevo International Airport to Tbilisi, Georgia. Three hours fifteen minutes later, after passing through passport control and customs, he was met in the arrival lounge by his daughter Sasha and his two grandsons Luka and Anri. The welcome he received always made the journey well worthwhile.

Once he had arrived at the family home and settled in, he emailed his son Sergei of his safe arrival in Tbilisi, using his daughter's laptop.

"The weather is a good deal warmer than Moscow, which was -6c with snow when I left earlier in the day. Sergei, all the family are looking forward to seeing you, please let us know when you will be arriving."

Sergei immediately texted Jack on his mobile phone with the news, just as he was relaxing in the dressing room prior to going on stage at the Club Med.

"Great news my friend, I will check out flights to Georgia tomorrow. As soon as I have arranged everything I will call you. I am about to go on stage at the Med Club."

Olga was her usual self and Jack felt no vibes that she was up to anything. In fact, he was disappointed to see her leave his apartment just after eleven the following morning and head back to Puerto Banus. He had never met a woman like her, always calm and in control of her actions apart from when she had consumed too much red wine and had sex.

When Jack arrived at Cobra Jewellery shortly before mid-day, he went straight to his office and telephoned a local travel agent about a one way flight ticket to Tbilisi, Georgia.

"There is a flight leaving this Friday at 17-55hrs with Turkish Airlines, with a two hour stop over at Ankara Turkey."

"How long does the flight take?"

"Normally around 10hrs 50min, this includes the stop over."

"Are there no direct flights?"

"I am afraid not Sir, the girl was most apologetic, no airline flies direct to Georgia."

"I understand. Will you book me a one way ticket in the name of Sergei Aslanov for this Friday's flight?"

"Certainly Sir, would you like me to email the flight ticket to you?"

"No, I will call in later today and pay you when I collect the ticket."

"That will be fine, would you mind calling after four."

As soon as Jack came off the phone he called Sergei and gave him the news.

"You can start packing; I have just booked your flight home to Georgia."

"Thank you Jack, I appreciate what you have done for me, I will give you the money for the flight ticket when I see you. By the way how much do I owe you?"

"One hundred and sixty Euros,"

Aslan was delighted with the news. "As much as I like Sergei, I am more than happy he is returning to Georgia. There has been immense pressure on me with the death of George and Freddie, so perhaps now that Sergei will be returning home, life will soon return to normal?"

Jack smiled. "Let us hope so."

"Jack, have you had lunch?"

"No, not yet, I was going to nip out in about twenty minutes."

"Do you fancy joining me?"

"I would love to."

The harbour lights created eerie shadows as sisters Olga and Tanya slowly made their way back along the harbour side to Tanya's apartment. The dark sky was cloudless with thousands of bright stars twinkling in the heaven above; there was even a full moon. All of a sudden a fairly strong cool wind started blowing in from the sea, causing several of the luxury Ocean going cruisers and yachts moored at the harbour side, to gently rock up and down in the water. As they continued with their walk back to the apartment, the girls covered their bare arms with their hands because of the sudden drop in temperature.

"Did you enjoy your meal?"

Olga looked at her sister and smiled. "It was lovely darling, next time it is my treat."

Just as Tanya was about to reply Olga's mobile rang.

"Hi Kaz what can I do for you?"

"Do you still want me to pick you and Tanya up at the Harbour Tower car park in Puerto Banus tomorrow?"

"Of course we do, at 3-30pm and don't be late."

"Have you arranged accommodation for us at the Seacrest Hotel?"

"Yes, I did that yesterday. I have some more news for you. Pasha Belinsky, who owns the Seacrest Hotel with his wife Anna, also works at the Malaga International Airport in the flight reservation department. He informed me earlier this evening that Sergei Aslanov is booked on a Turkish Airways flight to Tbilisi at 17-55 on Friday."

"Kaz, we will have to inform Major Pavlov of this development."

"I have already sent him an email. He said he would call you tomorrow morning. Olga, there is a possibility that the Kremlin may want you and Tanya to take Sergei out. On second thoughts shall we just wait and see what Major Pavlov has to say?"

"Kaz, I will call you as soon as I hear from the Major and put you in the picture."

"Thank you Olga. I will see you tomorrow afternoon at three-thirty."

Once back in Tanya's apartment, the girls opened a bottle of red wine which they drank most of and talked for a while, mainly about what they had in store for Boris before having an early night.

As soon as Jack arrived back at his apartment from Cobra Jewellery on Wednesday evening, he called Miles Coburn at MI6 in London. The call was redirected to Miles's mobile phone.

"Good to hear from you Jack, you are working late."

"I have some news for you Miles." He then told him he had arranged Sergei's flight to Georgia for late afternoon on Friday.

"Good man. Make certain you and Pedro take him to the airport and stay with him until he goes through passport control, and then it out of your hands."

"I shall be speaking to Pedro shortly."

"Jack, you must only use the Glock pistol for your own protection. The PM does not want the Spanish police to be involved."

"I understand."

"When all this is over, take a month off and return to the UK. When you arrive home call in and see me, I need to speak to you."

"Fine I will do that, I intend to return home for Christmas and the New Year, I need to visit my sister Lilly and family in Ludlow."

Later in the evening, after he had cooked himself a ham omelette, he called Aslan at his villa.

"Is there anything wrong my friend?"

"No, not really, I just needed to speak to you and Sergei about this Friday."

"One moment whilst I switch on the speaker then Sergei can hear the conversation. Go ahead Jack."

"Pedro Gonzales and I will be running Sergei to the airport. Sergei's flight to Georgia leaves at 17.55, we need to arrive at the airport by 14.55 to allow for ticket, baggage and passport check in. We will both be with Sergei, until he goes through passport control into the departure lounge. Sergei will you make certain you are ready to leave by 12.45?"

"No problem Jack I will be ready."

"Aslan, you will need to ask Natalie to open up Cobra Jewellery on Friday, there is little point in you rushing back and forwards to the office."

"I am glad you mentioned it, it had slipped my mind." "Sergei, I have been asked to mention the co-ordinates again. Is there any change of mind?"

"I am afraid not Jack, you know my views about the Russians."

"Right guys that is about it, Aslan I will see you at the office tomorrow."

"Jack, can I offer you a lift in the morning?"

"Yes, gratefully accepted."

"I will be there at the usual time Jack."

Sergei then broke into the conversation. "Jack thanks for everything you have done for me."

"What are friends for?"

After the conversation had ended, Jack made himself an Americano coffee, and then watched the television for a couple of hours before turning in. Everything appeared to be running smoothly, perhaps too smoothly.

When Olga's mobile rang Major Pavlov's name came up, she was pissed off, why the hell had he not called her sister Tanya who was still asleep? It was only 9am, as her brain started to function, she remembered that Moscow was one hour ahead of Marbella.

"How are you Olga?" She recognised the Major's voice immediately.

"Half asleep, I don't normally rise before ten."

"It is ten here in Moscow," the Major started to laugh. "With a little luck you and your sister will be on your way home on Saturday. First of all, we have the little problem of Sergei Aslanov to resolve. Kazimir Baizhanov tells me that Sergei is flying home to Georgia on Friday. He has still not given us the flight co-ordinates we have been continually asking for. If we do not receive them by the time he is due to enter the departure lounge at Malaga International Airport, he has to be taken out. At the moment his departure to another world is on a knife edge, no decision will be made until the very last moment. Neither of you must act without my authority. Do I make myself clear?"

"Perfectly Major, by now Tanya had woken and was listening in on the mobile's loud speaker.

"Major, it is Tanya speaking. "When we return to Moscow, we will call in and see you and then take you out for lunch. It has been a wonderful experience coming to Marbella and we have had a fantastic time."

"You have done well girls, your country is proud of you. I will speak to you tomorrow, make certain your phone is charged and kept open at all times." The call then ended.

"Tanya we need to start packing."

Tanya started to laugh. Olga looked at her with a blank expression on her face. "I can't wait to find out if Boris is built like a donkey or if it is all talk."

"Neither can I darling," both girls then burst into laughter. After a light lunch, the girls went back to their apartment, and finished packing their wheelie suitcases. Once they had made certain they had left nothing behind, they made their way down the deserted side street to Pinks less than three hundred metres away.

Olga pressed the intercom buzzer. "Can I help you?" She immediately recognised Boris's voice. "It is Tanya and Olga."

"If you go down the side alleyway I will meet you at the staff entrance and then we can go through to my office." "Hi Boris," Olga then kissed him, Tanya did likewise.

Boris was quite a handsome looking guy in a rugged sort of way. His black short sleeved cotton top and tight jeans showed off his trim physique to the maximum, at six two he had the physique of a body builder rather than a strip club owner. For once he was happy and charming. Olga was convinced he had been drinking or had taken some drug to enhance his sexual appetite. After following him into his office he offered the girls a drink.

"Darling we both love Spanish red wine."

"Give me one moment girls."

Boris then went to the bar in the club and took out a bottle from the cooler. Whilst he was out of the office, both the girls slipped out of their jeans and boob tops. A few minutes later he returned with their drinks which he almost dropped, both the girls were completely naked apart from each wearing a narrow black G-String.

"Christ, you both look incredible; I never get tired of looking at you two girls."

Putting the drinks down on the office table, he then turned to the girls and ran his hands over their large firm breasts and shapely bottoms. He then stood back and looked at them.

"I have always thought you two girls are very much alike, now I can see you both at close quarters you look more like sisters than good friends. If you both had your hair the same colour you could pass as twins."

"Darling we are twins. This is my twin sister Tanya we both come from Moscow." Olga then ran her hands over Tanya's body. "Well darling are you built like a donkey or is that all talk?"

Without another word, the girls began to remove his top and jeans leaving him naked apart from his dark blue tight fitting stripped trunks. The girls then stood back and looked at him in amazement.

Tanya was the first to speak. "The girls at Pinks were not exaggerating, Boris what a big boy you are. Strip off and sit on the chair."

As Boris stripped off and sat on the chair, both girls picked up their glasses of red wine and took a long drink before removing their G-Strings. Tanya immediately straddled Boris, pushing her breasts into his face. Shortly afterwards Olga did the same, the horny Russian was in ecstasy. To say the girls were extra rough with Boris would be an understatement, but he appeared to enjoy every moment. After about thirty five minutes whilst Olga was sat on top of Boris, Tanya, who was stood immediately behind her out of Boris's view, reached into her pink shoulder bag and took out a long silver hat pin. Olga glanced over her right shoulder whist Boris was oblivious to what was going on and smiled at her sister. Tanya had the long hat pin in her hand, without any hesitation she took hold of Boris's erect penis in her left hand and thrust the hat pin into it.

Acute pain then suddenly overtook Boris's lust, as he cried out in agony. Pushing Olga out of the way he stood up and looked down at the hat pin protruding from side of his penis. "What the fucking hell have you bastards done to me. Are you trying to kill me?"

As he pulled the hat pin out, blood rushed out covering his legs. The girls stood looking at him and then suddenly burst out laughing.

Tanya then passed him his mobile phone off the office desk, which he then accidently dropped onto the grey tiled floor. "You need to call the paramedics at once otherwise you may bleed to death."

"Why the fucks sake have you done this to me?"

"To teach you a lesson you will never forget. Since we have been here working for you at Pinks, you have treated us like shit. Most of the other girls working here say the same; they only have sex with you to keep you off their backs. You are sex mad, at least now you will not be able to have sex for two or three months. All you have to do is treat the girls well and they will look after you."

Blood was now starting to drip onto the floor. Boris was starting to feel faint and unsteady on his feet. "You are both psychopaths. If I get my hands on you I will fucking well kill you."

"You are in no fit state to kill anyone. We could have killed you if we had wanted too. We are just teaching you a lesson so you will never forget us."

Boris then moved towards the girls but the pain was excruciating and he fell to the floor. "Please call the paramedics, I beg you."

Olga looked at her sister Tanya. "Should we save him or let him bleed to death."

Olga then picked up Boris's mobile and rang the emergency number 061 and gave them the details where Boris was. "We have a guy with us who has had a bad accident whilst have sex, he could be bleeding to death so please be quick."

Tanya then knelt down by his side and whispered in his ear. "We don't kill fellow Russians, it is your lucky day, you will survive. Olga who had already got dressed then turned to Tanya. "Get your cloths on and let's get out of here before the paramedics arrive."

As they were leaving the office, Olga called out to Boris. "We will see you in Moscow when you return home."

"My friends back home will hunt you down when they discover what you have done to me."

"I don't think so when they find out who our uncle is, if I was you I would not say anything. Otherwise you will be known as the guy who could not handle his women. Is that what you want?"

"Fuck off both of you, I don't want you in Pinks any longer."

"Don't worry Boris, you will not see us again," remarked Tanya.

Leaving the side entrance door wide open, they walked down the alleyway to the main street just as the ambulance pulled up. Two paramedics jumped out.

"Tanya go to the apartment and get our suitcases down stairs, I will be with you in a few minutes." She then turned to the paramedics. "Guys, follow me, my girlfriend and I were having sex with him, when he burst a blood vessel."

After taking the paramedics into the office, Olga quickly disappeared whilst they were busy and re-joined her sister at her apartment.

"One more suitcase to go and that will be it."

"I will give you a hand. What about the key for the apartment, what do we do with it?"

"Drop it through the letter box at the first floor flat. The woman there owns all the flats."

Five minutes later Olga and Tanya were making their way through the deserted side streets of Puerto Banus to the Harbour Tower car park. As they stood by the entrance a white Seat SUV pulled up.

"Can I give you girls a lift?" It was Kaz.

Once out of the vehicle, he loaded the girls' suitcases into the boot and then headed for the coastal highway and the Suncrest Hotel Marbella. Olga glanced at her watch it was three-thirty, she could not help thinking how Boris was. The strong autumn sunlight was glaring through the Seat's windows, so all three of them slipped on their dark shades.

The Seacrest by Marbella standards was a modest twenty five bedroom two storey bed and breakfast budget hotel, with a small swimming pool set in its own grounds about a mile from the Cobra Jewellery Head Quarters. At this time of year the hotel had very few guests, so Olga and Tanya were allocated their own bedrooms. Olga had a great deal on her mind, so as she was alone in her bedroom she made a call to Jack at Cobra Jewellery.

"Darling it is me Olga, can I come to your apartment this evening; I need to speak to you."

"No problem if you arrive around seven, it will give me time to get home from work. If you like we could go out for a meal to the Albatross."

"I would love that, see you later darling."

Tanya was not particular happy when Olga informed her that she was going to see Jack. I thought we were going out for a meal together?"

"I am sorry darling but I have to go and see Jack, I can't just walk out on him. You have already told Roberto that you are returning to Moscow."

Tanya smiled at her sister, she knew she was right. "Roberto thinks that I am on my way home now."

"Did you tell him you would be returning to Marbella?" "Yes, I said in a few weeks and I also used the explanation we both agreed on, for having to return home. In any case we have to come back, don't forget the diamonds we put in the safe deposit box in the Bank of Santander in Marbella."

"That is our nest egg darling when we eventually leave the FSB." Olga then hugged and kissed her sister Tanya. "Kaz will take you out tonight for a meal, he has always fancied you."

Olga looked stunning when she arrived at Jack's apartment. As usual they kissed passionately and it did not take long before they were romping on the king size bed in his bedroom having sex. Rather than take a taxi to the Albatross they decided to walk down the Esplanade Paseo. For late autumn it was fairly mild. Jack was surprised how busy the restaurant was for a Thursday at this time of year. After ordering drinks and their favourite dish chicken paella, Olga took hold of Jack's hand.

"Darling, I have some bad news, I am returning to Moscow tomorrow. If you recall, I told you a few weeks ago that my visa expired at the beginning of December."

"I thought you had sorted it out."

"No, I ignored it. Last night the police visited Pinks and checked out all the girls for work permit and visa irregularities. I was given forty eight hours to leave Spain or face arrest if I stayed. Poor Boris could be up for the high jump for breaking the law." Olga then squeezed his hand. "Sorry darling I have no choice."

"When will you return to Marbella?"

"In three to four weeks but it all depends on getting my visa renewed. To be honest with you, I am thinking of moving here permanently and opening a girlie club like Pinks." Olga then took a drink of red wine; Jack did likewise with his Budweiser. "Would you like me to stay the night?"

Jack almost replied yes without thinking. "I would love you to stay but I have to catch an early morning flight from Malaga to the UK. My sister Lilly is not well and I need to see her, we have always been very close. I will be back in Marbella on Monday." Jack then leaned across the table and kissed her. "Don't forget to send me a text before you leave Spain."

"I won't." She then kissed him again.

It was shortly after eleven thirty when they left the Albatross and called a taxi. Roscoe Rodriguez the proprietor was conspicuously absent. He could not help wondering where he was. Jack still found it hard to believe that Olga was two different people. One moment, tender and loving, the next moment a deadly assassin. When the taxi dropped him off at the Marbella Beach Apartments, tears ran down Olga's beautiful face as they parted company. Whether it was genuine or not he had no idea but if it wasn't, she was a brilliant actress.

36

Med Beach Club boss Pedro Gonzales picked Jack up in his hyacinth red metallic C-Class Mercedes outside the Marbella Beach Apartments main entrance at twelve thirty. It was another mild day with strong sunshine.

"Good to see you Jack. Is everything ok?"

"I am fine, though I must admit I am a little concerned about today."

"Jack, if it is of any help to you I feel the same, it is the unknown which concerns me. We need to be fully alert and look out for us being followed which could be a car or motor bike." Jack nodded his head in agreement. "When we arrive at Aslan's villa, we need to speak to the security guard and see if he has seen anyone acting suspicious in the area. Before I forget there is a loaded Glock pistol under both front seats."

Jack then placed his right hand under the passenger seat and brought out the pistol. After checking the mechanism of the pistol and the chamber for bullets, he placed it back under the seat.

"Remember what Coburn said, the Glock pistol must only be used if our lives are in danger, the UK PM does not want a diplomatic incident."

"Fifteen minutes later they arrived at Aslan's villa. The security guard immediately waved them through the gates into the complex parking area. Once they had got out of the Mercedes, Pedro walked over to the security guard and asked him if he had seen anyone checking out of the villa. It did not surprise him when the reply was no. As he was walking away the guard called to him.

"Four days ago a guy in a white van, fitted a CCTV camera to that wooden telegraph pole over there. I actually went over and spoke to him; he told me that the local council in Marbella had asked him to fit it to improve security in the area."

Pedro walked over to the telegraph pole and looked up at the CCTV camera. "I live in the villa further up the road and we certainly need more security around here." Pedro then walked back to Jack, who was waiting by the Mercedes. "That is a private camera not the type normally fitted by the local authority. I would imagine our Russian friend Kazimir Baizhanov is monitoring the villa twenty four hours a day, he is probably watching us right now." Pedro sighed. "There is very little we can do now, come on let's walk up to the villa and pick up Sergei, the sooner he is on his flight to Georgia the happier I will be."

Aslan met them at the entrance to the villa. Embracing them both he invited them in. "Sergei is in the lounge waiting for you, I will tell him you are here."

Aslan then left the hallway, a few minutes later he returned with Sergei who was carrying a large black and red sports bag. Dropping the sports bag to the floor he embraced both Jack and Pedro.

"Guys, I really appreciate what you are doing for me."

Aslan turned to Jack and Pedro. "Can I get you a coffee before you leave?"

Pedro glanced at his watch. "Thank you for the offer but I think we should be on our way."

Aslan and Sergei were quite emotional as Sergei put his sports bag into the boot of the Mercedes.

"I have a great deal to thank you for my friend. You gave me a job and welcomed me into your home. I can never repay you for your generous hospitality."

"Sergei, we must keep in touch. Perhaps one day when this current situation has blown over we will meet again." "Let us hope so."

The two friends then embraced; there were tears in both of their eyes as Sergei got into the rear of the Mercedes. Within minutes, they had left the villa compound and were heading along the highway towards Marbella and the Motorway.

Road conditions were perfect. The weather was still unusually dry and mild for the time of the year. Compared with the summer months the motorway was relatively quiet, Pedro said they should make the thirty two mile journey to Malaga International Airport in less than forty five minutes.

Jack and Sergei spoke continually during the journey, mainly about the happy times they had spent together in South Africa.

"When I have settled in my new home in Tbilisi, you must come and visit me. At the moment I live with my elderly aunt, who is more like the mother I never knew. I intend to find myself a wife, buy a house and have a family. My life will start again but this time with my father and sister also being a big part of it." Jack smiled; he really hoped his dream would come true.

"Sergei, I have to ask you again, have you changed your mind about the flight co-ordinates the Russians want?" "Jack, as I told you before I do not trust them. As soon as I arrive in Georgia, I will text you the details. Trust me I will not let you down."

"Jack, look in your side wing mirror. There is a white Seat SUV following us. It is about a quarter of a mile behind. It slipped onto the motorway with us at Marbella."

"Are you certain it is tailing us?"

"I am fairly certain, when I pick up speed it does the same, when I slow down the Seat slows down."

Apart from the possibility of being tailed the journey was uneventful. Six and a half miles from Malaga city centre they followed a steady stream of traffic which took the airport sign. The drive along the duel carriage way, which was lined with office buildings, modern warehouses and small Palm trees, took less than ten minutes before they arrived at the airport.

Jack turned to Pedro as they pulled into the main car park opposite the terminal. "The white Seat appears to have disappeared unless he is purposely holding back."

"When we have parked, stay in the car for ten minutes and we will see if he turns up."

There must have been a thousand cars on the car park. Luckily they found a vacant slot close to the entrance. "Sergei, when you get out of the car please keep close to Jack and I, as soon as we enter the terminal building check- in at the Turkish Airline desk. We will then stay with you all the time, until you have to go through passport control to the departure lounge."

"Look who has just driven into the car park. The white Seat SUV."

"I noticed it as well. Apart from the driver, I am unable to see anyone else in the vehicle."

"He could have dropped his passengers off at the terminal before parking."

"That is a possibility. Jack did you recognise the driver?"

"No chance, he wore a baseball cap, dark shades and a high neck Bomber Jacket."

"Did you see where he parked?"

"No, but it will further back as the car park is very busy." Jack then whispered to Pedro in a low voice. No way did he want Sergei to hear. "Should we arm ourselves?"

"Yes."

Pedro then reached under the car seat with his right hand, picking up the Glock pistol he placed it in the gun holster inside his brown bomber jacket. Jack did likewise but as he had no holster, he tucked the pistol inside his leather belt and then zipped up his black leather jacket.

Once out of the Mercedes, Jack and Pedro escorted Sergei who was carrying his sports bag towards the terminal building. As they walked through the car park Jack took the opportunity to send a text to Miles Coburn in London.

"We have just arrived at Malaga Airport. Sergei still refuses to give me the landing strip co-ordinates. He is still adamant, that once he arrives in Georgia he will text the details to me immediately. Please inform the Russians."

The reply came back, "Message received, informing the Major."

There was little else he could do. It was now up to him and Pedro to protect Sergei from any possible attack.

It was twelve minutes passed two when they walked into the terminal. Jack was surprised how busy it was. Though it was out of season, Malaga was still a very busy airport with over eighteen million passengers a year.

Twenty five minutes earlier on the motorway, Tanya and Olga were in the rear passenger seats of the white Seat SUV travelling to Malaga International Airport when Major Ivan Pavlov of the Russian FSB called Olga on her mobile.

"Where are you now?" he asked abruptly.

"With my sister Tanya in a Seat SUV which is being driven by Kaz on the motorway travelling to Malaga Airport tailing Sergei Aslanov. You sound most stressed Major?" "So would you be, that fucking Georgian has still not come up with the landing strip co-ordinates in the Ural Mountains, I am certain he is taking us all for a ride."

"Just give us the word Major and we will take him out." Our President wants the diamonds back so that is our priority; once we get the co-ordinates we can then recover the diamonds. Sergei Aslanov will only be taken out as a last resort, do I make myself absolutely clear."

"Darling don't get stressed or you could have a heart attack. I promise you, we will not harm a hair on his head unless you give us the ok."

The Major started to stutter before regaining his composure. "Good, as soon as you arrive at the airport and make visual contact with Sergei call me. Make certain your sister Tanya and Kaz know all the details of this conversation."

"Have you got Kaz's mobile number?"

"Of course I have. Tell him that I will speak to him shortly. Olga, make certain I can always keep in touch with you."

Back in the terminal at Malaga International Airport, Sergei joined a queue of about sixty at the Turkish Airlines check in desk. Jack and Pedro positioned themselves about five metres from Sergei on either side of the queue, carefully watching for any unusual activity. Once Sergei's flight ticket had been scanned and his sports bag weighed in, the three men stood together and talked for a few moments.

Jack glanced at his watch before turning to Sergei. "We have a good hour before you have to go through to the departure lounge. Do you fancy a coffee at Starbucks and a bite to eat?" Both Pedro and Serge smiled and answered yes.

"If we make our way past the check-in desks towards the departure lounge, we will come to all the shops, café bars and restaurants. Sergei, would you stand between us for security?"

Jack could not help notice how many people glanced at them as they made their way to Starbucks.

"Sergei, walk a few yards in front of Jack and I, we are drawing too much attention."

This part of the airport was extremely busy, all the bars were full with noisy passengers many with young children, after a five minute walk they eventually came to Starbucks. Like all the other bars it was very busy with a long queue at the counter.

Sergei pointed to a table close to the front. "That family are about to leave."

Once they had got seated Jack spoke to both Pedro and Sergei. "Right guys, what type of coffee do you want?" Latté came the reply, "what about a sandwich?"

After running their eyes over the table menu they ordered three roast ham and cheese sandwiches.

"I will join the queue."

"Jack, I will give you a hand."

"Sergei, I think you should stay with Pedro, I can manage by myself."

The queue was not as bad as he first thought, fortunately another young female assistant had just joined the two other girls and an older guy behind the counter. Fifteen minutes later Jack returned to the table, Pedro and Sergei were deep in conversation.

"Sergei was just saying that he is considering applying to Georgian Airways, to see if they will take him on as a pilot as they have vacancies."

"An excellent idea you are highly qualified in that department. You will just have to make certain you never fly to Russia otherwise you may get arrested."

Sergei laughed out loud; a woman at a nearby table gave him a strange look. "It did cross my mind."

The coffee was excellent, the sandwiches passable but a little dry.

"I have not seen any sign of the girls or Kaz but they must be about. They are probably watching us from one of the other cafes waiting for an opportunity to strike"

Sergei looked at both Jack and Pedro. "Do you really think they will make an attempt to take me out?"

"It is highly likely my friend but whilst you are with Jack and I it is doubtful, they could not risk a shootout as there are too many police patrolling the airport. They would never get away with it; they would either be arrested or killed in any shootout."

Time was flying by quickly, within the next ten minutes Sergei would be called to passport control and customs before entering the departure lounge.

Sergei stood up. "Guys, I need to visit the men's washroom before I leave you and head to the departure lounge. I noticed my flight details to Georgia have just come up on the flight information display screen."

Pedro stood up. "I will walk you to the washroom."

"No need to, you can see the entrance to the male and female washrooms from here. There are too many people about for someone to attack me." Neither Jack nor Pedro objected. "Don't worry guys I will be fine."

Ten minutes earlier Olga and Tanya had taken up positions on either side of Starbucks when Olga's mobile rang. It was their FSB boss Major Pavlov.

"MI5 in London have just informed us, that Sergei still has no intention of disclosing the flight runway co-ordinates in the Ural Mountains, until he is in Georgia. The President does not believe he will then, he has given his authority for him to be taken out. No guns are to be used only PV44. Once you have achieved your objective get out of the airport. Kaz will drive you to our Embassy in Madrid, where you will both stay overnight before flying home to Moscow on Saturday. Good luck." The phone then went dead.

Seconds later it rang again, it was Kaz. "Sergei has left Starbucks alone and is heading to the men's washroom he is now inside, both of you get into position. You will only have one opportunity to strike, if you fail he will head to the departure lounge and your mission will be a failure."

"Kaz, Tanya and I never fail."

Pedro glanced at his gold Omega watch. "Sergei has been too long, something is wrong, it has been over ten minutes."

Both men jumped up from their chairs almost colliding with nearby tables. Within seconds they were both running across the greyish white tiled floor of the check-in lounge to the washroom facilities. When they arrived Sergei was bending down towards the floor, picking up a box of doughnuts, which had spilled onto the floor.

"What the hell has happened, we thought you were in trouble?"

"I was rushing out of the men's room, when I accidently collided with an attractive young women, knocking the box of doughnuts out of her hand. It was completely my fault; I could not leave them all over the floor." Picking the last doughnut off the floor Sergei put the box and its contents into a nearby disposal bin.

"What happened to the woman?"

"She said she would have to go, as her boyfriend was waiting for her, they urgently needed to get to the departure lounge for their flight to Madrid."

Pedro turned to Sergei, "I am afraid you need to be heading to the departure lounge, your flight details are now up on the flight display screen."

As they started to follow the departure signs, Jack looked up at one of the screens, and the first flight to Madrid was not until eight. The girl was lying, alarm bells started to ring in his head.

"Sergei, the woman you bumped into, have you any idea how old she was and could you describe her."

"She was very attractive probably no more than twenty five maybe twenty six, very slim and wore tight jeans, black leather boots and a pink baseball cap."

"Was her hair long or short?"

"Sorry I have no idea. It was hard to tell because of the baseball cap. She spoke to me in Spanish with a broken accent, she sounded like she was Russian or from one of the old Soviet Republics. As she left she touched my right arm and said 'Thank you darling'."

Jack smiled but did not continue with the conversation. Pedro who was listening stared at Jack with a look of horror on his face.

"I had better head to the departure lounge. I shall miss you guys, you have been incredible to me whilst I have been in Marbella, I can't thank you enough. Jack we must keep in touch and don't forget to come and visit me in Tbilisi, Georgia."

Sergei then shook Pedro's hand and embraced him. Turning to Jack he did the same, as they embraced he whispered in his ear, "You are a true friend Jack Sinclair, I will never forget you."

Without another word he turned and walked towards the departure security gate. Just before he went through, he turned and waved. Both Jack and Pedro waved back. "Let's get out of here Jack we have done our duty, he should be safe in the departure lounge. I also told him to be very weary of anyone who approaches him for no apparent reason, especially at Ankara if they have to embark from the plane."

As they walked towards Pedro's Mercedes in the airport car park, he turned to Jack. "The Russian girl Olga is always using the expression 'darling' do you think the mystery girl could be her?"

"It is highly likely but if you recall she has an identical twin Tanya, she could use the same expression as well."

Fifteen minutes later they hit the motorway for Marbella. The temperature had dropped dramatically and it was now quite cold and windy but thankfully no rain. Pedro switched on the car's heater and turned the radio on low.

Shortly after, Jack took his mobile out of his jacket pocket and sent a text message to Aslan. 'Sergei now safely in the departures lounge, waiting for his flight to Georgia.'

Aslan replied. 'What a great relief.'

There was little traffic on the motorway and they were making good time.

"It is going to be dark early tonight, it is looking very overcast."

"I would not be surprised if we don't get some heavy rain in the next couple of hours, December can be a very unpredictable month," remarked Pedro.

About twenty minutes from the Marbella exit, Jack's mobile pinged. It was a text message from Sergei.

"Hi Jack, I promised you the runway flight co-ordinates once I returned home, well I have changed my mind, you can have them now. You never know what happens in life, the plane may crash or I could even drop down dead, only the good Lord knows our destiny. Please make certain your friend at MI6 receive them and passes them onto the Russians, perhaps then they will call their hounds off and I can have a peaceful life with my family. When we first met in Johannesburg, South Africa, it was amazing how we clicked as friends though we are both from a very different culture and back ground. We have a true friendship which I never want to lose. As I am sat here in the safety of the departure lounge I feel so relaxed, all I can think of is being reunited with my family again and seeing my adopted mother my elderly aunt. Thank you again Jack and God bless you."

Pedro glanced at Jack. "Is there a problem?"

"I don't think so, would you give me one moment."

Jack then texted the co-ordinates to Miles Coburn.

'Please inform the Russians immediately.'

Five minutes later he received a text reply back. 'Major Pavlov informed and acknowledged.'

Shortly after, the Mercedes came off the motorway at the Marbella exit. Twenty minutes later Pedro pulled up outside the Marbella Beach Apartments; it was just leaving five forty-five.

"You were going to show me the text message from Sergei."

Jack passed him his mobile. Pedro read the text message and then sighed. "Christ, I hope that girl at the airport was not one of the twins. There is nothing we can do now but hope and pray for his safety."

Jack shook his head. "I should have accompanied him to the gent's washroom."

"With hindsight we should have both insisted in going with him."

"Jack, I am going to have to leave you now, I need to get a bite to eat and a shower before I go to the Med Club, Friday night is always a busy night. Before I forget can you put the Glock pistol back under your seat?"

"Good job you reminded me. At least we did not have to use them." Pedro nodded his head in agreement.

Earlier when Olga answered her mobile the adrenalin was still flowing, like her sister Tanya she loved her job and the excitement it brought. Major Pavlov's name came up.

"Olga, put your phone on the speaker and then Tanya and Kaz can hear the conversation. Abort your mission immediately Sergei Aslanov must not be harmed, we have received the flight landing co-ordinates in the Ural Mountains from him. No way must he be harmed. Do you hear me?"

"You are too late Major; we carried out your instructions around three forty-five Spanish time.

"Shit, there is going to be hell to pay for this. Which of you carried out the assassin?"

"Really Major you don't expect me to tell you. Tanya and I work together and share the glory equally whoever makes the kill. As I told you earlier Major we are the best and we never fail."

"Where are you now?"

"About sixty miles from Malaga on the A4 Motorway heading towards Madrid. It will take us about five and a half hours before we arrive at our Embassy."

"I will speak to you both when you arrive in Moscow." The phone then went silent.

"Shit! I hope the Major does not end up before a firing squad. At least not until we have had some fun with him." Both the girls started to laugh.

Kaz who was driving the Seat SUV never spoke when the Major was on the phone but now was the opportunity. "Fucking hell girls someone is up for the high jump. When we arrive at our Embassy in Madrid, leave the two Beretta pistols and the PV 44 lipstick files on the front passenger seat. I will dispose of them. Where are they now girls?"

Tanya was the first to speak, safely in our pink rucksacks darling."

Earlier when Sergei finally got through passport control and customs, he was relieved to have finally arrived safely in the departure lounge. The lounge was extremely busy with passengers waiting to fly off to destinations worldwide; eventually he found a vacant seat near a woman with three children. By five he suddenly started to feel extremely tired, he had never felt like this before and was most concerned. He felt the urge to close his eyes and rest, but he was worried that he would fall asleep and miss his flight. At five fifteen a girl came on the public address system, and asked all passengers who were flying on Turkish Airline flight TA106TG leaving at 17.55 to go to gate nine. Sergei's legs appeared to buckle beneath him as he stood up almost causing him to fall over. The young woman who was sat nearby with the children stood up and came over to him. "Are you all right, can I help you? You don't look very well," she said.

"Thank you for your concern but I will be alright."

It took a monumental effort for Sergei to walk down the corridor to gate nine, but he intended to board the Turkish Airline he could see through the window, on the tarmac below. His legs were now causing him great pain as he stood in the queue of passengers waiting to board. In front of him he could see two smartly dressed girls with head scarf's checking passengers' boarding passes. His chest was starting to ache and acute pain was shooting down both arms, he was even having difficulty breathing, it was as though someone had their hands round his neck. As he passed his boarding pass to one of the girls, she looked at him with a shocked expression on her face. Sergei then held his hand to his chest and cried out in pain falling to the floor, within seconds he was dead. His dream of seeing his father and sister were gone forever.

When Jack received the call on his mobile from Aslan he was in the Picasso Café Bar having just finished his meal, it was around nine thirty. Aslan had great difficulty speaking as his voice was full of emotion.

"Sergei is dead," he cried out. Jack did not answer. "Did you not here me? Sergei is dead."

"It is impossible for him to be dead, Pedro and I saw him walk through security to passport control and he was absolutely fine then. Who told you about Sergei?"

Aslan appeared to gain his composure a little. My phone number was in Sergei's mobile phone in his pocket. An Inspector from Malaga police called me with the news, there can be no mistake it was certainly Sergei." "Do you know what happened?"

"Yes, several of the airport staff witnessed what happen. It appeared he was becoming seriously ill shortly before he made his way to the flight departure gate. Witnesses say he was very unsteady on his feet, several of them even thought he had been drinking. As he joined the boarding pass queue, he was seen to be holding his chest in pain. Seconds later he cried out and fell to the floor. The paramedics think he was probably dead before he hit the ground."

"Where is he now?" Jack could feel tears in his eyes starting to well up and trickle down his sunburned face.

"He is in the mortuary at Malaga Police Head Quarters. Tomorrow they will carry out a post-mortem."

"Aslan, what you have gone through again is horrendous. "Would you like me to call round to your villa; I can be with you in half an hour?"

"Jack, I would appreciate that."

"Have you spoken to Pedro?"

"No, as soon as the police contacted me I called you, as you knew Sergei better than anyone."

"Thank you. I appreciate that. Don't worry about Pedro I will call him. I will see you later."

"Is everything alright?"

Jack looked up. It was Alberto the owner of the bar.

"I have just received some tragic news about a friend of mine. Unfortunately I am going to have to leave as I have several phone calls to make."

After settling his bill, he went outside and sat on one of the bar's dark blue plastic chairs whilst he phoned Pedro. When his friend answered the line it was very noisy and he could hardly hear him speaking. "Jack, I will call you back in two minutes from my office."

Walking onto the Esplanade Paseo he sat on the low wall overlooking the Mediterranean Sea. The wind was strong but at least the rain had kept away and his head was now starting to clear.

Just as he thought Pedro had forgotten to call him back his mobile rang.

"Jack, what can I do for you?"

Pedro listened to Jack in disbelief. "I am absolutely horrified, it is our fault he died and we allowed the Russians to assassinate him. If we had accompanied him to the men's washroom he would still be alive."

"Maybe you are right, but remember Kazimir Baizhanov is a highly trained sniper, and it is more than likely he would have attempted to take Sergei out himself if the girls had failed. We will now never know."

"Jack, you are going to have to excuse me."

He could tell from the way his friend was now speaking and the tone of his voice, the situation was starting to get to him.

"Where are you now Jack?"

"Outside the Picasso Café Bar, I have just had a meal. As soon as I have contacted Miles Coburn with the news I intend to call in and see Aslan."

"Jack, would you tell Aslan that I will see him tomorrow around mid-day."

"Of course I will."

Miles Coburn answered his mobile immediately when Jack called him.

"How are you Jack?"

"Not good Miles, Sergei Aslanov is dead." Coburn did not speak. "He became ill in the departure lounge and then collapsed and died, as he was about to board a Turkish Airline flight to Georgia. There were a number of witnesses. Paramedics at the scene suspect a heart attack."

"Fucking hell there is going to be big trouble over this. His father is a national hero in Russia; someone will get his balls chopped off for allowing this to happen. With the two Chechens and now Sergei, that is now three young people on the list dying from heart attacks. Jack, how the hell did they get to him?"

"Both Pedro and I were with him all the time, until he went through security to passport control. It is quite possible someone got to him in the departure lounge, whoever it was could then have disappeared on an outgoing flight. There is no way of checking flight passenger itineraries as the PM does not want to involve the Spanish Government. It looks like the perfect crime." Coburn then sighed. "It is not your fault or Pedro's, poor Sergei was just too late giving the Russians the information they wanted. An hour earlier and he would still be alive."

"Miles you need to inform Sergei's family."

"I will speak to the Georgian Embassy in London tomorrow, they will sort everything out. Jack, I will call you on Monday, we need to have a talk. In the meantime you take care."

Walking to the nearby car park he put a call through to Benny for a taxi.

"Hi Benny, it's Jack, is there any chance of a taxi to Aslan Maskhadov's villa."

"Give me ten minutes Mr Ramos and I will be with you. Where are you?" he said almost as an afterthought.

Jack could not help but smile. "In the small car park by the Picasso Café Bar, I will meet you by the entrance."

It took less than ten minutes for the taxi to arrive. "Thank you Benny for picking me up; you appear busy to-night."

"For the time of the year I am but I will never complain." Fifteen minutes later the taxi pulled up outside Aslan's villa. "Here we are Mr Ramos, if you want a lift back later to the Marbella Beach Apartments, please give me a call."

"Keep the change Benny."

"Thank you boss,"

Once out of the taxi Jack pressed the illuminated security buzzer on the small black door by the main entrance.

"This is security, can I help you?"

"You certainly can, it is Jack Sinclair."

"Please enter Mr Maskhadov is expecting you."

All the security lights came on as Jack walked up to the villa, the manicured garden and swimming pool looked spectacular. As he walked across the Indian slate patio, the door to the main entrance to the villa opened.

"Good to see you Jack, please come in." The two men warmly embraced. "I am just about to make myself a coffee, why don't you join me in the kitchen?"

"Thank you, you have had a hell of a time this last two months."

"It has been horrendous Jack, more like a horror story.

You don't take sugar with your coffee?"

"No just milk please."

"Sergei's death must have hit you hard Jack?"

"It has, we had been good friends since we first met in South Africa almost four years ago, I am finding it hard to believe he is no longer with us."

"If he has been assassinated as we suspect, how did they manage to get to him?"

"That is the question. The only time we were not with him, was when he entered the men's washroom. If they struck there, it had to be a man who took him out. Otherwise the only other place for an attack would have been in the departure lounge. The assassin could easily have struck and then boarded an outgoing flight. Personally I do not think we will ever know." The two men then took a drink of their coffee.

"You make a good coffee." Aslan smiled.

"I spoke to my Iraqi friend Dr Mohammed Abadi shortly before you arrived. He said he would take a sample of Sergei's blood and call me with the result on Monday." Aslan took another drink of his coffee. "It does not look good does it?"

"I spoke to my contact in London about Sergei. They said they would be in touch with the Georgian Embassy, who would contact his family. When his body is released by the Coroner the embassy will arrange for him to be flown home."

"That is a relief. Thank you for all the trouble you have gone to."

"Would you like me to cover for you at Cobra Jewellery tomorrow?"

"Thank you for offering but I need to do something to keep my mind off what has happened." Aslan then paused for a moment. "My sister-in-law Gabrielle is due to arrive next Sunday, do you think under the circumstances I should ask her not to come?"

Jack shook his head. "No way, it will do you the world of good to have a woman around the house."

"Thank you for your advice Jack. I must be honest I am looking forward to her coming."

An hour later Jack called Benny for a taxi. He was glad when he arrived back at his apartment, tomorrow he would call his sister Lilly and brother Lex but in the meantime he needed to get some shut eye. The last few hours had been very stressful and upsetting, so much that the memory of losing his beloved parents once again tormenting his mind. When sleep finally came it was a welcome relief.

Pedro Gonzales called him around two the following afternoon; he was just walking back to his own villa after visiting Aslan.

"Did you manage to contact Miles Coburn?"

"Yes, he does not blame us for Sergei's death. At the moment we are all presuming that he died of a heart attack like George and Freddie, but until we get the pathologists report, no one can be certain about his cause of death." He then gave Pedro a summary of what he had said to Coburn.

"Jack, you have done extremely well for your first assignment, in the next few days Coburn will probably be recalling you to the UK."

"When we spoke last night, he said he would be calling me on Monday, he will probably break the news to me then."

"Have you decided about your future?"

"More or less, I intend to return to the UK a week on Sunday for three weeks. I will probably spend Christmas and New Year with my sister and her family and then return to Marbella the second week in January. Aslan has offered me the position of General Manager with Cobra Jewellery, which I intend to accept. If you are still in the market for a House Music DJ next year then DJ Ramos is certainly available."

"Excellent, I am personally delighted you will be returning to Marbella. Next year if you agree, DJ Ramos will be performing on Thursday night at the Med Club until Easter before moving back to his regular Tuesday gig for the summer season. I will get Jose and Selena to make an announcement on Tuesday with it being your last gig of the year."

"Pedro you have made my day." His friend laughed.

"We can sort out your fee and any other details next week."

"No problem, I will see you on Tuesday."

On Sunday evening, Aslan texted with an offer of a lift to work on Monday morning, which he readily accepted. During the night there had been a heavy rain storm with a strong wind, which battered the beachside bars and restaurants. The manicured gardens of the Marbella Beach Apartments were littered with leaves and broken tree branches. The weather now was by far the worst he had seen since his September arrival on the Costa del Sol. Dodging a very heavy shower of rain, Aslan and Jack quickly made their way to the Cobra Jewellery HQ from the car park. Natalie was on reception.

"Good morning Mr Maskhadov. Good morning Jack." "Aslan, can you spare me ten minutes."

"Of course Jack come through to my office."

"Now what can I do for you?"

Jack got straight to the point. Aslan listened intently as Jack explained what he intended to do over the next few weeks. A broad smile crept over his face as he stood up and shook his hand and embraced him.

"Welcome to Cobra Jewellery my friend. If you are still as enthusiastic in six months, I will make you a director in the company. What about the Club Med, will you still be appearing there?"

"Yes, one night a week, I find it most therapeutic. Will you be able to cope whilst I am away in the UK?"

"No problem, most of our regular customers have already bought stock in for the festive season. Natalie is a real help and a quick learner. In January next year, she is going on a day release course at Malaga University, to study for a business degree."

"Excellent she will do well."

"It is a pity you will not be here to meet my sister-in-law." "I more than likely will return to Marbella early, so there is every possibility, we will meet then."

"Jack, can I ask you a question which has been on my mind for some time? If you do not want to answer, I understand."

He did not have to be told what the question was. He had been expecting this for some time.

"Please go ahead."

"Do you work for MI6?"

Jack smiled. "Let us just say, that I have very close contacts with them. My late father used to work for them but apart from that I would rather not say anymore."

Aslan smiled and changed the conversation. "Do you want to meet for lunch?"

"Most definitely, I will remind you at one. Now if you will excuse me, I need to get some work done."

An hour later Miles Coburn called on Jack's mobile, he was his normal happy self.

"You will be pleased to know your adventure in Marbella is now over, you can now return to the UK on the next available flight."

"I am one step ahead of you. I have already booked a flight for this Sunday the nineteenth." He then told Miles about his intention to return to Marbella, and the job offer he had accepted with Aslan Maskhadov."

"You have been busy. I need to see you in the office once you return, should we say Tuesday at two. By the way, feel free to stay in the apartment as long as you want. I will see you next Tuesday, take care."

Shortly before four, Aslan came into his office.

"I have some news for you about Sergei's death. My good friend Dr Abadi tells me the cause of death was a massive heart attack. The doctor then carried out tests on a sample of Sergei's blood, as he expected it was identical to the samples taken from George and Freddie. There is no doubt in Dr Abadi' s mind, that Sergei was assassinated with a nerve agent."

"It is hard to believe the Russians can be so ruthless." "They are no different now than when they were at war with Chechnya."

Once Jack arrived back in his apartment after work, he called both Miles Coburn and Pedro with the pathology and blood test report on Sergei. Neither was surprised with the results.

The week flew by quickly. On Thursday he phoned Thomas, the security officer at his Thames Plaza Apartment in London, who was looking after his Range Rover Sport.

"Mr Sinclair, your vehicle is still in immaculate condition. Would you like me to pick you up at the airport, Sunday is my day off?"

"You have no problem driving my vehicle?"

"No Sir."

"Then I accept your offer with thanks. I will call you with my arrival time in the UK on Saturday. Thank you again Thomas."

Lilly and Lex reaction was completely different when he told them he was returning to England for Christmas on Sunday.

Lilly was over the moon. "You must stay with us for both Christmas and the New Year," she said excitedly. Jack had not got the heart to tell her that he would be returning to Marbella. Lex on the other hand was disappointed, that Jack would not be with them at Christmas, but was delighted when his brother told him he would be returning in early January.

At six on Sunday morning, Benny picked him up in his white BMW at the Marbella Beach Apartment. Forty five minutes later they arrived at Malaga International Airport.

"When I return probably the second week in January, I will give you a call and you can pick me up if you would." "No problem Mr Ramos." Jack laughed; he liked Benny he was a great guy.

Once he had checked in at the EasyJet desk, he went straight to passport control and customs before going to the departure lounge. Later he bought a coffee and a couple of croissants at Starbucks, and waited for his flight at nine to come up on the large display screen. As he sat there, he could not help thinking how his friend Sergei must have felt as the nerve agent slowly crept through his body.

37

The flight to Gatwick Airport was quite eventful due to a hen party of twelve young women returning from a boozy week in Marbella. As soon as one of the girls recognized Jack as DJ Ramos, after visiting the Med Beach Club and told her friends, they went crazy. All the girls insisted in having their photo taken with their arms draped around him. Jack was soon the talk of the plane. Now he really did know what it was like to be a famous celebrity with everyone smiling at him.

Two hours forty-five minutes later, the fully laden Boeing 737 touched down on runway one and taxied to gate six. The weather was not good when he left Spain, but now it was even worse in England, dark, cold, wet and miserable. Once through passport control, he headed to the baggage carousel, collected his sports bag and suitcase and made his way through customs into the arrival lounge. He immediately saw Thomas who was stood by the WH Smith stand.

"Good to see you again Mr Sinclair." The two men shook hands.

"You look well Thomas."

"I try to keep fit with plenty of exercise. Let me give you a hand with your luggage, we need to be out of here fairly quickly, before I get a parking ticket."

Once Jack got into the passenger seat of the Range Rover he glanced at his watch, it was just leaving one.

"Are you glad to be back in London Mr Sinclair?"

"Please call me Jack. In answer to your question yes, mainly because I shall be driving to Ludlow on Thursday to spend Christmas and New Year with my sister Lilly and her family. I am looking forward to that. The second week in January, I shall be returning to Spain but I intend to return frequently to visit my sister and family, we are very close."
"Would you like me to keep an eye on your Range Rover whilst you are away?"

"Thank you I would appreciate that."

An hour later they arrived at the underground car park at the Thames Plaza. Jack then handed Thomas a slim white envelope. "My appreciation for your excellent service." "Thank you Jack," then placed the envelope into the inside pocket of his grey jacket.

"That is for all the trouble you have gone too, I appreciate what you are doing for me."

Thomas smiled and again replied thank you.

After taking the elevator to the third floor, Jack used his key card to gain entrance to his apartment. Everything looked the same; it was as though he had only been away for a long weekend. Dropping his baggage in the middle of the lounge floor, he walked over to the balcony doors and opened them wide. Cool air immediately rushed in as he stepped outside. The view across the Thames, which he never got tired of was still the same, numerous water taxies and working barges were still there, so was the iconic MI6 Head Quarters on the Albert Embankment, it felt good to be home.

The next few days were going to be hectic, on Monday he needed to phone Jim Richardson at Franks and make an appointment to see him on Wednesday. He already had an appointment with Miles Coburn at MI6 on Tuesday and in the meantime he needed to do a little Christmas shopping for cards and presents for his family in Ludlow. It was too late to send Lex and his family a Christmas card in the normal way to Spain, so he arranged one over the internet via Moonpig.

Once he had unpacked his luggage and settled into his old routine, he nipped out to a twenty four hour convenience store to buy some provisions, mainly for breakfast as he had no intention of cooking his own evening meal. By six he was beginning to feel quite hungry as he had not eaten all day, apart from the two croissants at Malaga International Airport. It was time for an early evening meal and there was only one place to go, his old haunt Joe's Café Bar, which was less than ten minutes' walk from the Thames Plaza Apartments.

Slipping on his black soft leather zip jacket, Jack headed outside into the chilly December weather. After a brisk walk along the Thames embankment he came to Joe's Café Bar, though there was no one sat outside, inside was busy. Slowly he made his way to the bar, owner Sophie had just served a couple of guys. When she saw Jack, a huge smiled crossed her face.

"Jack, I can't believe it is you." She then came from behind the bar and gave him a hug and a kiss. When did you arrive back?"

"About four hours ago."

"Are you dining with us?"

"Yes." Jack then nodded towards the bar. "Your customers are getting inpatient so you had better serve them." Then she touched his arm and went back behind the bar.

"Your usual drink Jack?"

"Please."

"I will let Mattia know you are here when I have a minute to spare."

Jack's usual stool at the end of the bar by the wall was not taken, so he took the opportunity to seat himself there.

"Jack, your pint of Peroni,"

"Thank you Sophie,"

"You look good Jack. Your short beard and longer hair certainly suit you." Jack smiled.

"Did you know you are now famous in the UK?"

"Really, you surprise me."

"Along with many of our customers, we have been watching your live Tuesday night House Music gig over the internet from the Med Club in Marbella. You are incredible."

"How did you know that I was performing there?"

"Several of our customers where on holiday in Marbella in early October and saw you at the Med Club. Since then we have been following you every week."

Jack then raised the glass of Peroni to his lips and took a long drink. The refreshing cool liquid slowly brought him to life.

"Good to see you have returned safely Jack or should I say DJ Ramos." Mattia shook his hand warmly. "How are you my friend?"

"I am fine."

"And you."

"Good." The two friends embraced again.

"Have you returned for good?"

"Not at the moment. I will be here for just over three weeks before I head back to Spain. I will be spending Christmas and New Year with my sister Lilly and her family in Ludlow. I shall be driving down on Thursday." The word had now got around that DJ Ramos was now in the bar so many of the customers were looking in his direction and acknowledging him.

"Mattia, you are now needed in the kitchen," whispered Sophie.

"I will see you later Jack."

"Do you want to order?"

"Yes, if you would, a chicken omelette."

Jack enjoyed his evening at Joe's Café Bar, it was good to be back, but you could not compare it with dining outside at the Albatross in Marbella on a warm evening with the beautiful Olga by his side, whilst listening to the nearby Mediterranean Sea crash against the rocks below the sea wall.

When he walked back to the Thames Plaza shortly after nine thirty, it was cold and wet. Even his apartment was cold, so he switched on the heating for an hour and watched television before having an early night.

The following day he was up by eight, after a light breakfast he showered and got dressed. It was his intention to walk into the city centre and buy Christmas presents for Lilly and her family, but before he went he needed to call Franks and make an appointment to see his former boss, the chairman Jim Richardson.

June the lovely looking young woman on reception answered the phone. "Jack, is that you?"

"It certainly is, good to speak to you June."

"When did you return?"

"Sunday afternoon."

"Have you returned for good?"

"May be. "I need to see Mr Richardson on Wednesday if possible"

"Let me just check his diary for appointments. Yes, he is in his office all day. What time would you like to see him?" "Would eleven in the morning be ok?"

"That would be fine, I will see you then."

June was always a breath of fresh air, it was a pity she was happily married.

Oxford Street was packed with Christmas shoppers, every store he visited had long queues. Fortunately the weather was dry, and it did not feel as cold as when he arrived back in the UK yesterday. In the end he was more than happy with the family presents he bought.

Rather than drive to the imposing MI6 Headquarters on the Albert Embankment in the Vauxhall district of London, Jack took a taxi as parking was always a problem. One thing he noticed on arrival at the building was how security had been tightened up. Instead of one armed police officer with a sub machine gun, there were now two on duty. After checking his ID pass, he then passed through a security scanner before entering the foyer.

Walking up to one of the two attractive and smartly dressed girls on reception he introduced himself. "My name is Jack Sinclair and I have an appointment with Miles Coburn at eleven."

"One moment please Mr Sinclair." She then checked the PC computer screen in front of her before picking up the green internal telephone. "Mr Coburn is expecting you, would you please take a seat he will be with you shortly." Five minutes later a jovial Miles Coburn walked into the foyer.

"Good to see you Jack." The two men shook hands and embraced. Would you please follow me?"

Once through two sets of security scanners which included finger print and eye retina identification, they went through a door into a long grey tiled corridor.

"My new office is on the second floor overlooking the Thames. I always use the stairs; it helps to keep me fit." Jack smiled but did not speak.

Coburn swiped his security key card into the door lock then they entered the room, which was quite bare. Painted white, there were three picture on the walls, two of London and one of Her Majesty Queen Elizabeth. The later was on the wall behind a light oak modern office desk. There were two telephones on the desk, one PC and an Apple laptop. A built in wall filing cabinet and four dark red leather chairs, one of which was behind the desk.

"Take a seat Jack. Firstly I would like to congratulate you on a job well done. It was a very difficult first assignment. I have no doubt the Russians will discover their diamonds now they have the landing strip co-ordinates, and life will get back to normal. It is a great pity your friend Sergei lost his life but mistakes do happen and life has to carry on."

There was a knock on the door and Coburn's assistant Richard Montague walked in with two lattes.

"Jack for the record, I need you to run through all the details about how you and Pedro escorted Sergei to Malaga Airport."

For the next ten minutes, Jack detailed everything from the minute they left Aslan's villa to their arrival at the airport and Sergei eventually entering the departure lounge.

"So to recap again, Sergei was either injected with the nerve agent in the men's washroom, if that was the case the assassin had to be a male or someone already in the departure lounge got to him." Coburn then took a long drink of his coffee before leaning back in his chair. "Personally I believe it is time to draw a line under your Marbella adventure. Both you and Pedro have done one hell of a job." Jack smiled and then took a drink of coffee. "Are you intending to go back working for Franks?"

"No not at the moment. Aslan Maskhadov, who owns Cobra Jewellery in Marbella, has offered me the position of General Manager in his company, which I have accepted. I also intend to carry on working for Pedro as DJ Ramos one night a week at the Med Beach Club."

Richard Montague, who had been sitting there like a mouse listening to the conversation, suddenly spoke. "My sister Kelly and her girlfriends saw you at the Med Club last week; she has never stopped raving about you."

"Kelly should be my PR girl," everyone smiled.

"When are you returning to Spain?" The green phone on his desk suddenly rang. "Right Jenny thank you for your call, I will let him know. Jack that was our accounts department, just to let you know that the £50,000 bonus we promised you has now been transferred to your account."

"Thank you Miles, a most generous Christmas present from the company." Both Miles and Richard smiled. "You were asking me when I was returning to Spain." Coburn nodded his head. "The second week in January. I shall be spending Christmas and New Year with my sister Lilly and her family in Ludlow."

"We have a proposition for you, how would you still like to continue working for us in Spain?"

"Tell me more."

"Pedro Gonzales needs someone who he can train in the use of high tech surveillance equipment. You work well together; you will make an excellent team."

"What is it worth to me?"

"You can stay indefinitely at the Marbella Beach Apartments free of charge. Pedro will pay you 250 Euros a night for your gig at the Med Club and we will pick up half the bill, you will also get six complementary return air flight tickets a year to the UK, plus a generous expense allowance and a £25,000 a year retainer. Jack we need two men on the Costa del Sol, it is too much for Pedro as drugs trafficking is increasing by the week, we need to keep a track on the movements of the drug Barons, who frequently travel between the UK, Spain and North Africa. Part of your job will be to get to know some of these guys and the people who work for them. With D J Ramos being a celebrity on the Costa del Sol and you also working at Cobra Jewellery, it will be an ideal cover. What do you say? Are you interested?"

Jack did not even hesitated before standing up and shaking Miles Coburn's hand.

"I am your man."

"Good on you Jack, I knew I could depend on you. You will be pleased to know, that this time you will be liaising with the narcotic division of the Spanish police." Miles then glanced at his watch. "Time has flown by quickly, why don't you join Richard and I for a bite to eat?"

"I would love to."

When Jack arrived at diamond and gem dealers Franks in Hatton Garden on Wednesday morning at eleven to see his former boss Jim Richardson, he felt most apprehensive. Jim a close friend of his late father had been an incredible employer, now he was going to have to inform him that he was going to have to cut his ties with his company. After passing through Frank's impressive security system, the first person he saw was June on reception. She immediately gave him a hug and a kiss. "Good to see you again Jack."

"Lovely to see you June, you look really well."

"Mr Richardson will be with you in a moment."

Whist waiting, he stood by the reception desk exchanging small talk with her.

"Good morning Jack."

He recognised the chairman's voice immediately. "Good to see you Jim." The two men embraced.

"Come through to my office. June, when you have five minutes to spare, may we have two coffees, both with milk and no sugar?"

Once inside the office Jim beckoned to one of the red leather chairs. "I presume you have come to tell me in person, that you will not be returning to Franks at the moment."

Jack was shocked and slightly embarrassed. "How did you know?"

"My ministerial contacts." Jim smiled and then burst out laughing. "No, I just guessed, you are the double of your late father, and he could not resist a challenge. I don't want to know what you have got yourself involved in with MI6, but I can guess. If I may add one word of warning, be extremely careful, the last thing I want to see is your name in the obituary column of the Times."

"Thank you for your advice. I came here today to apologise for letting you down, I have enjoyed every minute I have worked for you."

"You have not let me or the company down, life has to move on. By the way, I meant what I said when I last saw you. If Cobra Jewellery ever considers selling their operation, Franks would definitely be interested. You could run it for us in Marbella."

"If I hear anything I most certainly will let you know."

"Jack you must keep in touch."

"Of course I will."

Jack liked Jim Richardson; he could see why his father spoke so highly of him. Forty minutes later he left Franks. June on reception had left for lunch, unfortunately he never got chance to say goodbye to her in person, but he would call her before he left the UK.

Shortly after mid-day on Thursday 23rdDecember, Jack left the underground car park at the Thames Plaza in his Firenze red and black metallic Range Rover Sport for Ludlow Shropshire. Having made the journey many times before, he expected to cover the one hundred and fifty miles in about three hours depending on the traffic. The weather was cold and dry, but thank goodness there was no heavy rain or snow to contend with. When he finally arrived in Ludlow it was shortly after three thirty, he immediately went to the local Tesco Supermarket and bought his sister Lilly a large bunch of flowers, as he knew she would adore them just like their mother Rachelle always did. A mile or so past Ludlow Castle he turned sharp right into the entrance of Castle View, the magnificent stone detached property, which held so many childhood memories. After gaining entrance by the intercom system, the large wrought iron gates swung open and automatically closed as he drove up the short drive to the property. When he pulled up outside the house overlooking the manicured gardens, his sister Lilly, her husband Bret, and the children were gathered to meet him. The welcome home was fantastic and it really dawned on Jack what family life was all about. For the first time in several years, Lilly and her husband dined out on Christmas Eve, when Jack offered to look after the children. Christmas Day was extra special, it reminded him so much of the happy times when he was younger and the family celebrations he had shared with his parents, brother Lex and sister Lilly. Every time he reminisced about the past, tears weld up in his eyes. At least he was delighted that the family Christmas presents he brought with him were received with great affection.

Apart from taking the family out for a meal between Christmas and New Year to the Charlton Arms on the bank of the nearby River Teme, most of the time was spent at Castle View.

Two days before New Year's Eve, Jack took the plunge and confessed to his sister that he would be returning to Marbella the second week in January.

"If you had told me two months ago, I would never have coped with you living so far away, but I feel so much better now. Jack, I know you have a life to live, at least we can talk on the phone or Skype each other and of course I will still see you every five or six weeks. You are just like our dad so ambitious."

"You must come over to Spain with Bret and the children and visit me. Lex is always asking about you, he says you are very welcome to stay at his villa."

"I promise you we will come over." Lilly then took hold of both his hands. "Tell me the truth. Dad used to work for MI6, are you also working for them?"

Jack looked into her eyes and replied yes. He had never lied to his sister and he had no intention of starting now.

"I love you darling, please be careful." She then gave him a hug. "I am extremely lucky to have such fantastic brothers as you and Lex."

"By the way, if you and your family ever go up to London you must stay at my apartment, you have the spare key."

"Thank you darling," she then kissed him. "Please be careful whatever you are doing in Spain, I love you so much.

New Year's Eve turned out to be another very special night. Lilly and her friend Kay prepared a fabulous buffet for eight of their closest friends, who arrived early evening with their children. Jack enjoyed the celebration which concluded with a spectacular firework display. It was not what he had been used to in recent years, but to be honest he was sorry, when the evening came to a close.On Sunday the 2nd January, it was time for Jack to head back to London. Leaving a love one at anytime is hard, but leaving an entire family you adored was even harder. As he drove back he had time to think, was he making a dreadful mistake by returning to Marbella? He had around eighty million in the bank, so it was not the money which motivated him. Lilly was right, he was like their father he could not resist the excitement of a challenge. Jack had only been back in London a couple of days, when he realised there was nothing to keep him in UK, his life at the moment was in Marbella. After contacting EasyJet on the internet, he booked an early afternoon one way flight to Malaga International Airport for Friday 7th January.

When he informed his sister Lilly, she was not in the least surprised. "Please give me a call when you arrive safely. I love you Jack."

"I love you sis."

His next phone call was to his brother Lex.

"You must come and stay with us. I will pick you up at the airport and run you back to Marbella on Sunday evening. Maria and I will look forward to seeing you."

On Wednesday, Jack spoke to Thomas the security officer at the Thames Plaza, who was back on duty after a few days off, and put him in the picture about his proposed back and forth trips from Spain to the UK.

"No problem Jack, I will take good care of your Range Rover. By the way thank you for the money you gave me, you were very generous. Jack smiled. "If you need a lift to and from Gatwick Airport at any time just give me a call on my mobile."

When Jack stepped out onto his apartment balcony shortly before going out for his farewell meal to his favourite Italian Restaurant Joe's Café Bar, he realised for the first time in his life as he looked across the River Thames, what loneliness was really about. There were thousands of people around him, but he was alone oblivious to everyone. He would have to do something about it; no way did he want to spend the rest of his life in a cocoon.

38

When Jack's brother Lex met him in the arrival lounge at Malaga International Airport, it was just leaving 5pm Spanish time. The weather was mild and dry and it felt considerably warmer than in London.

The two brothers embraced each other warmly. After putting his wheelie suitcase and sports bag into the boot of Lex's Firenze red and black Range Rover Sport, they headed to the families' magnificent villa on the nearby Malaga coast. As they drove along the coastal highway, Jack took the opportunity to text his sister Lilly in the UK of his safe arrival, and also told her that he was staying with their brother Lex and his wife for a couple of days.

She immediately texted back, "enjoy your stay with Lex, I love you all, speak to you soon."

Maria and their baby David gave him a lovely welcome. For the next couple of days he relaxed and enjoyed family life. On Sunday, he took his brother and wife along with baby David out for lunch to their favourite restaurant, the El Gato Lounge in nearby Torremolinos. At seven, Lex drove Jack back to Marbella.

When he entered the foyer of the Marbella Beach Apartments, there was a young security officer on reception who was not familiar to him, but he still acknowledged him with a smile. It always paid to be friendly. Once inside his apartment, he closed all the window blinds as it was completely dark outside, apart from the security lights. After unpacking his luggage he switched on the television and then the central heating as it felt quite chilly. As he was about to settle down on the sofa, he remembered that he had forgotten to call his boss at Cobra Jewellery. Picking up his mobile which was by his side, he called Aslan.

"Hi Jack, what can I do for you?"

"I have arrived back in Marbella."

"Did you enjoy the Christmas festivities with your sister and family?"

"Yes I did, it was lovely seeing them again. I actually arrived back on Friday, so I spent a couple of days with my brother Lex, his wife and young son, at their villa near Malaga. I will be back in the office first thing tomorrow morning. How did Christmas go with you?"

"I spent most of my time with my sister-in-law Gabrielle. We visited a few restaurants, called socially on Pedro and Nada and dined out with my good friend Leroy Cardoso. We enjoyed the Christmas festivities." Aslan paused for a second before continuing. "Jack, take another day off from the office, I would like you to meet my sister-in-law Gabrielle. Perhaps you would join us for lunch?"

"I would love to."

"Excellent, we will pick you up at one."

Jack enjoyed his meal out in Puerto Banus with Aslan and Gabrielle. He recalled seeing a photograph of Aslan and his late wife in the lounge of his villa; he was amazed how much she resembled her sister, it was quite uncanny. No wonder Aslan was drawn to her. Gabrielle said she loved the Spanish way of life, but on Saturday she would be returning to Chechnya for **a** few weeks to sort out her affairs, before returning to Marbella. The couple told him in confidence, that they would most probably get married in late March or early April.

Aslan arranged to pick up Jack at eight fifteen on Tuesday morning. He had the shock of his life when he entered the Cobra Jewellery Head Quarters.

"Let me show you the new General Manager's office." Jack laughed. "Whilst you have been away in the UK, I have had the spare store room to the left of the foyer overlooking the car park, converted into a new office for you."

Jack was taken aback when he entered the room. It was very similar to Aslan's but slightly more modern.

"I am most impressed. What have you done with my old office?"

"It is being converted into a secure strong room."

"An excellent idea, we need it. Who is the lovely looking black girl on reception, has Natalie left?"

Aslan laughed. "No my friend, I took your advice and promoted her. She is now personal assistant to both you and I. She will still cover on reception when Amara has a day off.

"Where is Amara from?"

"Algeria, her parents were refugees many years ago. She is the youngest of four daughters; her father is a lawyer in the city."

"She is certainly a beautiful looking girl."

"I might add she is twenty three, single with no regular boyfriend. Oh! She is also a big fan of DJ Ramos. She used to visit the Med Club every Tuesday evening until you went back to the UK for Christmas."

On the way back through the foyer, Aslan introduced Jack to Amara.

"Jack, I am going to have to leave you now, I can't leave Gabrielle at the villa alone all day, I will call you later"

"So you are the famous DJ Ramos." Her large wide dark eyes appeared to come alive as she spoke. Jack smiled.

Amara had a beautiful smile with showed off her white teeth. At five-five she was slim with a perfect figure. Her hair, which was long and black and partly platted, fell several inches past her shoulders. The blue and white dress and high heeled shoes she wore, gave her a look of sophistication and elegance.

"Lovely to meet you Amara, if you need to speak to me I will be in my office. Before I forget, Mr Maskhadov tells me that you normally come to my DJ gig at the Med Club. Don't forget to say hello to me."

"I most certainly will Mr Ramos." Jack smiled. Amara had the same look of excitement in her eyes as Olga.

Jack was pleased that Aslan had employed a black person, it was good for racial equality and Amara would be a great front of house asset to the company.

After leaving the reception he went to find Natalie and congratulate her on her promotion.

Jack's life was even busier since his return to Marbella, his promotion to General Manager at Cobra Jewellery and the added responsibility it gave him motivated his work ethos. Even so he still found time to call his sister Lilly every week in Ludlow and attend every Malaga FC home match, usually with Aslan in his private box. His brother Lex, Malaga's manager, was confident that his team would still finish the season in the top four or five of the La Liga, though their recent away form was disappointing. Next season Lex said they would have to bring in several younger players as they had an ageing squad.

Over the next couple of weeks Jack had several meetings with Pedro Gonzales, who patiently explained how the sophisticated surveillance equipment worked.

"Do you recall the Israeli mobile interceptor dish which we discovered attached to Aslan's villa?" Jack nodded his head. "Our boys at MI6 have recently developed a small thin box, similar to a light switch but smaller, which will replace the dish. Miles Coburn informs me, that we will be issued with a couple of these sophisticated new mobile phone gadgets by the end of the month. Also next Monday evening at the Med Club, I have arranged a meeting with the undercover Spanish narcotic police officers, who we will be working with." He then took a long drink from a bottle of Andalusian Spring Water on his office desk before continuing. "It is not going to be easy tracking down these drug dealers, as the clubs and bars along the Costa del Sol are full of guys who look like crooks. Jack, most of the big time drug dealers normally keep a low profile, apart from when they have something to celebrate. Then they usually invite all their friends to their villas and let their hair down, with a wild party by the swimming pool, once the weather gets warmer. This is where you come in Jack. They always need a mobile disco with a top DJ."

"Tell me more?" Jack started to smile.

"An entertainment agent friend of mine Lucas Morales, who owns Costa Music, would love to represent DJ Ramos for private functions. He has contacts all over the Costa del Sol and further afield. Once you start gigging the word will get around and sooner or later you will meet the guys we are looking for. You will always have a roadie to help you; needless to say he will be an armed undercover cop."

The more Jack thought about what Pedro had said, the more it made sense.

The glamorous Isabella Lopez from Barcelona was rarely out of his mind. Now he was back into some sort of routine he decided to make contact with her. They met on several occasions with Jack flying to Barcelona to be with her, but the friendship was doomed from the start. She made it quite clear, that whatever developed in their relationship she would never leave Barcelona. Jack had no intention of moving there and to be honest, he was not even sure he would still be in Spain in twelve months or even six months' time. The relationship fizzled out before it had really started, but they continued to be good friends, with Izzie always contacting Jack and dining out with him when she visited her doctor brother and his wife in Marbella. Perhaps it was now time for him to ask assistant manager Kelly or DJ Selena out at the Med Cub or even speak to his brother Lex, and meet his wife Maria's younger sisters?"

Olga was still at the back of his mind, though he had gradually got used to her not being around. She was a stunning looking woman with an incredible sexual appetite, so to say he did not enjoy her company and did not miss her would be lying. Was she responsible for Sergei's death at Malaga International Airport or was it her sister Tanya? He would probably never know, but he prayed it was not Olga.

Shortly after Jack had returned to Marbella in early March, after making a flying visit to see his sister Lilly and family in the UK, Gabrielle arrived back from Chechnya. A few days later Aslan announced to close friends, that they would be getting married on Sunday the 10th April and asked Jack to be his best man. The wedding service and a small reception would be held at the exclusive Marbella Beach Hotel.

The weather was improving and the days were getting longer with temperatures starting to hit 23c. Tourists were starting to arrive in Marbella and along the rest of the Costal del Sol.

D J Ramos, who had been performing on a Thursday night at the Med Beach Club during January, February, and March, had recently reverted to Tuesday night. It was as though he had never been away, with the punters flooding in. Jack happened to be in Pedro's office prior to going on stage, when Boris's name who ran Pinks in Puerto Banus, came up in their conversation.

"I have it from a reliable source that Boris is returning to Russia. He has never been the same man since he disturbed two intruders in his club one Friday afternoon. One of them attacked him and plunged a knife into his groin. He told a friend of mine that Pinks' owners in Moscow, who are said to be the Russian Mafia, are considering an offer for the club."

Pedro's close contact with entertainment agent Lucas Morales, the owner of Costa Music was certainly paying off. DJ Ramos even at 1,200 Euros a gig had many wealthy clients wanting him to perform at their poolside villa parties. The doors were slowly starting to open. Photos secretly taken with a spy camera at several of these events by his roadie showed several of the guests were on police wanted lists both in Spain and the UK, mainly for murder, fraud or tax evasion and also the trafficking and importation of cocaine.

Aslan and Gabrielle marriage was very private with only thirty close friends invited. The following day the couple left in Aslan's Bentley convertible for a week's honeymoon in Gibraltar and Cadiz. On returning, Aslan had a heart-to-heart talk with Jack about Cobra Jewellery.

It was agreed that Aslan for the moment, would take more of a back seat and leave the day to day running of Cobra Jewellery to Jack. Aslan was naturally very concerned about Gabrielle adjusting to life in Marbella, whatever few friends she had in Chechnya, she had now left them behind for a new life. Jack suggested that for the next few months Aslan should work a three day week, which would allow Jack to leave the office early on a Tuesday to prepare for his evening DJ gig at the Med Club, before returning to work on Wednesday afternoon. Aslan eagerly accepted. This would also allow Natalie to become more involved with the business.

Out of the blue his pop star friend Boy George called him from London; it was good to hear from him. After a lengthy conversation George got down to the reason for his call. "If you recall Jack, when George Michael and I spoke to you at the Med Beach Club last year about my forthcoming new album, we said we wanted DJ Ramos on the album as guest celebrity. You will be delighted to know that we have written a brilliant song for you, all we have to do now is to go into the studio and put the track down."

"When do you want me to fly over to the UK?"

"No need to, George has a friend who owns The Cable Recording Studio in Marbella. In two or three weeks we will fly over for a few days, go into the studio, and record the track."

"It sounds fantastic. By the way how is George?"

"He is working his balls off writing songs for his own new album as well as producing this album for me. As soon as we are ready to record your track, I will give you a call and let you know when we will be coming over to Spain. Jack you take care of yourself, we both send our love and will speak to you again soon."

When Jack came off the phone he was elated, it was like a dream come true, no way in a million years did he ever think he would be recording a track with both Boy George and George Michael.

It had been a particularly busy Thursday, with unusually high April temperatures and strong sunshine, which caused him to partly close the window blinds in his office, but unfortunately obstructed his view of the car park. The green internal phone rang on his desk, it was Amara on reception.

"Mr Sinclair there is a girl on the outside line who wants to speak to you, she says she knows you. I told her you were very busy but she insisted."

"Amara don't concern yourself, would you please put her through to me."

Jack then picked up the white telephone on his desk. "Who is speaking please?"

"Hi darling it is me, I told you that I would return."

She did not even have to say who it was, he knew Olga's voice and her Russian accent anywhere, but then a thought suddenly crossed his mind. Was it really Olga he was speaking to and not her identical twin sister Tanya?

"Where are you?"

"In the car park at Cobra Jewellery, darling open your office blinds."

About the Author

Sean Dylan has been a well-known Entertainment Agent in Northern England for over forty five years. During this time he has had the privilege of working with many of the most famous stars in Show Business. Now retired from the industry, Sean spends most of his time writing. This, his sixth book, *They Had To Die*, was first published in 2021.

Other Books by Sean Dylan

The Rizzleman

The Rizzleman - Retribution

The Politician and the Mafia

Saddam Dead or Alive

Handful of Diamonds

Available worldwide online and from all good bookstores

www.mtp.agency

Printed in France by Amazon
Brétigny-sur-Orge, FR